# —— THE ——
# EXCEPTION

**THE EXCEPTION**
Edited by: Jessica Royer Ocken
Proofreading by: Elaine York, www.allusionpublishing.com, Julia Griffis
Formatting by: Elaine York, Allusion Publishing, www.allusionpublishing.com
Cover Model: Shaun Collins
Photographer: Michelle Lancaster @lanefotograf
Cover designer: Sommer Stein, Perfect Pear Creative

# THE EXCEPTION

VI KEELAND

—— CHAPTER ——

# ONE

Sutton

**"P**lease tell me you didn't bring that hideous brown dress to wear to the wedding."

No *hello*, no *how are you*—just straight to the point when I answered. It was one of the things I loved about Miles Hartley, except when his *point* was a critique of me.

I took a step forward in line. "It's a beautiful dress."

"It is. You should wear it to bingo when you go down to visit your grandmother in Florida."

I rolled my eyes, but chuckled. "I hate you."

"No, you love me. You *hate* when I'm right. Which is often, when it comes to your life. And because you love me so much, I'm currently in your room digging through boxes looking for the red dress you *should've* brought. I'll bring it in my bag tomorrow. Also, why did you answer the phone? I thought I was going to leave you a message. Shouldn't you be in the air by now?"

"Hang on a second." I took another step and handed the gate agent my boarding pass.

She scanned it. "Have a good flight."

"Thank you." Once I entered the jet bridge, I lifted my phone and returned my attention to Miles on FaceTime. "Weren't you just wearing blue glasses a minute ago?"

He shrugged. "These match your panties."

I couldn't help but laugh. My best friend had a collection of more than a hundred pairs of glasses, each more colorful than the last. He had a penchant for matching them to his outfits, but pairing them with my panties was a new one.

"I thought your flight took off at eight?" he said.

"It's delayed an hour. And you better pack everything back up and seal the boxes when you're done rummaging through my life. The moving company is coming tomorrow morning to bring me those."

"*Ooh*. When did you get this red mesh bra? Does it have matching panties?"

"Can you please stop going through my underwear?"

"Seriously, this thing is hot as fuck. It might even make my gay ass a little hard if you put it on."

"Wonderful. I can finally achieve my life's goal."

"If there aren't matching panties, I'm going shopping and finding you some. Because *this* is what you're wearing under the red dress at the wedding."

"I'm not wearing the red dress."

"Then how are you going to bang the best man?"

"I am *not* banging Brendan's brother."

Though I was definitely overdue for a good banging. *Way, way* overdue. And I hadn't mentioned to Miles that I planned to remedy that problem sooner rather than later.

"Why not? His underbite doesn't make him look as much like a bulldog as it did before the braces."

I boarded the plane and found my row. "I have to go. I just got to my seat, and I need to put my luggage in the overhead bin and get situated."

"All right. But promise me one thing."

I sighed. "What?"

"You won't have a couple of glasses of wine and respond to the jackrabbit's text. You get emotional when you drink."

"I am *definitely* not responding to Brendan." I was stopped in the aisle with my luggage, and the woman behind me didn't look happy. "Gotta go. I'll see you tomorrow."

After I hung up and stowed my bags, I settled into my seat. The flight from LA to New York was five and a half hours. I'd been annoyed when my mother had called the airline pretending to be me and upgraded my ticket to first class, but the big, comfy seat that reclined to a bed now made this section seem more and more like a little slice of heaven. Especially when the flight attendant walked over carrying a tray.

"Would you like orange juice or champagne before we take off?"

"Oooh. I love mimosas. I'll take both."

She nodded. "Good choice."

It had been a year since I'd flown home to New York, and I'd forgotten how big these planes were. Boarding went on for a full half hour. So when the flight attendant returned with the bottle of champagne and offered a refill, I happily nodded.

"Yes, please. It'll help take the edge off."

She smiled. "Nervous flier?"

"No. But I'm going home for a wedding I'm not looking forward to."

"Is there someone you don't want to see attending?"

I nodded. "The groom. He's my ex."

She wrinkled her nose. "Yuck. You must be a bigger person than me. Not sure I'd go to my ex's wedding, if I was invited."

"I don't have too much of a choice. He's marrying my stepsister."

Her eyebrows shot up. "Oh my."

I sighed. "Tell me about it."

She refilled my champagne flute to the brim and set the half-full bottle on my tray table. "It's going to be a bit before we get to pull away from the gate. The runway is backed up since we missed our time slot. I'll just leave this here. My name is Aileen. Buzz if you need anything else."

I smiled. "Thanks."

She leaned down to me. "My ex-boyfriend is a pilot. I got stuck on a flight with him last month, and I *accidentally* spilled the soda he ordered on his shirt when I was bringing him his dinner. It didn't make it any less awkward, but it made me happy to look at the stain every time I had to see him after that. Maybe you should have a little accident at the wedding."

"Who should I bump into, the bride or the groom?"

She smiled. "Both. And maybe order a Bloody Mary instead of a soda before you do."

"I might just do that."

We wound up sitting at the gate for another forty-five minutes, during which time I polished off my second glass of champagne and the remainder of what was left in the bottle. I was feeling no pain by the time we started to taxi toward the runway. Unfortunately, I was also feeling—*damn Miles for always being right*—emotional. So after I switched my cell to airplane mode, I pulled up Brendan's text. It had come in a week ago, and I'd read it at least twenty times since then.

> **Brendan: Hey. Could we get together to talk when you get to town? Your mom said you're coming in Thursday. Maybe we could meet for a drink at Buvette?**

A few minutes later, a second text had come in.

**Brendan: I'd appreciate it if you didn't mention this conversation to Colette.**

The latter had made my blood boil. I'd kicked around taking a screenshot of the text and sending it directly to my stepsister, but I wasn't up for the drama that would inevitably ensue. I also didn't want Colette to think I was jealous or petty. Even though *petty* was exactly what you *should be* when your boyfriend of three years marries your freaking stepsister. I shook my head and swiped the text closed, deciding to watch a movie to keep me distracted. At some point I must've dozed off, because when I woke up, the movie was no longer playing and there was only a little over an hour left in the flight. My new friend, Aileen, appeared at my side.

She smiled. "Good nap?"

"Definitely. Exactly what I needed."

"Glad to hear it. I'm about to wheel around the ice cream cart, so you woke up at the perfect time. The only thing better than champagne and a nap is having a hot fudge sundae when you wake up. Can I get you anything to drink?"

"Ice cream sounds great. And just some water, please."

While I waited for the flight attendant to come back, I dug out my phone and connected to the free Wi-Fi so I could check email. As soon as the three little bars illuminated, a text popped up in preview.

**Miles: Who's better than me?**

There was a paperclip at the bottom corner of the message, so I clicked to see the attachment. A photo of my best friend appeared on the screen—he was beaming, holding a pair of red mesh underwear that seemed to match my bra perfectly. I snorted. *Only Miles.*

Maybe he was right. Maybe I should've brought the red dress—though not to lure Brendan's little brother. What I needed was a *stranger*, a quick fling with someone who was good in bed. *Great* in bed, even. My mind leaned into the idea. No-strings-attached, anonymous sex. No names, no numbers—hell, no faces would work at this point. It could be hot if he wore a mask. I just needed to have sex with six inches that *didn't* require batteries. Tonight, I was planning to go to a bar and not come home alone. I wasn't sure why I hadn't shared that tidbit with Miles. He'd been my best friend since elementary school and knew everything else about my life.

Aileen wheeled over the ice cream cart, interrupting my thoughts. I ordered vanilla with peanut butter sauce and chocolate chips, and it was *freaking delicious*. Devouring it, I decided maybe I shouldn't object so much in the future when my mother wanted to throw her husband's money around and spoil me.

There wasn't enough time left on the flight for a second movie, so I opened the internet browser. Spooning the delicious sundae into my mouth, I checked my email, did the daily Wordle, and finally googled *best bar in Manhattan to meet a man for a one-night stand*. I was pretty surprised how many hits came back, and not just your typical Reddit chats either. There were articles in legit magazines and entire websites dedicated to the subject. Yelp had a *Top 10 Best Hookup Bars in NYC* list. Too bad they didn't have Yelp ratings for the men who frequented them. I clicked into one website that had a map of all the different neighborhoods of Manhattan, and each of those had a clickable list of bars. I double tapped into Gramercy Park and scanned the six places listed. Bullets underneath outlined the reasons each place was good to meet someone. While I was reading the write-up of the last bar, an animated ad popped up showing a bird inside a cage. The door opened, and a bright red finch fluttered its wings and flew out. It was cute and colorful. Underneath read: NY Loves DARE—*dating freedom.*

Though I'd decided tonight was the night I was finally going to find a man, it had never crossed my mind to use a dating app. I'd joined a few after Brendan and I broke up, but something about the constant cut-and-paste introductions I'd received turned me off. Yet this one had me curious. So I clicked and read. DARE wasn't your typical swipe-right-and-swipe-left-type deal where you judged people in two seconds based on their looks and a few sentences. Instead, you had to answer a ton of questions before your supposed matches were presented to you. Users didn't even see photos until the matches had been selected. The site claimed to be *ultra exclusive* and charged a whopping $599 a year. Considering I was no longer employed, that price was too rich for my blood. So I clicked the X to close out of the site. But rather than shutting down, a banner flashed on the screen: Try free for five days.

Hmmm... *What the heck?* Why not? I had another hour to kill. It might be fun to see who a computer would pick as my perfect match. Lord knows I hadn't had luck finding the guy on my own. So I clicked to redeem the offer and started entering some basic data. The first few questions were simple—age preference, type of looks and physique I was generally attracted to, religious beliefs, languages spoken, hobbies, rating the importance of salary and different values.

I was moving right along until the question about what I was looking for in a relationship gave me pause.

There were three choices to select from—a long-term partner, an occasional companion, or no strings attached. I knew the answer, yet it took me a full five minutes to find the courage to check the last box. I'd never had a fling. As I continued, the questions became more personal—did I like a dominant lover in the bedroom, was I open to multiple partners at once, and did pain turn me on. Let's be real, I had no idea what I truly liked after wasting all those years with Brendan. Yet I chewed my lip, considering my answers anyway. Multiple partners at once? Definitely not. I wanted someone with more experience than I had, so a lover who took control sounded good—*yes to dominant partner*. And who knows, a little spanking might be fun. The rest of the questionnaire took another fifteen minutes, and by the time I was done and hit submit, I had to admit, I was a little excited. An hourglass appeared on the screen with sand falling from one globe to another. Eventually a message flashed. *We've found your match.*

Match? Just one? Not match*es*? Why did I think I was going to be given a smorgasbord of men to choose from? I'd wasted almost half an hour for one measly guy who was probably going to be creepy? I sighed, but clicked anyway since curiosity had already gotten the best of me. I was certain I was about to be shown some troll based on a dumb computer algorithm deciding who was my Mr. Right.

But the man whose photo appeared was most definitely *not* a troll.

Wow...just wow. This had to be an AI photo, right? Real men weren't this beautiful, certainly not any of the ones I'd run into lately. I lifted my cell to my nose for a closer inspection. Pictures generated with AI, or ones that were heavily retouched, tended to be too smooth or overly blurry. They were also usually missing shadows, or the background lighting was unnaturally even. But this guy wasn't like that at all. I could see the texture of his skin, the sexy stubble of his five o'clock shadow. The ocean was also in the background, and the water reflected the sun. Not to mention, different shades of blue and turquoise revealed the changes in depths beneath. I was almost certain the photo wasn't generated by AI.

*Jesus, that means this guy is actually real?*

I scanned down to his short bio, assuming that was where I would find his blatant flaw, some big smoking gun. His hobbies probably include stalking his exes and poking dead things with a stick.

Though what I found made my jaw fall open.

Hobbies: Snowboarding, scuba diving, and travel.

Those were the same three things I'd written. Astounded, I kept reading. Jagger L.—even his name was sexy—had a well-written bio. It was personable, yet funny. In the *languages fluent* section he'd written "sarcasm," and in the *looking for* section he'd written "no strings attached, except the one you allow me to tie you up with."

This guy seemed like *exactly* what I was looking for—even more than I'd thought possible. But it couldn't be this easy, could it? I was still mulling around the potential pitfalls—he's a catfisher and using someone else's photos, he's made up everything in his bio. Or what if his profile isn't even real—the company made it up to get people to pay their exorbitant $599 fee. That was probably it. The people at DARE dangle a seemingly amazing guy in front of your face for five days, and it's only *after* that when Mr. Perfect responds and says he's not interested. *Yeah, that's probably it.* My eyes slanted to the message button. I was just about to type a short note, see if the guy would even respond, when a chime sounded, alerting *me* of an incoming message from my new match.

• • •

*God, why didn't I bring the stupid red dress?* I looked in the mirror one last time. I looked nice, but not Jagger L. nice. That man was a dozen echelons up from *nice*. Though I did look better than I had earlier. I'd blown out my long, chestnut hair and used a curling iron to style a few loose waves into it, swept eyeshadow across my lids that made my green eyes pop from my warm Italian skin, and lined my lips in a bold red. I had on a blue dress that wasn't as dull as the brown one Miles had forbidden me to wear. This one hugged my curves nicely, but it was high necked and didn't show any cleavage or anything. Though there wasn't much I could do about that now. I was already going to be late to meet my perfect match by the time I grabbed a cab and got to the bar. So I took a deep breath, swiped my purse from the counter, and forced myself to walk out the door.

When I arrived, the Copa bar seemed pretty busy for a Thursday night, but what did I know? The last time I'd lived in this city, I wasn't even legally allowed to drink. My heart raced as I scanned the room looking for my date, though part of me still doubted my perfect match would show. And if he did, I probably wouldn't be able to find him since he likely looked nothing like the amazing photo in his profile. But then my eyes landed on a man seated at the corner of the bar, and my galloping heart came to an abrupt halt.

Holy. Freaking. Cow. *He's real.* And the man might've been even better than his picture, if that were possible. My eyes met with Jagger's, and his lips curved to a seductive smile. He stood, but it took a few beats for my frazzled brain to get my feet to move. I somehow expected the sparkle of his looks to dim as I moved closer, but the exact opposite happened. His broad shoulders and custom three-piece suit hit every one of my hot buttons.

My date waited for me to make my way over, all the while keeping that delicious smile on his face. It was slightly crooked, considerably mischievous, and told me more about him than his bio already had. This man had *oodles* of confidence. At the risk of sounding like a sappy romance novel, I felt the air shift as I stood across from him.

He extended his hand, exposing a chunky watch and silver cufflinks, and I stared at his face, unable to form words. Or...apparently function at all. After an extended period of time with his arm outstretched, and me obviously incapable of completing basic etiquette tasks, he leaned forward and smirked.

"I don't bite." His deep, raspy voice lowered, and he winked. "Unless you want me to."

I blinked a few times, finally managing to place my hand in his. "Sorry. I...I...it's been a long day."

I'd come for a hook-up, even checked the box that said as much, but suddenly I was a shy, nervous wreck. A man this spectacular had a lot of experience and probably wanted a woman with equal skills—which I didn't have.

While I stood there drooling and acting like a complete idiot, my date seemed completely at ease. Jagger pulled out the chair next to him, and I miraculously managed to plant my ass on it without falling off. It seemed like a monumental accomplishment in the moment.

The bartender walked over and dropped a coaster on the bar in front of me. "What can I get you?"

*Alcohol!* Oh! Yes, yes, I definitely needed alcohol! Wine wasn't strong enough to calm these nerves. "I'll take a vodka cranberry, please."

Jagger put his hand out. "Would you give us a moment before taking her order?"

The bartender shrugged. "Sure thing."

My face wrinkled in confusion as I watched him walk away.

Jagger's sexy smile was now gone. He looked me in the eyes and spoke matter-of-factly. "No alcohol. Please."

I felt my brows knit. "What?"

"I don't want you to have any alcohol."

My eyes shifted to the bar, zoning in on the half-full drink sitting in front of him. I motioned to it. "You have a drink? Why can't I have one?"

"Because it's my preference."

"Your...preference?"

His eyes narrowed. "Is that a problem?"

Not having a drink wasn't a problem, but him *telling me* I couldn't have one certainly was. I didn't care how good-looking this guy was, no man was going to push me around. I folded my arms across my chest. "Do you have many other preferences I should be aware of?"

A ghost of a smile feathered onto his lips. "I do, actually."

His lips were curved, but there wasn't a trace of laughter in his tone.

"I'll humor you," I said. "Let's hear them."

"The most important of my rules is no alcohol or anything else to impair your judgment and blur the lines of consent. Other than that, I keep things simple. I demand punctuality—my time is too valuable to be kept waiting. And you'll also need a safe word."

"A…safe word?"

Jagger's eyes swept over my face. Two lines formed between his brows. "Why does it seem like it's the first time you've had rules like these?"

"Umm…because it is."

He tilted his head, looking as confused as I felt. "You're new to the community?"

"You mean the DARE dating app?"

"I mean the dominant-submissive community in general."

My eyes bulged. "The what?"

He rubbed his bottom lip with his thumb, maintaining eye contact, but I could see the wheels in his head spinning. "You have no idea what type of site you joined, do you?"

"Isn't it a dating site?"

"It is, for people with specific tastes."

"What kind of tastes?"

"DARE stands for Dominants, Alphas, Roleplay, and Exhibitionism."

"Dominants? Exhibitionism?" My jaw dropped open, and my hand flew up to cover my mouth. "Oh my God. I guess that site isn't the best place for a virgin."

—— **CHAPTER** ——
# TWO

Sutton

"**G**et. The. Fuck. Out of here."

Miles stamped punctuation at the end of each staccato word. I didn't think I'd ever seen him so shocked.

I chuckled and shoved a French fry into my mouth. "Last night's humiliation was almost worth it, just to see your face look like that."

"What happened after he realized you had no idea what type of dating site you'd joined?" He paused and shut his eyes. "Wait, no. Tell me how tall he was before you answer that."

"Pretty tall. I'd guess about six-two, maybe six-three."

"Yum." Miles took a deep breath and smiled before opening his eyes again. "Okay, I'm banking that visual for later. Now, tell me how he reacted."

"Believe it or not, he was actually pretty gracious. He raised his hand to get the bartender and ordered me the drink he'd stopped me from having. Then he apologized, paid the tab, and left. The funniest part was when he was leaving. He took a few steps, stopped, and turned back to ask, 'You're *really* a virgin?' As if the most shocking part of our encounter wasn't that he was into whatever it was he was into or that I'd had no idea when I joined. *Virgin* was what he couldn't get over."

"I love you, cookie. But you *are* twenty-four. Your V-card should be in a museum by now."

I whipped a fry at him. "I'd rather have my V-card than the frequent-flier pass you have."

Miles grinned. "Flattery will get you everywhere with me."

I chuckled. "I was prepared to be disappointed that my date looked nothing like his profile picture. But I was *not* prepared for him being a Dom or whatever."

"Are you opposed to getting tied up or a little spanking?"

"Honestly, I probably would've let this guy do whatever he wanted to me. He was *that* gorgeous." My belly fluttered just remembering his bright blue eyes and Superman-esque jawline. Though it was more than that, something about the guy just oozed sexy.

Miles gestured to my phone on the table. "Show me a picture of him."

I called up the app, unsure if I'd still have access to it. Maybe my perfect match had told the gatekeepers I was a virgin and they'd kicked my sad ass off. But Jagger's face popped up on my screen as soon as the app opened.

Miles swiped my cell from my hands. "Holy shit. He's freaking *hot*."

I leaned forward and stole a fresh glance, then shook my head. "I know. Such a shame."

"I usually like to be the one in charge, but hell, I'd let this guy whip me and tell me what to do."

I took my phone back. I wasn't about to mention it to Miles, but I'd gone back home thinking the same thing last night. Hell, I'd almost told the cab driver to turn around more than once. And I'd tossed and turned all night long, feeling hot and bothered by images of Jagger L. putting me on my knees and over his.

Stealing one last look at my phone screen, I sighed before closing the app. "I really wanted to lose my virginity before this painful wedding."

"I brought the red dress. I still vote you bag the jackrabbit's brother."

I wrinkled my nose. "The thought of seeing Brendan's brother naked makes me ill."

"Pretty ironic, considering who the jerk is marrying tomorrow, huh?"

I frowned. "He's getting married, and I can't even find a one-night stand properly."

Miles patted my hand. "Of course you can. You could have a one-night stand by walking into any bar or going on any of the normal dating apps. You just decided you needed to finally get laid three days before flying off to New York, and then you happened to pick some weird-ass app."

"I hate the thought of going to the wedding of the asshole who made me wait all those years while still being a stupid virgin."

Miles pointed to my phone. "Go on Tinder. Three swipes and you too can be a fornicator."

I laughed and finished off my lunch. Deep down, I knew Miles was right. It wasn't hard to find a hook-up. It was my own fault I was still a virgin. After three years in a sexless relationship with holy-roller Brendan, I should've gone hog wild when I was finally single. But instead, I'd wallowed and let it become this *thing* that was now bigger than it should've been.

"Let's get out of here," Miles said. "I want to see your new apartment before we have to get ready for the rehearsal dinner tonight."

Twenty minutes later, we walked into my doorman-equipped building. Miles whistled as he looked around the modern lobby.

"Fancy. You're really moving on up in the world."

"My mother has great taste in real estate—when she's buying it with other people's money."

Mia Holland—actually, it was Mia Newport now—had purchased this co-op in Gramercy Park a decade ago with money from her divorce settlement from husband number three, Peter Swenson, heir to a shipping empire. We'd lived in it for a few years before she met husband number four, and then she'd decided to keep it in case things didn't work out and she needed somewhere to live while searching for husband number five. Fortunately, that hadn't happened.

"Good afternoon, Ms. Holland." The uniformed guy behind the desk tipped his hat. "Ms. Newport has arrived and is waiting upstairs."

I stopped. "My mother's here?"

The doorman's face fell. "You weren't expecting her?"

I wasn't, but I absolutely should've been. I forced a smile, not wanting to make the poor guy feel like he'd done something wrong. "I was. She's just...early."

His smile returned. "Have a good afternoon."

Once we were in the elevator and the doors slid closed, Miles looked at me. "You had no idea she was coming, did you?"

"Nope. But shame on me. I should've. This was one of the reasons I wanted to get my own apartment. My mother isn't good with boundaries."

Miles pointed to the elevator panel. I hadn't pushed a button yet. "What floor?"

I took out a keycard and slipped it into the slot. The floor illuminated automatically. "PH. What else?"

The apartment door wasn't locked. I took two steps inside and stopped short, finding two men in the living room. Then I spotted my mother in the kitchen, laughing and drinking from a champagne flute. *I would've preferred a burglar.*

She threw her arms in the air. "There she is! My beautiful daughter."

I steadied myself and walked in the rest of the way. "Hi, Mom. I didn't know you were coming."

"Of course you did. I told you Pablo and Mario were going to get us ready for the party tonight." She looked at the taller of the two. "Isn't she stunning? I had her when I was eight, of course."

My mother engulfed me in a hug before moving on to my friend. She pressed her cherry red lips to his cheek. "Miles! How have you been, darling? Have you gone straight yet?" She wagged her finger. "I'm holding the husband-number-five spot open for you."

A lot of gay men would find that type of comment insulting, but thankfully Miles was a good sport. "If I was going to switch teams for a woman, it would be you, Mia. You look as amazing as ever."

She rubbed lipstick from his cheek with her thumb. "When are you going to move back to New York like my Sutton?"

"I *didn't* move back, Mom. I'm only here for the summer for my internship."

My mother ignored me. She walked over to the kitchen counter and lifted two big garment bags. "I brought you a selection of dresses for tonight and for the wedding."

"I have a dress for tonight and one for the wedding."

She smiled. "Not Monique Lhuillier and Christian Dior."

"Nice," Miles hissed.

I whipped around to look at him. "Don't encourage her."

Mom lifted a third bag. "And I brought you a new suit, Miles. It's navy with a light pink check. I hope you brought those Barbie-pink glasses I've seen you wear."

"I don't leave home without them." He kissed her cheek. "Unlike your daughter, my loyalty can be bought. I can't wait to try on my new duds."

My mother and Miles disappeared down the hall, while I went to the kitchen and uncorked a bottle of wine. Mom came back when I was halfway through a glass.

"Honey." She frowned. "You know alcohol will make you puffy."

"I'm not worried about it."

She took the wine glass from my hand and sipped. When I looked at her as if to say, *how come you can drink it then?* she waved me off. "My face is too frozen with Botox and filler to puff."

I laughed as I stole the glass back and drank. "Are you going to be popping in like this all the time? Should I get the locks changed?"

She winked. "Only the owner on the deed can authorize a lock change."

I rolled my eyes. "Great."

Her face grew serious. "How are you holding up, my love?"

"Well, this morning when I went to the ATM, I considered robbing the bank so I would get arrested and not be able to go anywhere for the next few days."

She frowned and stroked my hair. "I'm sorry this is so hard on you. If it makes you feel any better, I bought you and Miles new outfits for tonight, but not Brendan and Colette. I have to play nice because she's my stepdaughter, but I'll never forgive either of them. Edmund is still embarrassed about what his daughter did. He hates that he has any part of seeing you upset. And I don't think he'll ever be able to talk to his soon-to-be son-in-law without clenching his teeth. He calls him the *speedbump*, because that's what he was hoping Brendan was when his daughter first started dating him—a bump on the road to finding a real man."

I smiled sadly. "Thanks, Mom. But I'm not even mad at them anymore. Not really, anyway. I'm more mad at myself for not moving on yet."

"Have you been dating?"

"A little."

Her eyes sparkled. "I have a nice man I'd like you to meet. Jack's a friend of Edmund's from work. He'll be at the wedding."

I waved my hands. "No fix-ups, Mom. That's the last thing I need."

"He's an attorney—a little older, but I think older is better for a husband."

"Dad was two years younger than you."

She threw back the rest of the wine in the glass. "Exactly. I learned my lesson."

• • •

Miles held out his elbow as we walked through the restaurant door that evening. I'd chosen to skip the actual rehearsal since I wasn't in the bridal party. I'd been so relieved when Colette had told me she was only doing a maid of honor and best man—no bridesmaids or groomsmen. Of course, her identical twin sister, Chloe, had the honor. There was no way in the world I would have been able to stand up at the altar and smile while watching my first and only love promise eternity to my stepsister. Even if I now realized Brendan and I would've never worked long term, and if what they'd both sworn was true—that nothing happened until after we broke up—it was a tough pill to swallow.

"You look amazing," my best friend whispered. "You got this."

I stood a little taller, grateful that Miles knew what I needed in the moment. And he was right—I did look amazing, thanks to Mom's glam team and this incredible dress. She'd picked out a simple burgundy slip dress, silky with a loose, flowing fit that seemed effortless, yet elegant, but paired it with a set of vibrant turquoise sky-high heels that made a statement. I never would've thought to put the colors together, but then again, I didn't have Mia Newport's style. Maybe that's why she was on husband number four, and I was still a damn virgin.

"Thank you." I nodded and took a deep breath. "I'm ready."

The dinner was being held in the private back room of a popular restaurant. The double French doors were shut as we approached, but I could see Brendan's mother through the glass. She spotted me, and a look of pity crossed her face. That was the absolute last thing I needed or wanted. The next forty-eight hours were definitely going to be a challenge.

Husband number four, my stepfather Edmund Newport, must've noticed us walking through the restaurant. He opened the door with a welcoming smile. "Sutton, it's so good to see you, sweetheart."

I kissed his cheek. "You, too, Edmund."

Mom's husband of seven years was in his mid-sixties—fifteen years older than she was. He had salt and pepper hair and a slightly crooked nose, but he was handsome in his own way. "You remember Miles, right, Edmund?"

"Of course. How are you, son? My wife was so excited you could make it back for the wedding. Mia absolutely adores you."

"The feeling is mutual, sir."

Chloe walked over and hugged me. "Eep! I've missed you!"

"I missed you, too." The last time I'd seen my stepsister was when I'd come home and found out about Brendan and Colette. Chloe was supposed to come out to California to visit this spring, but then she got the flu and postponed the trip, and it never happened.

"I'm so excited that you're back for the summer," she gushed. "I have big plans for us. We need to go out to my dad's house in Montauk on weekends. We can get tans during the day and go clubbing in the Hamptons at night. I think there's also a wreck out at Culloden Beach, if you want to go diving."

"That sounds great."

Edmund chimed in. "The owner of my company is a diver, like you. I could ask him about diving spots."

Chloe leaned close to me and whispered. "His boss is also gorgeous. I might forget to invite Ryan that weekend."

I knew she was teasing. She was head-over-heels for her boyfriend of five years. The only reason they weren't engaged already was because Ryan had just finished medical school.

From the corner of my eye, I spotted Brendan and Colette. They looked at each other, said something, and started to make their way over, hand in hand. Miles must've noticed, too, because he snaked his arm around my waist and squeezed my hip. The happy couple had only been together a year and a half, so I'd never actually seen them together—at least not clothed, in the upright position, in public. It felt like someone had punched me in the stomach by the time they got to me.

"Hi, Sutton!" Colette hugged me. "You look beautiful."

"Thanks." I forced a smile. "So do you."

An awkward silence fell, and all eyes shifted to Brendan. He leaned forward like he was considering hugging me, and Miles stepped in and squashed it by extending his hand and offering a curt nod. "Brendan."

I knew the last thing in the world my best friend wanted to do was make nice with my ex, so his sacrifice made me love him even more. Not wanting Brendan to go for a second attempt at physical contact, I offered an awkward wave when he finished his shake with Miles. Thankfully, he took the hint and stuffed his hands into his pockets, and Edmund jumped in to make small talk.

"Everyone at Apex is looking forward to meeting you on Monday, Sutton."

I smiled. "I'm a little nervous, but I'm excited to start."

"Did you see the article that included Apex on the list of most-coveted summer internships in the financial world?" Miles asked. "Nine-thousand MBA graduates applied for the six open spots."

"And she landed the position without my help, I might add," Edmund said. "Sutton didn't even tell me she'd applied until she got the spot."

All of this was common knowledge in our family. Miles was just trying to make me feel good about myself because he knew seeing Brendan and Colette arm in arm made me feel the exact opposite. He also probably loved shoving my professional success in Brendan's face, because he knew my ex had applied for a job at Apex after college and didn't even get a callback for a second interview.

"Speaking of Apex," Edmund said. "I see that the boss has arrived."

I thought it was odd that my stepfather would invite his boss to the rehearsal dinner—the wedding, yes, but tonight was a small gathering of only family. Though from what I'd heard from Mom, they spent a lot of weekends schmoozing with businesspeople. Relationship-building was part of her husband's role as CFO of one of the biggest new investment firms.

Colette lifted her chin. "Jagger owns this restaurant. It's one of the most popular in the City right now. He canceled a reservation they already had on the books, just for Dad."

*Jagger?* That had to be a coincidence.

But when I glanced up and my eyes met a set of piercing blues, my heart nearly stopped. *Holy shit.*

The guy from the bar last night was my stepfather's boss?

# —— CHAPTER ——
# THREE

## Sutton

Miles turned toward me. "That's not..."

I covered my mouth. "Oh my God."

He traced Jagger's line of sight. There was no mistaking it—he was staring right back at me. "Holy shit..."

If it were possible, the man was even more breathtaking than I remembered. Slightly tousled, inky-black hair fell almost to his shoulders. It gave a rugged, effortless vibe that contrasted starkly with the bespoke three-piece suit he had on this evening. He flashed a very slight, cat-that-got-the-canary smile before breaking our gaze to speak to Edmund, who had walked over to greet him.

I hadn't yet picked my jaw up off the floor when the two of them walked straight toward us. *Holy crap. Holy crap. Holy crap!* What the hell was I supposed to do? I considered feigning sickness and making a run for it, but unfortunately their strides were too long, and before I could come up with an exit plan, they were upon us.

"Jagger..." Edmund motioned to our group. "You've met Chloe and Colette, and Colette's fiancé, Brendan."

The adonis nodded. "Good to see you."

Colette smiled. "Thank you for arranging for our group to use the private room tonight, Mr. Langston."

"Not a problem at all."

The men turned their attention to me, and I felt all the color drain from my face. "And this is Sutton," Edmund said. "The stepdaughter I told you about. She starts the internship program at Apex on Monday."

Jagger's gaze slid over my face, snagging on my lips for an extra heartbeat. He put out his hand. "Very nice to meet you."

*Okay, so this is how we're going to play it*—last night never happened. My hand shook as I raised it to meet his, and I had to clear my throat to get words out. "Nice to meet you, too, Mr. Langston."

His eyes gleamed. "Jagger, please."

My stepsister's brows pinched ever so slightly. Apparently, I wasn't the only one who noticed he hadn't told *her* to call him by his first name.

I managed to push out another smile and nod, but my insides were doing somersaults. My body had the same intense awareness of being near him as it did last night at the bar. It was a lot to handle—especially standing in front of my family. I glanced around for a reason to excuse myself— something, *anything*. Not finding one, I figured leaving the room completely was even better. I looked at Chloe. "Would you be able to point me to the ladies' room, please?"

She motioned behind me. "Straight out the doors and to your right."

"Excuse me," I said to no one in particular, but I *definitely* avoided eye contact with Edmund's boss.

In the bathroom, I splashed some water on my face and looked in the mirror. *How the hell is this happening?*

There were something like eight-million people in New York City. And yet I'd signed up for an app—a random app that I had no business signing up for—and got matched with my stepfather's boss? My heart raced as I realized Jagger Langston was more than that. He was also the CEO of the company where *I* was about to spend the summer as an intern...

Oh God.

I actually felt queasy.

A loud chime from my phone startled me, though I was holding it in my own damn hand.

> **Miles: Are you okay? Do you want me to come to the ladies' room? Better yet, I can send Mr. Langston, and he can bend you over the sink...**

*This is no time for jokes, Miles!* Before I could respond, a second text came in.

> **Miles: I can feign sickness and tell Mia you're going to take me back to the apartment.**

While the offer was absolutely tempting, I was going to have to suck it up and deal with this disaster. I could handle it. I could handle anything—I was here handling my stepsister marrying my ex, wasn't I? Well...sort of. Though on the bright side, that calamity no longer felt like a big deal compared to this new hot mess. I typed back to Miles.

> **Sutton: No, but thank you. I'm just going to take another minute to get my head screwed on straight and then I'll be back.**

> **Miles: OK. Text me if you need me.**

I shut my eyes, took a few deep, cleansing breaths, and gave myself a last-minute pep talk. *You can do this. Hell, he's probably gone already.* After all, the CEO of a Fortune 500 company wasn't about to hang out at the rehearsal dinner for the daughter of one of his employees on a Friday night. I was certain he had a million other things to do.

*Like meet women on that app.*

*And have sex.*

*Hot, sweaty, kinky sex.*

A pang of unexpected jealousy hit me. Ugh... My heart started racing again, only this time for a different reason. I needed to get a grip. So I forced my eyes shut a second time and took a few more cleansing breaths while I talked myself into believing he was gone already.

Only, when I swung open the door of the ladies' room, Jagger Langston was absolutely *not* gone. In fact, he was standing in the hall, waiting for me.

"May I have a word, please?" he asked.

I thumbed behind me. "Is going back into the ladies' room and crawling out the window no longer an option?"

His lip twitched as he reached for my elbow. "Definitely not."

Jagger guided me down a dimly lit hall in the opposite direction of the rehearsal dinner. He opened a door marked *emergency exit*, and we were suddenly outside, in a small courtyard. *God, why didn't I crawl through the bathroom window when I had a chance?*

"I take it from the look on your face when I walked in that you had no idea who I was when we met last night?"

"No! Of course not! It's bad enough that I signed up for some weird app. I had no clue you were also Edmund's boss."

His gaze slid over my face. "You shouldn't knock someone's sexual proclivities until you've tried them."

I shook my head, attempting to backtrack. "I didn't mean weird. I meant... I don't know—not a normal app."

Jagger arched a brow. His voice held a hint of amusement. "Not normal? Is that supposed to be better?"

I was screwing this all up. But how the hell was I supposed to think with this man so close? He had such a powerful presence that it made me feel unsettled... *unmoored.* I have no idea what possessed me, but I blurted out, "Does my stepfather know?"

"Know what?"

"About your...proclivities?"

A smile graced his handsome face. "I don't make a habit of discussing my sex life with the people who work for me." His eyes dropped to my lips and returned to meet mine with a gleam. "Although, I believe *you* work for me now, so I suppose I can make an exception when warranted."

An exception? Was he...suggesting *we* discuss his sex life? A slight breeze blew, wafting his cologne to my nose. *Great, he smells amazing too.*

"Look." I shook my head, attempting to clear it. "I had no idea who you were when I agreed to meet you, and I'm not going to say anything to Edmund, if that's what you're worried about."

"I wasn't worried about it."

"Then why did you follow me to the ladies' room?"

"I wanted to know who the man you're with is."

"Man? You mean Miles?"

He nodded. "Is he your boyfriend?"

"Miles is gay."

"So just friends then?"

"Well, I'm not a man, so of course. But why do you want to know?"

We stared at each other. I tried to figure out what was going through his head, but he wasn't an easy man to read.

Ignoring my question, he held his hand out and gestured to the door. "You should be getting back. Someone might come looking for you."

Why was it that everything that came out of this man's mouth was the last thing I expected? When I didn't immediately head to the door, he put a hand on my lower back and guided me to walk. Electricity shot through me, and I looked at Jagger to see if he felt the same thing. If he did, he was better at hiding it.

He opened the door, and two steps into the hallway, Miles turned the corner at the other end. The three of us continued to walk until we met in the middle. I stopped, but Jagger kept going, passing without a word. Miles and I both turned and watched as he stopped at the hostess station and then kept right on going out the front door of the restaurant.

My friend turned back to me. "What the hell was that about?"

I shook my head. "I have no damn clue."

•  •  •

Saturday morning, I was already in the living room when Miles walked out. He stretched his hands over his head.

"Morning, cookie."

"Good morning. How'd you sleep?"

"Like a baby with visions of sugar-Doms dancing in my head."

I chuckled and gestured to the kitchen. "There's coffee in the pot."

Miles poured his caffeine fix and looked out the window. He grinned. "It's raining on their wedding day."

"They say that's good luck."

"Only to make the brides with frizzy hair feel better." He tilted his mug to me. "You want a refill?"

"No, thanks. I've already had two cups. Any more will make me jittery. Or should I say *even more* jittery."

Miles sat down on the chair across from me and slurped his coffee. "Do you think the Daddy Dom is going to be at the wedding?"

"I thought you were calling him Dungeon King last night?"

"I'm still trying on names. Haven't found the perfect fit yet. But I'm thinking it should have an alliterative twist." He sipped from his mug. "So he has to be invited, right?"

*That* question had kept me up for hours. "A few months ago, when Mom mentioned there were going to be three hundred and fifty people at the wedding, I asked who the heck they all were because our family isn't very big, and neither is her husband's. She said Edmund has a lot of business associates. So I think there's a very good possibility his boss might be one of them."

"Have you done a deep dive on him yet?"

"What would make you think that?"

Miles shrugged. "You've done it on everyone else you've gone out with."

"But I'm not going out with Jagger."

Miles grinned. "What did you find out?"

I rolled my eyes and turned my laptop to face him. "He was in the military."

"*Reall*-y?" He got up from the chair and sat next to me on the couch. "Did you find any pictures of him in uniform?"

"No, but one of the articles mentioned he was a *troubled youth*, whatever that means."

Miles tucked his feet under his ass. "Hot *and* a bad boy. Me likey. Tell me more."

"Well, he's thirty-two, went to state college—not some Ivy League school—and he did his bachelor's degree in thirty months, rather than taking the full four years."

"An overachiever, just like you."

"Overachiever? It took me *six years* to get my four-year degree."

"But only because you took a little break. You're brilliant and gorgeous. He's brilliant and gorgeous. Sounds like a match made in heaven, if you ask me. You should tell him you graduated high school at sixteen and got a perfect SAT score. That'll impress a fellow member of MENSA."

"I'm not a member of MENSA."

He sipped his coffee. "But you could be."

I shook my head. "Anyway, he sold his first company at twenty-four for fifty-million dollars while he was still in school, yet he stayed and finished his degree. He'd started late since he was in the military for four years."

"God, why would anyone do that? Who needs college with fifty mill in the bank?"

It's funny. I obviously didn't know the man, yet the fact that he finished what he started seemed to fit. He exuded determination. That thought—and the way he'd looked at me last night when we were outside—made my skin prickle, in a good way.

"I guess he just wanted to finish what he'd started."

Miles smirked. "Oh, that man can *finish*. Trust me."

I chuckled.

"I'm *dying* to know what he's into. I checked out that app after you told me your story, and it could really be anything. Do you think he's into BDSM? Or just has some kink or fetish? Or maybe he likes to be *watched*." Miles licked his lips. "I could help him out there."

I shut my laptop. "Well, I doubt we'll ever find out, so you're just going to have to make up fantasies in your head."

"I wouldn't be so sure of that. I felt something between that man and you."

"I think your imagination is getting the best of you. Again." I stood. "What do you want for breakfast?"

Miles finished off his coffee and popped up from the couch like a spring was attached to his ass. "Mimosas!"

"I meant *food*."

"Your stepsister is marrying your ex in a few hours. I think alcohol for breakfast is what's on the menu."

He had a point. "Okay. But I need some food, too. You know how giggly I get when I'm drunk *and* nervous. I *cannot* burst out in laughter during the ceremony."

Famous last words...

—— CHAPTER ——<br>FOUR

Sutton

"If anyone can show just cause why these two may not lawfully marry, speak now or forever hold your peace."

"Heeheehee." *Shit.* I slapped my hand over my mouth, but it was too late. All heads in the church turned to the second row, including the bride and groom's. Colette's brows pinched, but when she saw who the sound had come from, her face softened with sympathy. I waved a hand and pointed to my throat. "Sorry. Just a tickle."

Meanwhile Miles sat next to me, about to blow. The two of us had been giggly guzzlers since eighth grade when we stole a bottle of tequila from my mother's liquor cabinet to celebrate his thirteenth birthday. We'd gotten caught because we couldn't stop laughing in math class. Miles's shoulders started to shake, and I just knew that if he got started, neither of us was going to be able to stop. Luckily, it was nearing the end of the ceremony, and I managed to keep any further outburst under lock and key. Though by the time the priest pronounced the happy couple husband and wife, a full-on belly laugh was dying to escape. The minute my stepsister and her smiling groom walked up the aisle, I made a beeline for the side door I'd been eyeing for the entire ceremony and let out a hyena-like laugh that ended in an unattractive snort. There was no way I could do the receiving line.

A voice startled me. "What's so funny?"

I looked up to find none other than the Daddy Dom standing there. And was that a *joint* he was smoking? At church? I forgot all about the shock of finding someone outside and fell into a second round of laughter. Tears rolled down my face as I released all of the alcohol-driven fits of giggles. My entire face was probably streaked with mascara, but I didn't care.

Jagger watched in silence, looking amused. When I finally got ahold of myself, he tilted his head. "Care to let me in on the joke?"

"This entire day is one big, fat joke."

He squinted, but said nothing, waiting for me to elaborate. I didn't.

"What are *you* doing out here?"

"I don't like weddings."

"Then why did you come?"

He tapped the lit end of the joint against the brick exterior of the church, extinguishing it, before turning his attention back to me. "Why is today a joke?"

I took a deep breath in and let out an audible sigh. "My stepsister just married my ex-boyfriend."

"Come again?"

I smiled. "You heard me right."

"And that's...funny?"

"No. Yes. No." I shook my head. "I don't know. Maybe it's not? I just get the giggles when I drink." Jagger's jaw flexed. I pointed to it. "Oh that's right. You don't like when I drink. It's your *preference.*"

His eyes narrowed. "Are you mocking me?"

"What if I am? Will you put me over your knee and *spank* me? Is that what you're into?"

Something flickered in his eyes. He took a step forward, but before he could say or do anything else, the door I'd spilled out of burst open again—this time producing my partner in crime, Miles. The newly anointed Daddy Dom retreated a step.

"Oh." Miles grinned from ear to ear. "Sorry to interrupt."

"Don't be." Jagger adjusted the knot on his tie. "If you ever see me near your friend again, please, make a point of interrupting." Then he turned and walked away. Miles and I stared after him. He looked as confused as I felt.

"What the hell was that?" he asked.

"Yet again, I have no damn idea."

• • •

Two hours into the reception, I had a hangover, even though I hadn't slept. The party was held in a giant, swanky loft on the top floor of a skyscraper. The elevator had an electronic sign that gave the hours for a rooftop garden, so I decided to go in search of some quiet before it closed. Outside, twinkling lights lit up New York City, while the Hudson River sparkled below. It was peaceful, at least until I was joined by the last person I wanted to see.

Brendan smiled. "There you are."

I rolled my eyes, anger pulsing through my veins at the sight of him. "I think you're confusing sisters. Your bride is inside. She's the one wearing the fluffy, white gown. But I could see why it might happen, given your history and all."

He frowned. "This must be tough on you. I'm sorry. I never meant to hurt you, Sutton."

I hadn't slept well for the last week, my head was pounding, and I had a year and a half of anger built up inside me. It all bubbled to the surface together. I turned and put my hands on my hips. "What do you want, Brendan?"

"I don't want you to be upset."

"Why would I be upset? Because I wasted three years of my young life in a sexless relationship with a God-fearing man only to walk in on him three months after we broke up fooling around with my stepsister?" I paused. "I didn't buy you a wedding gift, so here's some advice instead: The clit is not a golf ball that you whack once and it takes off. You should know, you never once gave me an orgasm, not with your hand or mouth. I faked them *all*. I hope you do better for poor Colette."

Not wanting to be near the jerk a second longer, I turned to walk away, but two stomps in, I crashed directly into something that felt like a brick wall. Or *someone*. I didn't even have to look up at the face, the delicious smell gave it away.

I closed my eyes. "How much of that did you hear?"

Jagger's tone was laced with venom as he glared at Brendan. "Shouldn't you be with your new *wife*?"

The two men were such polar opposites. Brendan's blond hair, sinewy runner's body, and boyish looks made him seem like a child in the shadow of Jagger's manliness. My ex was a junior Ken doll, and the man currently looking down his nose at him was brawny GI Joe. It made me wonder how I'd ever been attracted to *that* when guys like Jagger Langston existed.

Brendan had always been intimidated by successful men—his father, his boss. It was something I'd disliked about him. But right now, I was glad he was a wimp. He nodded at Jagger and swallowed. "You're right. I should find Colette."

Then it was only Jagger and me on the rooftop, and I stared straight ahead looking out at the City. "How much of that conversation did you hear?"

"Enough."

I sighed. Great. First, I show up for a date completely unaware of what kind of a dating app I'd joined, then I run into the man bolting from a church drunk, and now... Now I've revealed that my ex never gave me an orgasm. "How many times can I possibly humiliate myself in front of one person in twenty-four hours? I have to be near a record."

"Pretty sure *he's* the one who should be embarrassed for not being able to get you off."

I closed my eyes and laughed—because if I didn't, I'd probably cry. "I feel like you should tell me your most intimate secret, so we're even."

Jagger was quiet for a moment, but I felt his gaze slide over my profile. "What would you like to know?"

"Anything." I shrugged. "How about what you're into? Why are you on that dating app? Because my imagination has been running wild, and you have a collection of new nicknames—Dungeon King, Daddy Dom, and most recently Ball-gag Boss."

Again, he stayed silent for a long time before speaking. "I like rules and order."

I turned to face him with a wrinkled nose. "What does that mean? You're like a Dominant?"

He smiled. "The correct term technically would be *top*."

"A top?"

"What did he want?"

The quick change of subject confused me. "Who?"

"Your stepsister's new husband."

"Oh. I have no idea. I think he probably wants me to make him feel better, to absolve him of guilt or something." I looked around for the first time. It was still just the two of us on this roof. "What made you come up here?"

"I saw him follow you. He's been keeping tabs on you all night when he should be paying attention to his new bride."

"How do you know that?"

Jagger's eyes bounced back and forth between mine. "Because I've also had my eyes on you all evening."

I tilted my head. "Why?"

A smile tugged at the corners of his lips. "Because apparently, I can't keep away from trouble."

My belly did a little flutter. "I'm not trouble."

"You're a twenty-four-year-old virgin who now works for my company and whose stepfather is one of my executives, yet I can't seem to keep my distance like I should. You're the definition of trouble, sweetheart."

I felt so drawn to him. I couldn't quite put my finger on what it was, other than the obvious—he was gorgeous. It was more than a physical attraction, though. Maybe it was curiosity, because he seemed to know exactly what he wanted, and I was still trying to figure out who I was.

I met his stare, and a question tumbled from my mouth. "What did you do after you left the bar the other night? Did you use the app to meet someone else?"

I saw the wheels in his head spinning. Since the question was a pretty simple one, I assumed he was deciding *if* he should answer at all. The muscle in his jaw flexed before he spoke. "I went home."

An unexpected rush of relief flooded me. It was absolutely illogical and ridiculous, but I couldn't help what I felt. I smiled. "Me, too."

"How long were you with the Ken doll?"

My smile broadened at the description he chose. Maybe Miles was right and we were a little alike. "A little over three years."

"That's a long time to not have an orgasm."

I looked away, feeling my cheeks heat pink. "I had them. I just had to give them to myself."

Jagger grumbled something I couldn't make out, then cleared his throat. "We should get back."

I looked out at the City once again. "You go. I'm going to stay up here for a few more minutes until the rooftop closes. I need to clear my head."

He nodded and shoved his hands into his pockets. "Don't worry about the rooftop closing. I own the building. I'll let the guard know you can stay up here as long as you'd like, and I'll tell him to make sure no one else comes up, especially a douche in a tuxedo."

I smiled. "Thanks."

I stayed for another fifteen minutes, enjoying the sights and fresh air. It didn't actually clear my head, but at least when I went back downstairs, there was a little less time to go at this awful wedding reception. My mother spotted me almost as soon as I returned to my table. She latched onto the arm of some guy I didn't recognize and began to steer him to where I was seated. *Ugh.*

"Sutton, darling, I've been looking all over for you." She batted her eyelashes at the man she'd dragged with her, and a feeling of dread washed over me. "This is Jack Gallo. He's an attorney at Edmund's company. Edmund was actually Jack's mentor when he first started at Apex."

The guy was handsome. Two days ago I might've even said he was my type—tall, lean, and clean-cut. But suddenly he seemed ordinary, like I'd lose him in a crowd of a thousand other handsome men. I really wanted to kill my mother, but for now, I had no choice other than forcing a smile. "Hello. It's nice to meet you."

"Jack started as an intern at Apex, too," she said. "But now he has a herd of attorneys working for him."

Jack smiled, yet I sensed he was uncomfortable. "It's not quite a herd, more like a small band of nerds. I have three staff attorneys and a paralegal who's way smarter than me."

His honesty brought out a genuine smile. "My mother likes to exaggerate."

"I didn't when I told him how beautiful you are," she said. "Right, Jack?"

"Mother, must you keep going until you make *everyone* uncomfortable?"

She pointed across the ballroom. "Oh, look... There's Mary Harper. I haven't had the chance to speak with her yet. You two, excuse me, please."

My mother floated away, leaving me standing alone with Jack. I sighed. "I'm sorry about that. She isn't the most subtle person. I'm pretty sure Mary Harper wasn't even invited to the wedding."

Jack laughed. "It's fine. She's very sweet. And for the record, she didn't exaggerate when she told me how beautiful you are."

The compliment was nice, though it didn't make my belly flutter like when a certain CEO gave one. "Thank you."

He lifted his chin toward the middle of the room. "Would you like to dance?"

"Um..." I looked around for Miles, for someone or something to use as an excuse. Finding nothing, I forced another smile. "Sure."

Jack led me to a corner of the dance floor while a full twelve-piece band played "Perfect" by Ed Sheeran. He held me in his arms but kept a respectable distance between us. He was graceful on his feet, and unlike most men under fifty, he knew how to lead.

"So your mom told me you just moved back to New York to start an internship at Apex."

I shook my head. "My mother has a habit of saying things that she *wants* to happen as if they're true. I didn't actually move back. I'm only in New York temporarily, for the summer. I live in San Francisco."

"Oh. Is that where you're from?"

"No, I was born here in the City. I went to college in California and decided to stay out there after I graduated."

"Where did you go to school?"

"Stanford."

"Impressive. So it's probably not just my paralegal who's smarter than me..."

I chuckled. "How about you? Are you from here?"

"Born and raised out in Amagansett—on the east end of Long Island. I moved into the City to go to college, and like you, I never left."

"How do you like working at Apex?"

"I love it. I work a lot of hours, but it's been a great experience so far. Usually the first few years out of law school, new attorneys do a lot of monotonous grunt work to put in their time. But Apex has so many holdings and has grown so fast that I've been involved in dozens of different lines of business and transactions. You really get to dig in and get your hands dirty from the beginning. What about you? What department are you doing your internship in?"

"My MBA is in quantitative analysis, so I'm interning in the data-science department."

"Nice. I work with them a lot. Maybe we'll get a chance to work on a project together."

Our conversation came to a natural lull, and I found myself looking around the room over Jack's shoulder. Guests seemed to be enjoying themselves, smiling and laughing, eating and drinking. I scanned through the happy crowd until I found a set of eyes that were definitely *not* smiling. I swallowed a surprise gasp. Jagger Langston was staring right at me. His face was completely unreadable, and he made no attempt to hide what he was doing, even when I stared back. He lifted a glass to his mouth and drank as he watched, never taking his eyes off of me. The man had an unmistakable quiet intensity about him, one that unnerved me yet also sent a shiver of excitement down my spine.

My dance partner said something, which I had to ask him to repeat, and then we turned and Jagger was no longer in my line of sight. Though ten seconds later, when the view came back, he was waiting—as he was after every turn for the rest of the song. When the song ended, I took a step back, thanked Jack for the dance, and told him to have a good night.

I was happy to find Miles in his seat as I made my way back to the table. "You disappeared for a while," I said.

"I got stuck talking to your cousin Rachael."

"With the eight cats? Better you than me."

Miles shook his head. "She has ten now. Where were you?"

"My mother tried to fix me up with some guy who works at Apex."

"Was he cute?"

I shrugged. "He wasn't bad."

"Nice guy?"

"Seemed like it."

Miles sipped his wine. "Perfect. Bang him."

I laughed. "What? No!"

"Why not? You were desperate enough to use some random app to meet a guy to get one under your belt. Someone who works with your stepfather is probably safer. I'm sure they vet people, and you know he has a job. He's already got more going for him than the last guy I hooked up with."

My friend had a point, but my mind was stuck on a different man who worked with Edmund. My eyes made their way back to where Jagger had been standing while I was on the dance floor. He was gone now. I scanned the surrounding area, but he was nowhere to be found. A bereft feeling came over me.

"*Safe* doesn't sound like very much fun anymore."

—— **CHAPTER** ——
# FIVE

Sutton

I arrived at the Apex building a half hour before starting time on Monday morning. I would've been an hour early, since I'd gotten up at five AM, but I'd changed my outfit three times. I wanted to look professional, but maybe with a side of chic. In the end, I'd gone with a black pencil skirt and a simple, cream silk blouse with a big, pretty bow on one shoulder, and paired it with Christian Dior slingback pumps my mother had gifted me to wear on my graduation day. I'd twisted my hair into a sleek bun and added a few layers of simple gold chains to put the finishing touch on my look.

"Good morning." I stopped at the security station. "My name is Sutton Holland. Today is my first day at Apex, so I don't have a badge yet. HR said my name would be on the daily visitor list."

The security guard picked up a clipboard and scanned the top sheet of paper. When his finger stopped, he looked up. "Just need to see some ID, Ms. Holland."

"Sure thing."

After receiving a temporary badge, I pressed the button on the elevator panel for floor fifty-eight, the second from the top. As the doors slid closed, a wave of nerves surged, and my heart pumped faster with each floor we climbed. I'd done my interviews from California over Zoom, so this was my first time actually being in the Apex building. I knew my stepfather's office was on the top floor, and it made me wonder if *all* the executive offices were up there.

When the doors slid open, I took a deep breath and stepped out. A receptionist smiled in greeting.

"You must be Sutton."

"I am. But how did you know? There are six interns starting today, right?" My heart sank. "Oh, no. Am I the last to arrive? I hope people aren't waiting on me."

She laughed and stood. "No, nothing like that. You're actually the first to arrive." She counted on her fingers. "But our six interns are Tyler, Rasheed, Matt, Kyle, Ben, and Sutton. It wasn't too hard to figure out which one you were." She walked around the desk and gave me the once-over. "Great shoes. I'm Amara, by the way."

"Thanks. They're actually comfy, too."

She waved for me to follow. "Come on, I'll show you around while it's still quiet."

The fifty-eighth floor housed the data-science and finance departments. Amara walked and pointed things out. "It's Monday, so a lot of people tend to work from home. We have flexi-space two days a week, so the employees can vary which days they want to be in the office, and flexi-hours every day, which means you have to put in your eight hours, but it can be any shift—starting as early as five AM and ending as late as nine PM. It's great for people with kids."

"I bet."

"The interns, unfortunately, have to be in the office every day, but you can still shift your hours after orientation is finished the first week. Most tend to work the schedule of their manager. You'll also be assigned an executive mentor—whom you'll meet with weekly during your internship." She pointed to the ceiling. "The big guys work one floor up."

"All of them?" I asked.

She nodded. "Yep. Their offices are super posh. HR is going to give your group a full building tour later today. It takes a while, and I can't be away from the front desk for more than a few minutes. Otherwise I'd show you."

My pulse picked up at the prospect of seeing Jagger during the tour later. I'd thought about the possibility of running into him a lot yesterday, and it *might've* had something to do with why it had taken me so long to pick out my outfit this morning. Though I tamped down the excitement that started to grow in the pit of my belly, intent on keeping my focus on business and making the most out of my internship. I really was excited that I'd scored such an amazing opportunity. Amara answered the phone remotely from her headset as we toured the floor. When another intern arrived, she showed me to my cubicle and said my manager should be in shortly, and I should help myself to coffee in the breakroom we'd passed.

I was busy admiring the amazing Nuova Simonelli espresso machine when a familiar voice interrupted.

"That thing should be on the fifty-seventh floor, not this one."

I turned to find Jack, the attorney I'd danced with at the wedding, standing behind me. "Oh, hi."

"Good morning." He lifted his chin toward the counter with the sparkling, stainless-steel machine. "Part of every employee's annual review is a rating for being a team player. They average the employees from each department's rating for that category, and the group with the highest number gets their choice of some expensive item for the breakroom on their floor. That damn machine goes for ten grand, but it's worth every penny, if you ask me. I wish it was one floor down, though. You want me to show you how to use it? It's kind of confusing."

"Oddly enough, I know. I spent two years in college working at a coffeehouse. We had almost the same machine. I'm also addicted to cappuccino."

Jack held his hand out. "After you."

I worked to prepare my caffeine fix while he waited. "Do you come up here to make your coffee every morning?" I asked.

He shook his head. "I usually bring it with me, but I was running late this morning. I'm actually part of your morning meeting today. Each intern gets assigned a mentor from the executive team. I'm not an executive, but I'm filling in for my boss for a few weeks. She had a skiing accident and had to have knee surgery, so she's going to be out for a while."

"Do you know who you're mentoring yet?"

He smiled. "No, but I've been hoping for a certain intern since Saturday night."

I smiled back, but inside I silently hoped he was assigned to someone else, though I wasn't quite sure why. I finished making my cappuccino, said goodbye, and went back to my desk. Not long after, the rest of the interns arrived, and then finally Ellie Loring—the manager I'd interviewed with. The other interns seemed really friendly, and I'd started to relax by the time ten o'clock rolled around. We were given a fifteen-minute break before a kick-off meeting for the mentor program. I ate a granola bar, went to the ladies' room, and grabbed a notepad to take with me to the conference room.

Jack was already inside, standing at the front of the room with Ellie and a few older people we hadn't met yet. I joined the other interns seated around the table.

Tyler was seated to my right. He leaned in. "I heard the guy who does this program from the IT department is a hardass and gives you homework assignments no one else gets. I'm hoping I don't get him as my mentor."

"How do they match people up?"

"I asked that during my interview. She said they go through the candidates' resumes and profiles and look for commonalities with the mentors—like schools and experience or whatever."

Ellie called the meeting to order and began with introductions of the executive team members who would act as our mentors. There were only five people up there, aside from Ellie, so I wondered if one of us would be assigned to her. She told a little about how the program started and how it's evolved over time. Then she explained some of the logistics of how it worked.

"It's really up to you and your mentor how often you'll meet. There's a weekly meeting at a prearranged time that has already been set up on all of your calendars, but we encourage the mentors to involve you in as many things as possible, whether that's accompanying them to a meeting or allowing you to take part in an ongoing project. Today you'll also be having lunch with your mentor offsite to get to know them a little better. But you'll get to know each of the executives. They're the group that will be deciding which of you will be offered a spot in the Apex executive training program, which begins at the conclusion of your summer internship." She gestured to the people standing beside her. "If it's okay with you all, I prefer to hold all questions until the end and move on to having each mentor participant tell you a little about themselves." She smiled. "When they're done, I'd like to play a little game and see if you can figure out who you've been matched up with and why."

The first executive to speak was Jim Matthews, the vice president of human resources. He gave an abbreviated version of his resume and then talked about his hobbies and family. Considering his hobbies included golf, geocaching, and coin collecting, and nothing on his resume had anything in common with mine, I didn't think he would be my mentor.

Three more executives took their turns. One had gone to Stanford like me, so I thought perhaps he might be the one I was assigned to, but then Jack stepped forward.

"My name is Jack Gallo, and I'm a managing attorney here at Apex. I've been with the company for five years. It was my first full-time job out of law school, but my interest was always corporate law. I did internships at the SEC in the compliance department, and also at the law firm of Simon and Rugg in their transactional division. My boss, Kirsten Volpe, is usually one of the mentors, but she's going to be out for a few weeks, so one of you unlucky interns is stuck with me until she returns. My hobbies include skiing, snowboarding, mountain biking, and rock climbing."

Of course, the one person I *didn't* want to be matched with was the only person I had a hobby in common with. At least if I were assigned to him, it would only be temporary, until his boss was back.

Ellie looked at her watch. "And we have one more executive mentor. He's also a fill-in. Our VP of sales went out on maternity leave earlier than expected, so this morning we had to scramble to find someone. I guess he couldn't make this meet—"

She was interrupted by the conference room door opening. And my heart nearly stopped.

Ellie smiled. "Perfect timing. Here's our final mentor now. The founder and CEO of Apex, Jagger Langston."

$$\text{---- CHAPTER ----}$$
# SIX

### Sutton

His hair was slicked back in an old-Hollywood way, and he had on yet another bespoke three-piece suit. I imagined he had a full wall of a walk-in closet lined with them, probably color coded. Jagger Langston looked every inch the powerful CEO he was, and my mouth went instantly dry. His eyes scanned the interns seated around the table, and when they landed on me, the slightest hint of a smirk curled his lip.

"Good morning." He nodded. "Sorry I'm late."

"Your timing is actually perfect." Ellie smiled. "Each mentor gave an introduction, and we just finished up with the last person. So, if you're ready, the floor is yours."

I'd listened to everything the mentors had said so far, but suddenly I sat up a little taller, eagerly awaiting what this mysterious man might have to say.

He took a step forward. "Good morning and welcome. My name is Jagger Langston, and I founded Apex seven years ago. I started this mentorship program because I remember what it felt like to be overlooked, to be young and full of fire but have no idea what to do with it or where to aim." He smirked. "Or in my case, to aim at the wrong place and get yourself into trouble."

Everyone chuckled, and he continued. "My mentorship program was a little different than this one—mine was in the United States Marines—but the three principles you'll learn here are the same." He counted on his fingers. "One, you'll be trusted with responsibility, even though you'll think you're not ready. That will teach you confidence and the power of your voice. Two, you'll learn to value your team members. Right now, many of you are looking at the people sitting around the table as your competitors, but they're not. They are your best resources. And three, you'll learn strategic thinking. You'll see how small decisions can impact the bigger picture and learn firsthand why it's important to have a long-term goal and make sure that each initiative you engage in is a step toward achieving that goal.

"I started this program six years ago and acted as one of the mentors," he added after a moment. "The following year, I was traveling a lot, so I took a step back. I've been meaning to participate again, but something always comes up. So when this fell into my lap two hours ago, I took it as a sign." He looked over at me and held my eyes. "In a world full of distractions, sometimes we're redirected and forced to focus on what we're meant to see."

Then Jagger looked away as if he hadn't just rocked my world. He went on for probably another ten minutes, but I was stuck on his introduction. Did he think *I* was what he's meant to see? Or was I reading into what he'd said, hearing something innocent the way I wanted to hear it? Either way, my whole body was still buzzing when he finished.

"Thank you, Jagger," Ellie said. "If you don't mind, would you also share your hobbies with everyone? I play a little game where the interns have to guess who they've been matched with. The winner gets a fun prize."

He nodded. "Of course. I pretty much like anything outdoors. I'm an avid snowboarder, master scuba diver, and I love to travel." His eyes moved back to me. "I guess you could say I'm adventurous—the kind that always takes the dare over the truth."

*DARE*. My eyes widened, and I sucked in a sharp breath that was so audible, I had to cover it up with a fake cough.

Jagger smiled at the interns sitting on the other side of the table, but the look on his face was unmistakable. The mention of *dare* was definitely not a coincidence. And I'd forgotten about our similar hobbies. That's what had gotten us matched up to begin with. My heart started to pound.

Ellie told us all to write down who we thought each intern's mentor might be, and then she announced the pairs. I got three out of the first four right, and then it was down to just me and one other unassigned intern—who happened to have gone to the same college as Jagger. But Jack hadn't been matched up yet either. So it could go either way. Anxiety pulsed through me as I waited for Ellie to announce the next pairing. I wasn't sure whether I was nervous that Jagger might be my mentor or that he might *not* be.

"Ben," Ellie said, "your mentor will be Jack Gallo."

• • •

"Have a seat." Jagger gestured to the guest chairs on the other side of his desk. "I need to speak to my assistant for a moment."

He stepped out of his office, leaving me to look around. Tall windows showcased the New York City skyline. I bet it was amazing at night. There was a conference table to the left with eight chairs around it, and the right side of the room held a more intimate seating section with a couch and two matching upholstered chairs. Built-in bookshelves lined the wall behind the desk. I leaned forward for a closer examination of those.

Four of the six shelves were packed with books. I perused the titles with interest. What someone reads can tell you a lot about the person. Jagger's were mostly nonfiction—bestsellers about Bill Gates and Warren Buffet, books about coding and the stock market, nothing uniquely personal. The shelves above held some awards and framed photos—one of him in a cap and gown, standing with a woman I thought might be his mother, one of him surrounded by people as he rang the bell at NASDAQ, and another of a woman with her arms around two little girls. But the one I spent the most time checking out was of him in military fatigues. He was smiling, his arms stretched out around a group of six men. He looked different, younger and with short, buzzed hair, but there was no mistaking those striking blue eyes and the sharp cut of his jawline. Next to it was a small framed photo of a little boy wearing only a diaper and a military combat helmet that was five sizes too big for his head. I picked it up to look for resemblance, wondering if it was him, but there was none.

Jagger came back into the office, shutting the door behind him. He shrugged his suit jacket off and swung it over the back of his chair before sitting. He unbuttoned the cuffs of his crisp, white dress shirt and began to roll up the sleeves. My eyes found unexpected lines of black and gray ink wrapped around muscular forearms. I didn't even realize I was staring until his voice startled me.

"Most are from the military."

My eyes jumped to meet his. "Hmmm?"

"You were looking at my tattoos."

*Yes, but only because they're attached to the sexy arms.* "Sorry. I'm not sure why, but I guess I didn't expect you to have any."

He flashed a hint of a smile. "Expectations usually lead to disappointment, Ms. Holland."

"Not in this case." *Oh, Jesus Christ. Did I really just say that?*

Jagger raised a brow. "Good to know."

I shook my head. "Sorry. That was inappropriate."

"I appreciate candor." He tilted his head. "Do you?"

"Yes, very much."

"Good." He smiled. "So let's both be candid for a moment, shall we?"

"Oh-kay…"

"There's an attraction here." He motioned with two fingers back and forth. "Between us."

I blinked a few times before shifting my focus over his shoulder to the framed picture of the little boy with the helmet.

"Look at me, Sutton," he said sternly. "Eyes over here."

I adjusted my gaze to meet his.

"Thank you. As I was saying, there's an attraction here. Perhaps if we acknowledge it, it will be easier to deal with each other over the next few months. The cat-and-mouse game doesn't work as well when you take the mystery out of the chase."

Jagger was clearly waiting for me to speak. But I was at a loss for words. "I'm not sure how to respond."

"With honesty. Are you attracted to me?"

My cheeks heated. But Jagger's stare didn't relent, and I wound up looking away again.

"I'm about ten seconds away from coming around to that side of the desk and pulling my chair right next to yours so you can't avoid me, Sutton. If you don't want that, you might want to redirect your attention right now."

My eyes jumped back to his, and the jerk flashed a triumphant smile. "Good. Perhaps I should go first? I'm very attracted to you. I was from the first time I saw your photo, but there's something more here. Do you agree?"

It felt like he could read my mind with the way he was looking at me, so I had no choice but to be honest. I nodded.

"Excellent." He smiled. "Now, that wasn't so difficult, was it?"

"Maybe not from where you're sitting."

"That's a very good point. I'm in a position of power, and while that's the way I prefer things normally, you technically work for me, and I don't want you to be uncomfortable. So at any time, if you'd like me to recuse myself from being your mentor, just say the word, and I'll have someone else assigned. I'll tell Ellie it turns out I'm too busy. Understood?"

I nodded.

"Would you like to end this now and have someone else assigned as your mentor?"

I shook my head.

"Good. Then let's get back to business. We met under very different circumstances, outside of work, and we're attracted to each other. But for obvious reasons, nothing should come of it. How am I doing? Are you in agreement so far?"

I swallowed. "Yes, I work for you."

Jagger's eyes gleamed. "That wasn't the reason I was referring to. I wouldn't give two shits if that were the only obstacle."

"Then...what?"

"We have different needs."

"What do you need?"

His eyes narrowed. "Do you really want me to answer that?"

I swallowed and nodded.

He leaned forward and lowered his voice. "I like to play games and fuck hard, Sutton. You need a man who will be gentle with you and take his time, someone who wants something more from you than your submission."

*Fuck hard. Submission.* I felt an ache grow between my legs. I couldn't remember a time I'd been so turned on, and yet this man was basically telling me I was inexperienced, and nothing was ever going to happen. My body's reaction was laughable, really.

Jagger studied my face. His jaw clenched tight. "Christ, I need my head examined being near you right now."

I felt my brows pull. "Right now? Why?"

"Because it's dangerous when you look at me like that."

I was genuinely confused. "Like what?"

"Like you might like it my way."

A knock at the door interrupted our conversation. Jagger sat back in his chair and cleared his throat. "Come in!"

His assistant opened the door. "I'm sorry to interrupt. Your noon appointment is here early. I put him in the conference room."

"Thank you. Tell Jim I'll be a few minutes."

She nodded and pulled the door shut.

"I need to go to that meeting," Jagger said. "We're supposed to go to lunch with our mentees today. But perhaps we should postpone until tomorrow, to give you some time to consider whether you'd like me to step back from the mentorship program." He stood and pulled his jacket from the back of the seat. "I hope you enjoy the rest of your first day."

My head was spinning as I climbed to my feet. Jagger walked me out. He put his hand on the knob, but didn't open the door.

"If you decide to have me as your mentor, I'd appreciate it if you wouldn't wear that perfume. It's the same one you wore at the wedding."

"Oh. I'm sorry. Are you allergic?"

He smiled. "No. I fucking love it."

•  •  •

"Are you freaking kidding me? I can't believe he said that." Miles lifted his hand and called over the bartender. He hadn't gone home yet, so we'd met after my first day of work for drinks.

"Another round?"

I'd already had one dirty martini, so a second was not a good idea. I looked at Miles. "I think I'm going to switch to merlot."

He nodded like he was in agreement and turned back to the bartender. "We'll have two more dirty martinis."

The bartender looked to me. I rolled my eyes, but nodded to tell him it was okay.

After he walked away, I lifted the toothpick from my empty glass and used my teeth to scrape an olive off. "I have to work tomorrow. You know I'm a lightweight."

"I have to work tomorrow, too. And I'm taking the redeye back in a few hours. But wine isn't going to cut it to discuss your new boss. You need something stronger."

"I'm pretty sure what I need is complete sobriety when it comes to Jagger Langston. The man makes me feel drunk when I'm anywhere near him. I'm not joking. I get lightheaded and woozy."

"God, I'm so damn jealous. It's been ages since I felt that kind of excitement about boinking a guy."

"I'm not boinking Jagger Langston."

Miles took the toothpick from my hand and stole the last olive. "Yes, you are, honey. And I'm so glad your first time is going to be someone with experience. My first was with *Evan Redman*. His mother called while we were fooling around, and the idiot answered. My engine was already running, and I couldn't stop it even though *we'd* stopped. I finished before he hung up. I wasn't even touching myself. I just ejaculated."

I chuckled. "A week ago, I might've thought you were exaggerating. But I can totally see how it could be possible to finish just by being around Jagger Langston. If I keep him as my mentor, I'm going to need to bring a change of panties with me."

"What do you mean *if*? You're definitely keeping him."

I shook my head. "It's a really bad idea."

He grinned. "I know. But think of all the interesting stories you're going to have when we FaceTime in the evenings. You owe me this much, leaving me alone in California for the entire summer."

I did feel bad about that. Years ago, Miles had picked up and moved across the country to be roomies with me when I'd needed him most, and now I was spending three months back in New York. "I'm sorry I'm deserting you."

The bartender delivered our second dirty martinis. Miles picked up the toothpick skewered with olives and held it to my mouth. I slipped off the repayment with my teeth.

"It's okay," he said. "Although when I get arrested for breaking and entering at two in the morning because the woman you sublet your room to calls the cops after I stumble into your bed naked instead of mine, you better come bail my ass out."

I laughed. I'd started sleeping in Miles's room a few months ago after finding spiders in my room on four different occasions. We couldn't figure out where they were coming from, but after two weeks Miles just started sleeping in my bed. He said he liked it better, so we'd ended up switching rooms. But sometimes after a night of clubbing, he got up in the middle of the night to go to the bathroom and wandered back into his old room naked.

"Maybe if you sleep with underwear on, she'll go easy on you."

He scrunched up his nose. "You know that's not happening."

We chatted a while longer as we finished our martinis and then headed outside to wait for Miles's Uber to JFK.

"Good luck with your photoshoot this week," I said.

"Forget wishing me luck. I'm a genius when I'm behind the camera. Wish me a boss who looks like yours."

A white car pulled up, and Miles opened the door without even checking the plate. I shook my head. "How do you know that's your car?"

"I have a sixth sense."

The driver leaned back. "Miles? JFK?"

"See?" He winked and pulled me into a hug, then held out a curled pinky. "Promise me something."

We'd been pinky swearing since we were kids. "What?"

"You will *not* come home from New York a virgin."

"I'll do my best."

"Forget your best. *Do* the boss."

I shook my head. "That is such bad advice."

He kissed my forehead. "Maybe. But some storms are meant to be danced in, not dodged."

Jagger
14 years ago

**"S**hould we go in?" Marla asked. The two of us were waiting outside the courtroom. My joke of a public defender was nowhere to be found, and the court officer had just called my case for the second time. I walked over to him.

"I'm Jagger Langston. You called my name, but I don't know where my attorney went. He was here a few minutes ago on his phone."

"Who's your attorney?"

"Leonard Adams."

The court officer frowned. "He's probably down the hall with a different client. That guy will find a way to squeeze someone in if you go to take a piss."

"What should I do?"

"I can push you down on the calendar. I still have two more cases to call this afternoon. Hopefully he'll turn up by then."

"Thanks. I appreciate it."

I walked back over to Marla, who was biting her nail again. "Stop doing that. You're making me nervous."

"*I'm* making *you* nervous? My parents don't know you were arrested again, and if they find out I've been keeping your secret, we're *both* in hot water. And your dumb, disappearing lawyer called Judge Hanover Judge *Hammer* because of how hard he is with sentencing. Why the heck did you and your stupid friends break into the school anyway? You usually get in trouble for *not* going to school."

I shrugged. "It was cold out. We wanted to play basketball."

Marla shook her head. "You have to stop hanging out with those guys—and that new girl you're going out with, too."

"What's wrong with Lexi?"

"Last week, I was watching a soccer game on TV when she came over. You weren't home yet, so she sat down and started watching with me. I asked if she liked soccer, and she said no, she only really likes bolly-ball. It took me almost five minutes to figure out she was referring to *volley*ball. She's seventeen and seriously had no idea that the word isn't *bolly-ball*."

I sighed. "Lots of people get things wrong. Remember when you thought that Rihanna song was 'chips and dip excite me', instead of chains and whips?"

"I was *ten*! And Lexi played on the *bolly-ball* team for two years in middle school."

"You're making that up."

Marla made an X mark across her chest. "Cross my heart. Ask her!"

After we both had a good laugh, Marla seemed to study my face. I thought maybe something was on it, so I swiped at my cheek. "What?"

"You have dark circles under your eyes. You're having trouble sleeping again, aren't you?"

"I sleep just fine."

She frowned. "Sure you do."

Forty-five minutes later, there was still no sign of my lawyer when the court officer came out again. He looked at me. "You're up, buddy. Still no sign of Lenny?"

"Nope."

He gestured for me to follow. "Just take your place at the defendant's table, and when the judge asks where your attorney is, tell him he's MIA. You're better off with no attorney than not appearing."

*Great.* This judge didn't like me to begin with. The last time I was in front of him, my attorney had told me the max I could get as a repeat juvey was two-hundred hours of community service, but that he'd never had anyone get more than eighty. I got the full two hundred, along with a twenty-minute lecture. But what could I do now?

I made my way into the courtroom. Marla took a seat in the spectator section, while I pushed the swinging wooden half-door to get to the other side. The court officer stood in front of the judge's bench and called out a bunch of numbers, along with my name. I glanced behind me, hoping the buffoon of an attorney I had would show at the last second, but no such luck. I wiped my sweaty palms on the dress pants I'd borrowed from Marla's dad's closet after he left for work today.

Judge Hanover pushed his glasses up from the bridge of his nose.

"Mr. Langston, where is your counsel?"

"I don't know, your honor. He was here an hour ago. We were waiting in the hall and—"

"Stop." He held up his hand and turned to the ADA. She was kind of hot for a woman who could get me locked up. "Ms. Atkins," he said, "is the State prepared to hear the Court's sentencing?"

She nodded. "We are, your honor."

The judge's eyes slid back to me. "Mr. Langston, this is your second time in my courtroom and your fourth time in this courthouse for various arrests. The State submitted your school records to show that you are not only out causing a ruckus, but you're also often truant."

"Your honor, I—"

He again put his hand up. "I'll give you an inch of leeway because your counsel is not here at the moment. But you do not speak while I'm speaking. Is that understood?"

*Fuck.* I hung my head. "Yes, your honor."

He pushed his glasses up his nose again. "As I was saying, the State submitted your school records to show that you're a terrible student. But do you want to know what I noticed?"

I looked at the judge, unsure if he actually wanted me to respond.

He sighed. "I asked you a question, so you may speak now, Mr. Langston."

"Yeah, I want to know."

"The word is *yes*, not yeah. And what I discovered on your record is—contrary to what your actions may lead one to believe—you are not dumb." He picked up a paper and pointed to the top corner. "Did you have an SAT tutor?"

"No, sir."

"Did you take a review course?"

"No, sir."

He shook his head. "I've spent five grand on private tutors to try to get my son to a number that is a hundred points less than your score. Did you cheat on the exam, Mr. Langston?"

My eyes narrowed. "No."

"Then you're on your way to becoming what I like to call a Machiavellian Master. Do you know who that is?"

I nodded.

The judge frowned again. "Of course you do. You could probably write a whole paper on it even though you were absent the day the teacher taught about Niccolò Machiavelli." He shook his head yet again. "Normally, I would throw the book at someone who has been arrested four times in a year. Your little Class D felony has a sentencing guideline of one to seven years. But today is your lucky day. I'm going to give you two options and let *you* decide your own fate, since you're so smart. How does that sound?"

"Uh, I guess it depends on what my two options are."

Judge Hanover's mouth twisted to a sneer, and he wagged a finger. "See? You *are* smart. That's why I'm giving you the choice of two islands."

The courtroom door behind me burst open, and I turned to find my dumbass lawyer rushing in. Leonard took one look at me standing alone and the judge's annoyed face and swallowed. "I'm sorry, your honor. I was down the hall for what was supposed to be a two-minute calendar call and got held up."

"You joined us just in time, Mr. Adams. I was about to tell your client what was behind doors A and B."

Leonard pushed through the swinging gate and dumped a half-dozen files on the table. "I'm sorry—door A or B?"

The judge rolled his eyes and shifted his focus back to me. "You're probably the smarter of the two at that table anyway, Mr. Langston, so I'll explain it to you. Walk through door A, and you get an all-expense-paid, seven-year vacation at the lovely Riker's Island, compliments of the hardworking people of the state of New York. Walk through door B, and you get a four-year travel tour that kicks off at the lovely Parris Island in South Carolina and could end with you having a fighting chance in life."

"Parris Island? Is that a jail?"

"No, Mr. Langston. It's Marines boot camp."

—— **CHAPTER** ——
# EIGHT

Sutton

The following morning, I arrived at Apex early and dropped my stuff at my desk before heading to the breakroom for some much-needed caffeine. Jack Gallo was again inside. My footsteps stuttered, but the clickity-clack of my heels made him turn.

He smiled. "Good morning."

"Hey." I forced a smile—not sure *why* it had to be forced. Jack was a nice-enough guy. "Came up for the good stuff again, huh?"

He poured a drop of cream into his mug and lifted it to his lips. "I forgot how much better it is than the crap I buy on the street. How was your first day?"

"Good. Though I was introduced to so many people, I'm not sure I remember any of their names."

He smiled and patted his chest. "I'm Jack."

I chuckled. "I remember yours."

He stepped away from the big espresso maker to make room for me, but leaned a hip against the counter, not going anywhere soon. "I was disappointed that we didn't get matched together."

I nodded. "We have a few things in common, so I thought it was a possibility."

He sipped his coffee. "You would've been better off with anyone than the match you got."

"Oh? Is Jagger not a good mentor?"

He shrugged. "He's just difficult overall. He's arrogant and thinks he knows better than everyone. The guy has an expensive management team in place to advise him, yet he does whatever the hell he wants."

I felt oddly defensive. "Considering he made the Forbes Top 100 CEO list and is worth more than most of the Kardashians and Jenners, it sounds like whatever he wants must work pretty well."

"I guess." Jack shrugged. "I just hope he makes time for you. I know I would've."

I finished making my morning cappuccino, feeling ready to end this conversation, but Jack walked out of the breakroom with me and followed me to my cubicle.

"Are you going downstairs for the morning management briefing?" he asked.

I nodded. "They said it was optional, but it sounds interesting. That's why I came in early."

Every day, Apex held a fifteen-minute management briefing on the tenth floor, though it was open to anyone. It had been described during yesterday's orientation as the *morning news*—with highlights and a few stories getting a deeper dive—but of course all the news was Apex related. I thought it was a cool idea, a way to get staff at all levels invested in everything going on across all the different lines of business.

Jack lifted his chin to the cubicle next to mine, where his assigned intern sat—or would sit, when he got here. "Guess you're the only one who thinks it's interesting."

I smiled but wasn't about to badmouth my peers. Tucking my purse into the drawer, I picked up a pen and notebook. "Do you attend the morning meeting every day?"

"Not usually. I go to the gym in the morning, so I don't generally get here until closer to eight." He put a hand out for me to walk first. "But I'm going to make an effort to get here now."

I didn't ask why as we headed for the elevator. Jack pressed the button, and a few seconds later the doors slid open. There was only one occupant inside the car, *Jagger Langston.*

My pulse sped up. He was looking down at his cell, but when his head lifted and he saw me, a slow grin curved his lips. Though when his eyes shifted to the man standing next to me, that grin flattened to more of a grim line.

"Morning, boss." Jack put his hand on my back, guiding me to enter. It was innocent enough, but the way Jagger's eyes seized on it made it feel anything but. Tension radiated from the boss, filling the car as we stepped in. I smiled, but he just offered a curt nod and went back to his phone. It wasn't hard to figure out why Jack had said what he'd said about him earlier.

Awkwardness set in as the doors slid closed, so I did the only thing I could do—held my breath and stared up at the illuminated numbers, willing them to move faster.

The entire encounter probably took less than twenty seconds, but by the time the doors opened, I desperately needed air. Jack again put his hand out. "After you."

I started to take a step, but a hand at my elbow stopped me.

I turned to look at the man holding it. "I'm going to the morning briefing."

"We have an appointment this morning," Jagger said.

Jack was still standing next to me, waiting for me to get off the elevator. The boss glared at him. "*You* may go."

"Uh..." Jack's eyes flickered between Jagger and me. He seemed hesitant to leave me alone, but I didn't want this to turn into a scene, so I smiled and tapped my temple.

"Silly me. I completely forgot I'm supposed to meet with my mentor. Probably not the best thing to do on the second day of my internship."

Jack gave me a look, and I got the feeling he didn't believe me, but at least he stepped off the elevator. "I'll see you around."

I continued staring straight ahead until Jagger pressed the button for the top floor, and the elevator doors closed. Then I yanked my elbow from his grip. "What are you doing? We don't have any appointment, and you just made me look like a jerk."

"I told you to figure out what you wanted, whether you preferred I step back from the mentorship program or not."

"So? That doesn't mean you can manhandle me in the elevator!"

"I didn't manhandle you."

"You grabbed my elbow and told Jack I had an appointment, which we both know is not true. What else would you call it?"

Jagger's eyes swept over my face. The stern façade he'd had since he saw me with Jack fell away. Both his face and tone softened. "I apologize. I didn't mean to offend you."

I sighed. "You didn't offend me. Just...just don't do that in front of people who work here."

The elevator doors opened at the next floor. Thankfully, no one was waiting. Though at the last second, a wing-tip shoe slipped between the closing doors and they bounced back open. The owner of the foot attempted to step inside, but Jagger showed him his palm.

"Wait for the next one."

The guy's forehead wrinkled. "Uh... Okay. Sorry."

Jagger leaned forward and pressed the button for the top floor, though it was already illuminated. I waited for the doors to slide closed once again before speaking, since the man he'd just rejected was still staring at us.

Once we were alone, I turned. "Why did you do that?"

"You told me not to touch you in front of people who work here. He works here."

I wanted to be pissed off, but he was dead serious. For some unknown reason, I burst into laughter. "You don't care about making people uncomfortable, do you?"

He stilled. "I'm making you uncomfortable?"

"Not me!" I flapped my hands in the air. "That guy you just barred from the elevator."

He dragged a hand through his hair. "Let's just go speak in my office."

Neither of us said another word as we rose to the top floor, got off the elevator, and wound our way through a series of halls to get to the big corner suite. Jagger closed the door behind us. I took the same seat as yesterday, but he didn't this time. He moved the guest chair beside mine and turned to face me head on.

"What have you decided?" he asked. "Do you want me to recuse myself, or do you want me as your mentor?"

I'd been feeling prickly, but being this close to Jagger made me feel something entirely different. Electricity crackled inside of me. "I probably should ask you to recuse yourself."

Today's bespoke suit was navy. It brought out the color of his eyes more than usual—and that was saying something, because his irises were the color of an Alaskan glacier. Our chairs were set two feet apart, but Jagger's long legs were only inches from mine. It made me want to lean forward and brush my knees with his, just to see how he reacted.

"That's not a yes."

I rolled my eyes. "I've never been very good at doing the things I should do."

His lip twitched once again. Why did I love that so much? "I'm sure you're good at anything you set your mind to."

I sighed. "You scare people, you know."

"Who?"

"People who work here."

"Do I scare you?"

I thought about it and shook my head. "Scare me? No."

He shifted in his chair, leaning forward until our knees touched. When they did, his eyes stayed firmly focused on the contact for a long time before lifting to meet my gaze. A wicked smile spread across his face. "Are you sure about that?"

Electricity zapped from my knee to...*other places*. I swallowed. "Yes."

I thought he was going to delve further into the subject. Even if he bought that he didn't scare me, it was clear he did *something* to me. Instead he adjusted in his seat, breaking the connection, and cleared his throat. "One o'clock today."

Had I zoned out and missed part of our conversation? I felt my brows draw close. "One o'clock?"

"For our mentor lunch, the one we were supposed to have yesterday. Meet me downstairs in the lobby."

"Oh. Okay."

Jagger got up and walked around his desk. It was the equivalent to what he'd done to Jack in the elevator without saying "*You* may go." Still, I took the hint, stood, and walked to the door.

I turned back to look at him. "You're sort of rude, you know that?"

I *loved* the surprised look on his face. Jagger's eyebrows nearly reached his hairline. "Is that so?"

"You asked if I was afraid of you. I'm not, but you're dismissive, and it makes people feel disregarded."

He stared at me for a full five seconds before shifting his attention to his desk. "I'll take that under advisement."

• • •

**Miles: How are things going with Daddy Discipline?**

I was sitting in a conference room with all the other interns, watching some mandatory HR videos on a big screen. I lowered my phone under the table and typed back.

**Sutton: I decided to keep him as my mentor.**

**Miles: I already knew that.**

**Sutton: How?**

**Miles: Because I *know* you. This guy is like the Rubik's Cube your mom brought home in fourth grade.**

**Sutton: I'm not following...**

**Miles: When something intrigues you, you can't stop playing with it until you figure it out. You pretended to have a stomach virus so you could stay home from school and solve it.**

**Sutton: Well, hopefully this puzzle is as easily solved, because I got bored with the Rubik's Cube after I made all six sides into solid colors.**

**Miles: Something tells me that man is neither easily solvable nor a toy you'll get bored with.**

HR videos weren't the most exciting things to watch, but it seemed to take forever for one o'clock to arrive. When it finally did, I stopped in the ladies' room to freshen up—like I would for any lunch meeting. *Sure, tell yourself whatever you want, Sutton.* Then I rode the elevator downstairs. The car was packed, and people got off and on at every floor, making the nerves I already felt fray a little more as the seconds ticked by.

Though the sight of Jagger Langston looking at his watch, impatiently waiting in the lobby, made me want to stay on the elevator and ride it up and down again. It probably wasn't a good thing that I felt a strange urge to make the CEO of the company bristle. I took a deep breath and stepped into the lobby.

Jagger's head turned, and his eyes immediately latched on me. He watched each step of my approach as if there weren't two hundred other people moving about in the busy lobby. He didn't seem to notice the half-dozen women whose heads turned as they passed him. The man was truly breathtaking—put a fountain around him, and he'd have more visitors than a Michelangelo.

"Hi," I said. "Sorry I'm late. The elevator stopped at every floor."

"The stairs are quicker at this time of day."

"Stairs? You work on the fifty-ninth floor."

"Where I spend too much time sitting." Jagger's hand settled on the small of my back, and he steered me through the lobby without another word. Outside, a uniformed driver leaned against a silver Maybach. When he saw Jagger enter the turnstile, he pushed off and reached for the back door. But Jagger waved him away. "Downtown, Sam. Seventeenth and Park."

"Yes, sir. Sure thing." The driver tipped his hat to me and offered a friendly smile, then quickly jogged around the front of the car and got behind the wheel.

I slid into the backseat first, and Jagger joined me, pulling the door closed behind him. It was a full-size car, but the inside suddenly felt very small. The smell of Jagger's delicious cologne permeated the air, making it impossible for me to relax.

"How was your morning?" he asked as we pulled away from the curb.

"Fine. And yours?"

He looked outside the window. "Distracting."

"Oh? Is everything okay?"

"That remains to be seen."

Jagger's phone rang. He looked down and frowned. "Excuse me. I need to take this."

The heated phone call lasted until we pulled up at the restaurant—something about the terms of financing for an investment.

"Sorry about that." He stuffed his cell into his jacket pocket and told the driver to stay in the car, then got out and offered me his hand.

"Thank you." I smiled as I slid out.

Tuccio's must've been a frequent stomping ground of his, because the attractive hostess lit up when we walked in, and she quickly routed us to a quiet table in the back without having to be asked. Jagger again displayed perfect manners by pulling out my chair. I thought it was interesting how his actions were in stark contrast to the way he seemed to disregard people in the office.

"Can I get you something to drink while you take a look at the daily specials?" The hostess handed us each a leather-bound menu.

Jagger looked to me.

"I'll have a seltzer with lime, please."

He nodded. "Same."

Once she disappeared, I perused the choices. From across the table, I felt Jagger's gaze searing into me. I tried to ignore it, but eventually I lowered the menu.

"What?"

He squinted. "What?"

"You're staring at me."

"You're sitting across from me. Where would you like me to look?"

"Maybe at the *menu*?"

There was an unmistakable gleam in his eyes. "I already know what I want."

"Oh." I picked the menu back up and tried to go about reading again, but it felt like an impossible task. My eyes scanned the words, yet I couldn't seem to absorb anything because my body was too highly conscious of the man sitting a few feet away. Once again, I lowered the leather book. "What are you having?"

"The grilled salmon."

My nose wrinkled. "I don't love fish. Any other recommendations?"

"The blackened chicken Caesar salad is always good."

"That I can do."

The minute I set the menu on the table, an attentive waiter came to take our order. When he left, he took the menus with him, and I had nowhere to hide. Jagger's intense stare made me squirm in my seat.

"So..." I said.

He smirked. I got the feeling he knew I was twisting inside, and damn it if he wasn't enjoying watching me struggle. I was grateful when he threw me a lifeline by starting the conversation.

"I spoke to Edmund yesterday afternoon. He was happy that I was going to be your mentor. I take it you haven't mentioned how we first met?"

I shook my head. "Definitely not."

"Thank you. I value my privacy very much."

"And I value people not knowing what an idiot I was."

He smiled. "So tell me what your interests are."

My pulse quickened. "My interests?"

He chuckled. "Not those interests, Sutton. I'm asking about your career aspirations. This is a mentorship, after all."

"Oh." I shook my head, feeling my cheeks heat. "Of course. Sorry."

Jagger leaned in. "Though if you'd like to share your *other* interests, I'm open to hearing them. I'm at a bit of an unfair advantage here, considering you know mine."

"I think you have to actually experience things to figure out what you're interested in," I mumbled.

Jagger tapped his finger on the water glass. It looked like he wanted to say something but was in the process of thinking better of it.

I sighed. "Just spit it out."

He squinted. "What?"

"Whatever you're holding back. I was thinking about your strategy yesterday—admitting there was an attraction between us in order to move past it. I think it's more than an attraction—there's also a curiosity, at least for me. Maybe if we both say what we're thinking or ask about what has us curious, we can move past that too. A friend recently reminded me that sometimes I get stuck on things I find intriguing. Perhaps we should go through the middle and stop trying to go around the problem."

Jagger studied me. "This is a business meeting, and I'm your boss. Or more precisely, your boss's boss's boss."

"Okay." I shrugged. "Then I quit."

His brows jumped. "You...quit?"

I nodded. "Now, can we speak freely for five minutes?"

Again I could see the wheels in his head spinning. After a long while, he reached into his jacket pocket and pulled out his cell. Punching a few buttons, he set it on the table between us. He smirked as he hit the button to start a five-minute timer and held out his hand.

"Ladies first."

"I can ask anything and you'll answer?"

He pointed to the ticking clock. "You're wasting valuable time."

I exhaled in a rush and nodded. So many questions about this man had swirled in my head over the last few days, but now that I had the opportunity to ask them—I panicked and drew a blank. "I pass. You go first."

A smile formed on his perfect lips. "Are you still a virgin?"

I rolled my eyes. "Yes. Would you have slept with me if I hadn't told you I had no idea what the app was for and that I was a virgin?"

His gaze was intense. "Absolutely. Why are you still a virgin? Is it a religious thing?"

I smiled. "You're really hung up on my virginity, huh?"

He practically groaned. "It's been difficult to think about much else for days."

I took a moment to let his comment sink in. But after a few beats, Jagger tapped the side of his phone, reminding me of the rapidly disappearing seconds. "Right. Sorry. I'm still a virgin because of my ex. Brendan comes from a super-religious family. His father is a deacon, so he wanted to wait until marriage." I paused. "At least that's what he told me. A few months after we broke up, I walked in on him and my stepsister. So apparently, the issue was more that he didn't want to have sex with *me* than he didn't want to have sex."

Jagger's eyes darkened. "The man is a moron."

I smiled. "Thank you. He also looked like a jackrabbit on top of her, so at least it doesn't seem like I missed out on much."

He smiled. "Your turn."

"Are you attracted to me?"

"Every time you walk into a room, I lose focus. I don't remember ever feeling so attracted to someone."

"Oh. Wow." I felt my cheeks heat again.

He tilted his head. "And you?"

"You have a mirror, don't you?"

"Is that your question?"

I shook my head. "No, definitely not. What are you into? Like, BDSM?"

"I'm more into the dominance and discipline aspect of sexual relationships than I am inflicting pain. But I do enjoy a good spanking when one is warranted."

I shook my head, looking away.

Jagger smiled. "Have you ever been spanked, Ms. Holland?"

"No." I glanced down at his phone just as the timer dipped under one minute. How could the time have gone so fast?

*Fifty-nine.*

*Fifty-eight.*

*Fifty-seven.*

My insides felt like a shaken bottle of champagne with the top about to pop off. "Have you ever slept with someone you work with?"

The muscle in his jaw tensed. "Yes."

"Someone who worked for you?"

He held up his index finger and moved it from side to side. "That's two questions. I believe it's my turn."

"Oh, right."

"Are you still on the prowl, intent to lose your virginity?"

"I wouldn't exactly call it 'on the prowl', but yeah... I'd like to get it over with."

"You deserve much more than getting it over with, Sutton."

Feeling bold, I tilted my head. "Know anyone available to help me out with that?"

Jagger's eyes dropped to my lips, then to the cell phone between us.

"Is that your question?"

*Twenty-two.*

*Twenty-one.*

*Twenty.*

*Nineteen.*

My heart pounded faster. "No."

"It appears you may only get one more question," he said. "Make it a good one."

I looked him straight in the eyes. "Ever sleep with an intern?"

Jagger's mouth curved to a wicked grin. "Not yet."

# — CHAPTER —
# NINE

### Sutton

Friday afternoon, Jack Gallo stopped by my cubicle. I hadn't seen him since the breakroom on Tuesday morning.

"Hey." He leaned his elbows on the half wall and smiled. "A bunch of us go out for happy hour one Friday a month. Tonight's the night, if you're up for joining."

"Oh. I, uh..."

"Your fellow interns are all coming. I came down earlier to ask everyone, but you weren't around."

The week had been long, and I was tired, especially since I hadn't yet adjusted to New York time and my sleep schedule had been wonky. "I'm actually kind of wiped out."

He shrugged. "If you change your mind, we'll be at the Copa."

"The...Copa bar?" How many bars were in New York City? It seemed like a dozen lined each street, yet happy hour was at the same bar where I'd met Jagger for our DARE date? That seemed like an awfully big coincidence.

"Yeah, do you know it?"

I shook my head, as if admitting I'd been there was going to give my secret away. "No, but it sounds familiar."

He nodded. "Probably because it's on the Apex Holdings website. The boss owns it."

"The boss?"

"Langston. He owns the entire building, too. That's the reason we all go. Free drinks. Happy hour is on him."

"Does he go?" The idea of running into Jagger Langston made the thought of happy hour more interesting.

But Jack shook his head. "He's never graced us with his presence, even though he lives on the top floor of the building."

I suddenly felt icky. *Isn't that convenient?* He lives in the damn building. A few drinks to loosen his dates up, and straight to the elevator they go. God, why did that irk me so much? It wasn't like he'd ever misrepresented his intentions on the dating site, saying he wanted to meet the love of his life. He was on a hook-up site where convenience was probably appreciated, not found appalling.

Jack rapped his knuckles on the top of my cubicle wall. "I have to run to a meeting. But we'll be there from six to eleven. Maybe come for one drink?"

"I'll try."

He disappeared, and I sat at my desk, struggling with my conflicting feelings. I hadn't seen Jagger since our lunch date—or lunch *meeting*, I suppose. After our bizarre five minutes of free questioning, we'd returned to discussing business. Twenty minutes later, he'd gotten a call that some big deal he was about to close was threatening to fall through, and he'd had to get on a flight to London to try to save it. He dropped me at the entrance to the Apex building, and that was the last I'd seen of him.

I'd told myself it was just as well. No good could come from me continuing to drool over a man like Jagger Langston. But it didn't seem to stop me from getting excited every time the elevator door opened, or I went to a management meeting that included the group "All Executives" in Outlook.

My desk phone rang while I was still lost in thought.

"Sutton Holland," I answered.

"Hi, Sutton. It's Edmund."

I hadn't seen or heard from my stepfather since starting at Apex. He'd been off on my first day, the Monday after the wedding, which now seemed like a lifetime ago, and then he'd been on a business trip the rest of the week.

"Hey, Edmund. How are you?"

"I'm well. I was meaning to get down to see you today, but I got bombarded the minute I walked in the building this morning."

"I didn't realize you were back from your trip."

"We hit a stalemate with the deal I was working on, so I caught a ride home on the company jet late last night with the boss."

I perked up. *Jagger's back.* "Oh. That's good. I'm sure Mom was glad."

His voice softened. "Yes, her day is always brighter when her coffee is hand delivered to her in bed before the sleep mask comes off her eyes."

I chuckled. That was my mom. I'd learned the trick to her morning happiness in grade school—bring her hot coffee in her favorite Tiffany's mug first thing in the morning, and I could ask anything and get a yes. "And that, in turn, makes everyone else's day brighter."

"It certainly does." I heard the smile in his voice. Edmund adored my mother. And I'd never seen her happier than with him. What's the old saying? *Fourth time's a charm?* "Anyway, would you have some time to stop up here so we can talk for a few minutes?"

*Uh-oh.* My stomach dropped. He'd taken the plane home with the boss, and now I was being summoned to his office. This didn't sound good. "Umm... Yeah, sure."

"Great. Pop in on your way out. It won't take long."

Forty-five minutes later, I rode the elevator up to the executive floor and swiped my card to enter the glass doors. My stomach was a knot of nerves as I walked into the empty reception area. I'd learned the layout of the top floor on my first day. It was a circle that could be entered from the right or the left. The most direct path to Edmund's office was to my right, but his office came before Jagger's, so if I went that way, I wouldn't pass the boss. I nibbled on my lip for a few seconds before settling on going left.

Halfway to Jagger's office, my steps faltered when I heard men's voices. Two suits I vaguely recognized from the corporate website walked into the hall, and I breathed a sigh of relief that neither was Jagger or Edmund. Though my breaths again staggered to a halt as I approached the big corner office located at the turn. Trying not to make it obvious I was looking, my eyes darted to the side. Disappointment hit as I found the office empty, but my legs kept going without breaking stride.

When I arrived at Edmund's office, his door was open. He sat behind his desk, talking loudly on speakerphone. When he saw me, he smiled and stood, waving me in while continuing his conversation. It wasn't until a few seconds later that I realized he wasn't actually on the phone. He was talking to someone sitting on the couch, which was now behind me. I turned, and that person was none other than Jagger.

I wobbled on my heels at the sight of him.

He stood, and I could've sworn there was a hint of amusement dancing in his eyes. "Good to see you again, Sutton."

"I...I didn't realize anyone was in the office but Edmund."

Jagger's shirtsleeves were rolled up, showcasing his muscular forearms covered in tattoos. His hair, which was normally slicked back and neat, was more disheveled than usual. It looked like he'd spent a decent amount of time raking a hand through it. I could've ogled the man for hours, but I didn't want to embarrass my stepfather, so I turned my attention back to him and thumbed to the door. "Should I come back?"

Jagger answered. "That's not necessary. We were just finishing up." He picked up his suit jacket from the couch and nodded to Edmund. "Thanks again for trying to put out the dumpster fire. I was initially disappointed, but the way their management team has acted in the last twenty-four hours, maybe things worked out for the best."

Edmund nodded. "Sometimes things go wrong so that better things can come along and make things right again."

Jagger's gaze shifted to me, and this time the amusement in his eyes was undeniable. "I agree."

He left with only a nod, and I made the mistake of watching him through the glass wall until he was out of sight—a mistake because Edmund had been watching me.

"Have you two gotten to spend any time together yet?" he asked. "Since he's your mentor?"

My first instinct was to say no—but then I remembered that everyone goes to lunch with their mentees their first day. I nodded. "We had lunch and talked for a bit, but he got a call and had to cut our conversation short."

Edmund nodded. "You should probably get used to that. That man is pulled in twelve different directions at any time. I was actually surprised that he called Ellie and volunteered to be part of the mentorship program this year. He works fourteen hours a day, and it's not nearly enough to manage everything he's got on his plate."

"He...volunteered? Ellie didn't draft him?"

My stepfather nodded again. "I think when he found out it was you who was out of a mentor, he stepped in out of respect for me. I appreciate it. You could learn a lot from that man. His brain works a lot like yours—takes in massive amounts of data and spits it out completely processed in the time it takes most people to look at the numbers on the page. But he also has the patience of a boiling kettle's whistle." He waved me closer to his desk. "Anyway, let me know if he doesn't make time for you, and I'll see what I can do about getting you reassigned to another exec."

"I'm sure that won't be necessary."

Edmund held his hand out for me to sit, then took the seat behind his desk again.

"I wanted to talk to you about your mom's fiftieth birthday coming up."

My shoulders relaxed at the change of subject. I sat. "You mean thirty-ninth."

His brows drew together. "She's fifteen-and-a-half years younger than me, to the day. She'll be fifty."

"And you won't make sixty-six if Mia Newport hears you saying she's going to be fifty out loud. My mother is perpetually thirty-nine. Didn't you know that?"

He chuckled. "Good point. And that's part of the reason I thought I should talk to you about how we should celebrate. I was thinking about a surprise party, but I wasn't sure how she would feel about that. Unless, of course, I called it her fortieth, perhaps?"

"I'm not sure she would be thrilled with a big party. I don't think she's taking this birthday lightly."

He sighed. "That's why I wanted to run things by you before setting anything in motion. What about a small group at my house in Montauk for the weekend? We could go over to Block Island or even Nantucket for the day? I know where I might be able to borrow a beautiful boat, rather than taking the ferry. Maybe I could surprise her and have her best friend, Patrice, and her husband come, and of course all you kids?"

The thought of being cooped up all weekend with Colette and her new husband made me feel seasick without having stepped foot off land, but it did sound like something my mom would love. "That sounds really nice. I think she would enjoy that."

"Wonderful." He smiled. "I think I'll leave my cell phone in the City for that weekend, so I can be present for a change. I've had a busy year so far, and even when I'm home, my head doesn't always get the message it's supposed to relax. I owe your mom more than a weekend."

I smiled at how thoughtful he was. "That sounds amazing."

He nodded and rose to his feet. "Consider it done then. I'll let you know about the boat, but bring your swimsuit either way. Now why don't you get out of here and go enjoy your Friday night in the City? Last time you lived here you weren't old enough to take advantage of the nightlife."

Out in the hall, I managed to turn right and head straight for the elevator. But as I waited for the car, footsteps approached and I *knew*. Without needing to turn around, I had no doubt who it was.

Jagger came to stand next to me. Up close, I could see how tired he looked. His normally bright blue eyes were dimmer and reddened. Stubble peppered his angular jaw, and a piece of wayward hair fell over his eyes. None of it took away from his undeniable attractiveness, though. If anything, it gave him a more genuine and approachable look.

"You look younger when you're tired," I said.

"That's funny because I feel much older, about eighty at the moment." He rubbed the back of his neck and stretched it right, then left. "I've never grown proficient at sleeping on planes."

The elevator doors in front of us slid open, and Jagger put a hand on the small of my back, steering me inside. I'd observed him with other women in the office. He had impeccable manners, always opened doors and gestured for them to go first, but he didn't touch them the way he did me. Like always, the contact caused a zap, an electric current that jolted my tired body to life.

He positioned himself behind me in the elevator, close enough that I got a whiff of his sinfully delicious scent, yet shy of actual touching.

"Plans tonight?" he asked.

Remembering what Jack said about him living in the building, I decided to dangle a carrot and see if he'd bite.

"I was thinking about going to the office happy hour—the one at the Copa bar." I was glad I was facing straight ahead and he couldn't see my face because my smirk was impossible to contain.

He was quiet for a beat. "I see."

The doors slid open at my floor. I still had to shut down for the day and grab my purse, so I stepped off. Jagger stayed firmly inside, unmoving. I had no idea what the hell possessed me, but I suddenly got a wild hair and met his eyes. "Maybe I'll get lucky this time and find someone willing to take care of my little problem."

Jagger stared at me with an unreadable expression, though the muscle ticcing in his cheek gave me a good idea that he was less than thrilled. I held my breath as the doors slid closed, half expecting him to stop them. When he didn't, a strange mix of relief and disappointment hit me. I really must be tired because clearly I'd lost my mind, saying what I'd just said to the CEO. Thinking about it, I started to laugh.

At first it was just small chuckles, but eventually it turned into a full-belly cackle that probably made me sound like I'd lost my mind. I kept laughing all the way to my desk and through locking my laptop away and taking out my purse. It was strangely freeing, and I felt a lot better after I'd gotten it out.

Outside on the street, I took a big gulp of the New York City air. I looked around at the people walking in all directions, the bumper-to-bumper cars honking even though there was no room for anyone to move, and realized how much I'd missed the endless energy. The feeling was contagious, and I found myself no longer wanting to go home and dive into my bed. Instead, I headed to the same place I had last week—the Copa.

Maybe this time, I wouldn't leave alone.

—— **CHAPTER** ——
# TEN

Sutton

**M**y phone buzzed as I walked up the stairs from the subway, a block away from the Copa. I answered with a smile on my face.

"I know you're calling at seven PM on a Friday night to make sure I'm not home alone wallowing, and you'll be happy to know I'm on my way to a bar."

"Shit," Miles said. "I guess you saw the post?"

"What post?"

The line went quiet. "Wait, why are you going to a bar instead of going home to wallow?"

"Because it's a work happy hour and I was invited?" I left off that the bar was the place I'd met Jagger and almost hooked up with him—and also happened to be the building he lived in.

"Oh. Shoot. Okay...forget I called. Go have a great time." He paused and then added an awkward, "Woohoo! Happy hour."

*What is he up to?* "No so fast. What post were you calling about?"

"Eh, it's not important."

"Miles Brighton Hartley, you know I can't just forget that you have gossip juicy enough to call me about."

He groaned. "Just this once, try. Keep off social media and enjoy your evening."

"Hang on a second." Of course, I did the *exact opposite* of what he'd just told me because now I needed to know. Lowering my phone, I was about to swipe to go on to social media, but a missed call stopped me. *My mother.* A pit formed in my stomach. If my mother was calling me, that meant—

I swiped the missed call away and went straight to Instagram. One, two...three scrolls in, and the reason for Miles's call smacked me square in the face.

Colette looking up at Brendan with a big smile—as she held out a sonogram picture. I stopped in place on the busy New York City sidewalk. Someone cursed and stepped around me.

"Move it, lady!"

"What the fuck!" another guy said.

"Get out of the damn way!" a woman spat.

After the third person yelled at me, I managed to step out of the flow of traffic and stand against a building. I'd almost forgotten I was on the phone until I heard a faint voice in the distance.

"Sutton, are you there?"

I lifted the cell back to my ear. "Sorry, yeah, I'm here."

"You just went on Instagram, didn't you?"

I nodded, though Miles clearly couldn't see me. "Why does it hurt? I mean, this was inevitable. He married her, for God's sake."

"Because you did all the hard work for nothing, that's why. That man would be wearing a gray zip-up hoodie and

Crocs if you hadn't helped him. It's like someone buying your fully trained dog after three years of you cleaning up its piss."

I smiled sadly. "I really need to move on."

"You *have* moved on. What you need is to move up and down."

I took a deep breath and let it out on a big sigh. "Yeah."

"I'm sorry I ruined your night, cookie."

"You didn't ruin it. I'm actually glad I found out before I had a few drinks."

"Are you still going to go for happy hour?"

I felt even less like mingling with strangers now, not to mention my feet were starting to hurt in these heels, but I knew myself—going home would only make it worse. "Yeah, I'm going to go for at least a little while."

"Excellent. Maybe find some dork who works in a different department with a face made for radio and a body made for the big screen."

"Why does he need to have a radio-worthy face?"

"Because men tend to only look in the mirror when they go to the bathroom, which means they just see their face. The homely guys forget they have a killer bod and feel like they have to work twice as hard in the bedroom to make up for it."

"I can't tell if you're a genius or you just make this stuff up."

"Only one way to find out. Bring a homely boy home and take him for a test ride."

I shook my head. "I'll call you tomorrow."

"You better."

I stayed in the same spot for a long time, staring at the people moving along the sidewalk, yet not really seeing them while completely lost in thought. Then I did the inevitable—called up Instagram again to take a closer look at the stupid picture. The sparkling diamond on the hand holding up the sonogram hurt less the second time, but my heart still had a welt on it from the first wallop. Somehow, though, I managed to tuck my phone into my purse, force one foot in front of the other, and walk the next block to happy hour. Or perhaps now more appropriately called *gloom* hour. Though a few buildings down from the entrance, my steps again abruptly came to a halt. This time, to watch a man open the door for a woman. Jagger put his hand on the tall blonde's back—*the small of her back*—and guided her inside. My heart sank. They walked side by side to an elevator bank where they waited, then disappeared, all smiles.

My heart twisted in my chest, and I felt tears threatening. Which was absolutely ridiculous—seeing a man I'd met less than two weeks ago with another woman should *not* hurt more than seeing that my ex was having a baby with my stepsister. Especially since Jagger and I had never done more than a little flirting. Yet I couldn't help what I felt. Disappointment left a deep pain in my chest, and I wasn't sure what to do next.

As if on cue, my phone buzzed from my pocket. Needing a distraction, I pulled it out.

> **Miles: Just wanted to say how proud of you I am for not letting the jackrabbit ruin your night. Also, I hate my homophobic father more than ever because he wouldn't let me try out for the cheerleading squad like I wanted to in fifth grade. Otherwise, I'd have pom-poms and would be waving them around right now because I'm your biggest cheerleader. Love you! XO**

*Damn him.* I sniffled back the stupid tears that threatened. Now I couldn't skip the bar, pick up a pint of

Ben & Jerry's Half Baked, and go home and eat the entire thing in bed like I was three seconds away from doing. I had to suck it up and do better. And I didn't want to. *Grrr.*

Taking a deep breath, I managed to make myself walk the rest of the way to the bar on the ground floor of *what's his name's building*. The last time I was at the Copa it was busy, but tonight it was packed. And I was pretty sure it was mostly Apex employees. I recognized a few faces as I made my way to the bar. Even if the last ten minutes hadn't packed a one-two punch, I usually needed a little alcohol to take the edge off of mingling with strangers. A glass of wine made my inherent awkwardness feel slightly less clumsy.

Eyeing an empty spot at the far end of the bar, I made my way over. The same bartender who'd been working the last time I was here approached and put down a coaster. "How you doing? What can I get you tonight?"

"I'll take a merlot, please." The image of Jagger touching the tall blonde's back flashed in my head, and I lifted my hand just as the bartender went to walk away. "On second thought, I need something stronger. How about a cosmo instead, please?"

He nodded. "Coming right up."

I surveyed the crowd as I waited. A few minutes later, the bartender came back with a frosty silver shaker and martini glass. He shook before pouring red liquid to the brim.

"You here for the Apex happy hour?"

"I am, actually."

"What's the password?"

"The password?"

He nodded. "They give out a new one each month so we know who we should put on the running tab and who we shouldn't."

"Oh. I didn't realize that. I just started at Apex this week." I lifted my purse. "No big deal. I'll just pay for it."

I was still digging for my wallet when a hand touched the middle of my back. I knew it wasn't Jagger because I didn't have goosebumps and the little hairs on my arms weren't standing up. But also because this hand placement was more innocent and not on my lower back—where Jagger's had also been with his date earlier.

"Hey there." Jack smiled. "Glad you decided to come."

I forced a smile back. "Yeah, me too. Thanks for telling me about it." I finally produced my credit card.

Jack pointed his eyes down to it. "The drinks are free."

"I didn't know the password."

"Oh, shit. Sorry about that. It's *Hercules* tonight." He looked to the waiting bartender. "She's with Apex."

He nodded. "I'll add it to the tab."

"Thanks." Jack leaned an elbow casually on the bar, facing me. "So what did you think of your first week?"

"It was a little overwhelming. Loads of meetings, but I learned a lot."

"The data-science department is pretty big. Do you want to be a financial analyst?"

I shook my head. "I like the backend side of finance. My master's is in mathematical and computational finance with an emphasis in quantitative algorithms."

Jack sipped his drink and grinned. "I don't even know what that means."

"It's just a fancy way of saying I'm a math geek who's good at building computer models that help simplify quantum trading."

Two guys I hadn't met before walked over. One slung an arm around Jack's neck. "Are you hiding in the corner trying to hog the pretty intern all to yourself?"

Jack rolled his eyes. "I'm going to apologize in advance for these two boneheads. They lost a bet at the office and have to do shots every half hour." He sighed and gestured between us. "Mo and Larry, this is Sutton Holland. The three of us work together in the legal department," he explained. "Mo is in compliance, and Larry handles employment issues."

The taller of the two held out his hand. "Ryan Seeling, and I'm actually the *senior* director of compliance, which is more superior than Jack's mere director position. I'm also single, have no children, own my own apartment, and have an eight-ten credit score."

I laughed. "What, no credit report for me to review?"

The other guy held up his hand. "Please. He has that and the results of his last physical saved in his phone. But I warn you, it's in the same folder with his dick pics, and I'm going to poke my eyes out if I accidentally see that little thing again."

Jack shook his head. "I work with idiots."

An alarm sounded. Jack held up his phone. "It's seven thirty. What's it going to be, boys?"

"Vodka," Ryan said. He looked to me. "Care to join us?"

Jack called the bartender over and ordered another round. I wasn't a big shot drinker—or a big drinker at all, for that matter—though it felt like it the last two weeks.

But what the heck? I needed to relax. Today had been a day.

"You know what? I think I will join you for one."

• • •

Ninety minutes later, I had a buzz going and I was about to knock back a third shot—or maybe it was a fourth—

when I felt a presence behind me. The change in Jack and his posse's demeanor told me who it was, even if I hadn't already felt it in my bones. They stood a little taller, faces falling sober.

"Gallo." Jagger nodded. "I hope you're not being inappropriate with our intern."

"No, sir." He shook his head. "We were just cutting loose a bit, that's all."

For all of his comments about the boss being a jerk, Jack certainly buckled fast enough in his presence. Though, not to worry, I wasn't that easy. I glared at the CEO.

He held my eyes for a few seconds. It looked like he was trying to read what was on my mind, but then his attention moved to the bar, where a gaggle of shot glasses sat—a dozen empty and four new, full ones that had just been delivered. He gave me the once-over, stopping to stare at the near-empty drink in my hand before moving to stand next to me, facing the three men head on. "Excuse us, please."

Jack hesitated, looking between me and the boss.

I shrugged, not exactly bothered by the thought of being alone with this gorgeous man—so I could tell him what a jerk he was. "It's fine."

Once it was just me and Jagger, I figured I needed the shot waiting for me on the bar more than ever. So I lifted it to my lips and sucked it back, slamming the glass back down.

"What are you doing here?" I asked. "Why aren't you upstairs whipping someone or whatever it is you do?"

His brows drew down. "Excuse me?"

I waved my hand. "Whatever. I guess they don't get to stay the night, huh?"

Jagger's eyes washed over my face. "How much have you had to drink?"

I wagged my finger at him. "Wouldn't you like to know."

My gaze slid over him. He was dressed casually, in a cobalt blue T-shirt and jeans, rather than the three-piece suits he seemed to have a penchant for. His hair was slicked back like he'd just gotten out of the shower, the inky ends curling upward, his face now cleanly shaven. I reached out and fingered a lock of hair, not stopping to consider that it was probably inappropriate.

"You look closer to my age when you're not dressed in a fancy suit."

"I'm *not* your age."

"I know. You're thirty-two."

"And you're only twenty-four."

"You say it like you're old enough to be my father. Eight years isn't *that* big of a difference."

"Maybe not in years."

I rolled my eyes. "I know. I'm a virgin, too. You're stuck on that."

"Is that why you came tonight? To change that?"

"Would it bother you if it was?"

Jagger didn't answer, but the hard flex of his jaw said it all. All of a sudden, a wave of nausea came over me, and I began to sweat. *Oh no, I think I'm going to be sick.*

"Which way is the ladies' room?"

He pointed, and my stomach quivered as I made a beeline for the door. Thank the Lord, the place was empty. I locked myself in a stall and crouched in front of the disgusting public toilet. The stench alone could've made me dry heave, even if I hadn't overdone it with shots. Instead, it helped the contents of my stomach come up with a vengeance. I was still gagging when the outer door creaked open and shut. A few seconds later, there was a light knock on the door of the stall.

"Are you okay?"

*Jagger.* In the ladies' room.

"You can't come in here."

He was quiet for a beat. "Can I get you anything?"

I spit the lingering taste of barf into the toilet bowel. "A reset button would be great, so I can start this night over."

"Open the door."

"Why? So you can watch me vomit? No thanks."

"No, so I can help you up and bring you somewhere that doesn't have urine stains on the floor around the bowl."

I leaned back and squinted at the base of the toilet.

Jagger sighed. "Stop looking for them and open the door, Sutton."

How the hell did he know? I leaned up and flushed the toilet, then pushed to my feet. Jagger stood just outside the door. "Can you walk?"

"Of course I can walk. I only had two drinks and a shot. It must've been something I ate."

"*Four* shots," Jagger corrected. "I asked the bartender, right before I fired him."

"What? Why would you do that?"

"Three men standing around one young woman like they're waiting to pounce, and he's letting them get her plastered?" He shook his head. "Not happening."

"He wasn't *letting* anything. I'm an adult."

Jagger put his hands on his hips. "There's a back door at the end of the hall. We'll go out that way so people from the office don't see you like this."

"See me like what? I'm fine now."

Jagger's eyes dropped to my shirt. I followed his line of sight and found vomit splatter—bright red, just like my cosmo. I shut my eyes. "I'm mortified."

He put his hand on my shoulder. "Come on. Let's get you out of here."

# — CHAPTER —
# ELEVEN

## Sutton

I didn't ask questions as we stepped into the elevator. Jagger slipped a keycard into the panel, and the door closed. I felt his eyes on me as we began to move.

"You feel okay?"

"My stomach, yes. My pride? Not so much."

He smiled. "You'll survive."

The elevator car picked up speed. "Where are we going?"

"I live in the building. I'll give you a shirt to change into."

"Oh." I nodded. "Thank you."

Jagger Langston didn't just live *in the building*. He occupied the entire top floor. My mouth dropped open as I walked into the marbled foyer. I wasn't a stranger to nice New York City apartments. My mother and Edmund lived in a three bedroom off Central Park, but this—this was something else. Floor-to-ceiling glass lined one entire wall of the spacious living room. The New York skyline was so crisp and perfectly on display, it made me question whether there was actually a barrier.

"Wow. Your view is incredible."

He held out a hand for me to walk first, and I went straight to the window, forgetting all about my puke-stained shirt.

Jagger came up behind me. "It's all one piece of glass—twelve feet high by thirty-two feet long. The previous owner had all the individual windows removed—he didn't want any panes or interruptions to the view. Sometimes when I stand here, I feel like a betta fish in a fishbowl."

I snort-laughed. "Wouldn't you be an *alpha* fish?"

Jagger raised a brow and smirked, shaking his head. "I'll go get you that shirt."

He came back to the living room with a pressed white dress shirt on a hanger in one hand and a T-shirt in the other. "This is the best I can do."

I reached for the dress shirt. "Thank you."

He pointed. "Bathroom is the first door on the left. Help yourself to whatever you need."

The guest bathroom walls were covered in sumptuous textured wallpaper, deep brown with raised gold cherry blossoms that shimmered in the lighting. I was so caught up in the impressive space that I almost forgot the reason I was in it—at least until I got a load of myself in the mirror.

*Oh my God.* I leaned forward and cringed. Not only was there a giant splatter of red on my shirt, but my hair was a disheveled mess and mascara streaked down one of my cheeks. No wonder he'd whisked me out of the company event. I spent the next five minutes trying to clean up as best as I could. But I remained a train wreck, and I dreaded going back out there.

Then came a soft knock at the door.

"You okay?" Jagger asked.

"I'm fine. Just...mortified after seeing what I look like."

"Even makeup down your cheeks doesn't make you less attractive. Trust me, it pisses me off." He paused. "Open up, if you're decent. I have an extra toothbrush, if you want it."

I unlocked the door and took the toothbrush and toothpaste. Jagger looked down at my shirt—*his shirt* on me. I'd tied it at the waist and rolled up the sleeves. He shook his head and grumbled, "Looks better on you."

A few minutes later, I emerged with a scrubbed face and minty breath. I found Jagger staring out the window with a glass of amber liquid in his hand. His feet were set wide in a power stance I really liked. He looked lost in thought, but more than that, he looked lonely. It made me wonder if he'd even enjoyed his time with the blonde. I walked over and stood with him. "Where did your date go?"

"What date?"

"The tall blonde?"

He squinted at me before recognition dawned on his face. "You mean Marla?"

I shrugged. "I wouldn't know her name."

"If you're referring to the woman I walked into the building with tonight, her name is Marla Emerson. She runs the London Apex office. We keep a guest apartment in the building for when executives from our other offices come to town."

"Oh." As if vomiting on myself wasn't bad enough. "Sorry. The way you touched her seemed familiar, and I just thought..."

"It should be familiar by now. Marla and I have known each other for twenty-five years. My mother had some mental-health issues when I was growing up. She went in and out of the hospital a lot, so Marla's parents became my foster parents. I stayed with them during the times my mom wasn't able to take care of me."

"I'm sorry." I paused, unsure what else to say. "I hope she's okay now. Your mom, I mean."

He went back to staring out the window. "How are you feeling? Has your stomach settled?"

"I think so. On the positive side, getting sick seems to have sobered me up. It was stupid of me to drink as much as I did, especially when I hadn't eaten anything." I paused. "Can I ask you something?"

"Do I need to set a five-minute timer?"

I smiled. "I don't think so. Maybe we can just ask what we feel like asking without the pressure of the clock."

"What's your question?"

"What made you come to the happy hour tonight?"

He looked over at me. "It's my company. Am I not allowed to attend?"

"Of course you can. I just heard you usually don't."

His eyes swept over my face. "I went to pick up the dinner I ordered from a restaurant and saw you in the bar through the window."

"Before or after you picked up your food?"

"Before."

"Oh my God. So you've been taking care of me while your dinner is waiting for you and getting cold?"

"It's fine. Is it my turn now?"

"Turn?"

"To ask a question."

"Oh. Sure."

Jagger caught my eye. "Were you really looking for a hook-up tonight?"

"Would it bother you if I was?"

"I came to the happy hour I never attend to foil your plans, didn't I?"

I smiled.

He pointed to my mouth. "Don't gloat."

"I'm not gloating." *I'm totally gloating.*

Jagger shook his head. "I answered your questions, but you didn't answer mine."

"No, I wasn't looking for a hook-up. I was looking to drown my sorrows."

"Why are you sad?"

"I'm not, really. Maybe *sorrow* isn't the right word. I was just feeling sorry for myself."

"Is the internship not what you expected?"

I shook my head. "No, the internship is great. It's not that. It's my ex, the one who just married my stepsister Colette. Apparently they're having a baby."

Jagger squinted. "The wedding was only a week ago. I thought the douche came from a religious family?"

I smiled at the term of endearment he'd used for Brendan. "He does. The only good thing about the surprise announcement is they are probably very disappointed in him."

Jagger looked into my eyes. "The man is really a damn fool."

He turned his attention back to the view, and after a minute, I started to feel awkward. He'd brought me up here to give me a change of clothes and stop me from making an idiot out of myself, and I didn't want to overstay my welcome.

"Well, I should get going. Thank you for giving me a shirt. I'll have it cleaned and return it to you."

"Don't worry about it. I have a closet full."

Jagger made no effort to move, so I took another ten seconds to enjoy the view before turning away. "I'll see you next week."

Halfway to the door, he still hadn't left his spot in front of the window. "Wait."

I stopped.

"I ordered enough food for two. Why don't you put something in your stomach before you travel home? It'll just take me a minute to go get it."

I really didn't want to leave yet. "If you don't mind, that would be great."

Jagger walked to the kitchen counter and picked up his wallet and keys. "You should wait here. The party is probably still going on downstairs."

"Oh." I nodded. "Yeah, right. It wouldn't look good if people saw the boss walking out with an intern, especially one wearing his shirt."

"I give no fucks what people think of me. What I do is my business. You're welcome to come, if you want. I just don't want to subject you to scrutiny."

"Thank you." I smiled. "Can I snoop around while you're gone?"

Jagger's lip twitched. "Knock yourself out."

I watched the elevator doors slide closed before spinning around to take in the apartment again. I'd just been given free rein to peek into the nooks and crannies of Jagger's personal life, and I suddenly felt like a kid in a candy store. I didn't want to waste a minute. The living room and kitchen were gorgeous, but those I could eyeball more when he was here. So I headed down the hallway where I'd gone for the bathroom and started to open each door.

The first room was a home office. It had an oversized desk and the same incredible skyline view as the living room. A quick peek at the bookshelves looked to be more of the same of what I'd already seen in his office, so I quickly pulled the door shut and kept going.

A big spare room on the opposite side of the wall. Nice, but nothing too juicy in there.

A gym as big as my apartment back in California.

Another guest room.

The last door on the end had to be his. I opened the door and flicked on the light. "Wow."

Deep charcoal walls gave the oversized bedroom a warm, rich feeling. The far wall boasted the same floor-to-ceiling sparkling skyline view as the living room and office, except this view had a set of double doors that led to an outdoor terrace with seating. I imagined Jagger sitting out there at night, a glass filled with the amber liquid he'd been drinking earlier. The windows were dressed in opulent deep burgundy linens, tied back by tasseled ropes. To the right, a sleek fireplace had been built into the wall. But the centerpiece of the room was a king-size, four-poster bed, with ornately carved dark wood, a velvet duvet that matched the walls but had thick burgundy piping, and a pile of textured throw pillows with a pop of color. I couldn't stop myself—I ran my hand over the soft bedding and salivated. *He probably sleeps here naked.* I got the crazy urge to rip off my clothes and roll around in the sheets.

That thought rattled around in my head for longer than it should've, and I smiled, imagining him climbing into bed after I was gone and smelling my perfume on his pillow. I needed my head examined because I took a moment to consider whether I had the small, roller-ball cylinder of perfume I sometimes carried in my purse with me. Though I stopped myself from actually going to find out and instead walked to the door on the other side of the room. I figured it was a bathroom or closet, and it turned out to be both—an amazing bathroom, with a shower big enough for a party and a separate tub across from double vanity sinks, and a door that led into an oversized closet with dark wood built-ins. A center island showcased perfectly folded ties and sunglasses under glass, and both sides of the closet were lined with rows and rows of clothes. Suits and shirts on one side, and casual stuff on the other. I'd thought I was organized until seeing this place.

I fingered through the suits, noting he had not one, but at least three tuxedos, and he favored Tom Ford and Brunello Cucinelli suits. It was all very nice, but also very expected, and didn't tell me much I didn't already know about the man. I was just about to turn around and take a run at the bedside nightstand—maybe that's where he kept his secrets—when I spotted an old black trunk tucked in the corner. I stilled, listening for any sounds to indicate Jagger had returned before dropping to my knees and creaking open the top.

*Oh boy.* My eyes flared wide. *Welp, I guess I found it—* his treasure trove of sex paraphernalia, that is. Though I would've expected more along the lines of floggers and silk blindfolds, not hot pink boas and tiaras. What the hell was he into? Playing princess-and-bodyguard or something?

"I knew you were young, but you're not that young."

I jumped, startled by the unexpected deep voice, and sprawled flat on my ass. My hand covered my pounding heart as I looked up and found Jagger looking pleased with himself.

"You scared the shit out of me," I said, incredulous. "You were only gone five minutes."

"The restaurant is right next door. I would've been faster, but they warmed the food up."

"I didn't even hear you come in."

"I didn't realize I had to knock."

He held a hand out to me, and I took it. The second he closed his fingers around mine, my pulse took off like a runaway train. I'd had that reaction to him before, but this time I could tell by his face and the way he stared down at our connection that he felt it too. Jagger quickly took his hand back once I got to my feet.

I felt certain my face was turning red, and I wasn't sure if it was from what his touch did to me or getting caught going through his private things. I brushed invisible dirt from my ass, looking anywhere but at him. "I...I...you told me I could snoop."

"I thought you'd be interested in my things rather than my nieces'."

"Your..." I looked at the still-open trunk—the tiara, the boas, the pink fabric I hadn't yet had a chance to pull out from underneath. "Nieces'?"

Jagger's eyes narrowed. "Did you think I wore pink princess costumes?"

"I...thought maybe that was your kink."

He looked at me for a few seconds before bursting out in laughter. It was such genuine amusement, I started smiling just watching him.

"You thought I liked women to dress up in tiaras and tutus?"

"What was I supposed to think? Your apartment is otherwise insanely organized, and I didn't find anything nefarious at all."

"Nefarious?"

I nodded.

Jagger thumbed over his shoulder. "I guess you didn't check the nightstand then?"

My eyes widened. "What's in the nightstand?"

He chuckled and put his hand on my back. "Come on, Columbo. The food is getting cold."

I let him lead me out of the closet, through the bathroom, and almost out the bedroom door. But when I saw the nightstand, I slowed. "What's in there?"

He tugged me the rest of the way into the hall. "Wouldn't you like to know."

A takeout bag sat on the kitchen counter. Jagger took out two plates, utensils, and glasses. "Are you vegan or anything?"

"Nope. I like meat."

He raised a brow and shook his head without commenting, then turned and opened the refrigerator. "What do you want to drink? I'm guessing wine or other alcohol isn't very appealing right now."

"Definitely not. I'll just take some water, please."

He busied himself in the kitchen and then brought everything over to the dining room table and peeled back the lids of the tins. A delicious aroma wafted through the air. "I have chicken Milanese and cacio e pepe. You want some of both?"

"Mmmm... I wasn't even that hungry until I smelled it. But yeah, I'll try a little of both."

Jagger prepared two plates and sat across from me. The poor guy must've been starving because he dug right in.

"So..." I said. "How many nieces do you have?"

"Two, Olivia and Amelia. They're four and five, and I had to buy that box of dress-up clothes because they were invading my closet and wearing my stuff for fun."

I smiled. "It's sweet that you keep a trunk of stuff for them here."

"They lived with me for a while. They're in Ohio now— or at least they were when I spoke to them a week ago."

"Wow. Really? Did just your nieces live with you or your sister, too?"

"Just the girls. My sister has some issues. Like my mom, she's in and out of mental-health facilities a lot."

"Oh." I frowned. "I'm sorry."

"I only told you half the story earlier when I said the company keeps an apartment in the building for corporate visitors. That's what we use it for now, but I originally had it for my sister and the girls. I was hoping they'd stay here so I could keep an eye on them."

"Your sister didn't want to live in New York?"

"She never stays in one place for long. Catherine is schizophrenic and struggles with paranoia. It makes her move around a lot, especially when she's not taking her meds like she's supposed to."

That didn't sound good. "But she's okay taking care of her daughters?"

"She is." Jagger met my eyes. "Until she isn't."

"That must be hard on the girls, and your entire family."

"It could be worse. There're a lot of people out there who struggle with mental health but have no support system. I had the Emersons growing up, and my sister has me. The hard part is navigating when I need to step in with the girls. Usually Cat will come to me when things are getting bad and let me help. But the last time, my five-year-old niece had to call me because my sister had spiraled to such a bad place. I wound up having to fight her in court to get temporary custody, and now I've become part of her paranoia. Some days she thanks me for helping and always being there for her, and other days she thinks I want to take her kids away from her because I don't have my own."

Ever since I walked into the Copa bar that first night, I'd felt a strange pull to this man. It was an attraction I'd never experienced before, and in this moment, the pull was so much more than physical. I wanted to know everything about him. I wanted to smooth out the little creases that marred his forehead when he spoke about his family and kiss the tension from his perfectly shaped lips. Ridiculous, I know, considering he was my boss, or more aptly, he was my *boss's boss's boss*. Not to mention my stepfather's boss, too. So instead, I opted to share something I rarely discussed.

"I was your nieces' age when I lost my dad, so I know how difficult it is to have a parent there one minute and gone the next."

He nodded. "I knew Edmund was your stepfather. I remember when I first opened Apex seven years ago and interviewed him. He said he had just gotten married two weeks before. But I didn't realize your father had passed away. Was he sick?"

I shook my head. "Car accident. My parents were already divorced at the time. He fell asleep at the wheel on his way home from his second job."

"Damn. I'm sorry."

I shrugged. "Like you said, it could be worse. I could not have my mom." I smiled. "I'm glad the girls have you to rely on."

He shook his head. "How the hell did we go down such a dark path in conversation?"

"I believe it was my fault, when I uncovered what I thought was your sex toy box."

He smiled and twirled his fork in his pasta. "Tell me how your first week went."

"It was good. I've learned a lot about the company. They showed us the simulator the analysts use to run models to optimize stock predictions, but next week I get to see pieces of the proprietary software that runs the algorithms. Ellie said she's going to see if we can watch the testing of the upgrade they're working on."

"I think they're at the end phase where they manually test the results. It's not too exciting—the team spends a week locked in a room with whiteboards doing math problems that take hours to compute and check *one* output on the new software. Probably boring to watch."

"Are you kidding? I'm a total math geek. I *love* stuff like that. Ellie said I can bring a notebook and do my own computations, as long as I'm quiet and don't disrupt the analysts."

Jagger smiled. "I used to get excited about quant models, too."

"Used to? What happened? Did you get burned out or something?"

He shook his head. "I don't have that kind of free time anymore. These days I go to a dozen meetings a day instead."

"You're the boss." I shrugged. "Just don't go to the meeting."

He smiled. "You make it sound so simple."

"Or..." I pointed my fork at him. "You're making it more complicated than it is."

He laughed. "Maybe you're right."

We managed to keep things light while we finished eating. After, I insisted on cleaning up. His dishwasher was empty, but I wasn't ready to leave that fast, so I washed the dishes by hand before drying them.

"Any good plans this weekend?" he asked.

I folded the hand towel. "Not really. I need to find a gym I can join for a few months."

"There's an Equinox right near the office."

"Let me rephrase that. I need to find an *affordable* gym for the summer."

Jagger smiled. "Apex employees get a pretty good discount if they join."

"Oh really? Maybe I'll check it out. What about you? Any plans this weekend?"

"Work all day tomorrow, hit the gym on the way home. Nothing too exciting."

I nibbled my bottom lip, debating asking what I really wanted to ask. *Screw it*—I'd asked this man if I could snoop around his apartment and then got caught doing so. Though I felt a heck of a lot more sober after eating, so I wasn't as brazen. I could still probably blame it on the shots. "No date?"

Jagger's eyes met mine. He shook his head. "Not this weekend."

A stab of jealousy hit. If he didn't have any dates lined up, wouldn't he have just said no? But "not this weekend" alluded to him having one another weekend, didn't it?

"What about next weekend?"

"What about it?"

"Do you have one then? You said not *this* weekend."

"I'd have to check my calendar. But I don't believe so."

"Oh." I looked down, suddenly feeling awkward—like I'd overstayed my welcome. "I guess I should get going."

Jagger's face was impassive. I had no idea what he was thinking. Yet I waited to see if he'd suggest I stay for a while. When he didn't, I felt deflated.

"Okay, then," I mumbled and checked my watch. "Is there a back exit to the building? Happy hour is until eleven, and I wouldn't want anyone to see me coming off the elevator and get the wrong idea."

"You're concerned about what people might think of you?"

I shook my head. "Not me."

"I told you, I give no fucks what people think of me." Jagger lifted his cell phone and texted while he spoke. "There's a service entrance, but you're not taking it. Sam will drive you home."

"It's fine. I can take the subway."

"Sam," he said firmly, "will take you home."

Something inside me stirred at the sternness of his tone. I liked it. *A lot*. Though I also found that confusing. If I'd told Brendan I was going to do A, and he'd told me to do B, it would've only made me want to do A more. Yet I found myself nodding and liking the smile on Jagger's face when I didn't put up more of a fight. "Okay."

"Good. He'll be here in five minutes."

Too soon, he walked me to the door.

"Thank you for saving me from making a fool of myself tonight," I said. "And for dinner."

"Not a problem. I enjoyed the company." He paused and caught my eye. "A little too much."

I tilted my head. "Is there really such a thing as enjoying yourself too much?"

Jagger smiled ruefully. "There most certainly is, Ms. Holland."

## — CHAPTER —
## TWELVE

Jagger

14 years ago

"**O**h my God. What the heck did you do?" Lexi demanded as I walked in. She was sitting on the couch in Zane's garage while Zane and Ryder played pool.

It was eleven o'clock in the morning, and we were all supposed to be in school, but Zane's father had a new girlfriend and didn't give a shit about much else. He'd been sleeping at her place the last two nights.

Lexi walked over and rubbed my stubbly head. "I loved your hair. Why did you shave it?"

"I didn't have a choice."

"Did you lose a bet or something?"

That was a good guess since Ryder's eyebrows hadn't fully grown back in yet—the result of a wager we'd made about who would win the Knicks game last month.

I shook my head. "I joined the Marines."

Lexi's eyes bulged, and my two buddies' heads swung toward me, their game forgotten. "*What?*" they all said in unison.

I shrugged. "Fucking Judge Hanover. He gave me two choices—prison or the military. I'd rather be the government's bitch for four years than the bitch of some three-hundred-pound biker named Viper doing life."

"But...but...what about us?" Lexi whined.

I liked Lexi. She was fun and up for anything, but the two of us weren't going anywhere except the backseat of her car. "Sorry. But you're better off. Maybe you'll meet a nice guy who isn't a fuckup."

"But I don't want a nice guy. I want *you!*"

Zane and Ryder walked over. Ryder even put down the beer he was drinking—before noon. The two of us had gotten arrested together for breaking into the school. He raked a hand through his hair. "Fuck. You think he's going to do that to me, too?"

I shook my head. "Probably not. It was your first time being arrested. You'll just get a slap on the wrist—some community service or something."

"Are you fucking with us?" Zane pointed to me. "You got lice or gum stuck in your hair, and you're just being your usual asshole self, aren't you?"

I sighed. "I wish I was, buddy."

"Damn, man. The Marines? That's some hardcore shit. Maybe you could be a SEAL or a Green Beret guy like one of the Hemsworth brothers was in *12 Strong*."

"SEALs are Navy, and Green Berets are Army."

"So what the fuck are you going to do then?"

I chuckled. It was the first time I'd been able to feel amused in the two days since I'd walked out of the courtroom. "I have no damn idea. I just got finished taking some tests down at the recruiting office. They place you based on your results." I shrugged. "At least that's what I think they do. I didn't ask too many questions because the answers didn't matter. I'm going in no matter what job they give me."

Ryder smirked. "What if your job is to clean toilets and suck the commander's dick?"

I shook my head. "You're an idiot."

Lexi was still pouting. "When are you going in?"

"A week from tomorrow."

"But that's your birthday!"

"I don't think the Marines give a shit that I'm turning eighteen."

"We were going to have a big party."

"Cancel it. Because the party is definitely over for at least four years."

•  •  •

"Take a seat, recruit."

A few days later, a guy who had to be six-six and wore dress blues pointed to the plastic chair on the other side of his desk. I sat down.

He opened a manila folder and scanned the paper on top. "I thought you cheated on your ASVAB."

I narrowed my eyes. "I didn't cheat."

His face grew stern. "That's I didn't cheat, *sir*. And if you're going to have that attitude, you aren't going to make it very far in the military."

God, I freaking hated this shit already. The guy kept staring at me like he was waiting for something. I managed not to roll my eyes, but the words still came out slightly mocking in tone. "I didn't cheat, *sir*."

He shook his head and went back to the papers in the folder. "You got a perfect score on every section of the aptitude test—math, science, reading comprehension, even mechanical comprehension. I've been doing this for nine years now, and I've never seen anyone with these kind of numbers."

I was surprised most people didn't score a hundred because the test was a total joke.

He continued. "A kid with your background and attitude gets sent to us from Judge Hanover and scores a hundred on everything we test for, it's only logical to assume you cheated. So I had your high school records pulled and dug into 'em." He leaned back in his chair, taking the folder with him, and flipped through pages. "Ten points from perfect on the SAT, yet barely above breathing level on the PSAT. Why is that?"

"I was hungover and fell asleep...sir."

The recruiter cracked a smile. "You were tested in elementary school for some kind of advanced program, and your IQ is genius level. Yet you barely passed your classes in high school. You also have transcripts from a half-dozen different places. Why did you change schools so much?"

"We moved around a lot...sir."

"Who is we?"

"Me and my mother...sir." It felt awkward to keep adding that word. If I was having a conversation with Zane or Ryder, I wouldn't say their name at the end of every sentence. "Do I need to add *sir* to everything I say? It feels weird."

"I'll tell you what, you're not a marine yet, and we're just having a casual conversation. So speak freely. But, yes, you will add *sir* when addressing an officer. It's a sign of respect. You'll get used to it."

"Okay."

"Tell me, is your father in the picture?"

I shook my head. "I've only met him once."

He frowned. "And your mother?"

"She has some problems."

"What kind of problems?"

"The kind that made her smash the phone I'd saved up to buy because she thinks the government is tracking us."

The recruiter's brows furrowed before his face softened. "Your address changed fourteen times during your high school career. Six times to the same place up in Yorkville. Is that where your mother lives?"

I shook my head. "That's where I go when she gets admitted to the hospital. The Emersons' house. They're my foster parents."

The recruiter tapped his pen against the desk a few times. It looked like he was mulling over what I'd said. "Do you have any career goals or aspirations?"

"I want to be rich."

He chuckled. "Don't we all, kid. Are you interested in anything specific?"

I shrugged. "I like picking stocks and seeing how much money I could've made if I had any to buy them."

"That's not exactly one of our areas. But I'll tell you what... I'm going to pencil you in for infantry rifleman. It's the most highly regarded specialty in the Marines. You'll learn leadership, discipline, and tactical skills—three things that will help you succeed in whatever business you figure out interests you." He pointed to me. "But I'm going to keep my eye on you, see how you do in basic training. If you prove you can be tamed, I'll make it happen. If not, get ready for four years of food service. You'll be slinging slop in a hot kitchen to the men who *can* control themselves." He looked down and started to write, waving me off with his other hand. "Now get out of here."

I stood and walked to the door. "Thank you, sir."

# — CHAPTER —
# THIRTEEN

Sutton

**K**nock, knock.

"Hang on a second." I slipped out of bed, continuing to talk on the phone. "I think someone is at my door."

"Are you expecting someone?" Miles asked.

"Not that I'm aware of."

"Then it's probably Mia."

My steps faltered. *Ugh.* I loved my mother, but she was the absolute last person I needed to see this morning. It was bad enough that my head was pounding. I didn't need a lecture about getting drunk at a work event. Lord knows I'd been berating myself all morning for the way I'd acted last night. I held the cell up to my face so Miles could see me again. "God, I hope not. She'll take one look at my puffy eyes and know I did something stupid."

"Who else would it be? We've been on the phone for fifteen minutes, and the doorman didn't call up to clear anyone."

I sighed. He was right, so I stopped at the hallway mirror and attempted to fix myself. But smoothing out my messy hair wasn't going to cure my puffy face and the dark circles under my eyes. *Crap. This isn't going to be fun.*

To my surprise, when I peeked through the peephole, it wasn't my mother standing on the other side. It was the building's doorman.

I opened with a relieved smile. "Hi, Nestor."

He tipped his hat with a nod. "Morning, Ms. Holland."

"I told you, it's Sutton, please."

He nodded and held out a brown paper bag. "This came for you this morning."

"What is it?"

"Not sure. A gentleman dropped it by and asked that I see that you got it."

"A gentleman? You mean a messenger?"

He shrugged. "I was on the phone with the company that services the elevators when he came in, so I missed having him sign in like I usually would. But he didn't look like the typical delivery guy. If he was, I'm in the wrong line of work because the gentleman had a fancy Maybach waiting out front for him."

*A Maybach.* "Thank you."

"Have a good day."

I closed the door. Inside the brown paper bag, I found two items: a bottle of Tylenol and an envelope. The latter wasn't sealed, so I slipped out the thick piece of stationery inside to read the slashy, bold handwriting.

*Figured you might need what's in the bottle before using the other.*

*Jagger*

I unfolded a second piece of paper from inside the envelope—a free, one-month gym pass to Equinox.

The rush of excitement that pulsed through me because Jagger had stopped at my building was positively ridiculous. I sucked in my bottom lip, forgetting all about my pounding head. And apparently also forgetting that I was still on FaceTime with Miles.

"Well..." he called. "What was delivered?"

I held the phone back up to my face. "Tylenol and a gym pass."

"From who?"

"Jagger."

"*Whoa*. That's above and beyond CEO duties to an intern. What the hell happened between you two last night?"

"Just what I told you." I went into the kitchen and propped the phone up on the counter so I could make espresso. "He saved me from making a fool of myself, fed me, and sent me packing."

"This guy is into you, Sutton."

I didn't have a ton of experience with men, and none with someone even remotely like Jagger Langston, but I felt in my bones that Miles was right. It was in the way he looked at me, the way he wanted to take care of me. Though none of that mattered.

I sighed. "Even if he is, he's not going to cross the line. He's the boss, and I'm an intern. Not to mention, he's totally hung up on me being a virgin. And then there's the Edmund situation."

"Remember Hugh Kempner, the editor at the magazine where I interned?"

"Hugh Kempner? The guy you renamed *Huge Member*?"

Miles laughed. "That's the one."

"What about him? You're not going to try to tell me my situation is the same, are you? You threw yourself at the guy. If I remember correctly, you walked into his office, locked the door, and gave him a blow job while he was on a conference call."

"It's *exactly* the same thing. Hugh was in a position of power. I knew he wanted me as bad as I wanted him, but he wasn't going to make a move. So I had to take things into my own hands." Miles smirked. "Or mouth."

I chuckled and frothed milk to make my morning cappuccino. "I'm not you."

"Says who? Reinvent yourself. Do things outside your comfort zone in New York. Become a siren."

I took my much-needed caffeine to the couch and popped open the bottle of Tylenol from Jagger. Swallowing two pills, I set the phone on the coffee table. "I wish I had your courage."

"You do, cookie. You just need to listen to your gut. Courage comes in all forms. Sometimes it's just a subtle whisper that tells you to go for it, even when everything else around you is shouting *stop*."

• • •

It took a full two days to feel like myself again.

Monday morning, I arrived at Equinox at five thirty sharp, determined to get my life organized. A young guy with hulking arms greeted me from behind the desk. He smiled. "You must be new here?"

"I am. But how did you know?"

"Because I offer every new member a free personal-training session, and I'd remember you." He extended his hand over the counter. "I'm Troy. One of the trainers here. And you are?"

"Sutton."

"Nice to meet you. Is today your first time here?"

I nodded. "I'm technically not even a member yet. I have a one-month guest pass."

He looked at his watch. "I'm just covering the desk for someone for a few minutes while she grabs coffee. If you want, I can show you around when she gets back. It'll give me a chance to pitch you for a complimentary personal-training session."

"I'm more of a Peloton-and-treadmill person than weight training."

He shrugged. "Your call. But I can still show you around."

"That would be great. Thanks."

"Let me have your guest pass, and I'll get you set up in the computer while we wait."

I took out the pass from Jagger and handed it over.

Troy looked down at the paper. "You're a guest of Mr. Langston, huh?"

I nodded. "I work at Apex."

"Well, if you're half as dedicated as he is to showing up here every morning, you're going to do great."

I perked up. "Is he…here now?"

Troy shook his head. "You just missed him. Out the door by five fifteen every morning. I could set my watch to it."

Disappointment set in. "Oh."

"I'll just need your license to put your information in the computer. We'll give you a temporary ID card so you can swipe in like everyone else."

I handed over my California license, and Troy got busy typing. Meanwhile, I looked around, checking out the gym. It was busy for so early in the morning, but there were still enough machines that I wouldn't have to wait. As I finished surveying the rowing machines near the door, it opened and a familiar face walked in. *Jack Gallo.* Instinctively, I turned away, hoping to avoid him seeing me. But this hadn't been my lucky month.

"Sutton?"

I did my best to feign surprise. "Oh, hey, Jack. How are you?"

He smiled. "Better now. Are you a member here?"

"I have a one-month guest pass, so I thought I'd check it out."

"Awesome. I come here five days a week." He paused. "Hey, I looked for you Friday night before I left, but you just disappeared. I didn't have your number, or I would've checked in with you."

"I...wasn't feeling so well." Was that ever the truth, and I wasn't about to share more.

"Sorry about my buddies and their dumb shot game."

"It wasn't their fault. I should've known better. I'm sort of a lightweight."

A woman walked behind the counter holding the biggest coffee Starbucks sold. "Thanks, Troy," she said.

"Good timing." He pointed to me. "Josie, this is Sutton. She has a one-month guest pass. I set her up in the computer. Maybe you can print out her ID card while I show her around? I don't know how to do that."

"Sure, no problem." She tucked her purse into a drawer.

"I can show Sutton around," Jack piped up. "We work together."

I suddenly became interested in personal training. "Actually, Troy was going to tell me about personal-training sessions while he gave me a tour of the gym."

"Oh. Okay." Jack shrugged. "I'll see you later then."

Troy came around the counter. He waited until Jack was out of earshot. "Have a change of heart or trying to avoid that guy?"

"Thank you for not calling me out," I said. "He's a nice guy. I just... I don't know."

Troy smiled. "If it's not there, it's not there. Come on, I'll give you that tour."

I didn't see Jack again until I was walking out an hour later. He jogged up behind me at the door and opened it. "How'd you like Equinox?"

"It's great. They have everything. Though I'm pretty sure I'll never use half the equipment."

"I don't use too much either. I alternate swimming laps with weight training. But the dry sauna and free shampoo in the showers are nice perks." He smiled.

We walked side by side a few doors down to the office, waited for the elevator, and rode it up together. I had no idea why I wanted to shake him off so badly. Jack was a nice guy, a good catch even. He was handsome, had a great job, seemed to have good manners. Yet when the doors opened at my floor, I had to work at not frowning as he followed me off.

"Going to make the good stuff with the fancy machine," he told me. "Want me to make you one while you settle in?"

"That's okay. I'll do it in a bit. But thank you."

Ten minutes later, he returned with two cups anyway. And then proceeded to stand around chatting for another ten minutes. When my phone rang, I was glad to have an excuse to bring our conversation to an end.

"Excuse me." I smiled. "I need to answer that. But thank you again for the cappuccino."

"No problem."

I blew out a breath before picking up my phone. "Sutton Holland."

"I thought he was never going to leave." Jagger's deep voice made all the little hairs on my arms stand at immediate attention.

I looked around. "How did you know someone was at my desk?"

"I came down earlier and saw him standing there. I managed to stop myself from telling him to go do some damn work and returned to my office instead. But I did need to speak to you, so I checked the camera to see if it was safe to call."

My eyes darted to the ceiling. "What camera?"

"Turn to your right."

*Oh my God. He's watching me right now.* My eyes locked on a globe-type fixture on the ceiling. I opened my mouth to ask if that was it, but Jagger beat me to it.

"You got it. Pretty blouse, by the way. Blue looks good on you. It's my favorite color."

In a moment of temporary insanity, I briefly debated opening my legs for the camera. I was wearing a skirt and wondered what he would say.

"What are you thinking right now?" Jagger asked.

At least I *thought* the debate had gone on in my head, but apparently it wasn't the only place. I looked up, speaking directly to the camera. "Why?"

"Because the devil just made an appearance on your face."

"Jesus." I laughed. "That's some high-def equipment you have."

He chuckled, and the smooth sound flowed over me, making me warmer than a blanket. "It is. How did you feel on Saturday morning?"

I'd almost forgotten about the delivery. "Good, thanks to you. It was very thoughtful of you to drop off the meds and gym pass."

"You're welcome. I was in the neighborhood."

For some reason, I suspected that might not be the truth. And his watching me made me feel bold. I looked directly at the camera again. "Where?"

"Where what?"

"You said you were in the neighborhood. Where did you go?"

The line was quiet for so long, I was beginning to think he'd hung up. But then I heard his chair creak. "One of the analysts who was going to be part of the team that tests the new algorithm has the flu. So there's an open spot if you want to spend a week at the whiteboard."

My eyes flared. "Really? Not *watch* them do the testing, but be an actual part of it?"

"If you feel you're up for it. I recommended you to Will Twible who heads up the algorithm-engineering division, so you have the spot, if you want to participate."

I nodded my head fast. "Yes, yes. I definitely want to. I'm so excited."

"I can see that." I heard the smile in his voice. "You'll have to sign a mountain of legal papers that promise your first-born child if you violate our NDA since you'll be working with proprietary information. But they're starting at eight, so you should get going. Testing is being done in the quant lab, down on the seventh floor."

"Okay!"

"I'll have legal meet you there with the paperwork so you can get started."

"Perfect."

"And I'll make sure to send someone *other* than your new friend. He seems to know where you are at all times better than my eye in the sky."

I smiled. "Thank you for the opportunity."

"You're welcome."

I was about to hang up when I remembered he'd never answered my question. I lifted the phone back to my ear. "Jagger?"

"Yes?"

"Where were you going on Saturday when you stopped by my apartment?"

He was quiet for a few beats. "You're winning, Ms. Holland. But don't push your luck."

## Sutton

The testing team worked through lunch. And dinner, every day.

By the time Friday afternoon arrived, I had probably worked eighty hours. The whole algo team had, and I was in my glory. I couldn't remember the last time I'd been so full of energy, so full of passion. It made me realize how incredibly down I'd been for the last year and a half. I'd let everything that happened with Brendan really take its toll, and it felt good to take back control.

Will, the senior director of the algorithm-engineering team, was currently at the whiteboard doing manual calculations, and I was combing through layers of code, trying to find an error that had been eluding the team.

I raised my hand. "I think I found it!"

Will came over and crouched to look over my shoulder. I pointed. "It looks like there's a duplicate data name. If you run the math again but use this variable, we'll know for sure, but I think this is the issue that's causing the problem."

"It's like finding a needle in a haystack." He stood and patted my shoulder. "Good job. I raked over that code five times and missed it."

"Beginner's luck."

Will smiled. "Now you're just patronizing me. But thanks. My ego appreciates it. As does my wife, who is going to be very happy if I don't have to work all weekend. We're both in our forties with a colicky two-month-old. She needs a break."

He'd returned to the whiteboard and begun replacing numbers and re-rerunning the math when Jagger walked in. Everyone turned.

The boss raised his hand. "Keep doing what you're doing. I'm just checking on how things are going."

"Better now," Will said. "Thanks to Sutton." He shook his head and chuckled. "She might rival the processor speed in your head, boss. I haven't seen anyone fly through equations like she does in a while."

Jagger lifted a brow and looked to me. It had been four days since I'd seen him. Though I felt certain he'd seen me, through the cameras, at least.

I shook my head. "Will is being kind."

"I doubt it." He lifted his chin to the board. "I'm just going to watch. Don't let me interrupt the flow."

Jagger stayed in the back of the room while everyone went back to work. The team didn't seem half as distracted by his presence as I felt. I glanced over my shoulder a few times, and his stare always met mine.

After a while, he slipped into the chair next to me. "You've been putting in long hours," he whispered.

"Are you watching the cameras again?" I lowered my voice. "Did I just figure out you're also a voyeur?"

He grinned and leaned closer. "That's never been my thing...yet." His hot breath tickled my neck and set my body on fire. Actually, who was I kidding? Just him sitting this close was enough to do that. His breath on my skin was a bonus. "The card you use to swipe into and out of the building every day leaves a trail."

"And you were following that trail, looking for..."

Jagger took a deep breath. "Thought I asked you not to wear that perfume."

I grinned. "You did."

He chuckled. It was a deep rumble that vibrated, and I felt it between my legs.

Will finished plugging new numbers into the mile-long equation on the board and stepped back. "My brain is melting. Anyone want to work through this one?"

I raised my hand. "I'd love to."

He smiled and capped the dry-erase marker, setting it on the edge of the board. "You got it."

I got up, but Jagger stopped me. "Hang on a moment. Will seems to think I've lost my touch. What do you say we have a friendly competition?"

"What do you mean?"

He pointed to the board. "I'll take a picture and work through it with pen and paper over here while you use the whiteboard."

I grinned. "I'm in."

It took almost two hours for me to finish. Capping the marker, I raised my hands in the air. "Done!"

Will and the team laughed and applauded while Jagger folded his arms over his chest. "And did the result match what the algorithm produced?"

I nodded.

Will walked to the front of the room. "She not only found the error, she proved the updated algorithm works."

I smiled, and Jagger narrowed his eyes at me.

"You two should've made a bet," Will said. "The boss and I used to wager on IPO stock picks—me using a full day's math and him shooting from the hip—but I got tired of bringing him his morning coffee while wearing an apron that said *I'm the boss's bitch.*"

Jagger chuckled. "I almost forgot about that. I think I still have that thing in a cabinet in my office, if you want to go another round."

Will shook his head. "No thanks."

Jagger leaned back in his chair and looked over at me. "What would you have wanted to win if we'd bet?"

A thought not suitable for mixed company went through my head. I shrugged. "I don't know. It was just for fun."

Will pointed to me. "Don't forget you get bragging rights. Kicking that man's ass would be at the top of my resume."

Jagger rubbed his lip with his thumb. "I'll tell you what, I'll give you better than bragging rights. You let me know what you'd like as your prize, and I'll see what I can do."

Will patted my shoulder. "I hope you ask for a full-time job, kid. I could use you on my team." He looked at his watch, then at the other team members. "It's seven o'clock already. You all look wiped out. Let's get out of here. We'll clean this mess up on Monday. Thank you for all your hard work this week."

Everyone packed up. Jagger had been working out the problem on a yellow legal pad. He ripped the pages out and folded them into his pocket.

"Taking the evidence that I beat you with you?"

He wagged a finger at me. "What did I tell you about gloating?"

I smiled so wide my face hurt. "Who, me? I'm not gloating."

He chuckled and put his hand on my back. "Come on. Let's get you out of here."

Jagger and I were the only two who didn't work on the floor, so after we said goodnight to the others, we walked to the elevator together. As usual, the minute the doors slid shut, I felt his presence. The faint smell of his delicious cologne had me taking deep breaths as I tried to calm myself. Jagger stood behind me, and I made the mistake of glancing back, only to find him looking at me with the same intensity I felt. My skin tingled all over, and I found myself thinking of something Miles had recently said.

*"Listen to your gut. Sometimes it's just a subtle whisper that tells you to go for it, even when everything else around you is shouting* stop.*"*

I stared at the elevator panel. What would he do if I pulled the red emergency stop button, pushed him up against the wall, and climbed him like a tree?

Jagger leaned forward, head hovering at my shoulder. "You're doing it again."

"What?"

"Thinking something evil."

"It's not exactly evil."

"Oh no?" He arched a brow. "Then care to share?"

I pursed my lips, drawing a chuckle from him. "That's what I thought."

The elevator stopped at my floor. I hesitated, not wanting my time with him to come to an end. But after a few heartbeats, I had no choice but to step out.

Jagger put his hand on the doorframe, stopping the doors from sliding closed. "So what's your prize going to be?"

I nibbled on my lip. "It can be anything?"

"Within reason."

The words *I want to have sex with you* were bursting to break free, but I wimped out and shrugged instead. "Can I think about it?"

He nodded. "Of course."

"Do you...have any good plans for the weekend?"

"None as good as you."

I felt my nose wrinkle. "How do you know what plans I have?"

"Edmund is borrowing my boat. He said you guys are taking it to Block Island for the day to celebrate Mia's birthday."

"I didn't realize it was your boat he's using."

"I'm glad someone is getting to use it. I've barely had the time in the last year." He nodded and stepped back. "Enjoy your weekend with your family."

I wanted so badly to stop the doors and ask him to go for a drink or have dinner...or *something*. But of course, I chickened out. *Story of my life.*

## —— CHAPTER ——
# FIFTEEN

### Sutton

**"H**ey, Edmund." My stepfather was parked at the bottom of the train-platform stairs, waiting for me. "Thank you for picking me up."

I'd opted to take the Long Island Railroad out to Montauk this morning rather than drive with everyone after work last night. It was bad enough that I was going to spend a weekend in close confines with Brendan and his new bride. Squishing with the two of them in the backseat of Edmund's car while we sat in Hamptons traffic was more than I could handle.

Edmund hugged me and took my weekend bag from my hand. He tossed it into the trunk of his Range Rover and opened the passenger door for me before slipping behind the wheel.

"Is Mom still sleeping?"

He smiled. "It's only ten o'clock, Sutton."

I laughed. "What was I thinking?"

Edmund had a small house in Montauk's Ditch Plains, a low-key surfing area. I'd been there a few times and thought the route he was driving today was different than usual, but then again, I wasn't the best with directions. Though when he pulled into a ritzy-looking area with houses five times the size of his, I was certain we weren't heading the right way. "Are we going straight to the dock?"

"Not until a little later. Your mom said she'd be ready by eleven, so I'm guessing that means about one."

"This isn't the way to your house, is it?"

"I need to make a stop and pick up keys. I borrowed Jagger's boat. The captain I hired for the day was supposed to get them on his way out, but he wound up taking the train because he had car trouble, so I figured I'd save him the trip."

My horrendous day just got a little sunnier. "Jagger has a house in Montauk?"

"Sure does. The place used to be owned by Marilyn Monroe and Joe DiMaggio. It has a long history of celebrity visitors."

We drove for a few more minutes until we came to a sprawling house nestled on the edge of a cliff. Gray, salt-kissed cedar shingles gave the mansion a Cape Cod-style look. It sat far back, off a long, manicured lawn.

"Wow. This is incredible."

Gravel crunched under the tires as we pulled down the long driveway.

"You can wait here, if you want," Edmund said. "I'm just going to get the keys and we'll be on our way."

I would've liked a tour of the inside of the beautiful house, but instead I stayed in the car and watched Edmund climb the stairs and knock.

The tall door opened, and a shirtless Jagger appeared in the doorway. *Oh wow. I should've gone with him. I could've gotten a closer look.* Though the view from this distance was still pretty spectacular. I might've imagined how fit Jagger was more than once, but my vision didn't hold a candle to the real thing. The man was something else—broad shoulders, washboard abs, a narrow V waist... I leaned forward in my seat and squinted for a better look at the happy trail that ran from his belly button down into the waistband of his pants. Jagger Langston got me hot and bothered in a bespoke suit and wingtips, but I also needed to turn the AC up seeing him in a pair of low-hanging gray sweatpants and bare feet. The two men talked and then, mid conversation, Jagger looked over, and it was obvious he spotted me. Even from fifty feet away, I saw the hint of a smile that formed on his lips. Edmund followed his boss's line of sight and pointed to me. After another minute of conversation, both of them headed toward the car.

My heart started to race. Do I get out? Roll down my window? Was licking the deep etching of each of Jagger's abdominal muscles an option? In the end, I was lucky my brain managed to remember how to press the button to lower the glass.

"Hi." I lifted a hand to shield my eyes from the sun as I looked up.

Jagger smiled. "I was just telling your stepdad that I owed you a prize for whipping my butt yesterday."

Edmund's face filled with warmth and admiration. "I told you she was smarter than me. You should snap her up for the executive training program in the fall. I know her mother would love to get her back in New York permanently."

Compliments always made me uncomfortable. "Your house is beautiful."

"Thank you. I can't take any of the credit. It was this way when I bought it. It's an old house, but the previous owners took great care of it."

"Are you sure I can't talk you into joining us today?" Edward laughed and looked to me. "I've been inviting him to his own boat the last few days."

Jagger smiled. "I have a lot of work to do."

"If you change your mind, we aren't leaving for a couple of hours. Mia is a late sleeper and Brendan just left to go try to catch some waves at Ditch."

Jagger's eyes narrowed. "Brendan?"

Edmund nodded. "My new son-in-law."

Jagger's eyes slanted to me and then back to my stepfather. "Who else is going today?"

"My daughters—Colette and her husband and Chloe and her boyfriend, Ryan—plus Mia's best friend, Patrice, and her husband."

Jagger frowned. He didn't have to say what he was thinking because somehow I'd already learned his faces. This one said—*you're making this poor girl spend the day with her ex-fiancé and his new wife and three other couples?* His eyes moved back and forth between his watch and me a few times before returning to my stepfather. "What time did you say you were leaving?"

"Probably about one."

Jagger took a deep breath and exhaled. "I'll tell you what, I'll see how much work I can get done. Maybe I'll join you after all."

I seriously wanted to hug him. He was probably the only person who could distract me enough to make thirty-six hours with my ex bearable.

Edmund slapped his boss's back. "Excellent. You work too much. I hope you can make it."

Jagger nodded. "I'll try. But don't wait for me if I'm not at the dock by one."

• • •

I checked the time on my phone a dozen times. At 1:04, there was still no sign of Jagger.

Mom and I sat at the back of the boat with her best friend, Patrice, while everyone else was inside, still checking out the luxurious interior. I didn't know much about boats, but I was pretty sure this one qualified as a yacht. The seventy-five-foot Benetti was insanely beautiful. It had two cabins, a living room, a dining room, and a kitchen.

Edmund stood on the dock, getting ready to untie the lines so we could leave. He checked his watch. "I guess the boss got sucked into work. Shame. He could use a day off." He waved his hand and gestured to the captain, who was up top on the bridge deck. "You all ready?"

The captain nodded and yelled back, "Whenever you are."

Four dock lines kept us tied to land. Edmund untied the first rope from a cleat, and my eyes bounced to the wooden path that led to the parking lot. No one was coming. The same thing happened as he untied the second and then the third rope. When he got to the fourth and final one, there was still no sign of Jagger. My shoulders slumped.

Once we were untied, Edmund jumped on board and gave the captain a thumbs up. He shifted the throttle forward, and slowly we began to pull away from the dock. It felt like I was leaving all my hopes behind. But then I looked back one last time and saw a man jogging down the path.

I jumped up from my chair. "Edmund, stop! Jagger is coming!"

## CHAPTER SIXTEEN

### Sutton

You would've thought I had a disease.

Jagger kept his distance all afternoon. Though I was absolutely certain the same wasn't true of his gaze. Even with his dark sunglasses on, I could feel his eyes on me every time I went anywhere near him. I might've made sure of it, shamelessly stripping down to my bikini and sunning myself while everyone else still wore their cover-ups.

It was less than an hour ride to Block Island. The captain slowed the boat as we entered the five-mile-per-hour zone that led to the marina.

"Which beach are we going to?" I asked Mom. She'd been here before, but it was my first time.

"Mansion Beach. It's only about a ten-minute walk from where we'll dock. But I'd like to stop on Water Street and do a little shopping first."

Patrice lifted her sunglasses and smiled. "Did someone say shopping?"

Edmund chuckled. "I can give you kids directions if you don't want to shop. We can meet you at the beach when the ladies are done. There aren't that many stores, so we shouldn't be more than an hour."

"That sounds good to me," Colette said.

"Me too." Chloe shrugged. They both turned to me, waiting for an answer.

I had to spend time with Brendan and Colette because it was my mother's birthday. But if Mom wasn't going to be with them for an hour, neither was I. I pulled my cover-up out of my beach bag and shook my head. "I'm going to go check out these cliffs I read about while I was on the train this morning. Mohegan Bluffs?"

"Oh, they're beautiful," Mom said. "But we're on the north side of the island, and the bluffs are on the south side. It's probably at least a five-mile walk, right, honey?"

Edmund nodded. "Well over an hour, I'd say. Each way."

I wrinkled my nose. "Oh."

"There's a scooter rental shop right on Water Street, though," Edmund said. "Have you ever driven a scooter?"

I shook my head. "No, but it can't be that hard to learn."

Brendan scoffed. "You crashed the electric bike when we were up in Maine a few years ago and refused to get back on. And that thing doesn't go half as fast as a scooter."

Colette frowned. Apparently, I wasn't the only one who wanted to pretend I'd never dated her husband.

Jagger's jaw flexed. "I'm sure she'll be fine. I can give you a lesson before you go."

"But, honey..." Mom shook her head. "You really shouldn't rent one of those things by yourself. You have no experience riding a motor bike, and you also get lost pretty easily."

I nibbled my lip, looking at Jagger. "I actually don't have much of a sense of direction. Any chance I can talk you into going with me?"

He shrugged. "Sure."

Internally, I did a mental fist pump, while outside I did my best to look blasé.

Once the boat pulled into a slip, everyone grabbed their beach bags and piled off. The beach was in the opposite direction of the shops, and I was happy to be rid of Brendan and Colette for a while. Mom and Edmund and their friends went into a nautical-themed store, and then it was finally just Jagger and me.

He pointed to the right. "The scooter rental place is this way."

"Thank you for coming with us today."

"Your mom is great. Edmund is a lot more relaxed when she's around."

"Is that why you came? For my mom?"

Jagger looked over at me. "Did you really crash an eBike?"

"Just twice."

"Then how about we rent one scooter, and I'll drive."

*Hmmm... Let me see—picking rocks out of my knees after I crash, or wrapping my arms around this gorgeous man and getting to feel the abs I've been salivating over all day?*

I nodded.

We arrived at the rental place, and I zoned in on a powder pink scooter. "Oooh. Can we get the pink one?"

His lip twitched. "Whatever you want."

Fifteen minutes later, we both strapped on our helmets. Jagger straddled the pink scooter and released the kickstand before starting it. He pointed to the back. "Hop on."

I climbed onto the back, excited but also a little nervous. "How fast does this thing go?"

"About ninety."

My eyes bulged. "You're joking, right?"

Jagger looked back with a grin. "Yes. I don't know how fast it can go, but the speed limit on the island is twenty-five. I used to drive a motorcycle, so you can relax. You're safe with me."

My mind immediately conjured up a picture of Jagger on a Harley, rather than this petal pink scooter, and let me tell you, he looked really freaking hot. "Did you wear leather pants, by chance?"

"No, why?"

"No reason."

He shook his head. "You ready to go?"

I nodded. "Any instructions for me back here?"

He pointed down. "Keep your feet on those pegs. There's an exhaust pipe in the back that can get really hot, and you don't want to burn your calf. Other than that, just wrap your arms around my waist and hold on."

Jagger's sculpted abs were hard against my hands. I was dying to run my fingers up and down, feeling the peaks and valleys, but I managed to control myself. It had been *way* too long since I'd touched a man. But even if it hadn't been, I knew I still would've had the urge to touch this one all over.

We drove down a few side roads, and when we came to the corner that intersected with the main road, Jagger slowed to a stop. "You okay?"

"Yeah, I'm great."

"All right. The ride is mostly on that road, so we're going to go a little faster now."

"Okay!"

I clenched my jaw and hung on for dear life for the first minute or two. But as I got used to the ride, I relaxed and started to enjoy the wind blowing in my face and my hair whipping around. It felt amazing—so exhilarating and freeing. I had the impulse to lift my hands into the air like I was on a roller coaster, but there was no way in hell I was giving up a minute of holding on to Jagger's abs.

Sadly, less than ten minutes after we started, we pulled into a parking lot and parked.

Jagger took off his helmet and shook his hair out. "What did you think?"

"I loved it! Do you still have that motorcycle?"

He chuckled and held a hand out to help me off the scooter. Between the intimacy of having my arms wrapped around him and now taking his hand, I felt closer to him. I could almost pretend we were on a date.

"Do you want to just see the beach from up here or go down?" he asked. "It's a lot of stairs and a bit of a climb to get to the bottom. The stairs only take you to an overlook. You have to navigate rocks to get to the beach itself. But there's a rope to hold on to."

"Can we do both?"

He smiled. "I got the feeling you weren't exactly in a rush to get back anyway."

"You can say that again."

Jagger and I walked to the railing and took in the scenery from the top. "It's beautiful."

We were both quiet while we took in the panoramic view of the coastline. The cliffs rose sharply from the blue Atlantic, and the sound of waves crashing against the shore lulled me to relax. At least I *thought* we were both looking at the view. But when I turned, I found Jagger watching me and not the breathtaking ocean.

"What?" I smoothed my hair. "Am I a mess from the wind?"

He shook his head.

"Then what were you thinking just now?"

Jagger looked away. "Nothing."

There was definitely *something* going through his mind, but I wasn't going to push. Not when he'd salvaged what could've been a disaster of a day for me.

"Are you always this protective of people?" I asked.

Two lines formed between his brows. "What do you mean?"

"You only agreed to come today once you heard Brendan and Colette were coming. And then when Brendan chastised me about wanting to rent a scooter, you made sure I could rent one, safely."

Jagger's eyes dropped to my lips and lingered before meeting my eyes again. A faint smirk tugged at the corner of his mouth. "I think you're giving me too much credit. My intentions weren't as pure as you make them out to be." He put a hand on my back and guided me to start walking. "Come on. It's going to take a while to climb back up after we see the beach."

The descent to the bottom was a hundred-and-forty-one steps—I counted. But it was well worth the effort. After a pause, Jagger and I climbed the rest of the way down and walked along the beach to a quiet pile of rocks, where we sat. I looked around at the clay cliffs in awe.

"It's gorgeous. It reminds me of La Jolla Beach in California."

"I've never been," Jagger said. "I actually haven't been here in years, either." He was quiet for a moment. "I think that scooter might be the first thing I've driven in a couple of years, too."

"Really? You mean the first time you've driven something with two wheels?"

He shook his head. "I can't remember the last time I drove a car."

I hadn't given it much thought, probably because his house had multiple garages, but there hadn't been a car in his driveway when we pulled up. "How did you get out to Montauk? Did you take the train?"

He shook his head. "Sam drove. I didn't want to waste the hours in the car not working."

"I'm glad you came today then. It's too beautiful not to visit more frequently."

Jagger nodded, still looking at me. "You're right. It is."

—— CHAPTER ——
# SEVENTEEN

### Sutton

**"Y**ou hogging this view all to yourself?"

Jagger came over to where I was sitting on the bow of the boat, taking in the sunset on the ride back home. I smiled. "I'm pretty sure no one else is up here because most of the others aren't sober enough to navigate the narrow walk along the side to make it."

"True." He smiled and pointed to the spot next to me. "Mind if I sit?"

I shook my head. "I'd like that."

Jagger sat down, and we watched his incredible boat cut through the water, moving toward the glowing horizon in silence. The sky was lit in a gradient of orange and pink rays that deepened to a rich rust and burgundy as they melted into the ocean. The last bit of golden sun cast a shimmery trail across the top of the water. It made the ocean ahead sparkle.

"Haven't done this in a while either," Jagger murmured.

"Watch the sunset?"

He nodded.

"You know, all work and no play makes Jagger a dull boy."

He smiled, and we let the silence sit comfortably for a while. "Your mother seems like she had a good time today."

I nodded. "Edmund too. It's the most relaxed I've seen him in ages."

"Guess we both needed to take a break."

"And my day turned out to be nothing like I'd expected."

"What did you expect?"

"Pure torture." I laughed. "A day with my ex who married my stepsister."

"How did that go down, if you don't mind me asking?"

"Brendan and Colette getting together?"

He nodded.

I let out an audible sigh. "Brendan and I split about a year and a half ago. He's from New York, too, but we met out in California. We both went to Stanford. When he graduated, he moved back home, but I still had another semester left and wanted to do my master's out there after I was done. We tried the long-distance thing for a while, but it didn't work out."

"Whose idea was it to split?"

"In a way, I guess it was both of ours. He wanted me to move back to New York and do my master's at Columbia or NYU. I'd gotten into their programs, too. But I wanted to stay at Stanford and do my graduate work under a professor I'd TA'd for and really admired. Brendan gave me an ultimatum. If I stayed in California, we were going to break up. He wanted us to move in together in New York and get engaged. I didn't think he'd actually end things when I decided to stay at Stanford because if he loved me enough to want to propose, how could he just turn around and dump me because I was going to be gone another year? So I called his bluff by accepting the position at Stanford, and it turned out, he wasn't bluffing."

"How soon after that did he get together with your stepsister?"

"We broke up in August, and they were together by Thanksgiving."

"Were they seeing each other before you split?"

I shook my head. "I thought about that a lot in the beginning, but I really don't think so. They claim they saw each other at a bar one night about six weeks after we broke up. They'd met a few times at family events, so they already knew one another. When I found out, I got the *'we didn't mean for it to happen, I swear'* speech."

"Are you still in love with him?"

"God, no. I'm not sure if I ever was, if I'm being honest. Brendan was a safe choice for me."

"How so?"

"He was a nice guy from a good family and...he didn't want to have sex."

"You didn't want to be pressured?"

I shrugged.

Jagger studied my face. "I'm not going to judge you. Lord knows I have my own issues with sex. But if you don't want to talk about it, I understand."

"No, I..." I looked away, trying to decide what to tell him.

What I wanted was to tell him everything, which was truly crazy because I'd been through three therapists and never wanted to tell any of them anything. I'd opened up to the last one more than the first two, but I'd never *wanted* to share my story with anyone. To this day, not even Brendan knew what had happened to me. I'd only ever told Miles and my mother, and my mother had shared my story with Edmund. Yet right now I took a deep breath, ignored the churning in my stomach, and turned to face Jagger—and my own fears.

"I told you I was a virgin, but that's not technically true because I've had sex before. I just have never had it willingly, so I consider myself one."

Jagger stiffened. At least the top half of him did. His hands clenched into balls so tight, his knuckles turned white. "When?"

I looked down. "I was sixteen. I graduated high school two years early and enrolled at NYU. It happened during my second semester. Apparently, I was just as good a drinker then as I am now." I forced a smile as I started wringing my hands. "I was struggling, trying to fit into college life, so I didn't tell people my age. One night, I went to a party and started talking to a cute guy I'd never seen before. The party was in a fraternity house, and he'd said he was a member. I had no reason to doubt him. He looked like the rest of the guys there—preppy dress shirts, tapered shorts, and expensive loafers. After an hour or two, he asked me if I wanted to go up to his room. I said okay because I wanted to fool around. I didn't have much experience with boys because I'd skipped grades, and the people around me were always older and saw me as the brainy little kid. But when we got up to the second floor and went into his quiet room, I got cold feet and told him I wanted to slow things down. He said okay and offered to go get us some new drinks. He said we'd just hang out, get to know each other. An hour later, he was on top of me, and I couldn't move my arms and legs or speak. He'd given me some drug they use on animals that acts as a paralytic."

Jagger closed his eyes. When they opened, there was barely any blue left; his pupils had taken over. "What happened to him? Please tell me this story ends with him locked up or dead?"

I shook my head. "I wish. Afterward, I felt ashamed. Like it was my fault that it had happened. It was a bad decision to go up to his room while I was drinking at all, so I blamed myself. Plus, he took my license from my purse before he left and told me if I told anyone, he'd show up at my house while I was sleeping and do it again."

"Jesus Christ. His nuts should've been chopped off while he was under the same paralytic he gave you, so he had to lie there and feel as helpless as you did."

I swallowed, but the big lump in my throat didn't go anywhere. "Eventually, I confided in Miles about what happened, and he talked me into going to the police. There was no physical evidence anymore, but they opened an investigation. Turned out it wasn't the first time someone had told a story like mine. A few months earlier, there had been a similar case in a neighboring precinct where a kid pretended to be part of a fraternity and sexually assaulted a student at a different college. He also took her driver's license. Every year, he sent both of us cards on our birthdays."

"Are you fucking kidding me?" The vein in Jagger's neck bulged.

I shook my head. "A month later, I dropped out of school, and the sicko continued to send birthday cards for the next three years. They stopped when I moved to California to go to Stanford. So either he knew I left, or got bored with scaring the crap out of me once a year."

"Fuck..." Jagger got to his feet and started to pace. He pulled at his hair by the roots. "What did the police do? Ask a few questions and call it a damn day?"

I'd always been afraid to tell people what happened because I didn't want them to look at *me* differently. Jagger's reaction was nothing like I'd expected. He wasn't soft or tempered, afraid I'd break like glass; he was *angry*. And that hit my heart hard. A confusing rush of emotions washed over me, and tears spilled down my face.

Jagger was mid pace when he noticed. "Oh fuck." He dropped to his knees, lifted me into his arms, and held me close. Every other time this man touched me, even a simple hand at my back, I'd felt a rush of hormone-filled adrenaline pumping through my veins. But this touch was different. He held me so tightly it bordered on painful, yet every muscle in my body gave way. I buried my head against his chest and let it out.

My mind has always worked like a storm that never stops, spinning from one topic to the next, never taking a break to relax. But in this moment, the world slowed, and I thought about nothing except how good it felt to be held by Jagger Langston, how safe I felt.

Jagger and I stayed that way for a long time. The distant sound of my mother's party continued seventy feet away, the sky's pinks and purples faded to darkness, and yet it somehow felt like it was just the two of us.

Eventually, my sniffles slowed to a stop. I pulled back and looked up at Jagger with a hesitant smile. "Well, that... took a turn."

He smiled. "You okay?"

I nodded. "Actually, yeah. I haven't spoken about it in years. But it wasn't nearly as hard to tell you as it was Miles and my mother."

"Time helps heal most wounds."

My eyes rose to meet his. "Most?"

"I think some heal and we're able to move past whatever damaged us, and other cuts never fully close, so we have to figure out how to survive around them."

I had a funny feeling he might not be referring to *my* wounds, but his own. Though I didn't get the chance to ask before we were interrupted by Edmund's booming voice.

Jagger set me back down and walked over to the side of the boat the sound had come from. He immediately moved down the narrow walk that led from the bow to the stern of the boat.

"Whoa there," he said, disappearing from sight. He came back a few seconds later, holding onto Edmund. "You're gonna fall over, big guy."

Edmund's response was a hearty laugh. "I've already fallen, son." He placed his hand over his heart and began to sing some song about falling in love.

Jagger looked at me, amused. "It's Hootie and the Blowfish."

Edmund sang his heart out, while Jagger helped him sit down on the bow. My stepfather was a great guy, but his personality was usually somewhat stoic, definitely not the type who sang about being in love.

I smiled and enjoyed the playful moment of him bellowing with his hand over his heart, until his memory seemed to run out of words. After, he let out a hearty laugh, and Jagger and I joined in. It was impossible not to. And it was also *exactly* what I needed.

I moved over and put my arm around my stepfather. "I didn't know you could sing so well, Edmund."

"That mother of yours could make a grown man bark like a chicken."

I chuckled. "I didn't realize chickens barked."

He waved me off. "Whatever. I came to check on you. I feel like I've subjected you to so much these last few weeks—with the speedbump."

I smiled. "It's fine. I get it. He's married to your daughter."

He pointed his finger at me. "I'm going to make it up to you. Next time we get together, I'll make you my famous slow-cooked ribs, and it'll just be the three of us."

I loved that he cared so much. "You don't have to, but I'll also never turn down your ribs."

Edmund gestured to Jagger. "And this guy. This guy can come too. We need him to get to know you so he can see for himself how special you are."

Jagger winked at me, spreading warmth through my belly. "Pretty sure I already know that, Ed."

My stepfather slapped his hands to his thighs. "Welp, let me get back to my birthday princess."

Jagger took Edmund's arm, helping him up. "How about I make sure you get there in one piece?"

• • •

"Thank you for helping me herd everyone in and out of the car," I said.

Jagger and I stood in the kitchen of Edmund's summer house later that evening. My stepfather had driven to the marina earlier but hadn't been in any condition to drive home tonight. So I'd driven his car and the others had jumped in an Uber. Thankfully, Jagger had come with me, because Edmund had grown shaky on his feet by the time we got home. He'd just helped him into the bedroom.

"No problem. I'm glad they cut loose and had a good time."

"I think they might wish they'd had a little bit less of a good time when tomorrow morning comes around."

"True." Jagger smiled and pulled out his phone. "I'm going to call an Uber and get going."

"I'll drive you."

"It's fine. I don't want you to get lost. The backroads aren't lit out here."

I picked up Edmund's keys. "I know you haven't driven in a while, but we have this thing called navigation now."

He shook his head. "Wiseass."

"Come on."

Out front, I started to walk to the driver's side, but then thought better of it. "Hey, Langston?"

When Jagger looked up, I tossed him the keys to the Range Rover. "You drive. It's time you break the passenger-princess streak."

He chuckled, but waited for me to climb into the passenger seat and shut the door behind me. His grip on the steering wheel as we backed out of the driveway did all kinds of things to my libido. This evening had been the first time I'd been in Jagger's presence that I hadn't felt like a horny schoolgirl. But looking at his muscular forearms now sent me right back to the eighth grade. *Damn it.* He rested one hand on the gear shift, while the other wrapped around the leather wheel, and my mind drifted, imagining those confident hands touching me all over.

I needed my head examined when it came to this man. One minute I was telling him my deepest, darkest, secret, and the next I wanted to jump his bones.

When we pulled into Jagger's driveway, I wasn't anywhere near ready for the day to end. I looked up at his picturesque home perched on a cliff and sighed. "Your house really is incredible."

He shifted the car into park. "Thank you."

"Could I...see it?" I nibbled my bottom lip. "Maybe a quick tour of the inside?"

Jagger hesitated. "It's late. That's probably not a good idea."

It felt like he was making the responsible decision, yet something about the way he said it told me it wasn't the one he wanted to make. "It won't take long."

Our eyes met in the darkness. I could see he was still struggling, and I thought he was about to turn me down a second time. "Please?" I asked.

Jagger's jaw tightened, yet in the end he nodded. "Sure."

He led the way to the oversized, arched door, unlocked it, and flicked on lights before moving aside for me to enter first.

I took one step in and stopped. "Holy shit."

Soaring ceilings made the entry feel grandiose, but the real spectacle was the view. Standing at the front door, you could see clear through the massive living room and out to the ocean, even in the dark.

"It's so lit up outside."

"There are a ton of lights out back, including some spotlights installed on the bluff. I flicked on that switch along with the interior lights."

"Your view is the polar opposite of the one in New York City, yet there's still something similar about it."

He nodded. "It's the big windows as soon as you walk in. The rest of the house was a bonus. I knew I was buying this place the moment I stood here."

"I can see why."

Jagger ushered me in, yet he stayed several feet away as I looked around. An oversized, cream sectional with plush pillows acted as the centerpiece of the great room, positioned in front of a massive stone fireplace. White walls were decorated with colorful art, and a few antiques blended everything together. The only sign that anyone was staying here were the piles of paper on the glass coffee table.

I pointed. "Were you working from here earlier?"

He nodded. "I spend too much time inside working as is. The least I can do is take in the view while I'm doing it."

"Do you come out to Montauk year-round? I bet it's beautiful in the winter, with a big fire going, snow falling, and the ocean in the background."

"I should, but it's been a while since I've been out here."

"How long?"

"Not since last fall."

My jaw dropped open. "If this was my house, I'd be out here every weekend. Hell, if I were you, I'd move the office to Montauk."

Jagger smiled and nodded toward a hall. "Come on, I'll show you the rest of the house."

The remainder of the beautiful home was on par with the grandeur of the great room—a gourmet kitchen with not one, but two islands, a solarium-turned-office with a glass ceiling and walls, four bedrooms decorated to perfection with plush bedding and coastal-style furniture. All through the tour, though, Jagger kept more distance than usual. Perhaps it stood out to me because of how physically close we'd been earlier. When we came to the last unopened door, he opened it but stayed in the doorway.

While I walked in and looked around, he leaned against the jamb with both hands in his pockets. His broad frame filled almost the entire width of the opening. His bedroom had French doors that led to a deck with another incredible view, and there was an en-suite bathroom with a clawfoot tub and separate shower with a dozen heads. Jagger might have been across the room, but I felt his eyes follow my every step.

"This house is perfection, Jagger." I ran my hand along the plush bedding and made my way closer to the door. My pulse picked up when he didn't move. "Can I ask you something?"

His smile was lazy. "You just did."

I tilted my head and took a tentative step closer. "What made you come out here this weekend?"

Jagger pursed his lips. "You should probably get back home so Edmund doesn't worry."

"Edmund's sound asleep."

Jagger still hadn't moved from the doorway, so I took another step closer.

He cleared his throat. "It's late."

"You always do that," I said. "Ignore my question when it's one you don't want to answer."

"What would you like me to do? There are some things that shouldn't be said."

Another step. We were maybe a foot and a half apart now.

"Why shouldn't they be said?"

His eyes dropped to my lips and stayed there as he spoke. "Because they're highly fucking inappropriate."

I took another step, a baby one this time. Only a foot separated us.

"Did you come out to Montauk because I was going to be here this weekend?"

"It doesn't matter if I did."

"It does to me."

Another baby step. Six inches now. The air around us crackled. His breathing picked up, and I could feel it tickle my skin. Instead of making me nervous, it invigorated me. "Answer the question."

He stared at me while I wondered if I should take the last step. I was just about to do it when he closed his eyes. "You should go home, Sutton." His voice was stern, cold, and detached.

I took an immediate step back. Had I been misreading his desire? I suddenly felt like a troll rather than the temptress I'd thought I was just a minute ago. Heat crept up to my face. "Okay."

"I'm going to use the bathroom." Jagger stepped away from the doorway to let me out. "I'll meet you downstairs and walk you out in a minute."

My heart felt heavy as I returned to the living room. I thought about leaving before he came back, but that would only make me look like a petulant child. Instead, I took a seat on the living room sectional and forced myself to wait to say goodbye. Staring down at his piles of work papers, I felt so damn foolish, and I wasn't really seeing anything—at least until some pages ripped from a yellow legal pad caught my eye. They were sticking out sideways underneath a stack of clipped-together papers, and I recognized the computation since I'd worked through it myself just yesterday. I bent and slipped the pages out.

At the top, a number was written above the margin and circled. The answer—the *right* answer.

Did Jagger work through the rest of the problem after we left the conference room? For some inexplicable reason, I knew he hadn't.

I scanned the pages, eyeing rows and rows of computations. There were at least a dozen sheets of paper filled, and from what I could see at a quick glance, they were all right. I reached the last page just as Jagger returned to the living room. He looked at my hands before his eyes met mine.

"You let me win?" I asked.

He looked conflicted. So I asked a different question.

"*Why* did you let me win?"

"I figured it would help your confidence. Plus, I didn't finish that much faster than you."

"You even offered me a prize after I supposedly won—why add that to the mix?"

He met my eyes again. "I wanted to see what you'd ask for."

A fire lit inside me. "I think I finally figured it out."

"Figured what out?"

"The prize I want, assuming you're still giving me one since I now know you just let everyone *think* I won."

"That depends." Jagger's Adam's apple bobbed up and down. "What is it you want?"

"*You.*"

— **CHAPTER** —
# EIGHTEEN

Sutton

**"T**hat's not happening." Jagger folded his arms over his chest.

But his refusal did nothing to deter me this time. I retook the steps I'd surrendered upstairs and put my palms flat on his rock-hard chest. He flinched, but I knew it was because he felt the same jolt I did, not because he experienced any physical discomfort from my touch. His eyes sparked with lust, no matter what his words said.

"Why not?" I asked.

"Because you work for me."

"Nice try." I grinned. "You already told me you wouldn't give two shits if that were the only obstacle. Kiss me, Jagger."

His chest rose higher with each breath. "I can't."

"Can't? Or don't want to? If you're really going to stand there and reject me, you could at least be honest."

His eyes dropped to my lips and stayed there. "Can't."

"Why?" I looked down, noticing a substantial bulge. "It doesn't look like it's a physical problem."

"It's definitely not a fucking physical problem."

"Then what is it? Is it because of your...proclivities?"

He smiled sadly. "Sutton, putting my proclivities together with your history would be like setting two trains on the same track and waiting for them to collide. Plus, I'm the kind of man who sends jewelry and a thank-you note to say goodbye the next morning, not brings you flowers and asks for a second date. It's not a good idea."

"I'm not asking for hearts and roses." I lifted my other hand with the intent of wrapping it around his neck, scraping my fingers along his skin. But Jagger caught my wrist. His hand held me tight, and I liked the way it felt. No, I *loved* it.

"Then what are you asking me?"

I took a deep breath and looked directly into his eyes. "To fuck me."

His eyes closed, and he let out a string of mumbled curses. He was on the brink of giving in, and I would've stopped at nothing to watch him break. So I did the one thing I knew no man could resist. I dropped to my knees and reached for the button of his shorts.

"*Fuck...*" Jagger groaned. He looked down at me. "You look so fucking perfect like that."

His eyes were so intensely fixed on me, I wasn't even sure he noticed as I undid the button and took down the zipper. The tight boxer briefs underneath revealed the outline of his thick cock. I leaned over and placed a gentle kiss on it, leaving my lips against it as I spoke so he could feel the murmur. "I want you, Jagger. I want you the way you want to give it to me."

He tensed as I scraped my fingernail along the skin just above his waistband, but he didn't stop me when I reached in and wrapped my fingers around his girth. He was so hard and thick, it made me question whether I could even take what I was asking for. I was good at giving blow jobs after three years of being in a relationship without sex. But Brendan was *not* this size. Still, I ran my thumb over the tip and was rewarded with a trickle of pre-cum. Jagger hissed when I leaned in and swiped my tongue over it.

He exhaled raggedly. "Lick it. Lick my cock."

My entire body vibrated. I seriously could have come if I'd just reached down and touched between my legs for a second. I was *that* turned on already. I salivated at the thought of him giving me more commands.

Hooking my fingers into the sides of his waistband, I pulled down his shorts and boxers enough to free him completely and wrapped my hand around the root. Then I leaned in and did what I was told. I licked from the base to the crown. When I got to the tip, I opened wide and sucked him in with one long draw, until he hit the back of my throat.

"*Fuck*," Jagger hissed. He reached down, dug both hands into my hair, and fisted my locks so tightly it burned at my scalp. But I loved it. Loved, loved, *loved* it. The bite of pain made me want to please him even more desperately.

I pulled back, and Jagger took control. He held tight and maneuvered my head to bob up and down at a rapid pace. I was barely able to keep up, gliding my tongue along the underside and sucking while I jerked him with my hand in unison. On one thrust, he went deeper and stilled. His body shook, yet he pulled back again rather than have me take him all the way down my throat. I wasn't sure if his restraint was for my benefit or his.

"Good girl." His voice was a deep, throaty rasp. "Just like that. Take my cock."

I *loved* his praise. It turned me on more than I'd ever imagined pleasing a man could. My knees started to hurt from rocking back and forth on the hard wood floor, but they could've cut into my skin and there was still no way I would've stopped.

"Breathe through your nose, beautiful. I'm going to fuck your face."

I whimpered and squeezed my legs together tightly, desperate for friction. Jagger's hands stilled my head, and he pulled out and pushed back in harshly, burying his cock in my throat. His thickness stretched my limits, making my esophagus burn and my eyes water. I probably would've gagged if I had the chance, but Jagger pulled out and pushed right back in, over and over, going deeper and deeper. I had to wrap my hands around his thighs and hold on for dear life.

"*Fuck*," he roared. "Get ready. I'm going to come down your throat."

He'd given a warning, but there wasn't enough time to prepare. Then again, I could've had an hour, and I wouldn't have been ready for what he gave me. Hot spurts of thick cum streamed down my throat. It seemed to go on forever, and Jagger didn't stop pumping until every last tremor had wracked its way through his body. After, he pulled out, releasing his tight hold on my hair and struggling to catch his breath. I stayed on my knees doing the same, in awe that he'd barely softened after such an intense release.

After a minute, he reached down, slipped his hands under my arms, and lifted me to my feet. I winced when my knees extended, feeling the ache the hard floor had inflicted.

Jagger's post-release relaxed face changed in an instant. "Are you hurt?"

I shook my head. "My knees are just bony."

He steered me over to the couch and pointed. "Sit."

Jagger disappeared for a moment and came back with two ice packs and a glass of water. He set the drink on the coffee table and kneeled down on one knee to press the cold to my achy joints.

"I'll be fine," I said. "That's not necessary."

He frowned. "Let me take care of you." After a few seconds, he added, "Please. And drink some of that water. It will soothe your raw throat."

I swallowed, realizing for the first time that he was right—my throat was sore. I nodded and reached for the glass. "Thank you."

Jagger stayed quiet. He looked lost in deep thought, and I wondered if he was already regretting what we'd done.

"What are you thinking about?" I whispered.

He scoffed. "What a piece of shit I am."

"What are you talking about?"

"You deserve better than what I just did to you."

"What you just did to me? You didn't *do* anything to me, Jagger. I'm the one who started it, and I liked what we did. I *love* what we did, actually."

He searched my face. "You've been hurt more than once. I don't want to do it again."

"How would you hurt me?"

"I have a history of taking what I want from women and being done when I'm done. I'm not a romantic, Sutton."

"Who asked you to be a romantic?"

He seemed genuinely confused. "Then what do you want from me?"

I grinned. "More of that. And sex."

His serious face broke, and he laughed. "Are you saying you just want to use me?"

I took the ice packs from his hands at my knees and set them on the coffee table. Then returned his hands to my knees and inched forward. "Is that a problem for you?"

"Not at all." He put up a finger. "*But,* you have to trust me to know what you need."

"What is it you think I need?"

His eyes moved back and forth, staring into mine. "A first time the way it should've been for you. Not the way I like it."

He might not have thought he was a romantic, but I felt what he said in my heart. Jagger Langston had a hard shell, but inside was a soft center. His words brought a wave of emotions, and I tasted salt in my throat before nodding. "Okay." I leaned forward a little more until our faces were inches apart. "It's a deal. Now how about a kiss? Would that gross you out after what we just did?"

He licked his lips with a sinful smile. "Nothing about you grosses me out, sweetheart."

I inwardly swooned at the term of endearment. But didn't want him to see me getting all googly-eyed already. Instead, I tilted my head coyly. "Then what are you waiting for?"

He groaned, yet his smile widened. "You're gonna be trouble."

I opened my mouth with a witty retort in mind, but I never got the chance to share it. Jagger gripped the back of my neck, squeezed hard, and pulled me to him. His lips sealed over mine, and I melted into him. His tongue nudged my mouth open and dipped inside. He tasted insanely good, and the aggressiveness of his kiss, the way he dictated control in every way, had me sighing into his mouth. Jagger was still kneeling on one foot. He hooked an arm around my waist, slid me from the couch, and positioned me to straddle his knee.

I was in a complete lust-induced daze already, but when his fingers dug into my hips and he started to grind me back and forth on his leg—*holy shit*. My swollen clit had been desperate for friction, and it didn't take long before I was throbbing. My orgasm was so close, I started shamelessly gyrating my hips and riding his leg. But just when I thought I might fly over the edge, Jagger stopped, leaving me panting.

"Why are you stopping?"

He scooped me into his arms and rose to his feet. "Because I want you needy when you're beneath me."

I had been so bold tonight, but as I stood in Jagger's bedroom, a rush of nerves washed over me. The lights were off, though the room was still illuminated enough from the glow of the lighting outside to see clearly. Jagger walked to the French doors and opened them, letting in the tranquil sound of crashing waves before coming to me and taking my hand. He lifted it toward his lips, but stopped before reaching his mouth.

"You're shaking. Are you cold?"

I shook my head.

He frowned. "Do you want to go back downstairs? I don't want you to do anything you don't want to do."

"No, no." I shook my head vigorously. "Definitely not. I want this very much. I'm just...nervous, I guess."

He squeezed my hand and led me to sit on the edge of the bed. Crouching down in front of me, he stroked my skin with his thumb. "Talk to me. What are you nervous about?"

I shrugged. "I don't know. I guess I've just made sex this big thing in my head, and it feels overwhelming."

"I can understand that." He nodded. "We'll take it slow. Is there anything else? Are you sure you don't have any doubts?"

"Not really. Although now that I've seen the size of that thing in your pants, I might be questioning if maybe I should start with the beginner size and not jump right to the expert level."

Jagger chuckled.

My mind drifted, and I stayed quiet for a moment. When I spoke again, my voice was barely a whisper. "Can I ask you something?"

"Of course."

"When was the last time you made love to someone, rather than—you know, had sex?"

He squeezed my hand, prompting me to meet his eyes. "Tonight might be a first for both of us."

*Oh wow.*

Jagger smiled. "You've stopped shaking."

I hadn't even realized. "I guess I did."

He leaned in and kissed my forehead before standing and moving toward the nightstand. "I'm guessing you're not on the pill?"

"Actually, I am. But I just went on it a few weeks ago, and my doctor said you need to be on it for a full cycle before it becomes fully effective."

Jagger's brows drew down. "What made you go on it?"

"I was planning on taking care of my problem. Funny enough, that's why I joined that dating app and originally met you. I was determined to have sex and get it over with before Brendan's wedding."

He slid open the nightstand drawer and pulled out a strip of condoms. I counted six dangling and raised a brow. "Big plans?"

He shook his head. "You have no fucking idea, sweetheart."

The blood flowing to my clit had ebbed, but it all suddenly rushed back upon hearing Jagger sound as desperate as I felt. He strolled over and bent to one knee. My pulse kicked up as he lifted my foot and unbuckled my sandal, slipping it off. Placing a sweet kiss on my ankle, he set my leg back down and did the same to the other. *God, he's so damn sexy.*

Jagger held out a hand, and when I placed mine in his, he used it to help me up. Leaning down, he kissed my lips with the same gentle touch he'd been using since we'd decided to come upstairs. It was difficult to believe that this was the same man who'd been yanking my head around and *fucking my face* not too long ago. That had felt right, but somehow this moment felt right, too. Left to my own devices, I would've gotten having sex over with—a simple *wham, bam, thank you, ma'am* and goodbye virginity. I even would've let Jagger use the same gruff tactics he'd employed a little while ago. But I was thankful he was so thoughtful in considering what would be best for me.

He cupped my cheeks with his hands and brought his mouth down to meet mine. The kiss was languid and sensual, and the sound of the ocean drowned out everything but the moment. Even though Jagger was taking things slow, his lips were still demanding against mine. He started to unbutton my top and kissed his way down my jaw, nibbling a path over my chin, and sucking along my neck. It felt so incredibly good, I was on the verge of tears. But then Jagger nipped at my collarbone and made me gasp.

When I looked down, he winked. "I said I'd hold back from topping you, but making love doesn't have to be all soft."

He slipped my shirt from my shoulders, tossing it on the floor. I was thankful I'd packed a pretty bra and underwear set. The petal pink demi bra I had on made my B-plus cups look like full Cs that were anxious to spill over. Jagger continued kissing my shoulders, my arms, and the top of my chest as he worked slowly to remove my shorts.

When I stood in nothing but my bra and underwear, he stepped back, drinking me in from head to toe. "You're exquisite."

I flushed. "Thank you."

He knelt in front of me and slowly worked my panties from my hips, then stood and guided me to turn around. I probably should've been concerned that he unhooked my bra faster than I could've, but there would be plenty of time to overanalyze every moment tomorrow.

"Sit," he said. "I want to see all of you."

I took a seat on the edge of the bed, and Jagger again dropped to his knees. I wasn't generally self-conscious about my body, but when he nudged my legs open wide enough that the outer parts of my thighs were touching the mattress, I grew a little shy.

"You're so pink and perfect." He stroked his thumb over my clit, and I shivered.

"And so responsive. I'm surprised you've never been able to orgasm with a man."

"I'm starting to think I've never been with a man, only boys."

Jagger smiled. He slid his thumb down my slick center and gently pushed it inside me.

My eyes fluttered closed.

He massaged along my tender walls with slow, expert skill until he elicited a mewl from me. Then he pulled out and pushed back in with two fingers, leaving his thumb to stroke over my clit. I was already on edge, but when he leaned down and buried his face in my wetness, I throbbed from head to toe.

Jagger knew what he was doing. Again I had to tamp down thoughts of *why* he was so good at giving oral and focus on the pleasure I felt and how much he seemed to pay attention to my needs. When my breaths grew short and shallow, he flicked my clit with his tongue, making me clench hard with need. I dug my fingers into his hair and shamelessly ground against him.

*Oh my God.*

I'm going to come.

From a man.

Not from my own doing.

The pressure built and built. I felt like a tightly wound top about to spin out of control.

"Jagger…I'm going to…"

His fingers pumped in and out faster. The proof of my excitement was evident in the sounds of my wetness growing louder and louder. He sucked hard on my clit, and I exploded—fireworks-lighting-up-the-sky *exploded*. My body trembled, and I moaned my way through the most intense orgasm of my life—and my first with a man.

As I came down on the other side of it, Jagger kept lapping at me, drawing every last spasm from my body. After, it was all I could do to stay upright. My bones felt like they'd liquified from the heat.

"Holy shit," I panted. "I can't believe that just happened."

Jagger pressed kisses up my belly, stopping to nip at a nipple before pressing his lips against mine. "I can't wait to take all your other firsts," he murmured.

"All of my others?" I laughed. "I think there's only one left."

His smile was wicked. "We'll see about that."

Jagger slid his hands under my ass and lifted, scooping me into his arms and settling me back down in the center of the bed. "But for tonight, I'll play nice. You'll come whenever you feel like it instead of when I tell you that you can, and you'll tell me when you've had enough."

I didn't have time to let the meaning of his words really sink in because Jagger pulled off his shirt and shorts and settled on top of me, straddling my legs. He reached to the end table for a condom and ripped the packaging open with his teeth before rolling it on.

*Oh.*

*My.*

*God.*

The sight of him touching himself sent a ripple of pleasure between my legs. The full package that was naked Jagger Langston was a lot to take in. There wasn't an area of him that I couldn't spend hours admiring. Chiseled pecs led down to a wall of perfectly formed abs. I'd always heard the term six-pack, but Jagger had double that. His waist was narrow and sported that brain-frazzling V that made smart women make dumb choices. And I hadn't even gotten to his mesmerizing face yet. Though when I finally did, Jagger looked amused.

"Enjoying yourself?"

"I am. Do you think you can grab my phone so I can take a picture and stare at this whenever I want?"

"Later." He smirked. "I have much better things to do now."

Jagger stretched out his legs, covering my body with his, but being careful to keep his weight on his elbows. I felt the hot, hard length of him flush against my bare skin, and knew without a shadow of a doubt that the orgasm he'd been able to give me with his mouth was not going to be the last.

He brushed a lock of hair from my face and spoke softly. "You're beautiful, Sutton."

I smiled. "You're not so bad yourself."

"I have been trying to keep the hell away from you since I walked out of the bar that first night, but yet here I am, breaking all my own rules."

"Every rule needs an exception. In fact, my mother has a saying. 'Rules keep your life organized, but it's the exceptions that make life more interesting.'"

Jagger smiled before taking my lips in a kiss. Brendan had always brushed his teeth or avoided kissing after going down on me, so when Jagger's tongue tangled with mine and I tasted myself, I would've thought it would freak me out a little. But it did just the opposite—it turned me on. Kissing him back with everything I had felt like a thank you for the effort he'd put in.

Jagger pulled back and looked into my eyes. "You ready for me? I don't mean your body—that's primed, and I'll go slow. I mean *you*."

I nodded. "I have never wanted anything so badly in my life."

Jagger took a deep, steadying breath and pushed inside. His eyes never left mine as he eased in and out, being careful to go slow. I could tell from the strain on his face that it wasn't easy, but something told me doing the impossible was right up the man's alley. I was soaked and ready, so even though he was thick, my body stretched to accommodate him.

"Fuck. You feel..." His eyes briefly closed, and he swallowed. "You feel like...my first."

Emotions welled inside of me. I was really doing it. Having *sex*, and it was nothing like the get-it-over-with experience I'd imagined my first time would be. It was raw, and beautiful, and exactly what I didn't know I needed.

Jagger kept gliding in and out, each thrust in going deeper and deeper until he was fully seated. His arms shook as he buried himself to the hilt. "You good?"

I smiled and cupped his cheek. "I'm better than good. You don't have to be so gentle."

But Jagger continued at an unhurried pace. I wanted him to lose control, to feel the same thing that was happening to my body.

"Harder," I whimpered. "Please."

When he didn't listen, I grew desperate.

I nipped at his chin. "I'll beg if you want. *Please*, Jagger."

He mumbled a string of curses, but finally relented. Gentle thrusts grew rougher, and easing in and out became rooting deeply into my body. The one thing that didn't change, though, was the way Jagger looked at me. He stared into my eyes like he was able to really *see* me, and more importantly, he made me feel like I had nothing to hide. The moment was so intimate, like we were the only two people on Earth. Everything else faded into the distance as our bodies climbed in unison.

"Oh God!" I gasped, startling when I realized I was actually going to orgasm again. Today was exceeding all my expectations, and then some. I dug my nails into his back. "Jagger..."

He reached down and grabbed my thigh, guiding it to bend at the knee. Then he pushed up and angled himself so that when our bodies met, he also pressed against my clit. The friction sent me flying over the edge, and a toe-curling orgasm ripped through me.

"*Jagger!*" I moaned.

His response was to smash his lips against mine and kiss me through every pulsating muscle contraction. After, I looked up with hooded eyes, and Jagger quickened his pace, working toward his own release. It hit with such a roar that I thought he might've scared the fish in the ocean outside.

I obviously didn't have experience with the actual act of sexual intercourse, but Brendan had always collapsed after a blow job, his dick wilting to half-mast or fully flaccid before he would inevitably roll over and fall asleep. But Jagger kept kissing me for a long time, gliding in and out, even after his second orgasm with little downtime in between.

I flashed a goofy smile when our eyes met. "We did it, and you're still hard."

His lip twitched. "We did, and that's your fault. I've been semi-erect since I first laid eyes on you on that damn app. I had to stop watching you on the security feed because I kept having to jerk myself off in the private bathroom in my office."

I grinned. "Really?"

Jagger pressed his lips to mine firmly before getting up to dispose of the condom. "That's not a good thing. Especially the time I had a meeting with your stepfather right after."

I was still laughing when Jagger returned from the bathroom. He came back with a warm facecloth and pressed it gently between my legs. "Sore?"

I was, but not too bad. And I didn't want to admit it in case he might be up for a hat trick at some point. So I shrugged. "Just a little."

The adrenaline crash started to hit, and I yawned. I expected Jagger to distance himself now that the actual act was over. But he surprised me and slipped back into bed. He laid on his back and lifted me so my head rested on his chest. I listened to his heartbeat while he stroked my hair.

"Are you always able to do that?" I asked.

"What?"

"Give a woman two orgasms in as many hours?"

His hand stopped moving. "I'm not touching that question with a ten-foot pole, sweetheart."

I smiled and turned my head, propping it up on a fist on his chest. "I guess that was a you're-damned-if-you-do, damned-if-you-don't type of question."

He ran his thumb along my bottom lip. "How about this? What happened between us isn't the norm. It was special."

"Maybe you like it slow and sweet more than you thought?" I said.

Jagger cupped my cheek. I was expecting him to say something romantic, but instead, he used the hand on my face to turn my head and position it back on his chest. "Don't get your hopes up, sweetheart."

—— **CHAPTER** ——
# TWENTY

Jagger

10-1/2 years ago

"**C**all." Anderson tossed his cards on the table face up and grinned, reaching for the pile of chips in the middle. "Read 'em and weep, ladies."

"*Tsk. Tsk. Tsk.*" I put up a hand, moving my finger back and forth. "Not so fast, Corporal."

My buddy, Sergeant Nelson, leaned back in his chair and snickered. "Do you think we invited a *corporal* to play cards with us so you can take our money?"

Anderson shrugged. "I thought you invited me because I made corporal."

"We invited you because we were tired of Langston here only taking *our* money."

He looked down at the cards. "I have three aces and a queen high card. Sarge didn't even turn over his cards yet. How are you so sure he won?"

"Because he *always* wins."

I flashed a cocky grin and turned over five hearts, all of which happened to be consecutive numbers. "Straight flush."

Anderson groaned. "That's bullshit. You cheated."

I swept the pile of chips, along with a shoe Nelson had anted when he ran out of chips, over to my side of the table. "If I had a dollar for every time someone accused me of cheating, I'd still be smarter than you."

Nelson chuckled. "The only hand that beats Langston when he's on a roll is a lucky one. And you got shit luck, Corporal Anderson. You live in California, go out on leave for the weekend in New York and cheat on your girlfriend, and it turns out the woman is your girl's cousin."

Anderson's shoulders slumped. "That was fucked up."

I laughed and lifted my chin toward his pants. "You have any more chips hidden somewhere?"

He stuck his hands into his pockets and pulled out the lining. There was nothing but lint. "You cleaned me out."

"Good," I said. "Then go get Jace. He was promoted to lance corporal today. Tell him to bring his money to the sergeant's tent so he can celebrate next."

Anderson shook his head, but stood.

"Oh, and Corporal, if you warn him that he's going to have his ass handed to him playing with us, you'll be cleaning the toilet after Sergeant Nelson goes to the bathroom, and he's got IBS."

Nelson rubbed his pot belly. "It's the wheat. I'm gluten intolerant."

Anderson walked out, leaving just me, Nelson, and Sergeant Walker. Nelson and I had been buddies since boot camp. We both rose in the ranks and made sergeant together, and I'd accumulated a nice collection of his money playing cards over the years, along with other crap he sometimes raised when he was out of cash. But Walker we'd only met a few days ago. His platoon had just gotten back from the Middle East, where my fire team and Nelson's were heading together first thing tomorrow.

I looked over at him. "Got any pointers on how to bring home a team intact, Walker?"

He pulled out a hand-rolled cigarette and lit up, taking a deep drag and exhaling a thick cloud of smoke. "Sure. Pack sunscreen. You wouldn't want a sunburn to ruin your day while you're running through a field filled with IEDs and dodging a hail of gunfire."

"Great. Thanks. That's helpful."

He leaned up and clunked his elbows on the folding table. "Seriously though, the only advice I can give you is that complacency kills. We're sitting here shooting the shit without a care in the world right now. There are going to be times when it's quiet, where you feel like you can relax, maybe let your guard down for a night. That's when you become an easy target over there. Those fuckers are sneaky. They're always watching."

I nodded. "Good advice."

"Other than that, keep control of yourself. It's going to be chaotic in the field, and your team is going to take the lead from you on how to act."

"Keeping control is my specialty."

"For your sake, I hope it is."

• • •

This was the first time since we'd landed on foreign soil three weeks ago that the sky hadn't been lit up with what looked like fireworks. It was also the first time I'd slept for more than an hour straight, since there hadn't been explosions to rattle me from my slumber. My fire team must've felt the calm, too, because jokes and insults were flying around as we crossed through the desert in the back of a Humvee.

"Yo momma like a microwave," Corporal Anderson said to Private Wall. "Anyone can walk up and push a button, and she heats up."

"Oh yeah?" Private Wall pretended to slick back his hair. "Yo momma so stupid, I saw her staring at the juice container this morning because it said concentrate."

I chuckled and kept quiet as the other guys jumped in.

"Yo momma so stupid, she put a quarter in each ear to listen to Fifty Cent."

"Yo momma so stupid, she got hit by a parked car."

We slowed as we pulled into a small village. Sergeant Nelson and his team were behind us in a second Humvee. A couple of kids were playing jump rope with clothes tied together. It made me smile to see innocence after weeks of anything but. The kids saw the American military vehicles and started running after us, waving. Some of the guys waved back, but we kept on rolling.

"This is Khalari, the village we're supposed to check out," our driver yelled from the front.

"All right, pull over up ahead near that clearing."

Once we stopped, Sergeant Nelson jumped down from his vehicle, and together we looked around. "Doesn't look like too much of a threat."

"Maybe I'll finally get a chance to win back some of my money from Sarge," Corporal Anderson said.

"The line forms in back of me," Nelson said. "The man has been taking my money since freaking boot camp. I got a two-and-a-half-year-old who might want to attend college someday."

"I wouldn't worry about that," I said with a smile. "Not if he's got your brains."

"Bite me, dickwad."

I chuckled.

"What do you do with all the money you win?" Anderson asked. "I heard you don't got kids."

"I invest it."

"In what?"

"The stock market." In the three-and-a-half years I'd been in the military, I'd invested every penny I'd won in card games and turned my profits by twenty-fold.

"I don't have enough luck to even win at cards, much less win at the stock market."

"Winning at cards isn't about luck. It's about reading the table, same as the Dow."

Nelson shrugged. "If you say so."

I pointed to the area on the right. "Let's set up camp there. As of now, we're staying for three nights."

My team of six jumped off the Humvee and started to put up our tents. Nelson's did the same. The kids that had been jumping rope a mile back caught up and surrounded us, watching the platoon work. A few of them spoke broken English. I stood back when we were done and watched them convince Sergeant Nelson to jump rope. It was a good thing he had talent when it came to rifle skills because his combat boots kept getting caught in the rope with every swing.

I laughed, enjoying the much-needed levity of the moment. But then a wind gust kicked up out of nowhere and made a howling sound. It made the hairs on the back of my neck stand up as I looked around, searching the mountains for an enemy. Finding nothing, I disregarded the feeling, ignoring the advice I'd been given a few weeks ago during a card game—*"complacency kills"*—and went back to watching my soldiers let loose a bit.

Which was the reason that I never saw the ambush coming. And neither did the men I was responsible for keeping safe.

## —— CHAPTER ——
## TWENTY-ONE

Sutton

Wow. What a view to wake up to.

I sat up in bed for a better look, stretching my arms over my head. The morning sun cast a warm, golden glow over the green grass, and beyond that, the ocean stretched out endlessly in the distance. Unlike last night when the waves were crashing, the morning brought peaceful lapping and breaks that melted into the sand.

The beautiful view would have been much better, though, if the spot next to me were occupied. Jagger was nowhere to be found, and the sheets were cold where the imprint of his body remained. I took another moment to appreciate the breathtaking panorama outside before dragging myself from bed, wrapping a sheet around my achy body, and going in search of the man who'd made it that way.

Jagger was sitting out back on the deck with a cup of coffee, staring at the ocean. The doors were wide open, and a light breeze blew around some papers on the living room table, secured in place by a laptop. I padded over and leaned against the door. "Good morning."

He turned but didn't smile. "Morning."

"How long have you been up?"

He shrugged. "A few hours."

"What time is it?" I looked around the living room behind me. "I have no idea what I did with my phone."

"Almost eight." He paused and met my eyes. "You should probably go. Your family will be worried."

The statement and his chilly attitude felt like a punch in the gut. "Oh. Okay."

He turned back and resumed staring at the ocean, not even offering me a cup of coffee before he booted me to the curb.

Feeling fifty pounds heavier as I trudged up the stairs, I went back up to the bedroom and got myself dressed. I, at least, needed a pit stop in the bathroom before he kicked me out, and when I caught what I looked like in the mirror, I winced. My hair screamed *just fucked*, mascara was smeared under both eyes, and don't even get me started on the foul taste in my mouth. I did the best I could to wash up, smoothed down the chaos of my hair, and rummaged through the medicine cabinet to find toothpaste to use with my finger. A lone brown prescription pill bottle sat on the bottom shelf with a few shaving supplies. I tried to shut the door and ignore it, but I failed and instead reached in and turned the plastic enough to see the information on the label. Temazepam. *Huh.* I only knew it was to treat insomnia because it was one of the drugs the doctor had offered to prescribe for me when I'd had trouble sleeping after everything happened in college.

I returned downstairs and searched around for my purse. Jagger was still in the same spot, but when he heard the zipper on my bag, he turned and got up. I didn't want him to see the hurt on my face and wasn't sure I could hide it, so I buried my face in my phone as he came up to me.

"I'm just checking my messages to see if anyone has noticed I'm MIA at the house, and then I'll be out of your hair."

He didn't respond, so I kept scrolling. I had a million messages from Miles but none from Mom or Edmund, so maybe I'd be lucky and they'd both slept in. As per usual, my mother wouldn't likely see the light of day until early afternoon, but Edmund was usually an early bird. I tossed the phone back into my bag and continued avoiding eye contact. "Looks like I might be in the clear. Or at least they haven't called a search party for me as of yet."

I chanced a glance up and found Jagger staring at me. Still he said nothing, and it made me feel awkward. "So, uh...I guess I'll see you at work next week?"

He nodded.

I walked to the door, trying to ignore the horrible feeling in the pit of my stomach. I hadn't had many sexual interactions with men who weren't my boyfriend—or *any* for that matter. Maybe this was the norm. Maybe this was the aftermath of a hook-up. But when Jagger still didn't speak as I opened the door and stepped outside, I couldn't help myself.

"Did I do something wrong?" I huffed. "Should I not have fallen asleep here last night?"

Jagger shut his eyes and shook his head. "I'm just busy, and my mind has been elsewhere with work all morning."

I would've bet my last breath that he was full of shit, yet I let him have his lie and forced a smile. "Try to enjoy some of the nice day between all that work."

Jagger pushed his hands into his pockets and watched me walk to the car. I unlocked it and started to fold in, but then I remembered the pill bottle in the medicine cabinet and stopped. "By the way," I yelled. "How did you sleep last night?"

Even from fifty feet away I could see the wheels in his head turning. "Solid," he eventually said. "And you?"

"Good." I smiled. "I'm glad."

• • •

I parked in front of Edmund's house, rather than pulling into the driveway, so the noisy gravel didn't announce my arrival. The front door was unlocked—the way I'd left it last night—and I hoped that was a sign that no one was up yet. Gently pulling the door shut, I thought I might be in the clear. Until I found Brendan and Colette sitting on the couch.

I jumped, and my hand flew up to cover my heart. "God, you scared the shit out of me."

"We wouldn't have if you weren't sneaking around." My stepsister grinned. She popped up from the couch and walked over, hooking her arm with mine. "You dirty rotten stay-out. Tell me all the details."

Meanwhile, Brendan glared at me. "Where have you been?"

*Seriously?* My lips twisted in disgust. "None of your business."

He frowned. "You could at least be courteous and let the people you're with know you aren't coming back so they don't worry."

I rolled my eyes. "Sorry, *Dad.*"

Colette waved him off. "Ignore him. He's just cranky because my dad's snoring kept him up. But I want all the details. Did you hook up with Jagger? You never came back after driving him home. That house he lives in is the most expensive real estate property in all of Montauk."

I wanted so badly to look at Brendan and say, "Yep, the very rich, very gorgeous, *very well-hung* man fucked my brains out, and, oh by the way, his dick is twice the size of yours." But I didn't want to compromise Edmund's relationship with the boss. So instead, I shook my head.

"A friend from work invited me to go out in the Hamptons at the last minute. It was late by the time we got in, so I crashed on her couch."

Brendan's eyes narrowed. "Her? Edmund said all the other interns are men."

"I didn't say it was an intern." I shook my head. "And why am I answering you? I can do whatever I want."

Colette grinned. "I hope *whatever you want* was hot."

*Shouldn't these newlyweds still be in bed?* I looked over her shoulder at the hall that led to the bedrooms. "Is anyone else up? Edmund or my mom? Patrice?"

Colette shook her head. "Your secret is safe with us."

I was relieved not to have to tell more lies, especially since I'd pulled that one out of my ass, and Edmund probably knew everyone at the Apex office, so it wouldn't be hard for him to catch me. But I would've felt even better without these two around right now. I mustered as much of a smile as I had in me and lifted my chin to Colette. "I'm going to go shower."

A few minutes later, warm water sluiced over my shoulders, helping to ease the tension in my neck. I closed my eyes and let it work its magic, but it was impossible not to think of last night as my imagination wandered—Jagger desperate and needy, the erotic growl he'd let out when he came down my throat. The way he'd demanded control, and I'd eagerly ceded it to him. My breathing grew labored.

But then, the polar opposite behavior in the bedroom—something he said he never did. Jagger was warm and giving, soft and thoughtful, providing me a first time I would never, ever forget. Though it seemed *he* wanted to forget it already this morning.

That last thought shook me from my lust-filled haze, and I finished washing up. As I exited the shower, my cell rang. Miles was FaceTiming me. It was not even eight thirty here, so it was only five thirty on the West Coast.

I wrapped a towel around me and tucked it in at the corner before answering.

"Hey," I said. "Are you just getting home or up super early?"

Thumping bass in the background answered my question. Neither. He was still at the club.

"What a house!" he yelled.

I laughed. "Wow. That noise is coming from a house party? It sounds more like you're at a club."

"I was referring to the mansion on the bluff. Why haven't you called me yet to give me the details of you and bossman doing it? I'm desperate to know what kind of kinky shit he's into."

My jaw dropped open. "Back up. How did you know I was at a house on a bluff?"

"Find My Friends." He shrugged. "I stalk you every day, cookie. You were there last night *and* up until twenty minutes ago. I've been *dying* for you to get back to Edmund's place."

"But how did you know it was Jagger's house?"

"Oh. Find My Friends gives the address. I Google-imaged it to make sure you were safe, and then when I saw the house, I went down a rabbit hole and looked up the owner. Did you know it's the most expensive property ever sold in all of Montauk?"

I stared incredulously at my best friend. Meanwhile, he thought nothing strange of his behavior and kept on going.

"Spill the tea, girl. Did you dust off the cobwebs and open the bat cave? I left a Chappell Roan dance marathon to come outside and hear the deets."

I shook my head, wondering when the boundaries of our friendship had disappeared. Then again, I felt like I might burst if I didn't tell *someone* about last night. So I leaned close to the camera with a cat-that-swallowed-the-canary smile and lowered my voice. "It was *amazing*."

Miles screamed so loud, I wouldn't be surprised if he woke up the rest of the house I was in. I laughed. "Shhh... People are still sleeping here."

For the next fifteen minutes, I gave him some of the details from last night, concentrating more on the boldness of my actions, which I was proud of, than the details of our intimacy. Miles would often come home and give me the blow by blow of his hook-ups—sometimes literally—yet it felt wrong to do that with what happened between Jagger and me, at least the intimate and beautiful part in the bedroom.

While Miles and I chatted, I brushed out my wet hair and rubbed lotion into my legs. My hands stopped on my calf when I noticed something missing.

"Oh no. I lost my anklet."

"The gold one with the little star you always wear?"

I went into the bathroom to check the shower floor and the area rug where I'd dried off. "I know I had it on when we were on the boat yesterday. I remember seeing it when I put sunscreen on my legs."

"Maybe you lost it in the covers, getting dirty with Big Zaddy."

I sighed. "That's possible. I probably shouldn't be wearing it anymore anyway since Brendan gave it to me. But I really loved it. It's so simple and petite."

"Cookie, if I didn't wear jewelry from my exes, I wouldn't wear any at all. And don't even get me started on the clothes I borrow from my hook-ups and never give back. I go on a dating frenzy with men my size when my wardrobe needs replenishing."

I chuckled. "I gotta go. The train back to the City takes something like three-and-a-half hours, and I need to get groceries and do laundry when I get home. So I'm going to need an early start."

"Ugh. That sounds dreadful. I vote you go back to the mansion under the guise of looking for your anklet and bone the boss all day."

"I'm pretty sure last night was a one-time deal."

"You always underestimate yourself, cookie. You're addicting. Trust me, I know. I'm already counting the days until I come back to visit you. And I didn't even take your virginity. That man is not going to be able to stop himself from coming around for a lot more than seconds."

# TWENTY-TWO

## Sutton

The following week got harder with each day that passed. It wasn't like I'd expected flowers, but I'd stupidly gotten my hopes up that Jagger would make *some* contact. But it was already Wednesday, and I hadn't heard or seen hide nor hair of the boss. The fact that I knew he was somewhere in the building made it even worse. Because it would've been so easy for him to reach me.

My disappointment was palpable. There was a pet store a few doors down from the coffee shop I stopped at every morning to pick up a bagel, and this poor basset hound sat in the window staring outside, looking so sad. I'd realized today when I passed that I felt like he did.

I needed to pull myself out of this glum mood, but that was easier said than done when Jagger's name was frequently mentioned at work. Today it was because he'd been personally named in a lawsuit the DOJ had filed against Apex, alleging that their algorithm violated the rules against price-fixing stocks, though somehow without ever having direct communication with the companies themselves. It was way above my basic legal knowledge, but I'd listened intently as one of the executives explained the government's position during the morning briefing. A little while later, I was at my desk reading more about it when Jack stopped by.

"Hey." He lifted his chin to my screen. "I see my department isn't the only one trying to figure out how the hell the DOJ is making the connection between the algo and price fixing."

I smiled. "Yeah, it's definitely interesting."

He smiled and held up his mug. "I'm guessing this might not be my last trip of the day to fix myself the good stuff. Looks like we're going to be here all day and night. I already heard Langston is on the warpath and expects us to understand the nine-hundred-page document the DOJ put together by morning, even though we found out about it at the same time he did today."

Maybe this was the reason Jagger hadn't made contact this week. Maybe it had nothing to do with me. He was just tied up putting out a potential fire. I exhaled and nodded. "That should keep you all busy."

"I need to get back downstairs, but I've been meaning to stop by and talk to you. Have you ever heard of Big Snow?"

"I don't think so?"

"It's an indoor skiing and snowboarding place near the Meadowlands."

"Really? Indoor?"

He laughed. "I know, seems odd. But they have chairlifts and everything. A couple of my buddies and I went in May when they had a special snowboarding event, and we had a blast. I wanted to see if you'd be interested in going next weekend."

"That sounds like fun. Are your buddies who are going people from work?"

"Actually, my buddies went last time. I was asking if *you* wanted to go—just me and you next weekend."

"Oh."

I was grateful that my desk phone rang, interrupting our conversation. "Excuse me."

The digital preview told me the call was coming from inside the building, yet I still wasn't prepared for the voice that spoke.

"He has much more pressing things he should be working on."

*Jagger.* My eyes widened. He was watching me over the security feed again.

"Umm...hi."

I turned back around to face Jack, but my gaze stretched over his shoulder to the round globe in the ceiling. I hadn't realized how obvious I was until Jack turned and followed my line of sight. *Shoot.* Not wanting to explain, and definitely not wanting to answer the question he'd asked me while on the phone with Jagger, I pointed to the receiver and then covered the mouthpiece of the phone. "I need to take this."

He nodded and lifted a hand in a silent wave as he started to walk away, so I took my hand off the mouthpiece—just as he called over his shoulder, "Let me know about next weekend whenever you have time."

Jack was barely out of my earshot when Jagger's voice came through the line.

"What's next weekend?"

I looked up at the camera. "How long have you been watching me?"

"Today or in general? And you didn't answer my question."

"Well, both, I guess. And I'll answer your question after you answer mine."

The line went silent, but I knew Jagger was still there. "Since your first day, and you were later than usual this morning."

"I stopped into the pet store a few doors down to ask if I could pet one of their dogs that looked like he needed it."

"If you're interested in cheering up animals that look down in the dumps, maybe you should come up to the fifty-ninth floor today."

I smiled, still staring at the camera. "Don't tempt me, Mr. Langston."

"Fuck." He groaned. "Don't call me that while we're at the office."

My pulse picked up. "Where would you like me to call you that?"

"I'm guessing you know the answer." He paused. "Did you lose something last weekend?"

My brows dipped. "Lose some—oh wait, did you find my anklet?"

"Gold with a star?"

"Yes! I was wondering if I lost it at your place."

"If you wondered, why didn't you call and ask?"

I looked up at the security globe again. "If you found it, why didn't you call and tell me?"

Jagger's low rumble of a laugh shot through me like a rocket, the vibration doing all sorts of things between my legs.

"Touché," he said, and I heard the smile in his voice. "The anklet is broken, by the way. I hope it wasn't important to you."

"Not really. It was actually a gift from Brendan, but I liked it. I probably won't even get it fixed."

Again, Jagger was quiet a moment. "So what is next weekend?"

I'd gotten lost in our ping-pong match of a conversation, so it took me a few beats to catch back up. "Oh. Jack knows I like snowboarding, so he invited me to an indoor park. Apparently they have one in New Jersey."

More silence. "And? Are you going?"

I didn't even have to think about it. I wasn't going to go, not when it was a date and not with a group of people. But Jagger didn't need to know that. Turning back to my desk, so he couldn't see my face, I lied. "I haven't decided yet."

This time the phone line went dead quiet for a full thirty seconds. That might not sound like a long time, but on a call, it really is. During the stand-off, I tossed around telling Jagger I might not go if I got a better offer, but again, I thought better of it.

"Why did it take Jack stopping by my desk to get you to want to call me?"

"I've wanted to call you since five minutes after you left on Sunday morning. It's not a matter of want, Sutton."

"Then what is it a matter of?"

"Self-control. You're better off with someone who's capable of giving you what you need. I know that, so I'm doing my best to keep my distance. Yet for some reason that guy just irks me, and I snapped."

"What is it that you think I need, exactly?"

"A relationship with a nice guy who doesn't dream about fucking you while holding your throat in his hand so tightly you'll have to wear a scarf for a week."

I should've been scared, especially with my history, but the visual of him doing that turned me on so much, it made me a little dizzy.

Jagger's voice was gruff. "I have to go."

"But—"

"Go home on time tonight, Sutton."

• • •

Hours later, I'd just lifted my purse to my shoulder, getting ready to leave, when my desk phone rang again. My heart rate sped up, only to be disappointed when I saw it was the receptionist calling.

"Hi, Amara," I answered.

"Hey, Sutton. A messenger just delivered a package for you."

"Are you sure it's for me?"

"I'm looking at your name written across the top."

"Oh. Okay."

"I'd bring it to you, but I'm helping cover the overflow calls on the executive line. The phones haven't stopped ringing since that DOJ announcement this morning, so it's hard to leave my desk."

"No problem. I was just getting ready to leave anyway. I'll pick it up on my way out."

A small box wrapped in plain brown paper sat next to Amara at the reception desk. It made me laugh to myself as I approached because it looked like the same kind of discreet packaging my vibrators were delivered in. Though as soon as I saw the bold, slashy handwriting on the top, I realized it was something way better than a toy. *Jagger.*

"Secret admirer?" Amara smiled.

"No, uh, I forgot I ordered some supplies."

Luckily the phone rang and stopped her from asking any other questions, and I was able to scoop up the box and rush off to the elevator with it. I had no clue what could be inside, but too many people were in the car to rip it open and find out. I thought about ducking into a corner when I hit the lobby, but while I was looking around for a quiet spot, I noticed the security globe on the ceiling—the same kind as on my floor—and I wasn't sure I wanted to be watched while I opened whatever was inside. So I pushed through the turnstile and out onto the street, but it was five thirty on a weekday in New York City, and the sidewalks were bustling.

Since it didn't look like I was going to have a safe place to open the box until I got home, I attempted to ignore it and took the steps down to the subway. Though by the time I'd stared at Jagger's handwriting for six long stops, I was almost desperate enough to pop into one of the urine-scented bathrooms down here and open it. *Almost.* Instead, I called Miles as I made my way up the stairs to have him occupy me for the remaining two-block walk to my building.

He answered but told me to hang on while he spoke to someone else.

"Take ten, gorgeous. But don't go outside and smoke pot this time. Last time, your eyes were only half open. We're selling lipstick, not Cheech and Chong's new edibles." He came back on the line. "What's going on, cookie? You don't usually call during the day. I've been stalking your location like a fiend, and you haven't gone anywhere but home and to the office. So I know you didn't bang—" He halted midstream. "Wait. I'm a total idiot. You work together. Have you been banging the bossman at the office?"

I laughed. "Definitely not."

"Well, you owe me some good gossip now anyway because I just looked out the window, and my model either rolls her own cigarettes or just lit the joint I told her not to smoke." He sighed, and I heard the blinds rustling. "Aaaaand she's holding it in, so it's definitely not tobacco."

"Oh no. I'm sorry for interrupting."

"Eh, whatever. We'll just have to sell the brand manager on hooded eyes being sexy and pretend it was intentional. What's going on? Did you just call to chit chat?"

"I actually called to tell you about a box."

"A box? Or *your* box?"

I chuckled. "A box was delivered to the office for me as I was leaving. I'm ninety-nine-percent sure it's from Jagger."

"What's inside?"

"I don't know. I haven't opened it yet."

"Why the hell not?"

"Because I was on my way home, and then the streets were busy, and then the subway was even more packed, and what if it's something weird?"

"Weird like a dead bird, or weird like a nine-inch vibrator that plays Backstreet Boys music?"

"I'm not sure which one is weirder of those two choices, Miles."

"Trust me," he said. "It's the vibrator. To this day, I can't hear 'As Long as You Love Me' without asking *why* I went home with Wally Wallace. He had a framed poster of Brian Littrell in his bedroom. The name alone should've been a hint that he was an odd duck. What kind of person has the same first and last name?"

I should've called Miles before I even left the building. He had a way of taking my mind off of anything. I laughed. "Hopefully Jagger has better taste than Wally. What do you think he sent me?"

"I have no idea. How big is the box?"

"I don't know. Maybe eight inches by eight inches? It's wrapped in plain brown paper. Probably the same kind they used to send Wally Wallace his vibrator."

"I'm switching us to FaceTime so I can see it." A few seconds later, my phone rang to make the switch. I answered to find Miles wearing bright red glasses.

"Red, huh? Does that mean you're feeling sexy?"

"No, it means I sat on the black ones I wore today, and these were the only thing I could find in the car. They look terrible with my orange shirt. Now show me the box."

I held up the package.

"Interesting. Open it."

I laughed. "I'm a few buildings down from mine. Let me just get into my apartment."

"Now I know how you kept your virginity all these years. You love to torture yourself."

It wasn't too much longer before I was finally inside my apartment. I tossed my keys and purse on the kitchen counter, walked around the island to grab scissors, and propped up the phone so Miles could watch me open the package.

As I tore into it, I laughed. "It's going to be hysterical if I was wrong and it's not Jagger's handwriting on the top. Maybe we're both anxiously awaiting office supplies that someone ordered for me."

Inside the unmarked wrapping was a cardboard box containing two small, navy-velvet boxes. I lifted out the first and opened it. "Oh my God."

"What is it? What is it? I can't see."

I turned the box to show Miles. "It's my anklet. Jagger told me he found it at his house, but it was broken. He must've had it fixed."

Miles rolled his eyes. "Boring. What's in the other box?"

I reached in and took the other one out. My eyes widened upon finding another anklet—a diamond one.

"Nice bling," Miles said. "Bring that closer to the camera so I can see it better."

I held the anklet up to the phone. "Those are nice-sized stones," he said. "My guess is five carats. I guess that's a gift?"

"I don't know." I tilted the bigger box and took another look inside. On the bottom was a white piece of paper I'd missed before. "Wait. I think there's a note." I unfolded it and read aloud. "Thank you for a great time Saturday night. X Jagger Langston."

I frowned. "Seriously? A fucking kiss-off gift delivered by messenger?"

"I'm sure he didn't mean it that way. He's probably just sending you a gift because he likes you and wants to see you again."

I shook my head. "Today was the first time I'd spoken to him in three days, and he pretty much told me we weren't right for each other and hung up on me without saying goodbye. This is absolutely a parting gift—no different than the cash a businessman in a motel room leaves by the door for the sex worker. He's just got more money."

Miles shrugged. "If he wants to use me and send me diamonds, I'm available."

"Oh good. I'll let him know that—when I toss his stupid gift back at his face tomorrow."

## —— CHAPTER ——
## TWENTY-THREE

### Sutton

The anger didn't dissipate overnight. Just the opposite, it built and built, and now I felt ready to explode. Perfect timing, since I'd gotten to the office at six fifteen—knowing Jagger liked to start his day right after the gym—before anyone else got in.

I rode the elevator directly up to the executive floor and swiped inside. The receptionist wasn't in yet, so I walked around the desk and kept on going. The blood in my veins pumped faster with every step. I had no idea if other people who worked up here got in this early, though I definitely didn't want to make a scene and have my stepfather walk in. So I turned right to pass Edmund's office so I could double-check that he wasn't here yet. I'd already planned what I was going to say if he was, but thankfully his office was dark—as all of them seemed to be, except for the lone one shining a streak of light across the hallway floor. *He's here.*

My swift strides suddenly slowed. Part of me considered chickening out—stopping and turning around, hauling my butt back out the door, and taking the stairs so no one would even know I'd been on the executive floor. And I might've done just that if Jagger hadn't walked into the hall. He looked up, and his lips curved to a smile. Though it wilted when I brushed past him and walked into his office.

"Sutton, what's the matter?"

He followed me back inside, and I motioned to the entrance. "Shut the door."

He studied my face before pulling it closed. "Why are you upset?"

I took the diamond anklet from my pocket and held it out to him. "I'm not a whore."

He blinked a few times. "What are you talking about?"

I waved the box around. "That night meant something to me, even if it didn't to you. You could've just ignored me like you did for days after and left it at that. But instead you had to treat me like one of your fuck buddies."

"That's not what I was doing."

"Really?" I tilted my head. "You told me you buy a fuck-off gift for your playthings. Can you honestly stand there and tell me you've never bought one of them an anklet like this?"

Jagger's face fell.

I rolled my eyes. "Exactly." I tossed the box to him and started marching back toward the door. Jagger caught up to me just as I reached for the handle. He wrapped his arm around my waist and squeezed.

"Stop."

My anger suddenly morphed into hurt, and I didn't want to give him the satisfaction of seeing me upset. I tried to wriggle from his grip. "I need to go."

"Hear me out first."

I didn't agree, but I did stop trying to escape. Once I stilled, Jagger spoke in a low, even voice. "I'm sorry. I was wrong."

I swallowed back tears.

He continued. "You're right. I have sent that gift to women who didn't mean anything to me. But I honestly wasn't trying to do that with you. You said the anklet that broke was from your ex. As much as I would have preferred to throw it in the trash, I got it fixed because it sounded like it meant something to you. At the same time, I hated the idea of you wearing it again, so I wanted to give you an alternative. I should've picked out something more personal. It was stupid, and if the roles were reversed and you'd given me something you bought for other men, I would be just as upset." He paused. "Will you turn around and look at me now so I can apologize to your face?"

I wasn't ready to look at him, but I didn't fight him when he guided me to turn.

Jagger bent his knees slightly, so we were lined up eye to eye. "I'm sorry. Can you forgive me?"

I nodded.

"Thank you." He brushed the hair back from my face and smiled. "Just in case a small part of you is still uneasy and thinks I'm full of shit about you being different than other women I've spent time with, I'm going to show you something."

I let him take my hand and walk us back behind his desk. He pressed a key on his keyboard, and the monitor woke up from its screensaver. Jagger pointed to the top right corner, where the security feed from my floor was playing. "It's been there since last Monday." He shook his head. "I'm reading nine-hundred pages of bullshit from the DOJ that could mean the end of my company and meeting with lawyers all day long, and yet I can't stop watching this fucking thing."

I probably should've been freaked out that he'd just told me he'd been watching me, yet it made me feel just the opposite. It settled my nerves.

I stared at the screen for a minute, even though nothing was happening in the security feed since no one was in yet. Then I turned to face Jagger again. "Will you have dinner with me this weekend?"

His eyes reflected his hesitation. "We wouldn't be good together, Sutton."

"I thought we were pretty good together Saturday night."

He smiled sadly. "I'm a workaholic who's controlling and likes things a certain way."

"How do you know I don't like them the same way? *I* don't even know what I like yet, Jagger."

His Adam's apple bobbed, and he stared into my eyes for the longest time. Eventually his hand went to my hip, and he mumbled a string of curses as he yanked me flush against him. I felt his cock, hard and thick against my abdomen.

"Fuck it. Maybe this thing will finally go down on Saturday then."

I nibbled my lip. "I could...make it go down now."

He groaned. "We don't have time for that. I told everyone to be here by seven this morning to go over the DOJ filing. I expect Edmund will be walking in any moment." He reached behind me, grabbed my ponytail, and gave it a yank so firm that my head snapped back. "Seven PM Saturday. I'll pick you up. Now kiss me and get out of my office."

Jagger moved in fast, pressing his lips against mine. Within seconds, all the tension that had been swirling inside me was gone, and I melted into his tight hold. He groaned again. "Open your legs. I need to make you come quickly, or I'll never be able to think straight today."

I didn't even have to think about it. I widened my stance, and Jagger's hand dipped down and under my skirt. He sucked my tongue as his fingers pushed away my panties and stroked along my center.

"*Fuck.*" His voice was a sexy, low rumble. "You're wet for me already."

One finger pushed inside, and he started to massage along my walls. He added a second finger, and it didn't take long before I was a panting mess. I was on the edge of finding ecstasy, standing in the middle of his glass-walled office.

But then Jagger abruptly pulled away.

I reached for him, thinking he was playing some kind of a game—until I realized why he'd backed off. Someone was coming down the hall.

And it turned out to be my stepfather.

• • •

"Sutton." Edmund's eyes slid over my face before moving to Jagger. Luckily I'd put some space between us before he walked in, so at least we weren't caught standing inappropriately close. "Is everything okay?"

My stepfather misread my heated cheeks for something other than what they were. "Oh, yeah." I fanned my face. "I'm fine. I just came straight from the gym. It takes a long time for me to cool down after."

"Oh." He nodded, seeming to at least mostly accept my explanation. "What are you doing here so early?"

I'd made up one good excuse, but my brain was still misfiring from what had been going on thirty seconds ago, and I couldn't come up with a second one. Luckily, Jagger helped me out.

"I had my assistant call her last night," he said. "As Sutton's mentor, I thought it would be good for her to sit in on this morning's meetings. She was the first one to arrive."

That did it. My stepfather's face went from ninety-percent satisfied to one hundred. He looked at me and smiled. "Eagerness is a great asset in the workplace."

"Indeed it is." Jagger's eyes slanted to meet mine with a glimmer. He was lucky my cheeks were already red. Though Edmund thankfully seemed oblivious.

"I'm just going to get some coffee," he said. "Where are we meeting?"

"Board room," Jagger responded.

Edmund looked at me. "Did you get your morning cappuccino yet?"

I shook my head.

"Join me." He gestured toward the hall. "I'll fill you in on your mother's latest plans to set you up, this time with Patrice's nephew, so you can thwart them before she accepts a goat for your hand in marriage. That was all the two of them could talk about when she was over yesterday."

"Great." I rolled my eyes before exchanging glances with the boss. It was just my mother being my mother, but the glimmer of fun in Jagger's eyes was gone now, replaced with something I thought looked a lot like jealousy. It made me smile.

"I guess I'll see you at seven," I told him.

• • •

The seven-AM meeting went on for more than six hours. A team of in-house lawyers, outside attorney consultants, and every member of the executive team sat together, going through all of the details of the antitrust violations Apex and Jagger himself had been accused of. I got lost in some of the minutia of the law, but I definitely followed the government's theory when it came to the algorithm. Basically, they claimed that Apex and other large financial investment firms were colluding without having any direct communication just because there were some commonalities between their algorithms. This caused the companies to provide similar guidance to investors about the prices at which they should buy and sell stocks, thereby creating what looked like a conspiracy to fix prices. The problem was, in order to defend such a claim, Apex would need to prove that their algorithm differed from their competitors' algorithms, and doing that meant spelling out the secret sauce of Apex's internal system, which obviously Jagger did not want to do.

By the time the meeting started to break up, the boss looked like he'd been through a twelve-round fight, and he wasn't anxious about hearing the referee's decision. I hated the stress he was under, but it didn't stop me from admiring how he'd handled himself when his feet were held to the flame. Jagger Langston commanded a room full of men twice his age with twice as much experience, skillfully navigating between listening to their thoughts and opinions, weighing them, and managing to draw his own conclusions.

I'd been excited to spend the day near him for personal reasons, but in the end, I'd learned a valuable lesson in business. A commanding presence wasn't about having the loudest roar so your team followed in a straight line behind you. It was about earning influence and respect so they followed you willingly.

There had to be forty people in the room. I stalled as many of them cleared out with marching orders, hoping to get a few minutes with Jagger alone. Though when I realized there was a long line of more-important people ahead of me, I figured I should let him work and quietly made my way to the door.

Jagger's booming voice stopped me before I walked out. "Sutton?"

I turned, and he glanced over at one of the attorneys who had been brought in on retainer. "Excuse me a moment." Jagger looked back to me. "About the suggestion you made this morning to correct the issue we were discussing..."

It took me a few seconds to extrapolate that my *suggestion* had been dinner Saturday night and the *issue* we were discussing was my wanting to sleep with him again. At least that's what I assumed he meant. "Yes? Have you decided how you're going to handle things?"

There were still a dozen people in the room left, yet when he locked eyes with me, I felt that spark between us light again.

"Aggressively," he said. "I'll be in touch soon with plans."

—— CHAPTER ——
# TWENTY-FOUR

### Sutton

I didn't hear from or see Jagger again for the rest of the week. I was disappointed, but I understood. The office had been abuzz about the lawsuit, so I knew he'd flown down to DC to meet with the lawyers at the DOJ. The man had a lot going on. It wasn't realistic to think he'd have time for me in the near future.

I was at the gym Saturday morning when my phone ringing interrupted me watching him walk out of a government building last night on today's news. I didn't recognize the number but picked up anyway since it was a New York City area code.

"Hello?"

"Are you out of breath?" Jagger's deep voice sent a shiver up my spine.

"I'm on the Peloton at the gym." I kept pedaling even as I spoke.

"You might want to save some of your energy for later. You're going to need it."

I started to sweat, and it had nothing to do with my exercise. "Is that so?"

"It is indeed."

"I wasn't sure we were still on for tonight. I just watched you on the news. You're a very busy man. I thought you might be too tired."

"For anything else, I would be. But not for you."

Warmth filled my chest. "That's sweet of you to say."

"Don't confuse sweet with my need to fuck you senseless, Sutton, or this isn't going to work." He paused. "I'm still in DC. I'm meeting with my attorneys again in a little while before I head back. I just called to say I'll pick you up at seven."

I was so excited to see him tonight that I managed not to let his callous warning ruin my mood. "Okay."

"Mr. Langston?" I could hear a woman's voice in the background. "Mr. Finley is ready to see you."

His response was muffled, like he'd covered the phone. "Tell him I'll be there in a minute." He came back on the line. "I have to go. But stop by the doorman on your way into your building. He has a package for you."

"A package?"

"Wear it tonight. And no underwear. I'm not going to make it through dinner without touching you." He paused. "Until later, Ms. Holland..."

The line went dead, and I stopped pedaling, yet my pulse raced faster than ever. It didn't matter that I'd programmed forty minutes into the bike and only twenty-two had gone by. I was out the door as soon as I could grab my gym bag.

The doorman smiled as I approached my building. He opened the door and gestured for me to walk through. "Good morning, Ms. Holland. I have a package for you."

Nestor went behind the desk and opened a locked drawer, pulling out a small black bag with a silver logo I didn't recognize.

"Do you know who delivered it?" I asked.

"I can check the log. Everyone who comes in and out of the building is supposed to sign in, even Uber Eats guys."

He found the clipboard that contained the sign-in sheet and scanned down, tapping when he came to a name. "Sam Grover."

*Sam Grover*? It took a few beats, but then it hit me. Sam was Jagger's driver's name.

"Any chance you noticed if he was driving a silver Maybach?"

He nodded. "The Zeppelin model. It's a beautiful machine. Pretty sure that car has been here before."

"Thank you."

I managed to make it into the elevator car before digging into the bag, but there was no way in hell I could hold out until I walked into my apartment. Inside was a small box. I opened and found a beautiful anklet. Unlike the first one Jagger had sent me, this one wasn't full of sparkling diamonds. It was small and delicate, with tiny pearls strung every half inch of the thin, shimmery gold chain. I loved it.

Underneath the box was a small envelope. I ripped it open and read the card, which I was surprised to find in Jagger's own handwriting since he was out of town.

*The beauty of a pearl is inherent in the way it grows. When a grain of sand or some other irritant infiltrates the oyster's shell, it fights back and secretes a substance to protect itself. Over time, layers build up and form a pearl, making something beautiful out of adversity.*

*You're a pearl, Sutton.*

*X Jagger*

My hand covered my heart. The man could tell me he wasn't sweet all he wanted. But actions spoke louder than words.

. . .

"Hang on. I need a picture of that one." Miles flicked his wrist, gesturing for me to step back while we were on FaceTime Saturday evening. "Perfect. Got it."

"I guess you like this dress?"

"No, Mrs. Gutterman's cat keeps waiting in the hall and scaring the shit out of me when I walk in. I need something to scare him back. That frock is hideous. Remove it immediately."

I narrowed my eyes and leaned to the camera. "A simple yes or no would have been sufficient, drama queen."

He covered his eyes and waved his hand at the camera. "Seriously. Take it off. I'm feeling queasy looking at that pattern."

I gave him the finger, but peeled the dress off. "I should've asked how fancy the place we're going is. I have this royal blue silk two-piece set with a long skirt and halter top. It's really pretty but dressy."

"What time is he picking you up?"

"Seven."

"It's only six thirty. Ask him now."

"Okay, yeah. I'll do that." I swiped to my contacts and shot off a quick text while still on FaceTime with Miles.

**Sutton: Hi. What's the name of the place we're going? I'm trying to figure out what to wear.**

The little dots started jumping around.

**Jagger: Le Jardin. And I can help you with that. Open the door.**

I felt my forehead wrinkle.

**Sutton: What door?**

**Jagger: The one I'm standing in front of. Yours.**

My eyes widened, and I swiped back to FaceTime. "I just asked him, and he said he'd help me pick something out because he's at my door! But it's only six thirty!"

"Was he joking?"

"I have no idea." I grabbed my black silk robe and slipped it on, tying it at the waist as I rushed to the front door. Pushing up on my toes, I peeked through the peephole and gasped, then ducked down. Why did I duck? I have no damn idea. I whispered to Miles while still crouched. "Oh my God. He is here!"

"How did he get past the doorman?"

"I left his name with Nestor because the buzzer is hard to hear sometimes."

"At least your hair and makeup are done."

"I know but..." I rushed over to the mirror in the entryway and smoothed the mess my hair had become from trying so many outfits on. Then took a few deep breaths before opening the door.

"You're early?"

He looked me up and down. My skimpy robe barely covered the tops of my thighs. "I think my timing is impeccable."

"You said seven, didn't you?"

"I did, but our reservation is at seven thirty, and it will take us at least twenty minutes to get there. We haven't discussed your limitations yet, so I figured it was best to make you come in the privacy of your home rather than in a public restaurant." He tilted his head with a mischievous smile. "Invite me in now, Sutton."

I blinked a few times and stepped aside. "Uh, right. Come in?"

Jagger kissed my forehead as he entered. He looked around the living room while I tried to figure out how to close the front door. *Limitations? Make me come?* This man did stupid things to my brain. My hand was still on the doorknob when he turned back to face me.

"Are we alone?"

I nodded.

"Excellent." His eyes sparkled. "Take off that robe."

"Wow. This is fucking hot!" a man's voice said.

*Oh my God! Miles!* The phone was still in my hand, and he was still on FaceTime.

"But I'm hanging up now, cookie," he said. "I'd say have an exciting evening, but I'm pretty sure your date has that covered already. Toodle-oo."

Jagger's eyes narrowed on the phone in my hand before meeting mine. He didn't say a word, yet I heard his questions loud and clear.

"It was Miles. He was helping me pick out an outfit."

He nodded, then lifted his chin toward the phone still in my hand. "Is the call ended? Gay or not, I don't like the thought of him seeing you naked."

I glanced at my phone. "He's gone."

Jagger slipped his hands into his pockets. "Good. *Now* take off the robe." His words were so calm. He seemed so *in control* of the situation. He stood waiting while I wrapped my head around the moment. What did I feel about him telling me what to do? Considering my nipples could probably cut diamonds, and between my legs felt like an eye twitch was going on where there was no eye, I'd say it worked for me. Yet I still felt like I was *supposed* to push back and not take orders.

"It'll get easier once I earn your trust," Jagger said. "Look at me, Sutton."

My eyes moved to his.

"I will never make you do anything you don't want to. That's not what I'm into. Try not to get too in your head, and focus on listening to what your body wants."

That was easier said than done, but I managed to stop judging myself long enough to redirect that energy to feeling the changes in my body. It *liked it* when he told me what to do, and I didn't try to figure out why or if that was right or wrong. Instead, I went with it and took a deep breath, untying my robe. One of the outfits I'd tried on for Miles was strapless, and I hadn't put a bra back on yet. So when I slipped the black silk from my shoulders, it was just me and a black, lacy thong.

Jagger took his time tracing every inch of me. I watched as the rise and fall of his chest grew faster, and his tongue ran along his bottom lip. "Thank you."

He closed the distance between us and ran his thumb softly over one shoulder. "I have not been able to stop thinking about you all week—the way you looked standing in my office with my fingers inside you, the sounds you made... Someday soon, you're going to sit on my desk while I feast on you." He dropped a kiss on my shoulder, then moved his mouth to the shell of my ear. "My fantasies are so fucking torn between wanting the world to watch me own your body and the desire to punch any man who looks in your direction."

Jagger stepped back and shook his head. "You didn't listen to me about the perfume I told you to stop wearing. You have it on now, and you had it on in the office the other day." He locked eyes with me. "Did you forget?"

I probably could've recited every word this man had ever said to me. Still, I could've lied and said yes. But a part of me was curious to find out what would happen if I didn't follow his orders. So I shook my head.

Jagger's eyes lit with fire. He reached down between us and slipped his fingers into the side of my panties. Stroking through my wetness, he made a *tsk*ing sound. "You know what happens to bad girls who don't listen?"

Oh God. I hope they *come*, because one of his fingers had dipped inside me, and I felt desperate for more already. "What?" I breathed.

A wicked smile curved along his face, and I immediately regretted not lying. "They don't get to orgasm." He pumped once, twice, and on the third time he pulled away. Jagger lifted his hand to his mouth and sucked the fingers that had been inside me. His eyes closed, and he groaned like he was in pain. "Damn it, Sutton. I've been salivating to lick your cunt for days."

Oh God. No. *No. No. No.* He could *not* leave me like this. "I'll stop wearing it," I said. "I promise."

His response was to rest his hands on my shoulders and push me down. "You might not believe me, but this is not my first choice of things to do with you at the moment." Once I was on my knees in front of him, he brushed a lock of my hair behind my ear. "Suck me, Sutton."

Even through his trousers, it was evident that he was already rock hard. Fifteen seconds ago, I'd been desperate to come, but gazing up and seeing the way he looked down at me, that desperation changed. I shifted from ready to be pleased to wanting to do everything in my power to please him. Between my legs still throbbed to be touched, but it became secondary to satisfying this man.

I reached for the button on his slacks, pulled down the fly, and slipped my hand inside in a frenzy.

Jagger groaned as I wrapped my fingers around him and squeezed hard, then he bunched the back of my hair into a tight fist. "It doesn't look like you're feeling very punished at the moment."

Fearing he might decide I didn't deserve even this, I forwent the teasing in favor of lunging forward and taking him deep.

Jagger let out a string of curses. "Fuck. You love it, don't you? Look up at me while you suck my cock." His hand at the back of my head pulled hard, causing a burn at my scalp, and he slipped out almost to the tip before pushing me back down. "Just like that, baby. Take me deeper."

With every bite of pain, I grew needier and needier. The ache between my legs intensified, and I reached down to touch myself.

"No coming means no coming." Jagger spoke with a stern voice. "Now lock your hands behind your back and keep sucking."

I whimpered but did as he'd instructed and clasped my hands together above my ass. Jagger's gaze took in my new position and his eyes shut. "God, you look so damn perfect. I could come just from seeing you like that."

The strain in his face told me he was telling the truth. I'd been bobbing my head, meeting his thrusts, but now he abruptly stopped me from moving and took over. *One. Two.* On the third stroke, he buried himself deep and let out a guttural roar. It matched the intensity of the gush that rushed down my throat, nearly choking me.

We were both breathless after he pulled out. Jagger bent over with his hands on his knees like he'd just run a marathon while I unclasped my hands and leaned forward with my palms to the floor.

"Jesus Christ," Jagger mumbled. "I can't make you wait to get off after that."

I smiled. "It's okay. That got me off almost as much as you getting me off."

He shook his head with a laugh and scooped me into his arms, cradling me against him. "We're going to have to find a new punishment for disobeying."

### Sutton

Jagger Langston was a hand holder. Who would've guessed?

I looked down at our joined hands resting on top of his thigh in the back of his Maybach as we made our way to the restaurant in bumper-to-bumper traffic. My legs were crossed at the knee, and my eyes caught on the ankle bracelet he'd bought me.

"Thank you again for the anklet," I said. "It's beautiful, and I love the sentiment behind it."

He squeezed my hand. "You're welcome. It should've been the first gift I gave you."

"You made up for it with your note." I smiled. "By the way, when did you get it? You were still in DC when it arrived, but the card looked like your handwriting."

"I bought it the morning after you tossed my first gift at me, at a shop in DC." He glanced over. "To be clear, I've never purchased anything for anyone at that shop, and I've never given a piece of jewelry to a woman other than items similar to what I sent you the first time. And those were not the carat weight of what I sent you."

"How did you get this one to me?"

"I had Sam drive it back home to deliver it. He'd driven me down to DC."

"But you stayed?"

Jagger nodded. "I took a flight home when I was done so he didn't have to come back."

"It was very sweet of you to do all that."

He frowned. "What did I tell you about thinking I'm sweet?"

In the last hour he'd kissed my forehead, helped me pick out what to wear to dinner, and told me I was beautiful five times. People aren't who they *tell* you they are; they're who they *show* you to be. Though I kept my mouth shut.

A few minutes later, Jagger's phone buzzed. He dug it out of his pocket and looked at the screen. "Crap, it's an Ohio area code. I need to answer this. Excuse me."

"It's fine. Go ahead."

I looked out the window, but it was impossible to give him privacy while sitting in the back of a car. Even hearing only one side of the conversation, it was evident right away that something was wrong.

"Hello?"

Quiet.

He let go of my hand and adjusted to hold the cell in his newly free one. "Where are the girls?"

*Uh-oh.* More quiet.

"Have they ever met the family before?"

I could hear a woman speaking, but it wasn't clear enough to make out what she was saying. Though Jagger closing his eyes hinted that the news was getting worse.

"I could be there in..." He lifted his wrist to check the time on his watch. "Probably will take me at least four hours."

Silence again.

Jagger eventually nodded. "All right, if you're sure the family is safe and the girls won't be up all night crying. Because if that's the case, I'd rather come tonight, even if it's midnight when I arrive."

He listened before nodding more. "That would be great. If you could do that now, I'd appreciate it. If they're comfortable where they are, I'll come first thing in the morning."

Another pause, then, "Thank you. I'll wait to hear back."

Jagger swiped to end the call and blew out a ragged breath.

"That didn't sound good," I said.

He shook his head. "It's not. My sister went in on a fifty-one-fifty hold. It's a seventy-two-hour involuntary psychiatric hospitalization that gives the doctors time to evaluate someone and decide if they're a danger to themselves or others." Jagger leaned forward and spoke to his driver. "Sam, can you please pull over for a few minutes? We might be heading to the airport, which is in the opposite direction. I'll let you know momentarily."

"Of course, sir."

The driver pulled the car from the flow of traffic and slowed at the curb in front of a Trader Joe's. "I can't park here, but we'll keep it running and move if anyone gives us a hard time."

Jagger leaned back into the seat. "I'm sorry. They took Amelia and Olivia to a foster family. I've worked with this case worker before, and she's been pretty straight with me. She thinks it's better for me to pick the girls up in the morning, if they aren't stressing where they are since I wouldn't get there until the middle of the night. She said the family has a little girl the same age as Amelia and kids generally love it there, but she's going to call the parents now, see how my nieces are doing, and send me a text."

Without thinking, I reached over and took Jagger's hand again, lacing my fingers with his. He stared down but made no attempt to pull away.

"How often does this happen?" I asked softly.

He shook his head. "Too damn often. I tried to get custody of the girls a few years back when things got bad, but the judge refused. When he gave his decision, he warned my sister that she was one more appearance away from him siding with me. That's when Catherine up and moved back to Ohio. I think her piece-of-shit lawyer told her it would make it more difficult for me to get her in front of the same judge if she left the state."

Jagger's phone buzzed. He lifted it, scanned a text, and then let out a breath. "Olivia is sleeping already, and Amelia is painting with the daughter. The social worker wants me to leave them until morning since they've already had enough disruption for the day."

I nodded. "It's probably best they get a good night's sleep."

Jagger leaned forward and spoke to Sam. "You can continue to the restaurant now."

"You got it, boss."

Jagger swiped his phone again. "I just need to make arrangements for the morning."

"We don't have to go to dinner. You need your rest too, and it sounds like you're going to have an early start tomorrow."

He looked at me. "What I need is to take you out to dinner, then pin you to my bed and bury myself inside of you so the world stops spinning."

That simple sentence told me *so much* about what made Jagger the man he was today, with his need for control and lack of long-term relationships. But it wasn't the time to psychoanalyze him, so I smiled. "Okay. I like your plan better."

I wanted to do whatever I could to help Jagger get through this difficult time. Being the CEO of a major company had to be stressful enough, but to have the DOJ filing an antitrust suit against Apex, and now to be responsible for two young girls seemed like enough to break a person.

I wasn't surprised that Jagger was quiet for the rest of the ride and through appetizers at the beautiful French restaurant. Eventually we made small talk, but the mood was heavy. I debated sharing what was on my mind between sips of a four-hundred-dollar bottle of wine and looking at the two small lines that had formed between his brows during the car ride and never left.

"I want to help," I finally said.

The lines in his forehead deepened. "With?"

"I babysat for years. I'm good with kids, and I know CPR and the Heimlich maneuver."

Jagger smiled. "Thank you. But I can't ask you to do that."

"You didn't. I volunteered. I'm sure you have a million extra things to do with the DOJ filing. Were you planning on going back down to DC anytime soon?"

He nodded. "Tuesday. But I'll figure something out."

"You saw my closet. I'm an expert at playing dress-up. Plus, if I babysit at your place, I can finally find out what's in your nightstand drawer. My curiosity has been killing me."

Jagger's lip twitched. "Trust me. You're going to find out tonight when we get to my place."

I squirmed in my seat. "I'm being serious, though. I want to help."

"Why?"

"Because I care about you."

The change in Jagger's posture made me immediately regret what I'd said. He stiffened. I could see he was about to say something, probably remind me it wasn't a good idea to get attached, so I put my hand up. "I'm not proposing, Jagger. I care about my friends, too."

"Is that what we are? Friends?"

I had feelings for this man, deeper than I wanted to admit to myself. But wasn't the basis of any good relationship a strong friendship, whether it be dating or a marriage or whatever? So it wasn't a lie to say I also thought we were friends. I leaned forward in my chair and lowered my voice. "How about friends who fuck?"

Jagger's eyes darkened. "I like hearing you talk like that."

"Like what? Using naughty words? Do you like it when I tell you I really loved your cock in my mouth earlier?"

He reached across the table and took my hand, lifting it to his lips. I'd thought he was going to kiss the top but instead he nipped at my fingers. I yelped, which earned me a devilish smile.

"You're playing with fire, sweetheart," he warned. "I'm already hard under the table, and we haven't even been served our main course yet. Hours of you teasing me won't bode well for your ability to walk tomorrow morning."

I bit down on my bottom lip. "I don't mind."

"No? Then I think it's time we discussed what you do and don't mind. I need to know your limitations, Sutton."

My cheeks heated. "I'm not sure I know them myself."

"But you're interested in exploring what they are?"

I nodded.

"Tell me how you felt when I took over earlier, when you were sucking me."

"I liked it. A lot."

"It didn't make you feel like you were being taken advantage of?"

I shook my head. "No, because I wanted it, too."

"Do you trust that if you tell me to stop whatever I'm doing, I will?"

I didn't even have to think about the answer. "Yes."

He smiled. "Good. Have you considered that it might be triggering to not be able to move while I fuck you?"

My face wasn't the only thing on fire now. My body ached for him. "Right about now, I'd probably let you tie me to this chair and do whatever you want in front of all these people. I feel that desperate for you, Jagger. But I also don't think people are always aware of what might trigger them."

He nodded. "We should have a safe word."

"Okay."

The waiter walked over to refill our wine glasses and asked if we were ready to be served dinner. Jagger nodded, and then sipped his wine and studied me over the brim until the waiter was gone.

"What word would you like to use?" he asked.

"Can't we just use *stop*?"

"It's safer to use a word that's clear and won't cause an emotional response. I would imagine you used that word during a time you would rather not be reminded of."

"Oh, yeah, that makes sense."

"Does any word come to mind that you'd like to use?"

I met his eyes. "How about *pearl*?"

"That's perfect." He smiled, and his eyes dropped to my lips. "So you're open to having your body controlled. What about spanking?"

"I thought you said you weren't into inflicting pain."

"I never have been before, but the thought of my handprint on your ass..." He shook his head. "I want to leave marks."

"The thought of being able to do something with you that you've never done with anyone else makes me want to pull up my skirt and bend over your knee right now."

Jagger's eyes bordered on predatory. "You're lucky I feel territorial about anyone seeing you, or you'd be out of the chair already. How about toys?"

"What kind of toys?"

"Whatever kind I want."

I laughed and lifted my wine to my lips in an attempt to cool down. "That's a pretty big blank check you're asking me to sign, Mr. Langston."

He groaned. "I think I might need to forbid you from calling me that anywhere in public. It drives me crazier than your perfume."

I felt empowered that I could turn on a man who could have virtually anyone he wanted, just by using two words or spraying on a scent. "I'll tell you what, I'll sign that check if you promise to go slow with what you bring into the mix."

"Deal." He tilted his head. "Anal?"

I blinked a few times. "Not beating around the bush anymore, are you?"

Jagger smiled. "I want you to give me every part of your body, sweetheart. But it has to be given. I won't *take* anything from you, even though at times it may feel like I am. You will always have the power with me."

"Okay." I took a deep breath and nodded. "I've never done that before, but I'm open to trying with you. Again, though, I'll ask that you go slow."

The waiter appeared out of nowhere—or at least it seemed that way—with our dinners. He set them on the table and asked if we wanted fresh pepper, but Jagger's eyes never left my face, not even as he waved him away.

"You have no fucking idea how hard I am right now."

I felt a little lightheaded. "And you have no idea how wet I am."

He groaned and pointed to my food. "Eat. Fast."

I laughed but picked up my fork in a hurry. Jagger wasn't the only one feeling desperate at the moment.

## — CHAPTER —
# TWENTY-SIX

### Sutton

I felt buzzed, and it had nothing to do with the glass of wine I'd had at dinner.

Jagger led me to his bedroom by the hand. Once we were inside, he took a seat on the edge of the mattress and pulled me to stand between his open legs. "Undress for me."

My heart thumped. I didn't understand exactly why, but his authoritative tone sent a rush of goosebumps over my arms. I reached for my heels first, but he stopped me with a crooked grin. "Those stay on."

I nodded and swallowed, nerves really beginning to set in. The material of my silk two-piece outfit felt heavier than it was as I reached behind me and unzipped the skirt. But when I let it slip to the floor and looked up and saw Jagger's eyes filled with blazing heat, my confidence got a boost. He wanted me as much as I wanted him, and it didn't matter that I wasn't experienced in the art of a sultry striptease. Seeing his desire made me stand taller, be a little more daring and flirty as I peeled pieces of my clothing off one by one.

Once I was fully naked, Jagger leaned over and pressed a kiss to my stomach. His lips vibrated against my skin. "Such a good girl. I can't wait to reward you."

He slid open the nightstand and pulled out a set of leather handcuffs. Holding them up to me, he spoke softly, "I left the tag on so you can see they're brand new. I bought them for us."

I smiled. "Thank you."

Jagger set them aside and stood. He wrapped one of his big hands around my throat and used it to pull me in for a kiss. It was hard to believe I'd never been able to orgasm with a man before when I was on edge already from just a simple touch. His thumb stroked over my pulse line, and when he squeezed, relief washed over me. I *wanted* him to take control. I trusted him to.

Jagger broke the kiss by tugging the flesh of my lower lip between his teeth as he pulled away. "You test every last ounce of my self-control, sweetheart."

"I gave up on trying to control anything when I'm around you."

He brushed his knuckles along my cheek. "Good. I don't want you to hold back anything when you're with me." Jagger scooped me into his arms, setting me down gently in the middle of the bed before climbing on and straddling my hips, the handcuffs in his hands.

"They're padded inside, but you don't want to pull against them too hard, or you'll bruise and get chafed."

"Okay."

He lifted my arm, kissed the inside of my wrist, and slipped on the first cuff. The clicking sound of it tightening sent a lightning bolt through my body. He attached the other end to the headboard and moved to the next cuff. When he was done, my arms were spread in a wide V over my head.

"Pull," Jagger said. "Feel the restraints."

I did, and it surprised me how much I liked it—liked the restriction of movement and the pinch of pain from the cuff digging into me.

Jagger watched me and smiled. "We'll leave your legs free. *This time.*"

He climbed off the bed, and I assumed he was going to undress, but instead he headed for the door.

"Wait," I called. "Where are you going?"

"Shut your eyes and think about all the things I can do to you, and you won't be able to stop me."

*Oh God.* With my history, that statement should've scared the crap out of me, but again, I liked it. *A lot.* My breaths quickened, and I imagined giving up control, letting Jagger do whatever he wanted to my body—his cock sliding into my mouth, his mouth on me... I pulled against the tight cuffs, imagining how I would try to touch him as he thrust deep into me, but wouldn't be able to.

I was still lost in my vivid imagination when footsteps came back into the room. My eyes opened to find Jagger setting what looked like an ice bucket on the nightstand. He walked to the bottom of the bed and unbuttoned the cuffs of his dress shirt as he spoke.

"You can watch me undress. But when I'm done, you're going to close your eyes and not open them until I tell you that you can. Understood?"

I nodded.

"What happens if you open them before I say it's time, Sutton?"

"You'll punish me." Just saying the words made me aroused.

"And what will your punishment be?"

"I won't be able to come?"

He shook his head as he unbuttoned the last button on his shirt and pulled it off. "Your punishment will be whatever I decide it will be. Understood?"

I swallowed. "Yes."

My brain went haywire as his underwear finally came down. The man's body was a masterpiece, and my eyes jumped around, trying to decide whether I should thank God for his washboard abs first or his thick cock that reached up to almost his belly button. Jagger's lips curled at the corners.

"Right back atcha, sweetheart." He walked over to the nightstand and took an ice cube from the bucket. "Time to close your eyes."

I hesitated, partially because I didn't want to give up the view, but also because I was dying to know what was going to come next. But Jagger's voice was stern when he spoke again. "Sutton, eyes closed. Now."

I squeezed them shut and waited. Long seconds ticked by as my anticipation built. I felt the bed dip and heard him moving around, but wasn't sure exactly where he was. Then a warm hand touched my foot. I jumped at the unexpected contact. Jagger guided my leg toward the side of the bed and set it down gently before doing the same to the other. I'd never been so exposed in my life—my arms were cuffed into a V and legs were spread wide.

"You look beautiful," Jagger's gravelly voice slid along my bare skin. Maybe my other senses were more heightened because I couldn't see, but I could've sworn I felt his words caress me. "Better than I could've imagined. You look like mine to do as I please."

"I am yours." The words hung heavy in the air, and I wondered if I should add *to do with what you please*. But then the bed dipped again, and cold pressed against my inner thigh. I gasped. My skin was already on fire, and the ice felt like it was burning a path as Jagger slowly slid the cube up my leg. When he reached my center, he veered to my hip and kept going up. Circling my navel painfully slowly twice, he skated along my ribs until arriving at my breast, where he traced the outline of my pebbled areola.

Then suddenly the cold disappeared, and my body went on high alert, anticipating where it might return. It made its appearance at a place I didn't expect—in his mouth. Jagger sucked in one of my nipples, and the warmth of his mouth gave way to the hard, cold ice inside.

"Oh, God." I moaned as he pulled back, sucking hard on the withdrawal, and I heard the smile in his voice when he spoke.

"You can call me Mr. Langston."

The bed dipped yet again and next came the sound of ice rattling. I held my breath, expecting he was getting a fresh cube to do the same on the other side of my body. But instead I felt his hand hovering between my legs.

"Squeeze those eyes shut tight. I don't want them to open and spoil all the fun I'm having."

I'd barely had time to comply before something nudged at my entrance. At first I thought Jagger had slipped a finger into me, but then I felt a cold burn inside me. I arched off the bed at the odd sensation. "Jagger..."

"I'm going to work the other side of your body, then catch the drops that drip out of you with my tongue."

I wasn't sure how much more I could take. Jagger took his time tracing up and down the right side of my body. By the time he was done, I'd grown desperate for friction. He settled between my legs, lifting my thighs over his shoulders. His tongue lapped at me, slurping up the constant drips of water leaking from my body.

"Jagger, please." I lifted my hips from the bed and tried to maneuver my clit to his mouth, but he only laid a hand at my stomach and flattened me back to the mattress.

"When you're ready," he said.

"I'm ready now."

He *tsk*ed. "You'll be ready when I decide you are."

I pouted, but it did nothing to hurry him along. Long licks built me to a panting frenzy, and when his tongue speared inside me, I realized he might not have to touch my clit to set me off after all. My muscles tightened, and I felt the wave building. Just when I thought it was about to crest, Jagger's tongue disappeared.

"Oh, God," I cried. "No! *No. No. No!*"

The amused tone of his voice made me want to smack him. "Patience is a virtue, Ms. Holland."

"So is compassion, so I think you should put me out of my misery."

He chuckled. "You can open your eyes."

I squinted at him. "My whole body feels like there's a tickle I can't scratch."

His smile widened, and he crawled up and pressed his lips to mine. His cock pressed against me. It was so hard, so right there... *If I could just...* I wiggled beneath his weight, trying to position my hips so he was lined up at my opening.

Jagger sat up and looked down at me. "You're trying to test my control."

"No, I'm trying to break it."

He shook his head. "That's not possible."

Though suddenly, it hit me that I'd been going about things all wrong. I *did* have something I was certain he couldn't resist, and it wasn't my begging. I grinned up at him. "Yesterday was day twenty-eight since I went on the pill. Which means you can come inside me without a condom."

Jagger's head dropped. "Fuck. That's cheating."

I reached for him, but the tight restraints bit into my wrists. So I had to settle for lifting my head to his ear. "Come inside of me, Mr. Langston. *Please?*"

He growled. But it also did the trick. He sank into my body in one deep, hard thrust.

"You're so damn tight. You're going to get what you asked for faster than you want it."

But I'd been on edge since we started, and it wasn't going to take much to push me over. My legs wrapped around his back, and I held on for dear life as he ferociously pumped in and out. Seeing and feeling Jagger as desperate as I was made emotions bubble up inside of me. I reached for him, forgetting about the restraints, wanting to claw my nails down his back. The bite of pain made my body throb, and I moaned. Jagger shifted his hips, the thick length of him rubbing against a desperate ache inside of me.

"Come for me, Sutton." He groaned. "Now."

My body didn't have to be told twice. It twitched and convulsed its way through the most powerful orgasm of my life while Jagger watched me come undone. After, he sped up his thrusts, racing to his own climax. He came inside of me with a roar so loud that it vibrated and bounced off the walls. The feel of his hot cum spilling into me caused a new quake of aftershocks to jerk through my body.

Jagger was quiet as he unlocked the cuffs and freed my wrists. He stayed that way while he went into the bathroom and came back and cleaned me up. When he was done, he covered my body with his once again, looking down into my eyes.

"You made me lose control," he whispered before pressing his lips to mine.

"Is that a bad thing? I thought it was pretty amazing, and I didn't have any control."

"That remains to be seen. It's not something that's ever ended well before."

# TWENTY-SEVEN

Jagger
10 years ago

**"F**uck."

I raked a hand through my hair, wishing I was back at the Emersons', wishing I was anywhere but here.

My mother and Catherine's apartment was a damn mess—dirty clothes all over the place, dishes piled up in the sink, half-eaten frozen dinners with cigarette butts sticking up from what was left, and don't even get me started on the stench. It was a mix of sour, mildew, and... I sniffed again. I really hoped something hadn't died in here, too. Meanwhile, my sister was frantically writing in her journal and hadn't even noticed that I'd come in.

I stepped over a pizza box and cleared my throat. "Hey. Where's Mom?"

She looked up, confused. "How did you get in?"

I held up my set of keys. "These."

"But I had the top lock on."

I turned to look at the door. "There is no top—" *Jesus Christ.* Not one, but *three* shiny new locks. One was screwed on more crooked than the others. I thumbed to them. "You install these yourself?"

Catherine nodded. She got up and bolted all three locks, then looked around the apartment. "I guess Mom must've gone out."

My guess was that could've happened two days ago, and my sister wouldn't have noticed with the state she was in. Things had taken a turn during the four years I was in the military. I took a deep breath and started to collect the garbage strewn all over. "You need to clean up after yourselves or you're going to get bugs in here."

She tucked her feet under her ass on the couch and went back to writing in her journal.

I raised my voice. "Catherine? Did you hear me? You need to keep this place clean."

"You don't have to yell at me. Leave it. I'll do it. I've been sick."

*Sick.* I'd been back home for five weeks now, and I hadn't heard a single sniffle. And I stopped by every few days. I picked up one of the three prescription pill bottles sitting on the kitchen counter and twisted the cap open. Emptying the contents into my other hand, I counted the pills as I dropped them back into the canister. Twenty-nine left of the thirty-day supply I'd picked up five days ago. I walked over and stood next to the couch. "You need to take your medicine every day, too."

"I do."

I frowned. "I just counted them."

"They're trying to poison me, and you don't even care." My sister's eyes filled with tears.

I was frustrated and tired, but I knew Catherine wasn't just being difficult. She was ill. Managing her, or my mom, was like trying to catch a butterfly—I'd get close, but somehow they always slipped through my fingers. I sat down on the couch next to my sister. "Have I ever done anything to hurt you, Cat?"

She looked away but shook her head.

"And I never will. Look at me, Catherine."

Her eyes met mine.

"The doctor is not trying to poison you. Those meds will help you feel better. Are you having trouble sleeping?"

She nodded.

"Do you feel anxious in your chest?"

She nodded again.

"Does everything feel too loud again? Like the TV and people talking?"

A tear streaked down her cheek, and she nodded more.

I held up the pill bottle. "These will make you feel better. But they take time to work, and you have to take them consistently."

She still didn't look sold, so I unzipped my backpack, pulled out my own pill bottle, and pointed to the label. "See the name here? I take pills, too, Cat."

"Are you sick?"

"Not the kind of sickness you get, like a cold or the flu. I have something called PTSD. Post-traumatic stress disorder." I rubbed over my breastbone. "I get that same anxious feeling in my chest sometimes—usually when I'm trying to go to sleep, and then I wind up staring at the ceiling all night. These help me when that happens. It makes me feel like I'm in control again."

Catherine's shoulders relaxed. She scooched closer to me on the couch and leaned her head on my shoulder with a sigh. "Are we going to be okay?"

"We are. But in our own way. Not everyone's okay is the same."

### Sutton

Jagger's alarm went off at six the next morning, but I was already awake, lying on my side looking at him.

"Good morning." I smiled.

He stretched. "I don't remember the last time the alarm actually woke me up. I set it, but I'm always up before it goes off."

"I'm glad you slept well."

"You look like you've been up for a while."

"Not too long. Maybe an hour."

"Have you just been staring at me?"

"I've been thinking, actually."

He kissed my forehead. "Uh-oh. That doesn't sound good."

I smiled again. "I want to come with you today."

"To Ohio?"

I nodded. "I was serious when I said I'd like to help out with the girls."

"Sutton—"

I pressed two fingers to his lips. "Before you tell me the million reasons why you're not right for me and we shouldn't get too close, I should tell you that I'm not taking no for an answer."

His eyebrow quirked, and he nipped at the tip of my pointer. "Is that so?"

"Ow." I pulled my finger back and shook it. "And yes. If you want to continue to be able to tell me what to do in the bedroom, you're going to have to give elsewhere, so I don't feel like everything is completely one-sided."

Jagger grabbed my hand and brought it to his mouth, kissing the finger he'd just bitten. "I thought you enjoyed giving up control."

"I do. I absolutely do. But I need to be heard, Jagger. I want to support you. It doesn't mean I think you're going to propose, or that we need to do every little thing together, but I do need balance to feel like I'm not being used."

Jagger's face grew serious. He looked into my eyes, and by some miracle, I kept from cracking. Eventually, he nodded. "Okay."

My eyes widened. "Really? Okay? I thought you were going to be way more difficult than that."

His eyes narrowed. "Are you saying I'm a pushover?"

"No. No. You're more of a tyrant."

Both his brows popped this time. "A tyrant?"

"Well, yes. You're bossy."

He shook his head. "I think you should quit while you're ahead, Sutton."

I grinned and pressed my lips to his. "Thank you for giving in. I really didn't want to give up the mind-blowing orgasms."

Jagger chuckled. He looked so much younger when he was relaxed like this. "We have to get on the road by seven thirty. The social worker is meeting me there at eleven, and it's a two-hour flight."

"I need to run home and get a change of clothes, take a quick shower."

"Sam will take you. I'll have him drop you off, then come back and get me, and we'll pick you up again on the way to the airport. How does that sound?"

"Perfect. Thank you."

"I need to get in the shower and make a few business calls." Jagger pulled back the cover and stood. I hadn't really gotten the chance to check out his bare ass before. It was firm and sculpted like the rest of the man.

"Jeez. You must do a lot of squats."

He turned, and apparently his ass wasn't the only thing hard. I licked my lips without even realizing I was doing it.

"Stop looking at me like that or neither one of us is going to make it to the airport on time."

I nibbled on my lip. "Good point. But save that for later. Maybe I can join the mile-high club."

•  •  •

I'd never been on a private plane before. Jagger was finishing up a last-minute work call before we taxied to the runway, so I took a moment to snoop around. Supple leather seats that swiveled, two full-size couches that faced each other, a conference table in the back, not to mention a private bedroom. And everything was so nicely coordinated—the navy piping in the cream seats matched the throw pillows, and the blankets on the couch and the velvet bedspread in the sleeping cabin had the Apex logo monogrammed in cream.

The captain came back just as Jagger finished his call.

"We should get going. We have wheels-up in seven minutes or we're going to get stuck behind a band of traffic and get pushed to forty minutes."

Jagger nodded. "Ready when you are."

The captain went back to the cockpit. A minute later, the flight attendant came in holding two travel mugs with the Apex logo. She smiled. "Black for you, Mr. Langston, and cappuccino with one sugar for you, Ms. Holland. I'll serve breakfast after we've leveled out."

"Thank you, Renee."

She smiled at Jagger and passed me a mug.

"Thank you so much," I told her.

"I hope you don't mind, but I have a few more emails to get out," Jagger said. "Once the girls are with us, I won't get five minutes again until they crash tonight. The first day they're with me, they're always extra hyperactive. I think it's their nerves, because they usually settle within a day or two."

"Not at all. Do whatever you have to do."

I didn't particularly love the take-off part of flying, so once the plane started to move, I shut my eyes and kept quiet, focusing on taking deep breaths and staying calm. After we leveled out, my grip on the armrest of my chair loosened, and I opened my eyes.

Renee returned with a tray and sat it in front of me. "Breakfast. Would you like another cappuccino?"

"No, I'm good. Thank you."

She looked to Jagger. "I'll be back with yours, and I don't have to ask if you want more coffee."

He smiled. "Thanks, Renee."

I waited until we both had our trays to take the silver dome off the plate. Jagger's had a big omelet and sausage links, while mine had yogurt with a side of blueberries and honey. I'd thought it was coincidence that the flight attendant had brought me my coffee exactly the way I took it, but this couldn't be one, too.

"How did they know what I like for breakfast?" I asked Jagger.

"I texted them this morning after you left to go to your apartment and get ready."

"But how did you know? We've never had breakfast together?"

Jagger smirked. "The eye in the sky in the office. I've spent waaay too much time watching that damn feed."

*Wow. Just wow.* The busy CEO who not only watched me but *remembered* what I liked too. "What else did you learn about me from that thing?"

"Other than a member of my legal team has too much time on his hands and needs to be reminded of the no-fraternization policy in the employee handbook? I noticed that you often put your palms flat on your desk."

I blinked. "You noticed that?"

Jagger's eyes met mine. "I notice everything about you, whether I want to or not."

My chest tightened. "Miles has never even noticed that I do that. Honestly, I didn't realize it until a therapist pointed it out to me. Dr. French noticed after two visits. The night I was drugged, my hands were at my sides, and I kept thinking if I could only get my palms flat, I could push up and bang my head against his and try to get away. I sort of hyper-focused on it during the whole thing, but of course, I couldn't move."

Jagger's jaw flexed. "I'm sorry I brought it up."

I smiled sadly. "It's fine. I just can't believe you picked up on it. My therapist said it's called grounding. I actually do it with my feet as well. I don't even realize it most of the time. But it helps me relax."

Jagger nodded. He was quiet for a moment. "I used to shower four or five times a day when my mother would stop taking her meds and go off the deep end, ranting about the government watching us or some other paranoia tirade." He smiled. "I don't do it that often anymore, but it's one of the reasons I picked an office space with a shower. Every once in a while, when I'm feeling overly stressed, I take a shower mid-day at the office."

I smiled. "You must be clean as a whistle this week."

"Actually..." His eyes dropped to my lips. "I think I've found something better to relax me these days."

I knew Jagger was just talking about sex, but I liked the thought of being something that could help ground him. "Are you...feeling stressed now?"

His eyes darkened as they swept over me. "Finish your breakfast. Quickly."

I nibbled on my bottom lip. "Have you ever...on a plane?"

He shook his head. "No. I've never traveled with a woman other than a business associate."

"Not ever? What about on vacation or a weekend away?"

"I haven't taken a vacation in five years, and my previous relationship arrangements didn't include spending much time together outside of the bedroom."

A surge of jealousy twisted in my gut. It was stupid—I knew that. But I couldn't stop it from happening.

Jagger smiled. "I'm damn lucky you were a virgin, or I'd want to strangle every man who'd had you before me, too."

"How do you know what I'm thinking?"

"You wear your feelings on your face, Sutton." He pointed to my breakfast with his fork. "Now eat, and then get your ass to the back bedroom and strip naked."

•  •  •

An hour later, I was buckling my seatbelt when my eyes met the flight attendant's, who was in the front of the cabin. I quickly looked away and whispered to Jagger. "I feel like Renee knows what we did back there."

"So?" Jagger shrugged. "Are you embarrassed? I'd fuck you anywhere and not care who knows it."

"There's a double standard for women. If we sleep around, we're promiscuous, but if men do it, they're studs."

"I get it." He reached over and took my hand, bringing it to his lips for a kiss. "But we're also not sleeping around. We're sleeping with each other."

"Are we...exclusive now?"

Jagger had started to lower our joined hands but froze midway to the armrest. "Do you want to sleep with other men?"

"No, but I wasn't sure if you did exclusive."

"I wouldn't expect anything from you that I wasn't willing to give. And the thought of another man touching you? There aren't enough showers in the world for that."

I smiled. "Okay."

The pilot came on overhead and announced that we were beginning our initial descent into Cleveland Airport. A few minutes later, Renee came to collect our drinks. I looked out the window as we lowered through clouds and the land beneath came into view.

"Do you have family in Ohio? Is that why your sister is here?"

He shook his head. "Catherine spent a week here in the summer when she was thirteen. NASA has a research center in Cleveland. My sister used to compete in these science competitions, and one year she won a week of Space Camp. She got to spend a week shadowing astronauts and learning about everything NASA was doing. Cat's four years older than me, but I still remember my mom bringing us here that week. I was so pissed that they gave her all these logoed NASA clothes, and I didn't get any."

I laughed, and Jagger continued. "While she was here, Catherine found out that Ohio has more astronauts per capita than any other state, and she decided she wanted to be an astronaut and live here when she grew up. Things didn't turn out exactly as she'd planned. She's bounced around to a lot of cities, but she always finds her way back here."

"Where does your mom live?"

I knew before he answered that he was about to say something bad.

"My mother died a few years ago."

"Oh. I didn't know. I'm sorry."

He nodded and looked out the window. I thought that was going to be the end of the conversation, but a minute later, he surprised me when he turned back. "She accidentally overdosed on her prescription meds. At least that's what the death report said. But I've always assumed it might not have been an accident. Doctors always underestimated my mother because of her condition. The only time they saw her was at her worst, but at her best, she was an extremely intelligent woman. It was difficult for her to hold down jobs long term, but even working at the grocery store, she'd memorize the codes to key in for all the different fruits and vegetables the first day." He smiled. "She graduated high school two years early like some other smarty pants I know."

"Yeah, I'm so smart, you had to let me win when we did the algorithm calculation face-off."

"You're young and haven't spent years working through those like I have. Trust me, you blow the doors off my abilities at your age."

I didn't think that was true, but rather than say so, I squeezed his hand. "I really am sorry about your mother. I know from experience that it's difficult to move past things when there are still unknowns in your mind."

When Jagger and I first met, I'd thought we were complete opposites. I was a young, inexperienced, virgin intern, and he was the older, billionaire CEO who met women on kinky dating apps. But the more time I spent with him, the more I realized we had a lot in common—and not just the way we both seemed to like things in the bedroom. It gave me hope that maybe there could be more to us than just what Jagger was adamant we were.

# —— CHAPTER ——
# TWENTY-NINE

### Sutton

"**U**ncle Jagger!"

Two little blonde girls with unruly curly hair threw open the screen door and ran toward us on the porch of the foster home where they'd stayed last night. Jagger dropped down to a knee to catch them in his arms, and they practically knocked him over. I smiled and gave them space.

The smaller of the two squeezed her eyes shut. "Uncle Jagger! I dreamed that you came! And you did."

Jagger kissed her cheek and tapped the tip of her nose with his finger. "You did, did you? Does that mean I made your dreams come true?"

She dove back into his arms, nodding her head. Jagger's smile widened and he stood, taking both the little girls with him. Their feet dangled as they giggled. My heart swelled seeing how much they adored him. Jagger Langston was already a ten on any rating scale, but today he shot up to a thousand.

A woman stepped out of the house and smiled. "How're you doing, Mr. Langston?"

He nodded. "It's Jagger, please. And much better now."

"Girls?" the woman said. "Why don't you go collect your backpacks and say goodbye to Jenny? Jenny is the Breslins' daughter," she explained to Jagger and me.

"Okay!"

Jagger bent to set the girls down, and they took off into the house. He turned to me. "Sorry I didn't introduce you."

I waved him off. "They didn't even notice I was standing here because they were so excited to see you."

He gestured to me while speaking to the woman. "Octavia, this is Sutton Holland. Sutton, this is Octavia Moore, the social worker I coordinate with when the girls need my assistance."

I extended my hand. "Nice to meet you."

She nodded, and Jagger put his hands on his hips. "How'd the girls do last night?"

"Mrs. Breslin said they slept well. But Olivia wet the bed."

Jagger took a deep breath in and exhaled. "She did that the first night she was with me last time, too. When my sister isn't doing well, she sometimes stays up all night and rants. Amelia told me it scares them, and her sister is afraid to get out of bed to go to the bathroom."

Octavia nodded. "It's not unusual for children who are removed to have an accident. They're often afraid to get up in the middle of the night in their new surroundings. Also, you should know that Amelia has already been asking if she can visit her mother. She understands she's in the hospital."

Jagger shook his head. "They don't allow visits during a fifty-one-fifty hold."

"I know. I told Amelia the hospital was taking good care of her mother, but she wouldn't be able to see her for a while. Will you be staying in Ohio for a few days?"

"I can't stay this time," he told her. "I have some stuff going on at work. But I was able to get the same sitter who helped out when they stayed with me for a few months last year. The girls really liked her, and she's already familiar to them. I'll try to keep my workdays shorter than usual, but I'm going to need to be at the office, unfortunately."

Octavia nodded. "That's understandable. Caregivers, especially those who jump in right away when needed, like you do, have responsibilities. Will you be taking the girls to the same address as last time? I'll need to get some information from you, and we'll need to speak on a regular basis, like we always do."

Jagger nodded. "Same address, same contact info. And I already have a call in to Catherine's doctor. I'll let you know what he's thinking after I speak to him. Then we can start to make a longer-term plan."

"Unfortunately, you already know the drill," Octavia said. "CPS in New York will contact you, and they'll drop in on a regular basis and report back to me. Meanwhile, I'll be making an independent assessment about the safety of the girls being reunited with their mother. Catherine did call me directly and tell me she needed me to take the children, so that's a plus. But we'll need to see how things go."

Jagger frowned. "She used to call me, but ever since I took her to court to try to get custody, she thinks I'm the enemy."

Octavia smiled halfheartedly. "That's also not unusual, especially from a parent who struggles with Catherine's mental-health issues."

The social worker had Jagger sign a bunch of papers, and when the girls came back, he introduced them to me.

"Do you know how to braid hair?" Amelia asked.

"I do. I can even do a fishtail."

Her little nose scrunched up. "What's that?"

"It's an extra fancy kind of braid that sort of looks like a fish's tail. I can show you how to do it, too, if you want."

"Uncle Jagger has a dress-up box for us at his house," Olivia added.

Jagger gave me an inconspicuous smirk.

"I've actually seen it. I bet we can come up with a different hairstyle for each outfit in there. Do you think you can draw some of your favorite clothes from the box?"

Both girls nodded eagerly.

"Maybe on the way back to Uncle Jagger's house, you can do that, and we can sketch the hairstyle you want with each outfit?"

Their little eyes widened. "Uncle Jagger, can we stop to get paper?" Amelia clasped her hands into the praying position.

"And crayons," Olivia added.

He smiled. "Sure, why not?"

Jagger thanked Octavia and the foster parents, and the four of us went on our merry way.

I pointed to a strip mall on the right side of the road on our way back to the airport. "There's a craft store in there. We can get paper and crayons."

Jagger navigated into the parking lot. As we started to unload, his phone rang. "It's a local number. Probably the..." He pointed to the girls with his eyes.

"Take it," I said. "The girls and I will be fine in the craft store. Right, ladies?"

Olivia took my hand without having to be prompted. "We're going shopping!"

I chuckled. "We'll see you inside when you're done."

The craft store was a dangerous place to send me with two little girls. By the time Jagger caught up to us, we had sketch pads, crayons, colored pencils for Amelia—because crayons were apparently for babies—an origami kit, two bracelet-beading boxes, and four animal crochet kits.

He raised a brow. "I was only gone five minutes."

"Consider yourself lucky we're in Michaels and not a clothing boutique or a jewelry store."

It wasn't until we were back on the plane that Jagger and I had a minute to talk alone again. Olivia and Amelia were busy drawing the outfits they were going to wear so we could plan their hairstyles.

"How was your call?" I asked quietly.

"Catherine won't eat. She thinks they're putting something in her food, and she's upset because she believes the landlord is going to read her journals."

"Journals?"

Jagger nodded. "She goes through one or two notebooks a month. Has been doing it since she was a teenager. There are more than a dozen boxes of them in a storage facility. The first thing I do when she gets admitted into any hospital—after I make sure the kids are okay—is have a few blank journals delivered to her ward. It helps her to write down her paranoia."

The picture he painted kept getting bleaker and bleaker. I looked over at the girls. "It must be so hard on them."

"The worst part is never knowing what you're going to come home to. One day your mother is smiling and singing along with the radio when you get back from school, cooking your favorite meal, and the next she's unscrewed all the electrical outlets and pulled out the wires so no one can listen in on her conversations, and she just stares at the TV from the couch for four straight days."

I wasn't sure if that story was about his sister or his mother, not that it mattered. But I reached over and took his hand. Jagger looked down at our linked fingers for a long time. "Thank you for coming."

"It's my pleasure." I bumped my shoulder with his, trying to keep the mood light, though I felt myself falling fast. "I enjoyed coming earlier, too."

• • •

It was nine o'clock that night before the girls started getting ready for bed. We'd spent most of the day doing hair and playing dress-up. I was glad I'd stayed, not only because I was able to keep his nieces' minds off things, but because Jagger had gotten a half-dozen work phone calls and needed to go into his home office to speak in private. This really was the worst time for him to take custody of two little girls. And the last thing those little angels needed was to hear their uncle raising his voice and getting upset.

Jagger started getting the girls to bed in the guest room while I went to use the bathroom across the hall. I tied my hair up in a ponytail and slowed as I stepped out, hearing my name coming from across the hall.

"Is Sutton your girlfriend?" one of the girls asked.

There was a long silence before he answered. "She's a girl, and she's my friend."

"I like her," said Olivia, the younger of the two. "She makes pretty braids."

"That's good." I heard the smile in Jagger's voice. "I like her too."

"Is this your first girlfriend?" Olivia asked.

"I've had other girls who were friends."

"How come we never met any of them?" Amelia followed up.

Again, there was silence.

"I guess because none was special enough to meet you."

Warmth flowed through my belly. If I wasn't careful, I was going to fall so hard I'd never be able to climb back out of the hole I'd be in if Jagger Langston hurt me.

"How long is Mommy going to be in the hospital this time?" Amelia asked.

"I'm not sure, sweetheart."

"Why can't the doctors ever make her better so she doesn't have to go to the hospital anymore?" Olivia asked. "My friend Peyton who lives downstairs, her mom had her 'pendix out, and she didn't have to go back to the hospital again. She was holding her stomach all the time, and now she doesn't. They made her all better."

"Not all sickness is the kind you can see, and some take longer to make better than others."

I didn't want to get caught eavesdropping, so I quietly made my way out to the living room. It was another ten minutes before Jagger emerged. I stood at his wall of glass, looking out at the twinkling City lights. He came up behind me and wrapped his arms around my waist. He kissed my neck, and I let my head loll back against him.

"Long day," he said.

"I think they have more energy than either of us."

"I would've agreed five minutes ago, but my cock seems to have found his second wind the minute he felt your ass push up against him."

I chuckled. "We did it this morning on the plane."

Jagger turned me in his arms. "Once a day is not nearly enough with you."

I smiled. "If you keep things up at this pace, you're going to get sick of me."

"I'm not sure that's possible." He rubbed his nose with mine. "If I could bottle how thankful I am for you today, it would overflow endlessly."

My heart did a little pitter-patter. For a man who refused to believe he could be sweet, he'd certainly found the right words to melt my heart. "It was nothing. I'm glad I could help."

Though *sweet* didn't last too long. Jagger's hand slid up from my waist and grabbed my ponytail. He gave it a good, firm yank. "Let me thank you properly. My door has a lock."

I wanted to, *God, did I want to*, but I also didn't want the girls to hear us.

"I don't think I can be quiet."

"I'll cover your mouth."

"Not sure that would do it."

"Then I'll shove my cock in it while I eat your pussy."

*Ooohh.* The rawness of his voice almost did me in. But I forced myself to think of the girls and covered Jagger's mouth with my hand. "Don't say anything more. I'm trying to be the good one here, and you're making it very hard."

He nipped at my fingers. "I'm *already* very hard."

I laughed. "I'm serious, Jagger. Olivia and Amelia are barely settled, and I don't want them to hear us, or worse, run to your room if they get scared and find the door locked. I want you, too, but you're going to have to take a raincheck."

He groaned, and it made me smile.

I raised an eyebrow. "Mr. Always-in-Control needs to demonstrate some self-control. But I'll help you out with that. I'm going to go home. We could both use a good night's sleep."

Jagger pouted.

I pressed my lips to his. "The sitter is coming early tomorrow, right?"

"Yes. Louise. The girls know her pretty well. She's coming at six. I have a seven o'clock meeting I can't miss."

"Skip the gym and come by my apartment on the way to the office. I'll answer naked and ready to make it up to you in fifteen minutes or less."

# —— CHAPTER ——
# THIRTY

Sutton

**"I** love when your sleeves are rolled up like that."

I laid on the bed on my belly, naked, swinging my feet in the air as I watched Jagger get dressed for work. It was six thirty in the morning, and we'd just had a quickie—same as we'd done every morning this week so far.

Jagger finished rolling one sleeve and started the next one. "I don't have much of a choice today since you tore the button hole taking off my shirt."

"I was impatient. I wait for you naked every morning, but you come in a full suit."

"I go straight to the office. What would you like me to come in?"

"-side me?"

His forehead wrinkled, but he quickly got the joke and smiled. Jagger picked up his tie and wrapped it around his neck. "I have a call with my sister's doctor and Octavia this morning. Catherine is now telling them she plans to go home tomorrow."

"I thought she'd agreed to stay for a while?"

"She did on Monday, when she was still sedated, but now that they've ruled her not a danger to herself or others, they can't force her to take any meds or stay there, and she wants to leave."

"What will happen with the girls?"

"It depends on how our conversation goes today, but normally the court makes Catherine do some work on herself—like meet with a psychiatrist and counselor a few times and prove she's taking her meds regularly—before they'll even consider reunification. I can't imagine that would happen sooner than a month or two, but I'll know more later. I may need to fly down to Ohio tomorrow morning. I need to see her in person if she's getting out, to assess whether it's okay for her to be near the kids this quickly, even for a visit. If she's stable, I'll bring her back to New York, and she can stay in the guest apartment in my building and visit the kids as much as she wants, as long as someone else is present. But I'm not letting them go back with her too quickly this time."

"Will you take the girls to Ohio with you?"

Jagger shook his head. "I won't even let them know I'm going to see her until I figure out if she's stable. She's scared them enough, and I don't want to get their hopes up. Plus, either way, she and I are going to have a long talk that the kids don't need to hear."

I slipped from the bed and took over tying his tie as I spoke. "I can hang out with them while you're gone."

"Louise can probably watch them. I mentioned that I might need her on weekends when I asked her to come back."

"I want to do it. I picked up a bunch of hair accessories for us to play around with—butterfly clips, headbands, snap-on extensions…" I tucked Jagger's tie through the loop and pulled the knot up to his neck. "I like this tie on you. It brings out the blue in your eyes."

He pressed his lips to my forehead. "Thank you. And that was very sweet of you to pick up all that stuff for my nieces."

"I had as much fun as they did playing dress-up. It was always one of my favorite things to do as a kid."

"Oh yeah?" Jagger's hand snaked around my waist and slid down to grab a handful of my ass. He squeezed hard. "Maybe we should play together. I bet you dressing up would be one of my favorite things, too."

I laid my hands flat on his chest and bit my lower lip. "I might be able to arrange for a little playtime one morning, if you play your cards right."

"I'll tell the sitter to come an hour earlier tomorrow."

I laughed. "Slow down, cowboy. Don't you want to sleep in a bit on Saturday?"

"I'd rather spend the extra hours inside you than sleep. These fifteen-minute morning things don't cut it."

"Miles is also flying in tomorrow night. So I'll have a house guest."

Jagger frowned. "How long is he staying?"

"Until Tuesday. We have a tradition that we're always together at midnight the night before one of our birthdays, so we can be the first to say happy birthday."

"It's his birthday Sunday?"

I shook my head. "No, it's mine."

Jagger froze. "Why didn't you tell me?"

"I hadn't really given it any thought until Miles texted me his flight information two days ago. I don't really do big birthdays. It's Miles who thinks they're national holidays."

An alarm chimed from somewhere. Jagger pulled out his phone. "Sorry. I have to set an alarm now when I visit you in the morning, or I get carried away. Yesterday, I was a half hour late for a meeting with a team of lawyers. Probably cost me ten grand in fees." He took my chin between his thumb and index finger and pulled my face to him. "It was worth the extra time inside of you, but I need to run. I'm meeting Edmund this morning, and it's bad enough that I'm going to have his stepdaughter's taste in my mouth. I don't want to be late, too."

"I have an extra toothbrush, if you want?"

"No way. Tasting you is what gets me through the day lately." He gave me a chaste kiss. "We'll discuss your birthday later."

I didn't think there was any more to discuss, but I shrugged. "Have a good day."

Jagger reached for his suit jacket. "Wear a skirt so I can see your thighs on the security feed, and I will."

• • •

Saturday morning, I arrived at Jagger's apartment at seven. He'd offered to have Louise come over and watch the girls until I got there, but I didn't mind getting up early, especially not when Jagger opened the door, hooked an arm around my waist, and pulled me against him for a languid kiss.

"Wow." I smiled. "That's some greeting."

"The girls are still sound asleep, if I can convince you to let me say good morning with my mouth licking lower?"

"Not a chance, Langston."

He yanked me into the apartment and steered me to the kitchen, handing me a steaming mug before picking up his own. He must've started it when the doorman buzzed up that I'd arrived.

"The girls are excited for today," he said.

I held up the tote bag of stuff I brought. "I am, too."

Jagger chugged the rest of his coffee and rinsed the mug in the sink. "There's been a little change in plans though."

"What do you mean?"

His phone chimed. "Sam is downstairs to take me to the airport." He scooped up his wallet and keys from the counter. "I left you a keycard to get in and out, and Sam will be back to pick you and the girls up at ten." He walked toward the door.

I followed. "Wait. Where are we going?"

He cupped my neck and pulled me close for a kiss. "You'll see."

"I don't understand."

"You will, birthday girl."

"But my birthday isn't until tomorrow."

He winked. "That's why I'm saving your big gift until then."

An hour later, Olivia walked out from the guest room. I was sitting on the couch playing with my phone, and her eyes lit up when she saw me. She ran and jumped onto my lap.

"Sutton! We're going to get manicures and pedicures and have tea and go shopping and—"

Amelia walked out from the bedroom, rubbing her eyes. "You weren't supposed to tell her any of that, dumb butt."

Olivia slapped her hands over her mouth while her sister padded to the couch, dragging her feet and shaking her head.

"Good morning, Amelia," I said.

"Hi." She plopped down next to me and yawned. Unlike Olivia, who'd bounded into the room, full of energy,

Amelia seemed more my speed in the morning. Except she was too young for coffee.

"Uncle Jagger is going to be mad you spoiled the surprise," she said to her sister.

I smiled. "We don't have to tell him. But...tell me more. Where are we going?"

The girls filled me in on some of our plans for the day. Apparently, Jagger had made us manicure and pedicure appointments at The Plaza, where we also had a reservation for high tea, followed by going to some stores that neither of them could remember the names of.

"Wow," I said. "Well, we better start getting ready. Who wants their hair done for the big day?"

Both girls stretched their arms into the air. I laughed. "I brought a bag of goodies. Let's get you ladies washed up, and then I'll show you all the hair accessories you have to choose from."

• • •

Later that afternoon, I looked at the price tag of the dress I currently had on.

Bergdorf Goodman was definitely *not* in my budget.

The personal shopper noticed and leaned in to whisper in my ear. "When Mr. Langston made the appointment, he said to tell you that you're not to look at any tags." She smiled. "Today is his treat."

He'd already spent a few thousand dollars on the girls' new clothes, which they needed since they hadn't brought too much, though I would've taken them to Old Navy or somewhere more practical. But two grand for a summer dress, just because it had the Fendi logo on it, wasn't going to happen.

"It looks beautiful on you."

"It's not really my style," I lied and went back into the dressing room.

Amelia yelled from the other side of the wall. "Try on the green one!"

The green silk dress was absolutely beautiful. But when I lifted that tag, my eyes bulged from my head. Forty-eight hundred dollars for this? Was it sewn by royalty?

"I think I'm going to skip it and get dressed."

A voice I hadn't expected responded this time. "I'd really like to see it on you."

I'd already slipped off the other dress. I unlocked the door and stuck my head out. Jagger was leaning casually against the arched dressing-room entryway. "How did you find us?"

"Sam."

"Oh. Yeah, of course. When did you get back?"

"I came straight here from the airport." He spoke with the same even-keeled, commanding tone that had done me in from the beginning. "Put the dress on, Sutton."

Goosebumps prickled my arms, and I found myself nodding and shutting the dressing-room door. What kind of magic powers did this man have? All it took was a few words, and I became desperate to please him? I wasn't sure, but whatever it was, it had me pulling on a dress I'd had no intention of trying on only a minute ago. And I felt relief when it looked good. I even fluffed my hair a bit before unlocking the door and stepping back out.

"You look so pretty, Sutton!" Olivia jumped up and down.

"Gorgeous," the personal shopper said. "It looks like it was made for you."

Jagger stayed quiet, but he didn't really have to say anything for me to know what he was thinking. His eyes swept over my body and darkened. "We'll take it."

• • •

"I think Amelia is already snoring."

Jagger came back into the living room and sat next to me on the couch after putting the girls to bed.

I smiled. "They had a great day. So did I. You spoiled all three of us. Thank you."

He put his hand on my knee and rubbed his thumb back and forth. "It's my pleasure."

"How did things go with your sister?" It was the first time we'd had a chance to speak alone.

"Better than expected. She agreed to stay in the hospital for the length of time the doctors recommended, a month. They're adjusting some of her meds. She claims she stopped taking them because they made her tired all the time. We're going to see how things go before I bring the girls to visit, but hopefully she'll be well enough for me to take them for a few hours soon."

"What about after she's out? Will you bring her to New York?"

He nodded. "I want to protect the girls and make sure they're safe, not keep them from their mother."

"You're a really good uncle, you know that?"

"They're great kids. I hate that they're going through shit that's a lot like what I had to deal with growing up. But my mother was an only child, so there wasn't anyone else. I'm glad I can be there for them."

"Do you want children of your own?"

Jagger's eyes jumped to meet mine. I'd gotten good at reading what was on his mind. And now he was giving me a warning.

I held up my hands. "I'm not asking you to have them with me. Just wondering since you're so close with Amelia and Olivia."

He looked away. "If you'd asked me a few months ago, I would've said no."

"And now?"

He pushed up from the couch. "And now...I need a drink. Would you like one?"

I shook my head. I was disappointed at the abrupt end to our conversation, but tried to look on the positive side. He hadn't said *no*, and it seemed he was allowing himself to think about possibilities he might not have considered previously. So I didn't push.

I stood and walked over to stand on the other side of the kitchen island while he fixed his drink.

A text flashed on my phone.

**Miles: Honey, I'm home! Just landed.**

I smiled.

**Sutton: See you soon.**

"Miles just got to JFK," I said. "I should get going."

Jagger rattled the ice cubes in his glass as he stirred, then sipped. "When will I see you? I know you have dinner plans with your parents because I spoke to Edmund earlier. He and I are getting together for a few hours tomorrow afternoon to go over a strategy we've come up with that we think might satisfy the DOJ."

I nodded. "Mom pushed dinner to eight, but I didn't realize it was because Edmund would be with you."

Jagger came around the island and cupped my cheek. "I'd like to celebrate your birthday with you. Is there room for one more at dinner? I can see if Louise can babysit the girls. They'll be in bed by eight anyway."

I blinked. "You want to go to dinner with my mother and Miles and Edmund?"

"It sounds like that's the only way I'm going to be able to see you on your birthday."

"But...what about Edmund?"

"I was thinking I should have a conversation with him soon, anyway. He walked into my office and almost caught me watching the security feed this week, and I'd rather him not find out about us any other way than me telling him."

"Really? You want to tell him about us?"

"Do you have a problem with that?"

"No." I shook my head. "Not at all."

"Good." He pressed a kiss to my lips. "Then it's settled. I'll speak to Edmund in private before dinner tomorrow."

Miles had showed up at ten o'clock last night wearing sparkly gold glasses with a bottle of XO Patrón in one hand and two shot glasses in the other that read *Swallow It All Like a Lady*. Needless to say, Sunday morning I woke up with a bit of a hangover. I stayed in bed for an hour, scrolling on my phone until the smell of coffee wafting through the air coaxed me to my feet. I found Miles in the kitchen, standing under a *Happy Birthday, Bitch* sign that he must've brought with him.

"Happy birthday, cookie. May your day be gayer than the roller-skating party I went to during Pride in San Francisco."

"Thank you." I smiled, and he passed me a mug and looked toward the living room.

"That bag was delivered for you. It hasn't been easy to control myself the last hour while I waited for your lazy ass to get up. I already looked up the logo, so I know it's from an expensive jewelry store. Hurry and open it before I do."

I swallowed a healthy gulp of caffeine and carried the mug with me to the other room where a haughty-looking, matte-black bag was tied with a big red bow. Inside was a card and a box. I slipped the note from the envelope first and read, *Happy birthday, beautiful. I can't wait to fuck you with only this on.*

Miles peered over my shoulder. "That's hot."

I pulled the card against my chest. "Nosy."

"Open the damn gift already."

I shook my head as I slipped the black box from the bag and flipped it open. Inside was a stunning choker with three strands of pearls connected to a large, diamond-encrusted sapphire clasp. The center stone had to be fifteen carats.

"Holy crap." Miles gawked. "Is that...a collar?"

"What do you mean a *collar*?"

"It's a necklace a Dom gives his submissive. It's usually a leather choker or some shit."

"Oh my God, really?"

Miles nodded. "I'm pretty sure it means you belong to him."

I ran my finger over the sparkling sapphire. "Do you think this is real? The color is incredible."

"It's definitely real. I researched the store the minute Nestor handed me the bag. It's high end. Most of their stuff is one-of-a-kind pieces. They don't sell costume jewelry."

I lifted the necklace from the box for a closer look. "It's really beautiful."

Miles smirked. "Good thing you got a rich Dom, because the leather ones you see in the window of adult stores are pretty damn tacky."

I laughed. "I really don't think it's meant to be a collar. He bought me a pearl anklet too. The thought behind the pearls is actually really sweet."

"Would it bother you if that's what it was meant to be?"

I thought about it. I was crazy about the man. Not to mention, I was more than satisfied with how things were between Jagger and me in the bedroom. Plus, if I belonged to him, that meant he belonged to me. I shook my head. "I think I already belong to him, Miles."

A few hours later, my best friend and I were heading out for brunch when the doorman stopped me. "I just tried to call you, Ms. Holland. You got another delivery from a messenger."

"Oh?"

Nestor reached into a drawer and pulled out an envelope, extending it to me.

"Thank you."

He tipped his hat. "Have a good day."

"You, too."

Miles wiggled his brows as he opened the door for us. "Another gift from your master?"

I turned the envelope over, expecting to see my mother or Jagger's handwriting. But I froze with one foot out the door when I realized it wasn't from either of them.

"Oh my God." My heart pounded in my chest. "Miles, it's a birthday card from *him*."

• • •

Detective Wallace yanked up his pants by the front buckle as he paced in my living room. "So this is the first contact he's made in six years?"

Miles reached over and covered my hands with his, stopping them from twisting and wringing. I hadn't even realized I was doing it. "Thanks," I whispered before turning my attention to the detective I hadn't seen in years. "The last time he sent me anything was a card on my nineteenth birthday."

"Why do you think he made contact again after all this time?"

I shook my head. "Maybe because I'm back in New York for my birthday? I moved out to California to go to school six years ago this fall."

"But the cards stopped coming when you left?"

I looked to my mother, who had showed up an hour ago even though I'd told her she didn't have to. "Mom? Did they really stop, or did you just tell me they did so I wouldn't get upset?"

She shook her head. "They really stopped coming. I don't live here anymore, but I did for more than a year after Sutton left while my husband and I did renovations to his place, and no card came. Plus, I sometimes still get mail here and the doormen just hold on to it. Nothing's come."

Detective Wallace scribbled some notes in his flip-top pad. "So if he knew you weren't living here, this guy has likely been tracking you all this time."

A chill ran down my spine. "But how? How does he know I'm back?"

"I don't know." Detective Wallace pulled something that looked like a tweezer from his pocket and used it to pick up the card. "Hopefully he left some DNA on this so we can find out."

"What is she supposed to do?" my mother asked. "Sit here and wait for him to show up one day? What have the police done in the last six years to catch this man?"

"It's still an open investigation, ma'am. But there isn't much we can do without new evidence. Now we have some. We'll also have the security video footage pulled from the lobby and see if that gives us anything."

I looked to my mom. "Nestor said he was pretty sure the guy had been here before to deliver."

Detective Wallace nodded. "If he used a messenger service to drop it off, the company should have records where the envelope was picked up. If he brought it himself, hopefully we'll get him on camera."

I felt all the color drain from my face. I don't know why I'd assumed that the doorman recognizing him meant the card had been brought by a legit messenger. "You think he comes to this building so often that Nestor recognizes him? What does he want? What is he doing here?"

My front door burst open, and all four of our heads turned to watch Jagger storm in, followed by Edmund. I stood, and he rushed over and wrapped me in his arms.

"Are you okay?"

I nodded. "I'm fine."

"I'm going to find this fucker and kill him."

"That's probably not a good thing to say in front of the police, son." Detective Wallace stood and extended his hand. "Detective Richard Wallace. And you are?"

Jagger left the detective's hand outstretched while he patted me down like he was looking for holes. "Are you sure you're okay?"

"I'm fine. Just a little shaken up, that's all."

He blew out a breath and finally acknowledged the waiting detective, clasping the man's hand with his. "Jagger Langston."

"And your relationship to Ms. Holland is..."

"I'm her...boyfriend."

My mom's forehead wrinkled. "Umm... Did I miss something here?"

"I'll explain later, Mia," Edmund said.

Detective Wallace asked a few more questions, none of which any of us had answers to. Eventually, he flipped his little notebook closed and used a handkerchief to pick up the birthday card and put it into a plastic bag. "I'll be in touch once I know something."

Jagger folded his arms across his chest. "I've already spoken to Commissioner Frank about having my security team kept in the loop."

The detective frowned. "Great. You're one of those. I do my job the same whether I have the boss up my ass or not. In fact, all that does is take time away from going after the bad guys."

"Considering it's been *eight years* since Sutton was assaulted, and you still haven't caught the guy, I'm not entirely convinced that *doing your job* is enough."

The detective's face heated. Edmund noticed and stepped between the men. He laid a hand on Jagger's shoulder. "Everyone is just a little upset right now. Thank you for coming so quickly, Detective."

Wallace mumbled something I didn't catch, then nodded to me before walking to the door with Edmund following.

My hands were clammy, and I felt like my clothes were sticking to me, even though the apartment had central air. "I'm going to go wash up and get changed."

Jagger and Miles both stood at the same time, like they were planning on going with me. I smiled. "I'll be fine."

In the bathroom, I washed my face and doused my wrists with cold water, then I went to the bedroom and changed into a pair of yoga pants and an oversized sweatshirt. It wasn't lost on me that this had practically been my uniform for a full year after everything happened eight years ago. When I'd finally spoken to a therapist, she'd told me it was likely part of my PTSD, and I was avoiding wearing anything that might attract a man's attention.

I sat down on the bed, replaying the last hour in my mind until there was a knock on the door.

"Come in."

Jagger slipped inside, shutting the door behind him.

I smiled halfheartedly. "Are you coming to check on me or looking for a place to hide from my mother? I'm sure she couldn't wait to interrogate you about what's going on between us."

Jagger sat down on the bed next to me. "Both."

I leaned my head on his shoulder. "I can't believe this is happening. I thought I'd finally put this nightmare behind me and moved on."

"I'm sorry, but I promise you, I'm going to get to the bottom of this."

"I just feel so...violated. Like this guy has been watching me for who knows how long, and I had no idea. He might've been walking in and out of this building." I looked around. "Could he have been inside this apartment and I didn't know it? Am I that oblivious? I feel like such an idiot."

Jagger scooped me up and settled me on his lap. He brushed hair from my face. "You are not an idiot, and I don't want to ever hear you say something like that again. To be safe, I already called my security team and told them I want twenty-four-seven protection on you, at least until this guy's caught. I doubt he's made it into your apartment, but I'll also have them do a sweep of the entire place to make sure there aren't any cameras hidden or anything."

I felt all the blood drain from my face. "You think he hid cameras?"

"No, but I'm not taking any chances."

Jagger's thumb rubbed back and forth on my knee. It was one of the few times he'd touched me that my body didn't ignite. That made tears well in my eyes for an entirely different reason.

"I'm going to keep you safe, Sutton. I promise." Jagger caught my chin in his hand and tilted my head up so our eyes met. "Do you understand?"

I nodded.

"Good." He kissed my forehead and held me close for a long time before speaking again. "I'd just finished my conversation with Edmund when you called. About us."

I looked up at him. "How did that go?"

"He told me he'd kick my ass if I hurt you, whether I was his boss or not."

That made me smile. "He's my favorite of my collection of stepfathers."

"Unfortunately, he's witnessed me with a different woman on my arm at every event over the years. So I think it's going to take him a while to trust me with you."

My nose wrinkled.

Jagger kissed the tip of it and smiled. "The feeling is mutual, sweetheart."

· · ·

Hours later, we all sat around the dining room table eating Chinese food. We'd decided to order in, rather than go out for my birthday. My mother passed me the cardboard carton of Kung Pao chicken.

"I really hate the idea of you staying here."

"She's not," Jagger said. "She's staying at my place."

"Oh good."

I blinked a few times. "Hello? You two know I'm sitting here, right?"

Jagger frowned. "Do you want to stay here after what happened today?"

"No, but…"

He shrugged. "It's settled then. You're staying at my place. Miles can stay in the extra apartment. He's only here for one more night anyway, right?" He looked over at Miles, who nodded.

"Works for me." Miles shrugged.

"But the girls are at your place," I protested.

"What girls?" Mom pointed to another container. "Can I have the fried rice, please?"

"Jagger's nieces are staying with him."

"Aww…" Mom's eyes lit up. "Do you want kids of your own, Jagger?"

"Mom," I warned. "Please."

She shrugged. "What? We have a good nose. I'd like to see it passed on."

"I'll speak to Amelia and Olivia," Jagger said. "Neither of us is going to sleep tonight if you're here."

"I won't sleep either," Mom said.

Miles watched our exchange like a tennis match.

I sighed. "How about I stay in the extra apartment with Miles?"

Jagger frowned. "If that's what you really want."

"It is. Thank you."

"I'm putting a guard outside the door then."

I smiled, feeling loved and protected. "Okay."

"Works for me." Miles shrugged again. "Hey, Mia," he called from the other end of the table. "Did you see the necklace Jagger got Sutton for her birthday?"

"Oh my God." My hand covered my heart. "I forgot all about the necklace. I'm so sorry, Jagger. I didn't even say thank you. It's absolutely stunning."

"What do you call that type of design?" Miles smirked and gestured to his neck. "It's sort of like a collar."

I was going to *kill* him. Though when my eyes caught with Jagger's, there was a gleam there. I cleared my throat and looked at my mother. "It's a choker with a beautiful sapphire in the center. I'll show you after we finish eating."

"I can't wait." Mom beamed.

The five of us finished dinner and sat around talking for a while. Mom got to *ooh* and *ahh* at my birthday gift from Jagger, and I was honestly grateful when she said they were going to get going. It wasn't even eight yet, the time our dinner reservation had been, yet it felt like midnight. I was mentally spent and physically running on empty as I closed the door behind her and Edmund.

"I'm going to go pack my things," Miles said.

"Okay. I'll do that in a minute too."

Jagger was on the couch. The box containing his gift still sat on the coffee table. I gestured to it, standing before his spread legs. "Your gift was really overboard."

He shrugged. "When I saw it, I knew it was exactly what I wanted to give you."

I nibbled on my fingernail. "Does it...have any meaning to you?"

The corner of his lip quirked. "Like what?"

I squinted, trying to read him. Did he really not know what I was asking or was he just screwing with me? "Well, what made you want to give me that necklace specifically?"

He grabbed my hands and yanked. I yelped as I fell on top of him. Jagger rolled us so my back was to the couch, and he hovered over me.

"It means you belong to me."

"So it is...a collar?"

His smile was full of mischief. "Call it whatever you want."

"Have you always given the women that you were... seeing one of those?"

"Never."

"Why not?"

"Because I would never expect a woman to belong to me, unless I belonged to her."

The air rushed from my lungs in the most amazing way. "It's the best gift I've ever received, and I'm not referring to its monetary value."

Jagger leaned his forehead against mine. "I don't know what I would've done if something had happened to you today."

Tears filled my eyes. "I'm falling for you, Jagger."

He kissed my lips. "Then you better catch up, sweetheart, because today made me realize I'm already there."

Sutton

**I**t smells delicious in here."

Jagger tossed his keys on the kitchen counter and came around the island, wrapping his arms around my waist as I stood at the stove. He kissed my neck. "And I wasn't talking about the food."

I set the wooden spoon down and turned in his arms, linking my hands behind his neck. "I figured the least I could do is make you a homecooked meal, since you've been letting me freeload here all week."

"No need to cook." He pressed his mouth to mine and pulled back with the flesh of my lower lip between his teeth. "I'll just take the rent from your body."

"In that case, I might be paid up until the end of the month. I've been here for five days, and I think we've had sex ten times."

"I can't help it. I wake up hard thinking about you one floor down, and then I can't stop thinking about coming home and having you again." He slid a hand into the waistband of my yoga pants and palmed a handful of my ass. "I have to go out of town tomorrow afternoon for the night, so I may need to bank a few before then."

"How about I feed you first?"

"Your pussy? Perfect."

I laughed and gave his shoulder a nudge. "I'm serious. I made chicken piccata with gnocchi."

He pouted. "I'd rather have you."

"And you can. *After* you eat dinner."

Jagger had been slipping into bed with me each morning this week instead of going to the gym. We both worked all day, and in the evening, he stopped here before going upstairs and relieving the sitter. Last night I'd decided to go to bed wearing nothing but the choker he'd bought me for my birthday, and when he found me like that this morning, we'd both been a few minutes late getting to the office. I knew he had a million things going on at work, so the fact that he'd made this time for me meant a lot. Even though we were staying in two separate apartments, waking up to him and having him come home to me had settled us into a nice domestic routine that I loved. It allowed me to forget what happened last week and live in a fairy-tale-like bubble. But...it wasn't really reality, and it would soon be time for me to go home.

I pressed a chaste kiss to Jagger's lips and pointed. "Go sit. Dinner is just about ready."

Surprisingly, he listened. Jagger took off his suit jacket while I plated two dishes and opened a bottle of wine. His phone rang just as I set dinner on the table, and I loved that he sent the call to voicemail and turned the screen facedown so he couldn't see notifications coming through. We'd come such a long way together in a relatively short time.

"This is delicious." He forked chicken into his mouth. "Though if I keep skipping the gym in the morning and you keep cooking like this, you might not like my body so much anymore."

"I'm pretty sure that's not possible." Jagger had an incredible physique, but I was turned on more by who he was than his rippling muscles. There was something in the way he spoke to me, the way he looked at me, that made me feel like I was precious to him. This morning, he'd stared into my eyes while he pumped in and out of me and growled the word *mine.* I'd spent half the day hot and bothered just thinking about it. Even now, I felt my cheeks flush. So I lifted the chilled wine to my lips, hoping to cool off. Otherwise, the dinner I'd spent an hour making would be tomorrow's leftovers. I cleared my throat. "Where are you heading tomorrow?"

"I have to go down to DC to meet with the DOJ again. We think we found a solution to their concerns that we can both live with."

"You're going to tweak your algorithm?"

Jagger shook his head. "No, but we're going to propose a change in the information we feed into it. Right now, all of the big investment firms use data from the same group of sources—PitchBook, Bloomberg, etc. We plug their datasets and analytical tools into our proprietary algorithm to analyze the millions of different companies that exist in the world. It's not really that surprising that what comes out might be similar when we're all putting in the same thing. We're going to propose that we start using only information that is proprietary to us."

"You mean you'd do all the legwork to create the data in-house? Wouldn't that be an enormous undertaking?"

"It would be if we didn't buy an existing data and research platform. Tomorrow night I'm having dinner with the CEO of MSL—Market Search Link. They're smaller than the top three, but we've been using their data for a few years, and I think we can just add resources and bring it in-house fairly painlessly. If we can reach a tentative agreement, we're going to present the idea to the DOJ."

"Oh wow. And MSL is willing to sell?"

"It'll cost a small fortune—they realize we need them more than they need us right now—but it will give us more control in the end."

We spent the rest of dinner talking business, and then Jagger insisted I stay seated while he cleared the table and loaded the dishwasher. I did, though I moved to the stool on the other side of the counter to watch him. The man somehow managed to be sexy rinsing dishes and wiping counters.

"I spoke to Detective Wallace today," Jagger said.

The announcement was akin to throwing a bucket of water over me. I sat up stick-straight. "Oh?"

"They were able to get traces of DNA off the envelope. But it didn't match anyone in their systems."

The smile that had been on my face while watching the domestic side of Jagger faded. "What about the video?"

"The envelope was delivered by a courier who regularly works this route. The card was dropped off at their office, which is a shithole uptown, and they don't have any security cameras."

"So they have nothing? Again they hit a brick wall?"

He nodded. "But it doesn't mean that's what'll happen to me. They won't hand over the DNA profile they created from the envelope sample, but I asked if my security team can have the envelope to do our own search. My hands aren't tied by the law like theirs are. Of course, Wallace got pissed off and said no. But I went over his head, and I'm waiting to hear back. I think we'll get to do our own testing."

"I was really hoping they'd come up with *something* this time." I shook my head and looked down. "I've lived in fear for too long, and I can't let it rule my life anymore."

"I agree. Leave the worrying to me and my team."

I smiled sadly. "I appreciate that. I really do. But I can't stay holed up in this apartment and have security follow me everywhere I go."

"Why not?" Jagger seemed genuinely confused.

"Because I need to reclaim what I've lost. My fears aren't going to vanish overnight. I'm sure I'll still check over my shoulder for a long time, but taking the train to work instead of having your driver take me, and walking on the busy Manhattan streets, sleeping in my own place— those are all ways of reclaiming what he tried to take from me all over again."

Jagger walked over and held my shoulders as he spoke. "I'd prefer you stay here. I like having you here."

I turned my head and kissed his hand. "I like being with you, too. And I appreciate all that you've done for me. But it's time for me to go back home. I'll get my things after work tomorrow. You're not going to be here anyway. And besides, your sister is going to come in a few weeks."

"I don't give a shit. I own the building. I'll kick a tenant out if I have to so Catherine has a place to stay."

"That's sweet, but I need to go home, Jagger. Moving to New York and living on my own was a big step for me, one that was long overdue. After everything happened, I dropped out of NYU and spent the better part of a year inside my mother's apartment. When I finally was ready to go back to college two years later, I left New York to leave my past behind me. But even then, I wasn't standing on my own. Miles came with me, and we moved in together. Being back here and being independent is something I really needed to do, and I don't want to go backward." I reached for Jagger's cheek. "Can you understand that?"

He pulled his head back. "No."

I blinked a few times. "No, you can't understand that?"

"No, you're not going back to that building. He knows where you live."

Jagger's commands might be attractive in the bedroom, but they were *extremely* unattractive at the moment. It pissed me off that he thought he could tell me what to do. My hands went to my hips. "You know you aren't the one who's making this decision, right?"

"You're being unreasonable. It's safer here."

"How? If this guy figured out that I moved back to New York, don't you think he can figure out that I'm staying here?"

Jagger's face heated—and not the good kind of hot it got in the bedroom. "That's all the more reason for you to stay here, or better yet, come stay at my place where I can keep an eye on you."

"I need to go home, Jagger."

"There's a difference between want and need. You don't *need* to go home."

I rubbed my temples, feeling a headache coming on. "Okay, then I want to. And I'm going to."

Jagger studied me. Not finding anything that made him happy, he walked to the dining room and grabbed his suit jacket.

"Where are you going?"

"I need to make arrangements. If you're not staying, at least let me put extra security on your building."

I could see in his face he was bending further than he was used to. And he meant well. Plus, I didn't need to *leap* back into my life. Baby stepping was okay. I nodded, thinking we'd reached a compromise. "Okay. Thank you." I laid my palms on his chest. "But can't you make the calls after…"

Jagger shook his head. "No. I *need* to go."

I pulled my hands back. "You mean you *want* to."

"I'm glad you can see there's a difference."

He went to the door and didn't look back before walking out.

•  •  •

The next morning, I waited until six before getting out of bed. Something in my gut told me Jagger wasn't going to come today, even though he had every other morning since I'd come to stay. Still, I laid in bed, hoping. The latest he'd ever showed up was five thirty, yet I still listened for the door as I took a shower and got ready for work.

Full-blown disappointment had set in by the time I'd finished drying my hair and getting dressed. By seven, when there was still no sign of him, I decided to go upstairs.

Louise answered the door and said Jagger had already left for work, but Amelia heard my voice and came running.

"Sutton, will you braid my hair?"

"Of course."

I went inside, and Louise gave me a cup of coffee while I made two French braids, one on each side of Amelia's head.

"Is your sister still sleeping?"

Amelia nodded and rolled her eyes. "She took *forever* to go back to sleep last night. Uncle Jagger had a bad dream."

I stopped braiding. "He had a bad dream? Did it wake you?"

"I didn't wake up. But Olivia woke up when he yelled, and then *she* woke *me* up."

"Does that...happen often? Your uncle has bad dreams?"

Amelia shrugged. "Not that I can remember. But Olivia sometimes has them, and she wants to talk to me for hours after. It's *so* annoying."

I wanted to ask more questions—*What did your uncle yell? Did he go back to sleep? Did he say anything at all?* But I couldn't pump a little girl for information. And it seemed like she didn't think too much of her uncle having a nightmare, so the less questions the better.

As soon as I got to the office, though, I went up to see Jagger. Unfortunately, his assistant said he was in a meeting. I hesitated, unsure if I should leave a message or not, but in the end I did since he was going out of town to deal with the DOJ tonight, and I wanted to speak to him before he went.

By five o'clock though, I was wishing I hadn't, since he didn't call me back. Uneasiness settled in the pit of my belly, and I shot off a quick text.

> **Sutton: Hey. Just wanted to check in. Was hoping I would see you before you left.**

I stared at the phone for a long time before hitting enter and decided to add one more sentence.

> **Sutton: Good luck with your meeting tonight. Call me when you have time.**

I was just about to shut down my laptop when an email arrived from Jagger's assistant. I clicked and discovered it was a meeting cancellation notice. He was canceling our regular weekly mentor meeting for Monday. Disappointed, but not surprised, I tried to shake it off and had started packing up my desk when Edmund came down.

"Hey, sweetheart. You leaving?"

I zipped my laptop into my bag and noticed he also had his briefcase slung over his shoulder. "I am. Are you actually getting out of here, too? It's only five o'clock. I didn't think you ever left this place before six or seven."

"It happens every once in a while." He smiled. "You want a lift? I drove today."

"You did? I thought you always took the train?"

He shrugged. "Sometimes I take the car. Gotta start the battery and run it every now and then."

I lifted the strap of my bag to my shoulder, and Edmund put his hand out for me to go first. Together we headed to the elevator.

"Thank you for the offer, but I'm actually going to Jagger's building," I said. "Which is the opposite direction of your place, so I'll take the train. I'm moving back to my apartment today."

"That's fine. I can take you to get your things and then bring you back down to Gramercy Park."

*Wait a minute...* Edmund *happened* to be leaving on time today and he *happened* to drive, and now he *happened* to be available to run me all over the City? I stopped walking. "Mom put you up to this, didn't she? I spoke to her this morning and told her I was moving back home. She wasn't happy about it, but when I refused to change my mind, she tried to insist that she at least go with me the first time I went back."

"No." He shook his head. "Your mother didn't say a word to me."

I narrowed my eyes.

"All right, all right." He held up his hands. "I knew. But it wasn't your mother. It was the bossman."

"Jagger asked you to drive me?"

Edmund shook his head. "He told me your plans for today and asked me to keep an eye on you while he was gone."

We arrived at the elevator bank just as the doors slid open. It was pretty full, but there was room for two more.

"Can I give you a ride, please?" Edmund asked softly. "My car is in the basement garage."

I knew he meant well, so I nodded. "Sure."

Inside the car, I buckled and attempted to sound casual. "How was Jagger today?"

My stepfather put the car into gear. "How do you mean?"

I shrugged. "He was just...very stressed last night." I left off that I had anything to do with it and added, "He told me about the meeting with MSL tonight and the DOJ Monday."

"He's got a lot on his plate, that's for sure. But he didn't seem any worse for the wear than he normally does."

We got to the street-level parking garage gate, and Edmund inserted a card into the machine. The arm ahead of us went up, and we slid into the busy rush-hour traffic.

"I'm not going to lie, Sutton. When Jagger first told me about the two of you, I wasn't exactly happy. He's intelligent and hardworking, but he can also be difficult. Though now I can see he really cares about you. He has the DOJ on his ass, two little girls to take care of, and he was in my office at seven thirty this morning asking me to look after you. And that was *after* he'd stopped at the police station."

"He went to the police station this morning?"

Edmund's eyes flashed to me and back to the road. "Jagger said he'd updated you on the status of things with Detective Wallace."

"He did, but he didn't mention he was going there today. Do you know what he went for?"

"To put pressure on them about the investigation, I assume." Edmund smiled. "The things that I was concerned about between you and Jagger are actually coming in handy. He's being difficult on your behalf."

We rode uptown to Jagger's building and collected my stuff from the spare apartment, then drove back down to Mom's apartment where I'd been staying. I was nervous when we pulled up, but when I saw one of the guys from Jagger's security team stationed in front of the building and spotted another positioned near the elevator bank, I relaxed a little, grateful that Jagger was as stubborn as he was.

Nestor tipped his hat as usual, and the ground didn't crumble beneath me as I walked into the quiet apartment with my stepfather in tow. He stayed for a few minutes before I told him he should go home to his wife. He was gracious and told me to call him if I needed anything. Then I was alone.

Surprisingly, I wasn't scared, at least not for my safety. I knew the security team downstairs wouldn't let anything happen to me. Jagger had made sure of that. But as the hours went by and I still didn't hear from him, my fears started to grow.

Those fears had nothing to do with the man who had assaulted me resurfacing and everything to do with the man I'd fallen for pulling away.

— CHAPTER —
# THIRTY-THREE

Sutton

Saturday passed with only minimal contact from Jagger. He'd let me know he was back home from his trip now, and unfortunately, things hadn't gone as smoothly as he'd planned. His sister had checked out of the hospital sooner than she was supposed to and disappeared, and Olivia had wet the bed while he was gone. There were more things on his plate than ever. Yet still, in my heart I knew none of those things was the reason Jagger was keeping his distance from me.

Saturday night, I had dinner with my mom. She was still on a high, thinking her daughter was dating one of New York's most eligible, wealthy bachelors. I could've used someone to talk to about what was going on with Jagger, but I didn't want to disappoint her or make her worry. So when I got back to the apartment at ten o'clock, I decided to call Miles.

He answered, took one look at my glum face, and jumped up from the couch like he was about to run straight to New York, three-thousand miles away. "What's the matter? Did you get another envelope? Are you in your apartment alone?"

I attempted a smile, but it got tangled somewhere between my heart and my mouth. "I'm fine. Nothing happened."

"Then why do you look like that?"

I sighed. "I think Jagger is going to dump me."

"What? Why? That's impossible. That man is so into you. I saw it with my own eyes last weekend. He went all caveman-like when you got that card. I don't usually like the possessive type, but it was freaking hot."

"I know. I don't get it either. I feel like I have whiplash from how quickly things changed."

"Break it down for me. Something must've happened. Start from the night I left. Did you see each other Monday?"

I went through my week—summarizing how Jagger had slipped into my bed each morning and come home to me each night before going up to his nieces—until I reached the night before he left for DC. "Everything was going really great, or at least I thought so, until I told him I wanted to move back home."

"He's an alpha," Miles said. "He's probably just upset that you're not staying in his lair where he can protect you. He'll get over it."

"That's what I thought, too. But he didn't come down the next morning like he had been. I had the key to the spare apartment to give back, so I used it as an excuse to go upstairs before work, hoping I could talk to him. He was already gone, but Amelia asked me to braid her hair, so I wound up hanging out with her for a bit, and she told me her uncle had woken Olivia up last night yelling. She said he'd had a bad dream."

"Is that what really happened, or is that a little kid's take on something else going on?"

I shrugged. "I think it's what really happened."

"Did he ever have nightmares when he stayed with you?"

I shook my head. "Never."

"Hmm... Maybe it's all the stress? I saw the shit with the government on the news again, and he's got two little girls staying with him, and then all your shit on top of that."

"Great." I frowned. "So I'm the straw that broke the camel's back? Is that what you're saying?"

"No, not at all. I just meant the guy is busy. I think that just comes with the territory when you're dating a mogul."

"I guess." I chewed on my fingernail. "But he always seemed to be able to make time for me before. I don't know. Maybe I'm just overthinking things. It's only been a few days."

"He definitely doesn't seem like the beat-around-the-bush type of guy. Don't you think he'd tell you if there was a problem?"

"I hope so." I sighed. "Anyway, enough about me. Tell me about your week."

Miles's face lit up. "I met someone."

"You did? When? Why don't I know about it yet?"

"Because it was only three days ago, and he only left my apartment a couple of hours ago."

"He just left your apartment from last night?"

"No, from three days ago." He grinned. "Unlike your busy mogul, mine has all the time in the world. He's an actor. Of course, he's not currently filming anything, so I guess that technically makes his profession *unemployed*, but actor has a nicer ring to it, doesn't it?"

It wasn't the first time Miles had fallen for someone without a job. I was pretty certain the last time when it ended, he'd told me to smack him if he ever dated someone who didn't have a promising career and six figures in a 401k. But he seemed happy, so rather than remind him of that, we spent an hour deep-diving the guy's social media together. Unlike most of the men Miles dated, Rodrigo had photos of his family instead of pictures of him and five shirtless buddies drinking tequila from a shotski.

"I really like this guy," Miles said. "You might not believe this, but we didn't have sex for the entire three days he stayed here. He said he wanted to get to know me first. I can't remember the last time a guy actually wanted to talk to me instead of bend over."

I smiled. "I'm happy for you."

"I'm happy for you, too, cookie. Jagger is crazy about you. I saw it with my own eyes. He's just preoccupied, and you're worried because you're crazy about him too."

I forced another smile. "I'm sure you're right."

But my gut still told me there was more to it than just Jagger being busy.

•  •  •

Sunday came and went. I intentionally didn't text Jagger, though it killed me not to, to see if he would contact me. I busied myself with errands—gym, dry cleaners, Trader Joe's, the bookstore, and two trips to Starbucks. I checked my phone like a fiend, and the disappointment from not seeing Jagger's name weighed heavier and heavier on my heart as the hours passed.

I ate boxed macaroni and cheese, watched a movie starring Jim Carrey that I assumed would be funny because, well, *Jim Carrey.* But I found myself crying at *Eternal Sunshine of the Spotless Mind,* which turned out to be about a couple who split up and decide to undergo a medical procedure to have each other erased from their memories, only to realize they didn't want to forget the bad parts because it meant losing the good, too.

By Monday, I'd decided I was being ridiculous, pulled up my big-girl panties, and dragged myself to work. I went to the early-morning management briefing that was open to all employees. Jack was also there. I hadn't seen him in a while, and after the meeting let out, he jogged to catch up to me as I reached the elevator.

"Hey. Long time no see."

I smiled. "I know. Did you give up coffee?"

The elevator doors slid open, and he put his hand out for me to enter first. "Nah. I've just been up to my eyeballs with all this DOJ stuff."

My ears perked up. "Did you go to the meeting in DC on Friday?"

He shook his head. "Not to the DOJ meeting, but my team went to DC to work on the MSL acquisition."

When the doors opened at my floor, Jack stepped off with me. "We're in a holding pattern until we know if the DOJ will accept what Langston put together to drop the antitrust case, so today I can enjoy a good cup of coffee that takes a few minutes to make."

The security globe caught my attention as soon as we rounded the corner to my desk. *Good. Maybe this will get him to pick up the phone.*

"You need a refresh?" Jack pointed to my cup.

"No, thank you. But stop on the way back if you have time. I want to ask you a few questions about something they said during the briefing."

"Sure." He smiled.

I hated playing high-school games, but that's what I was resorting to now. Jack returned just as I'd figured out some stupid question to ask about the annual prospectuses they'd showed at the morning meeting. He stuck around, forearms leaning on the half-wall of my cubicle, for a solid ten minutes. I waited for my desk phone to ring, as it had the last few times Jagger watched this kind of exchange, but it never did. My attempt to get a reaction had backfired, leaving me feeling even worse than I had yesterday, because now I wondered if he was even watching me anymore.

When Jack finally left, I stared up at the globe for a long time before slouching back into my seat and forcing myself to work on the project I'd been assigned. Thankfully, I loved what I was doing, and before I knew it, it was two o'clock in the afternoon. I hadn't even eaten anything today, so I grabbed my purse and went to the deli next door to get a salad. My nose was in my phone as I walked through the lobby, and by the time I looked up, I almost walked straight into Jagger. And a woman.

It took a few seconds to go through my mental rolodex and register who she was—Marla, his foster sister who worked in the London office.

The look on Jagger's face made me wonder if he'd been going to try to walk right past me. Though he didn't get the chance when I stopped in front of him.

"Hi."

Jagger nodded. "Hello, Sutton."

Marla's head ping-ponged between us. "Sutton? As in..."

Jagger's jaw flexed. "Yes." He motioned to Marla. "Marla Emerson, this is Sutton Holland."

I put my hand out, but Marla went in for a hug. "It's so nice to meet you."

The fact that she apparently knew who I was soothed the ache in my chest, at least somewhat. I smiled when she stepped back. "It's nice to meet you."

Her eyes gleamed. "I've heard a lot about you."

I looked at Jagger. His face was filled with tension and gave away nothing. I attempted to sound casual. "Was I... the topic of lunch conversation today?"

She waved me off. "Unfortunately, not today. We had a boring business lunch. But I heard all about you last week."

*Last week. When things were still going well...* I supposed I should see it as a positive sign that he hadn't said anything negative since then.

Jagger put a hand on her back. "We should get going. The attorneys are waiting for us upstairs."

Marla rolled her eyes. "He just wants to keep me away from you so I won't tell you about the time he hotboxed the janitor's closet at school and tried to blame it on our eighty-year-old math teacher. Or the time he replaced the school song they played over the loudspeaker every morning with recordings of women moaning—I *still* don't want to know how he got those."

I smiled, but when I looked to Jagger and saw nothing on his face, my smile felt more like a sigh. Marla looked over as well, caught his stoic reaction, and returned to study my face before she frowned. "It was nice meeting you, Sutton."

Jagger offered a curt nod and clearly couldn't wait to get the hell away from me. I was left more confused than ever.

The rest of the day dragged on, and my feelings bounced between, *what an asshole, giving me the cold shoulder* and *what if it's really over—how will my heart come back from this?*

I attempted to throw myself back into the assignment I'd been working on, but my focus was no longer there. By six, the office started to clear out, and I stared at my screen, debating whether I should march upstairs and demand that Jagger speak to me. I must've been really lost in thought because I didn't hear anyone approach until a voice startled me.

"Sutton?"

I turned, and Marla smiled.

"Oh, hi, Marla."

She looked at my screen. The saver was on, which I hadn't even noticed. "I see you're as laser-focused on nothing as Jagger is."

There was something so honest and nonjudgmental about her. It made it easy to open up. "I might be able to focus if I knew why I was suddenly getting the cold shoulder."

Marla smiled sadly. "I recognized the steely face he had today from when we were kids. It's part of the wall he puts up when he's vulnerable and doesn't want to get hurt. Unfortunately, I saw it a lot back then."

"Did he say *why* he was shutting me out?"

She shook her head. "I tried to pry, but he did the same thing to me. When he was a kid, he built walls to protect himself, but as an adult I feel like they often act as a prison, keeping everyone out."

I frowned, and she continued, "I love the guy, but he can really be a stubborn ass sometimes. Anyway, I don't know what's going on, but I stopped down because I wanted you to know that he's never told me about a woman before. He's really crazy about you."

"He has a funny way of showing it lately."

Marla sighed. "I know. It's not an excuse, but Jagger fights a lot of demons. Eventually though, he always makes it through to the other side. And he's worth waiting for. He's stubborn, and arrogant, and he can be excruciatingly annoying. But he's also loyal and protective and patient." She looked at her watch. "I have to get going or I'm going to miss my flight. But I really enjoyed meeting you and hope to get to know you better."

I smiled. "Same."

She waved and turned to walk away. I replayed everything she'd said in my mind as I watched her go—stubborn, arrogant, *demons*.

"Marla?" I called.

She stopped, and I went over to her. "Has Jagger ever had any nightmares that you know of?"

Her face fell. "God, yes. They were brutal, but he'd never talk about them. He came to live with us for a month after he got out of the military while he figured out his next move. He seemed like such a different person after four years in the Marines—until I heard him in the middle of the night again. The nightmares hadn't changed, but they seemed to have gotten worse."

# THIRTY-FOUR

### Jagger
10 years ago

I woke drenched in sweat and bolted upright. It took me a full minute to realize I was in a bedroom at the Emersons' and not a tent in Khalari. My chest felt like an elephant was sitting on it, but it was only the weight of the dream—the same damn one I'd had for months now. It always ended the same way, with the crack of gunfire, followed by the thud of a body hitting the dirt. I never saw the aftermath of the gun going off. But I didn't need to; it was a moment seared into my brain forever.

I looked over at the end table, where I put my pills after I took one when I brushed my teeth at night, but the bottle wasn't there. Shaking my head, I scoffed at myself. *Great. You got your sister to take all her meds but forgot to take your own.*

My shirt was soaked through, clinging to my back. I peeled it off as I pushed out of bed and headed downstairs to the kitchen. Standing in the dark, I poured a glass of water from the tap, shook two pills from the prescription bottle that instructed me to take one, and popped both in my mouth. It was going to take them a while to kick in, and I needed something to take the edge off now. So I went back to my room, dug out my emergency stash of weed, and quietly rolled a joint in the dark. The Emersons didn't like me smoking in the house, so I opened the bedroom window, climbed out, and sat on the slanted roof.

Two puffs in, the window next to me opened and Marla swung a leg through.

"I smelled that with the window shut," she said.

"Sorry. Did it wake you?"

She took a seat next to me and held out her hand for the joint. "No." She inhaled and held her breath for thirty seconds before letting it out. "But your nightmare earlier did."

My eyes flashed to meet hers. "I yelled?"

She nodded and extended the joint back to me. "You've been doing it almost every night since you got back."

"Sorry."

"There's nothing to apologize for." Marla smiled sadly. "Do you want to talk about it?"

I shook my head. "Not really."

She bumped her shoulder with mine. "Shocker. You're such an open book, Langston."

I smiled and brought the joint to my lips.

"How are your sister and your mom doing?" she asked.

"I think they take turns making me nuts. I got Catherine back on her meds last week, but now my mother is off hers and MIA." I paused. "It's fucked up. I was gone for four years, and when I go there, it's like I never left. Nothing's changed."

"I know one thing that's changed," Marla said. I offered her the joint back, but she waved me off. "You. You've changed."

I looked over at my foster sister. "It's impossible to have witnessed the shit I've seen and be the same."

"But you're talking to someone, right?"

I'd gone to a doctor at the VA hospital to get sleeping pills. He wanted me to start talking to a therapist, but pouring my heart out to some guy who would ask me shit like "*And how does that make you feel?*" wasn't my thing. Though I didn't want Marla to worry, so I nodded. "Yeah, I got myself a doc."

"Good."

I'd already talked about myself more than I cared to, so I changed the subject. "How's the new job going?"

"Awful. My boss is a chauvinistic dick. He asked me to *fetch* him a cup of coffee. I'm not his personal assistant. I have a damn degree in economics."

"Accidentally spill it on him."

She smiled. "I should."

I took a long draw on the joint and spoke while holding it in. "Why don't you quit?"

"Because I'm not sure what I want to do or where I want to go. Actually, that's not true. I'd love to go live in London for a while."

"Really?"

Marla nodded.

"So do it."

She snort-laughed and covered her mouth. "Oh my God. I'm really stoned already. How are you still smoking that thing?"

I chuckled. "Bet you no one in London sounds like a hyena when they laugh."

She shoved me. "Shut up."

"Seriously." I inhaled again. "Why don't you find a job in London, if that's what you really want to do?"

"Because I'm not you, boy genius with balls of steel."

"I prefer man genius now."

She smiled and sighed. "Maybe you can open an office in London one day when you're rich, and I'll run it for you."

I shrugged. "Okay. I'll do that." Feeling pretty high myself, I tapped the head of the joint against a shingle to put it out. "But I'm going to try to crash now. I have a long drive ahead of me tomorrow."

"Where are you going?"

"To visit a buddy of mine's family."

"Oh." Marla's face softened. "Nelson. Mom told me about that. How come the Marines didn't ship his stuff home when he—"

"They did. But I have some stuff I won from him in a card game that I want to return."

She smiled. "You're a good friend."

If she only knew the truth. I wasn't a good friend or a good leader. If I had been, John Nelson would still be alive. I pushed to my feet and held a hand out to help Marla up.

"'Night."

I had one leg in my window when Marla called. "Hey, Jagger?"

"Yeah?"

"If you ever want to talk about your dreams or... anything, I'll always be here for you. Even if my window isn't next to yours anymore."

"Thanks, Marla."

•  •  •

The following morning, I got an early start on the drive down to Maryland. Sergeant John Nelson's family lived in a small town along the coast that looked really nice as I drove through. My heart grew heavy as I turned onto his street and passed a dad teaching his little boy how to ride a bike. My friend would never get to do that because of me.

Nelson's house was a small blue Cape. There was an old push-mower in the middle of the front lawn, which was almost knee high and only half cut. It looked like someone had given up in the middle of the job. The front door was open, except for the screen door, and I could hear a kid's show playing from a TV inside somewhere. I took a deep breath and knocked.

A woman who looked vaguely familiar came to the door and smiled. "You must be Jagger."

"Bridget?"

She opened the screen door. The bottom was wood, so I'd only seen the top half of her until that moment. When I saw the rest, my heart leaped into my throat.

"You're..."

She rubbed her very swollen belly and smiled. "Eight months along. John got leave to come home for our son's first day of kindergarten. It happened then."

I closed my eyes. "I had no idea."

"How could you? I hadn't even told John yet. I had so many complications with my first pregnancy and wound up bedridden for four months. John was such a worry-wart, and I didn't want him to not be focused while he was where he was, so I didn't tell him. He was supposed to be discharged when I was six months along, so I figured he'd come home to a big surprise."

I swallowed.

Bridget stepped back and waved me in. "Well, come on in."

I panicked and thumbed behind me. "Actually, could I...finish mowing the lawn for you?"

"Sergeant Langston, I can't let you do that, even if it does take me all day to get through it."

"It's Jagger. I'm not a marine anymore, so no need for the honorific."

She smiled. "My husband would disagree. He always said, *Once a marine, always a marine.*"

I looked back at the lawn. "I'd really like to mow, if it's okay with you."

She shrugged. "I'm not going to stop you."

I extended the box in my hand. "These are the things we spoke about on the phone."

Bridget took the box, and I took my time mowing the rest of Sergeant John Nelson's lawn. It was hot as hell today, but I didn't mind one bit. After, I put the mower back in the garage, and then I couldn't avoid his wife or going inside his house anymore.

Bridget opened the door with a tall glass of lemonade in her hand. "For you."

I nodded. "Thank you."

The contents of the box I'd brought were laid out all over the table—things I'd won over the last few years of playing cards. Most of it was stupid—a belt, a cell phone charger, one left sneaker, a toothbrush, a piece of paper with his Netflix password. But there was also a leather wallet I thought she might actually want to keep. Bridget lifted the sneaker. "I wondered why there was only one when they shipped home John's things."

I smiled. "I figured maybe the belt and wallet might be nice to have."

She picked up two small photos I'd never seen before and held them out to me. "These were inside his wallet."

One was a photo of me and Nelson with our arms around each other. I swallowed. "We took this the night we finished basic training."

She gestured to it. "Turn it over."

I recognized John's chicken-scratch handwriting. *Lucas, if I'm ever not around and you need something, call this guy.* My phone number was listed after.

*Jesus Christ.* There was a sting behind my eyes.

Bridget patted my hand. "You meant a lot to him."

"He meant a lot to me, too."

The second picture was of their son, Lucas. He had on his dad's helmet, which was five sizes too big for his little head, a diaper, and a smile.

Bridget pointed to the refrigerator. "That's one of my favorite pictures of Lucas. He looks just like his daddy. John had me make a copy to take with him."

"Would it...be all right if I kept it?" I asked. I wasn't even sure why I wanted it or what I would do with it.

Bridget smiled. "I'd like that. Would you like the photo of you and John, too?"

"No. That's for Lucas. You tell him to use the number on the back if he ever needs anything. Same goes for you, Bridget."

"Thank you, Jagger." She kissed my cheek. "You take care of yourself."

—— CHAPTER ——
# THIRTY-FIVE

Sutton

By the following week, Jagger had completely stopped answering my texts. His security guys were still guarding my building like it was Fort Knox, but I was losing sleep trying to make sense of everything. I knew he was busy and going through a lot, but I could no longer justify the way he was treating me. And I planned to tell him that today at our weekly mentor meeting.

Ten minutes before we were to get together, I went to the ladies' room to freshen up. I'd intentionally worn blue, Jagger's favorite color and one he'd told me more than once he liked me in. The dress also happened to be the same exact shade as the center stone on the choker he'd given me. I lined my lips in the mirror and put on a fresh coat of lipstick before taking a deep breath. It didn't do much to calm my nerves, but at least I looked good. As I went to the bathroom door, my phone chimed with an incoming email. My stomach had already been nervous, but it knotted seeing the message was from Jagger's assistant. *Another meeting cancellation?* Not five minutes before the start time! I shook my head. *No, just no.* He was not avoiding me again today.

I'd just pretend I hadn't seen the message and go upstairs as scheduled. And that's just what I did. Smiling bright, I opened the glass door to the executive floor and hoped the receptionist hadn't been told about the cancellation.

"Hi, Amara." I pointed to the back and kept walking. "I'm late for a meeting with the boss."

She smiled back, none the wiser. "Better put a move on. He's been grumpy lately."

*Gee, tell me about it.*

Jagger's assistant was in with him. He was reaching for something on the bookshelf behind him, so she saw me before he did. "Oh, hi, Sutton. Are you here for the mentor meeting? I'm sorry, but I sent you a cancellation a few minutes ago. You probably didn't see it."

Jagger turned, and our gazes locked. "Actually, I did. But I really need a few minutes with Mr. Langston."

"Umm..." His assistant's forehead wrinkled, and she looked to her boss.

He put his hand up. "It's fine. Shut the door on the way out, please, Laura."

She looked between us again but didn't say anything more. I stayed rooted in place, just a few feet inside the office, as she walked out and closed the door behind her.

Jagger gestured to the guest chairs. "Would you like to sit?"

"No, I don't want to sit. What the hell is going on, Jagger?"

He looked down at his desk and reached for some papers, shuffling them into a pile. "You'll have to be a little more specific. I have a hundred things going on these days."

"There's only one that I care about at the moment, and I think you know exactly what I'm referring to."

"I've been busy."

"You were busy last week and the week before, too. Yet you somehow always found time for me. What's changed?"

He met and held my stare for a long time before looking away. "I needed some space."

"Is it because I went back home when you didn't want me to?"

He shook his head and continued to avoid eye contact.

"Jagger." My voice cracked. "Can you please look at me?"

He turned to meet my eyes.

"Is it because of your nightmare?"

He blinked. "What?"

"I came up the morning after I told you I was going back home to give you the keys to the apartment, and Amelia mentioned it."

The mask he'd been wearing slipped, and for a moment he looked so vulnerable. His eyes filled with pain and sadness. Without giving it any thought, I walked toward him, wanting to touch him and offer comfort.

But Jagger's stern voice stopped me in my tracks a few feet away. He held up a hand again. "No."

"No?"

He shook his head. "I'm sorry, Sutton."

"Sorry about what? Avoiding me the last week?"

"No. I'm sorry I let things between us get out of hand. It was a mistake."

I'd been on the verge of tears until I heard that word. It felt like someone had sucker-punched me in the stomach, and it made me angry. "A *mistake*? A week ago you told me you'd fallen for me and gave me a gift you said meant I was yours."

He hung his head. "I'm sorry."

*This* was the way we were ending? Not even a reason? He owed me that much. "Why is it a mistake, Jagger? I *deserve* an explanation."

"I told you at the beginning I wasn't looking for more than sex."

"And neither was I!" I raised my voice. "But more than that happened between us, and you damn well know it."

I felt another rush of emotions coming, this time hurt more than anger, and there was no way in hell I was going to let him see me cry. So I turned on my heel, rushing for the door to at least keep a small piece of my dignity.

When I reached the handle, I stopped. "You were the first man I'd trusted in a long time," I said without looking back. "Thanks for the reminder that I was stupid, yet again."

### Sutton

2 weeks later

**"G**ood morning, Marcus."

The beefy bodyguard who had been in residence in front of my building for more than three weeks now nodded. "Morning, Ms. Holland."

"It's Sutton. And you're fired."

The corner of his lip quirked. "You have a good day, Ms. Holland."

I'd fired Marcus the first time on my way home the day I'd been kicked to the curb by Jagger. Now it had become part of my daily routine—that and the daily text I shot off to Jagger immediately after.

> **Sutton: Call off your dogs. I don't want your bodyguards following me anymore.**

I watched as it went from Sent to Delivered and then to Read. As usual, he didn't respond. The entire routine was sort of comical at this point, and maybe a little sad.

I shoved my cell into my pocket and headed to the subway. I didn't have to turn around to know Marcus had joined me for the walk. Usually he stayed almost a full block behind me. Sometimes I walked fast and tried to lose him, but then I'd inevitably see him getting out of the subway car next to mine.

I did my regular routine once I got to the office, making a coffee and going to listen to the daily briefing. To my surprise, today Jagger was already in the conference room when I arrived. He was in the middle of a conversation with Will Twible, the director of the algorithm-engineering division, but his eyes latched onto me as I entered.

I looked away, not giving him the satisfaction of thinking I was still pining over him, even if I was, and I was thrilled to see Jack standing on the other side of the room. Normally I kept my distance from him when I could, because I knew his interest was more than as a friend or coworker, and I didn't want to lead him on. But today I approached with an overfriendly smile and made sure to touch his arm more than once as we chatted and waited for the meeting to start. When I chanced a glance back over at the boss, Jagger's eyes were searing into me.

*Good. Serves you right.*

The meeting began, and the boss shared the news that Apex had reached an agreement with the DOJ. Everyone clapped and cheered, including me. Even if I wanted Jagger to suffer on a personal level, I admired everything he'd built and how hard he'd worked. While he spoke, I couldn't help but notice that he didn't look so good. His normally tanned skin was sallow, and dark circles rimmed his eyes. He was probably just exhausted from the chaos at the office and at home, but it hurt to see him looking that way.

After Jagger finished, a few more executives gave updates, and then the daily fifteen-minute briefing broke up.

"Are you going to happy hour tonight?" Jack asked as we shuffled with the crowd toward the door.

I wasn't feeling very happy, and a heavy heart didn't mix well with alcohol, yet I shrugged. "I'm not sure."

"Sutton?" A voice called. I turned to find Will waving me over. "Could you hang back a minute?"

"Uh-oh," Jack teased. "Are you getting in trouble with the teacher?"

"I hope not."

The room continued to empty out, and I waited as Will made his way over. Unfortunately, Jagger was by his side. Once they got to me, Jack waved goodbye. "I hope you come tonight."

Without turning, I felt Jagger's eyes burning into me and forced a smile at Jack. "Actually, I think I might."

"Excellent." Seeming completely oblivious to the scowl on the boss's face, Jack waved to him too. "Congrats on working things out with the DOJ, boss. Have a good day."

Not surprisingly, Jagger didn't reciprocate the well wishes. Up close, he looked even worse than he had from a distance. His eyes were bloodshot and puffy, like he'd been drinking, and I was pretty sure he'd lost weight. Though even at his worst, he was still a ridiculously attractive man, and my body felt a physical pull toward him.

Once the last person left the room, Will smiled. "I have some good news for you."

"Oh?"

"Apex has selected you for their executive training program. Congratulations."

My mouth dropped open. "What?"

Will shoved his hands into his pockets and laughed. "Don't look so surprised. You've impressed my entire team. You've taken the lead on projects. You're confident in your abilities without being arrogant, and you're adaptable and goal oriented. Not to mention..." He thumbed toward the man standing next to him and smirked. "You can kick this guy's ass in solving complex equations."

I looked at Jagger. We both knew that last part wasn't true. But like any other time he'd been near me in the last few weeks, he averted his eyes.

"I...I don't know what to say."

Will's smile widened. "Well, I'm hoping you'll say yes."

My head was spinning. I hadn't given the executive training program much thought since I started. And it was certainly the last thing on my mind lately.

"When do I need to let you know?"

"The deadline is the fifteenth, so only about a week."

I didn't want to come off as ungrateful, so I forced a smile. "Thank you so much for selecting me. I guess I'm just a little shocked."

"You shouldn't be. It's well deserved." Will patted my shoulder. "I have to run to another meeting, but congratulations. HR will be reaching out to discuss the details of the program and salary with you soon."

Jagger's eyes flickered to me. "Congratulations."

The two of them walked out, and I stayed in the conference room a few more minutes. The Apex executive training program was one of the most coveted positions in corporate America, but it meant staying in New York and being around Jagger all the time. I wasn't sure that would allow the gaping hole in my heart to ever heal.

• • •

Four days later, my desk phone rang, and a flash of hope surged before my brain could catch up and remind my body that Jagger didn't call me anymore. The realization left me feeling hollow as I answered.

"Hello?"

"Hi, Sutton. It's Linda, Edmund's assistant."

I sat back in my chair. "Oh, hi, Linda."

"Edmund is stuck on a conference call, but he didn't want to miss you before you left for the day."

"Is everything okay?"

"Yes, everything is fine. He just wants to speak to you. Would you be able to come up when you're on your way out tonight?"

"Sure."

"Great. He should be off his call soon, so pop in whenever you're ready."

I'd avoided my mother and Edmund as much as possible over the last two weeks. Eventually, I was going to have to tell them Jagger and I had broken up, but I hadn't felt up to that conversation yet. I had no idea what my stepfather wanted, though I couldn't avoid him when he'd specifically asked to see me.

At six, I finished the project I'd been working on and took the elevator up to the executive offices. The receptionist was already gone for the day, so I used my keycard to swipe in. As always, I reached the point where my choice was to go right and not pass Jagger's office, or go left and torture myself. My day had been fairly decent so, of course, I decided to self-sabotage.

I regretted my choice as I neared the corner office and saw that the lights were still on. But it was too late now. The best I could do was hold my head high and attempt to walk past his wall of windows without looking in. But even without turning my head, I saw through my peripheral vision that he wasn't alone. Marcus, the bodyguard I'd fired a dozen times, was inside, and the two of them were arguing. I couldn't help myself, I turned to watch their interaction as I kept walking.

Marcus handed something red to Jagger. "That's not a good idea, sir," he said. "You should leave this to the professionals."

Jagger's voice grew louder. "Don't tell me what to do. I'll take care of it myself." His gaze suddenly lifted over Marcus's shoulder and met with mine. He held it as he walked to his office door and slammed it shut.

*Oh-kay then. Asshole.*

My legs kept moving even though it felt like my heart stayed behind. I was busy trying to swallow the lump forming in my throat when Edmund stepped out of his office. He saw me and smiled. "Hey, sweetheart. I was just going to run to the men's room. Do you mind waiting a minute?"

"No problem. Take your time."

"Great." He gestured to his office. "Make yourself comfortable. I'll be right back."

I was glad for the short reprieve because I needed a moment to collect myself after the brief encounter with Jagger. I didn't understand the man at all. One minute he looked sad and broken, and the next he was hard and angry. Though seeing Marcus reminded me that Jagger and I needed to have an in-person conversation about ending my bodyguard service. Things had been uneventful since the birthday card was delivered, and it was time my life went back to the way it had been a few weeks ago.

Edmund returned from the restroom and took a seat behind his desk. "I wanted to talk to you about the executive training program."

"Okay..."

"Jagger filled me in on your personal situation with him, and I wanted to make sure you don't let it get in the way of making the right business decision. The program is a phenomenal opportunity."

"He...filled you in on our...situation?"

Edmund held two hands up. "I didn't ask. I don't want you to think I was prying."

"What exactly did he tell you?"

"Not too much. Just that you ended things."

"That I—"

"You should know, I didn't mention anything to your mother. I figured you'll tell her when you're ready. It's not my place to interfere in your personal life with her or your boyfriends. But I would like to give you some business advice, if you don't mind listening."

I was confused as to why Jagger would tell Edmund that *I'd* dumped *him*. Was it so he didn't look like the asshole and have Edmund get angry that he'd hurt me? Or was he doing it to protect me somehow? So many questions ran through my head that it took me a minute to realize Edmund had just asked me one of his own and was currently waiting for an answer.

I nodded. "Of course. I'll listen to any business advice you want to share."

My stepfather spent the next ten minutes telling me what a great opportunity the executive training program was. He fired off starting salaries at other Fortune 500 companies and compared the average executive compensation at Apex to the industry as a whole. I vaguely heard him speak about breaking glass ceilings, while doing my best to nod at appropriate times—all while my mind was totally somewhere else.

When he seemed to be winding down, he smiled. "I just want what's best for you. Your mind is extraordinary, Sutton, and I think this place will keep you challenged. And last but not least, I'll add one personal appeal: It would make your mother happy to have you nearby."

"I know it would." I smiled. "Thank you, Edmund."

He stood and came around the desk, engulfing me in a hug. "I'm proud of you, kid."

I tasted salt in my throat hearing the tenderness in his voice. "That means a lot to me."

I'd brought my bag so I could leave after meeting with Edmund, but I realized I'd left my cell phone in my desk drawer. So after saying goodnight to my stepfather, I stopped back down at my cubicle. My mind wasn't in any condition to brave the busy New York streets, not with so many things swirling around in it. And I didn't have a reason to rush home, so I sat down to gather my thoughts for a bit.

Why would Jagger lie about our breakup? I couldn't imagine he'd do it to save his own face. Angry at him or not, I knew that wasn't his style. Which meant he had to have lied to protect me. The more I thought about it, the more I stewed. I didn't need his protection—not from my parents, and definitely not with the bodyguards he still hadn't called off. In fact, maybe it was time I delivered that message in person. I stood, not giving myself time to rethink my plan, and set off for the executive floor once more, this time filled with righteous anger.

Hoping to avoid Edmund, I took a left at the split. Jagger's door was open now, but he was no longer inside. My stepfather's deep voice carried from down the hall.

"Yes, dear. I'm leaving right now."

I was pretty sure he was on the phone with my mother. I didn't want to have to explain why I was back up on the executive floor, so I slipped just inside Jagger's office and eavesdropped.

"I'll stop and pick it up and be home in twenty minutes."

A door closed and I stood still, listening as footsteps became fainter and fainter. I heard the reception door click open and closed, and then suddenly it was eerily quiet. I looked around, my heart racing when I noticed Jagger's closed bathroom door. Was he in there? I knew he sometimes showered when he was stressed, and he'd certainly sounded stressed yelling at Marcus earlier. I should've bolted and not risked being found out when he opened the door, yet instead I tiptoed to the bathroom door and listened.

Silence.

Except for the loud swishing of blood through my ears as I thought about getting caught in here. *What the hell am I doing?* Shaking my head, I realized how stupid I was and hurried for the door. But on my way, a flash of color caught my eye. A red folder on the round conference table. It looked like what Jagger had been holding during his heated exchange with Marcus.

I stopped and listened for the sound of anyone coming.

Silence again. Only this time it was the kind that made every tick of the clock, every creak of the floorboard, feel suspicious. I had no right to be in this office and certainly no right to look inside that folder. I glanced to the door, only a few feet away, willing my feet to move. But my eyes drifted back to the red again. Wondering what was inside felt like an itch I couldn't scratch. I moved slowly toward it, as if *slinking* would stop an imaginary alarm from going off. A few papers peeked out from the folder. They slipped back inside as I lifted it and opened, until the hallway creaked, and I snapped the folder shut. In my haste, one page fell to the floor. My heart thumped in my chest as I listened for more sounds, but there was nothing except the loud silence again.

*Jesus Christ.* What the hell was I doing? Who cared what Marcus and Jagger were having a heated discussion about? I bent with the intention of stuffing the paper back in the folder and getting the hell out of here. But that plan changed the second I got a look at the photo of a man printed on the page. It was a face I'd never forget, not even after eight years.

# —— CHAPTER ——
# THIRTY-SEVEN

Sutton

1*632*

   *1634*

*1636*

My heart thudded in my chest as I scanned the numbers on the apartment buildings. Cars drove by, horns honked, people carried about their day, but it all felt disconnected. Like I was underwater.

*1638*

*1642*

*1644*

I'd had to go out through the service elevator to avoid Jagger's security following me, but now I wished I'd brought them along. What was I going to do when I got there? I had no plan. Beat him up with my two fists? I lost an arm wrestle to Miles's eleven-year-old cousin a few months back, and I hadn't even brought a weapon to protect myself. Yet nothing could've stopped me from coming.

*1646*

*1648*

I lifted the now-crushed paper in my hand and double-checked the number, though I was certain I knew it. 1648 Dumont Avenue, Apartment 3F. This was the right building. Chipped bricks, sagging windows, and rusted fire escapes zig-zagged across the front. The only thing that had been updated in the last decade were the graffiti tags. The run-down, shitty building in the middle of a forgotten area of Brooklyn felt like a fitting home for Silas Clive. *Silas.* I'd never even known his real name until an hour ago.

The front stoop was missing half its bricks, and only one crooked railing remained. I took a deep breath and walked up to the door. A collection of beat-up doorbells with an array of crossed-out names lined the inner doorway. I scanned until I found *S. Clive*. Rather than ring, I reached for the door handle. Not surprisingly, it wasn't locked, and the door creaked open like something out of a horror movie. The vestibule smelled like urine and mildew, with maybe some weed mixed in, too.

I knew what I was doing was stupid. *Very* stupid. I didn't even understand why I wanted to see him. But it was like I was heading into an accident with no brakes, and all I could do was brace myself for impact.

I climbed the creaky wooden stairs up the first flight. When I reached the landing, a teenage boy came out of nowhere and brushed past me, nearly giving me a heart attack. I wasn't winded, and it wasn't hot, yet my forehead had a thick sheen of sweat and my palms were wet with perspiration. But I kept going, rounding the landing, down the dimly lit hall, and up the next flight of stairs. A cat meowed as I reached the top step, and I had to grab the railing to keep from falling backward.

*This is dangerous.*

*No one knows I'm here.*

Still, I kept going. My pace slowed as I reached the last stair of the third flight, and I took in a big deep breath as I stepped onto the floor where he lived. *Silas. Silas Clive.*

*3A*

*3B*

*3C*

*3D*

My heart felt like it was about to burst out of my ribcage, and I still hadn't released my breath.

*3E*

*3F*

The door was slightly ajar. I turned my head and put my ear to the opening. But there was nothing to hear except eerie silence. Was he waiting for me right on the other side? Did he somehow know I was coming? Was this *a trap*? The answers to those questions didn't really matter, though, because nothing could've stopped me from going in.

I pushed the door open ever so slightly, and it creaked as it scraped along the floor. I expected to find Silas Clive inside. But that wasn't the man I saw first.

"*Jagger!*"

He had the barrel of a gun in Silas's mouth, and Silas's eyes widened when he saw me.

"Get the fuck out, Sutton!" Jagger yelled.

"No! Stop! Don't do that!"

"*Get out!*"

I didn't know what to do. The man who eight years ago had taken something I could never get back, looked at me with fear in his eyes. I knew the terror he felt, the helplessness, the nightmare of someone having control over you with ill intent. It drew me closer to them.

Jagger yelled again as I neared. "Sutton, leave, goddamnit! Now!"

"No. I want to see him up close." An odd sense of calm washed over me. "I want to see the same fear in his eyes that he made me feel."

Silas was bent backward, his head pressed against a plastic dish-drying rack, his mouth stretched around the width of the gun. His jaw trembled, and spit glistened at the corners of his mouth. He'd also pissed his pants.

I leaned in so our faces were close. "How does it feel? Not being able to move and someone else holding your life in their hands?"

Tears spilled from the corners of his eyes. I allowed myself a few more seconds of vengeance before turning my attention to Jagger. I rested a hand on his shoulder.

"Please don't do this. He's already taken so much from me. Don't let him take you, too."

• • •

"You put a gun in his mouth?" I heard Detective Wallace ask Jagger from the other side of the room. The police had separated us as soon as they'd put the cuffs on Silas and hauled him out of here.

"Am I under arrest?"

"No, not as of this moment. But Mr. Clive said you broke into his apartment and assaulted him." Detective Wallace gestured to the door. "Front door has a busted lock. Story seems to check out."

"You're going to give me shit when you couldn't catch the guy for eight damn years?"

Detective Wallace frowned. "Just answer my questions, Mr. Langston."

Jagger looked over at me. "Can we please get her out of here? You're making the victim sit in the apartment of the piece of shit who assaulted her. Don't you think she's been through enough?"

"We can do that. But then we're going to have to go down to the police station so I can finish my questions."

"Great." Jagger lifted his cell. "I'll tell my lawyer to meet us there."

Detective Manning, whom I'd just met when he arrived with Detective Wallace, closed his notebook. "Sorry, Ms. Holland. We're going to finish taking your statement down at the police station."

I looked over, and my eyes met Jagger's. "Okay. I'll have my lawyer meet us there, too."

## — CHAPTER —
# THIRTY-EIGHT

### Sutton

"I think I'm going to head home."

My mother frowned. "What? No. You barely even slept last night."

I didn't point out that I actually hadn't slept a wink. How could I after the last seventeen hours? When we'd left Silas's apartment, I'd gone down to the police station, where Edmund's lawyer, Kent, had met me. It hadn't actually been necessary since I didn't have anything to hide, but I didn't want to say or do anything that might incriminate Jagger. The police detectives had asked me questions for about an hour and then thanked me and told me I was free to go. Jagger, on the other hand, was not. As far as we knew, he was still there now, at ten o'clock the next morning.

"I'll sleep better at home."

Edmund walked down the hall, fresh from the shower. I looked at him and didn't even have to speak. He shook his head. "Still nothing."

My shoulders slumped. "They can only keep him for a

few more hours, right? Kent said they could question him for up to twenty-four hours."

"Unless they decide to charge him. But if that's happened, we'd know about it because all hell would break loose in the media."

I blew out a heavy breath.

"That would be absolutely ridiculous," Mom said. "He had to do the police's job for them."

Edmund frowned. "He held the guy at gunpoint, Mia."

"The man is a violent criminal. He was just holding him until the police arrived."

I loved my mother for defending Jagger, but her point of view wasn't exactly correct. Jagger had had no intention of calling the police, and I couldn't even bring myself to think about what he might've done if I hadn't gotten there in time.

I stood. "I'm going home."

Mom pointed. "Edmund will drive you."

I shook my head. "I need the fresh air."

"You can put the windows down in the car."

I smiled. "Thank you. But I really need to do this on my own."

"I don't understand why—"

Edmund interrupted. "Mia, she's safe now. Give her a little room."

Mom threw her hands in the air. "Is anyone ever really safe in this City? We should think about moving."

I went to my mom and hugged her. "Thank you for everything." I smiled. "Don't think it went unnoticed that you were up at six o'clock this morning."

Mom pouted. "I would have puffy eyes for you every day if you needed me."

I smiled and kissed her cheek. "I know you would."

My mother's apartment was seven stops away on the Six train, but I got off after five so I could walk a little. The late-morning sun cast a golden glow over Manhattan, making it feel softer than it was, and the normally bustling sidewalks were sparse even for a Saturday. Manhattan felt mellow, as if it were exhaling along with me.

A young woman in pajamas and Uggs walked a poodle with its tail dyed pink while talking on her phone. An older couple strolled arm in arm, him wearing a gray-checked newsboy cap and her a red fascinator. A woman smacked the hood of a taxicab that had almost run over her feet turning against the light. Everything felt almost...normal.

A block from my building, my phone buzzed with the Google alert I'd set up last night for Jagger's name. My heart raced as I prepared to open it and find a headline saying he'd been arrested. But it turned out to be an article about Apex settling with the DOJ. Before I tucked my phone back into my pocket, I went to my contacts, scrolled to Jagger's name, and hit call. It went right to voicemail, without even ringing, same as it had the dozen other times I'd tried since last night.

I stopped at the food truck on my corner and picked up my third—or maybe it was my fourth, I'd lost count—coffee for the day and waved to Nestor, the doorman, who was on the phone as I walked in. I stepped off the elevator and checked my phone for the gazillionth time, hoping maybe my service had been spotty on the ride up and a message had come in. No luck. Still no text from Jagger. But two strides down the hallway, movement up ahead caught my eye, and I froze for a heartbeat thinking it might be Silas. At least until I saw the man rise to his feet.

"Jagger!" I ran to him and jumped into his arms. "Oh my God. Are you okay? Did they just let you go?"

He nodded. "I came straight here."

Jagger's eyes were rimmed with dark circles, as well as being bloodshot and swollen, and his hair was sticking up all over. It looked like he'd spent hours pulling on it. Yet he was still the most beautiful man I'd ever seen.

I pressed my lips to his, but when he didn't kiss me back, my heart sank. He gestured to the door. "Could we go inside and talk?"

I swallowed. "Yeah. Of course."

I unlocked the door, walked in, and put my keys on the kitchen counter. Jagger looked uncomfortable, standing just inside the doorway. "Do you want coffee or something?"

He nodded. "Thanks."

He took a seat on the couch while I buzzed around making a pot of coffee. We hadn't been together the last few weeks, but I thought him going after Silas had meant something. Perhaps I was wrong. He was a protective man, and maybe I'd read into his actions, making them mean more than they did. I'd been jumping out of my skin, anxious to talk to him, but now that he was here, I took my time preparing his mug because I was nervous about what he might say. Eventually, I couldn't stall anymore.

I passed him his cup and took the seat on the chair across from him, rather than the couch. "Did they charge you with anything?"

He gulped down half his coffee and shook his head. "Not yet."

"But they still might?"

Jagger shrugged. "My lawyer said it was a possibility. He doesn't think the detective believes I didn't do what the guy said I did, but I'm not sure they care." He caught my eye. "Thank you, by the way, for not telling them what you saw when you walked in."

"It's the least I could do after what you've done for me."

Jagger looked down for a long time before meeting my eyes. "Come here."

My heartbeat sped up. I wanted to be close to him more than anything, but I still had an ounce of self-protection left in me. "Why?"

"Because I *need* you, Sutton." His voice was raw and gritty. "So fucking much."

I moved to the couch, but left space between us. Jagger looked at the gap, then me, then the gap, and shuffled closer. The simple gesture said so much—Jagger was the kind of man who took what he wanted. If he wanted me close, he normally would just pull me to him. But now he was giving instead of taking.

I shook my head. "I don't understand what happened between us."

He nodded. "I know. There's a lot I need to tell you. Most of it doesn't have anything to do with you, but it might explain why I am the way I am."

"Okay..."

He reached for my hand. "Before I start, I need to apologize. I'm so sorry I hurt you, Sutton."

"It's okay."

"No, it's not." He shook his head. "I knew I was going to, but I'm so damn selfish, I couldn't keep away. There were a million red flags waving around, a million reasons why it was a bad idea to get involved, yet I fucking ignored them all."

"There might've been very good reasons to keep your distance, but there was a stronger reason for us to be together." I put my hand over my heart. "What feels right in here outweighs all the wrongs."

Jagger wrapped his arms around me and held me tight. I could barely breathe, but it didn't matter; I would've stayed like this forever. It felt so good to be in his arms again. Too soon, though, he pulled back. He looked into my eyes for a long time before taking a deep breath.

"When I was six years old, I learned to pick the locks on mailboxes because my mother believed the government was sending all of our neighbors a letter about her. I would break into a dozen a day and bring my mother the mail I found, and she would burn it all in the bathtub. When I was twelve, I convinced the guy who owned the pizza place I was fifteen and got a job delivering pies on my bike in order to pay the rent because my mother hadn't come home in a few weeks."

I squeezed his hand. "I'm sorry."

Jagger shook his head. "I'm not telling you this because I want you to feel bad for me. I'm telling you because I want you to understand what having control means to me. Paying the rent meant I was certain to have a roof over my head, and burning the mail meant my mother might not ramble all night and I could sleep. But I was also a dumb kid with no one watching me, so I was out of control. When I was a teenager, I got arrested four times in a year, and I wound up going into the Marines because it was that or prison. I hated the military when I first enlisted, but as time went on, I grew to appreciate the rules and order. And I realized if I did what I was told, I'd move up in the ranks, which meant I got to be the one making the rules instead of listening to them. But I never fully understood the gravity of what could happen when I fucked up."

He looked down, and when he looked back up, there were tears in his eyes. "I met my buddy John Nelson in boot camp. We had a team of men we were responsible for, but John always deferred to me when it came to tactical decisions. One assignment, we were supposed to be checking a village, making sure no insurgents were hiding out. We'd been there two days, and the only things around were a bunch of families and happy kids who liked to play jump rope. The night before we were supposed to leave, I made the stupid decision to let our men make a fire. I still have no idea what the hell I was thinking."

He paused, and his eyes became distant. It made me wonder if he was reliving what had happened.

"I woke up to gunshots. Insurgents had captured three of our men, including John. When I came running, they caught me. And they made me watch them execute each one of them." Jagger closed his eyes and continued. "They put the barrel of the gun in each of their mouths and pulled the trigger like they weren't even human."

"Oh, God." Tears streamed down my face. *Just like he was going to do to Silas.*

"I almost became the same thing they were."

"But you didn't do it, Jagger. You didn't."

"I'm fucked up, Sutton. You're better off without me. Yet here I am again."

I squeezed his hand. "I'm not better off without you. Just the opposite. I'm better because of you."

• • •

Hours later, we were in the bedroom lying down. We'd spent the entire day talking. Jagger had told me a dozen stories about John Nelson, and I'd opened up about how closed off I'd become to everyone except Miles after what happened to me in college. It was like once we weren't afraid to be honest with each other, we couldn't stop sharing truths.

We'd both been up for more than twenty-four hours, and I knew when Jagger looked at the time on his phone that he needed to go home to his nieces soon. He brushed a lock of hair from my face. "Move in with me."

"Isn't this how we got ourselves into this mess to begin with? You asked me to stay with you, and you pushed me away when I wouldn't."

"I asked you to stay with me because I wanted to protect you. But now I'm asking for the right reasons. I'm asking because I realize my day is better when I wake up next to you."

My heart melted. "That's really sweet. And I'd like to move in with you. Soon. Just not right away."

Jagger frowned. "Why not?"

"Because I've spent the last eight years being afraid, and I'm just starting to feel independent. When I walked home today, even just from the subway station, I felt different—freer knowing Silas can't get to me anymore. I'm still healing, still figuring out who I am. And I want to do that outside of us."

I could tell Jagger didn't like not getting his way, yet he didn't push. Though he wouldn't have been the successful businessman he was if he didn't try to negotiate. "How about two nights a week at my place?"

I smiled. "How about one, we exchange keys, and we can come and go from each other's places whenever we want?"

"And we make the relationship public at work so I don't have to keep my distance there since I won't be coming home to you at night."

"My internship doesn't have that much time left anyway."

"And then you'll be in the executive training program."

I sucked in my lower lip. "I'm not sure if I'm going to accept that offer yet."

Jagger sat upright. "Why not?"

"Because I'm not sure it will be healthy to work for someone I'm involved with. I feel like it might blur the lines. I like your bossiness in the bedroom, but in the office too? I'm not sure that would be good."

"I'm not bossy at work."

I smiled. "Yes, you are, and you know it. You'll just say anything right now to get your way."

"I can work on it."

"I need a little time to think about it all."

"Fine."

My smile widened. "You're cute when you pout."

"Oh yeah?" Jagger rolled on top of me. "Am I cute when I hold you in place by your throat and use your body for only my pleasure? Because that's what's about to happen."

I hadn't slept in more than a day, but suddenly my body felt fully invigorated. "No, then you're sexy."

He flashed a wicked grin that probably should've made me nervous. "Arms up. I need you naked." Jagger stripped me out of my clothes and took care of his as well. "Bend your knees and spread your legs."

God, I'd missed this. Missed *him*.

Jagger slid down and ran a finger through my center. "Wet for me already?"

"Well, you've deprived me for the last two weeks."

"I have a lot to make up to you then." He flattened his tongue and licked me from one end to another. It felt like a million little nerve endings woke up. I arched off the bed, and Jagger pushed me flat to the mattress. "Keep still or I'll tie your arms and legs down."

I thought about moving on purpose, but I didn't have cuffs or rope, and even if I had, those would've taken too long. I needed him fast. So instead, I closed my eyes and let them roll into the back of my head as he sucked on my clit. It didn't take long before I was panting. Digging my hands into Jagger's hair, I moaned. "Please, I need you."

"Fuck..." Jagger crawled up my body. "Say that again."

"*Please*, I need you."

He held my gaze as he pushed inside me in one rough thrust.

I gasped. "More."

Jagger wrapped a hand around my neck, his long fingers curling and almost meeting at the back, and then he squeezed—not tight enough to restrict my breathing, but so I felt completely at his mercy. He leaned close to my ear and murmured, "Don't come."

"No! You can't—"

My words were lost when he pulled out almost to the tip and slammed back in again. Then he slowed, stroking his cock in and out, rubbing against the tender spot he'd found on our first night together. When I let out a mewl, he leaned in again. "Do. Not. Come."

Somehow I'd gone from a woman who was unable to have an orgasm with a man to a woman who couldn't stop herself from having one. I was on the edge, so I decided he should be too and squeezed my muscles tight.

Jagger groaned. "Playing dirty. I like it." He ducked his head and caught my nipple between his teeth. Tugging, he bit down almost to the point of pain. It sent a lightning bolt shooting through me, and my body started to pulsate. I should've known better than to challenge him.

"Christ..." He looked down at me, his eyes caressing my face, moving over his hand around my throat. "You look so beautiful right now. You look like mine."

"I am yours. I have been since the first day we met."

That did it. Jagger smashed his lips to mine. His hand at my neck fell away, and he kissed me until I was breathless. What had started as hot and rough slowed to beautiful and intimate. He glided in and out tenderly and pulled back to look into my eyes.

"Come with me, beautiful. Come with me."

Jagger linked his fingers with mine and pulled my arms up over my head. He stared into my soul as my orgasm rolled through my body like a warm wave.

"Jagger," I breathed.

He sped up his thrusts. "Right there with you, sweetheart. Always right there with you."

After we caught our breaths, he glided in and out for the longest time. "I love you, Sutton."

"I love you, too. For years, I felt like I needed to be fixed, but when I'm with you, I feel like it's okay to be a little broken."

Jagger kissed my lips. "Neither of us needs fixing, sweetheart. We just need each other, exactly as we are."

# EPILOGUE

## Sutton

### Almost a year later

"**C**ome back here." Jagger caught the bottom of my bathrobe and yanked as I stood from the bed. "We're not done."

I snort-laughed and tugged the silky material from his hand, hurrying to the bathroom. "I have to get ready for work."

"It's Saturday."

"And? Since when does that matter? You often go into the office for a twelve-hour day."

Jagger pouted. "Not when I'm still hard, and you're naked under there."

I started to wash up at the sink. My bossy CEO had woken me an hour ago with his head between my legs. I'd returned the favor on my knees. "I really think you should get that thing checked," I yelled. "It's supposed to deflate after you finish, you know."

Jagger stalked into the bathroom. He came up behind me and tugged the tie of my robe. It opened and parted, exposing my breasts. "I'm never finished until I'm inside you."

Remembering the last time he'd come into the bathroom and made me late for work—taking me from behind while we watched each other in the mirror—I was tempted to give in again. But then I remembered the meeting I had at nine. I turned around and pressed my lips to his.

"I can't be late this morning. But I promise I'll make it up to you when I get home."

*Home* was now Jagger's penthouse. I'd finally agreed to move in with him two months ago. A lot had happened over the last year, and the timing had finally felt right. Amelia and Olivia no longer lived with their uncle, though they did live in the spare apartment in the building with their mom. It had taken Catherine six months to get back to a place where she could be with her daughters again. Once she was healthy, she'd moved to New York, but it took another four months before the girls lived full time with her. Jagger now had joint legal custody of his nieces, something his sister had actually agreed to, rather than going back to court. The girls were happy to have their mom back, but they still spent a lot of time with us. Which was the reason this bathroom was lined with pastel nail polishes, bubble baths, hair clips, and a million other little-girl things, not to mention all of my beauty supplies. Seeing the clutter spread out all over the vanity—in what used to be an immaculate, nearly sterile apartment—made me smile.

"If you worked for me..." Jagger pouted. "...you would be able to take off whenever you wanted."

Against the advice of everyone, including my stepfather and bossy boyfriend, I'd declined the Apex executive training program invitation. While it was the business opportunity of a lifetime, I knew it wouldn't be healthy for our relationship. And I valued what we had personally too much to put it at risk. Balance was important to me, and it hadn't been difficult to figure out where I preferred Jagger Langston to be in charge. He wasn't happy with my decision, but it had all worked out for the best. The week after my internship ended, Louise—the sitter who took care of Amelia and Olivia—had a family emergency in Florida. Her mom had broken her hip, so she went down south to take care of her for a while and wound up not coming back. I was able to step in so the girls didn't have to be introduced to a stranger. We had an amazing nine months together. And then when one door closed, another miraculously opened.

Remember Will, the head of the algorithm-engineering division at Apex? Well, he left and started his own company. Turned out, Jagger's loss was my gain. I was now an AI algorithm engineer at Alchemy AI, Will's amazing startup.

"I'll only be at work for a few hours. And then tomorrow you'll have me all to yourself for a full week."

"You better have ice packs and Epsom salt in your suitcase because you're going to need 'em."

"What else am I going to need?" Jagger had kept the destination for our upcoming vacation under wraps. "You, at least, need to tell me if I need a bikini or a winter coat."

Jagger slipped a hand inside my robe and pinched a nipple. Hard. "You're assuming you're going to be allowed to leave the room."

With that, he begrudgingly let me get ready for work, and I stopped in the living room on my way out. If I wasn't already head-over-heels in love with this man, the sight of him sitting shirtless on the couch with my dog snuggled up next to him, head on his lap while he snored, would've done it. I'd gotten Blue a few days after everything went down with Silas. Since I'd refused to move in with Jagger, he'd pushed me to get a dog. Of course, he was thinking more along the lines of a highly trained German shepherd or Doberman and not the lazy, extremely sleepy basset hound I'd picked up at the pet store a few doors down from the office. Blue was no longer lonely. Though I couldn't even train him to sit on command, much less attack someone. Still, I liked to believe he'd protect me if push came to shove.

Blue snorted, waking himself up, and proceeded to fall off the couch.

Jagger shook his head. "What a guard dog."

I bent down and kissed both my boys goodbye. "Why would I need a guard dog when I have a guard human?"

. . .

The following afternoon, I still had no idea where we were going when we arrived at the airport. Though I guessed it didn't really matter. I was just excited that Jagger had taken off work for a full week. It was going to be his first vacation in six years.

Renee, the flight attendant, met us at the door with two flutes of champagne. She passed me one. "Happy birthday, Ms. Holland."

It wasn't until tomorrow, but rather than correct her, I smiled and took the champagne. "Thank you."

The privacy curtain that led from the galley to the seating area was closed. She pushed it open so I could enter and...

"*Surprise!*"

My eyes widened. "Oh my God, Miles! What are you doing here?"

He wrapped his arms around my waist, lifted, and swung me around. "You didn't think I'd miss your birthday eve, did you?"

My best friend set me down and Rodrigo, his boyfriend of almost a year, hugged me. "Happy birthday, Sutton."

I turned to the man behind me. "I can't believe you didn't tell me about this."

"I knew you felt bad you wouldn't be with your best friend for your usual birthday-eve celebration."

I *had* felt bad, though I hadn't said anything. That was one of the things I loved most about Jagger—he knew me. He paid attention to the small stuff—the way my hands fidgeted when I was nervous, the way sometimes my silence said more than my words. Even when he had a million things going on in his chaotic life, he always knew what I needed.

Jagger kissed my cheek. "Don't get too excited. They're only coming for two nights. I'm not willing to share you more than that."

I smiled and whispered, "Thank you. This was so thoughtful."

After we took off and leveled out at cruising altitude, Jagger went in the back to use the bathroom. As soon as he was gone, Miles slipped into his seat. He weaved his fingers with mine.

"I could get used to flying private."

"You might need to fly this way soon so your boyfriend doesn't get flanked by teenyboppers. I noticed yesterday that his Instagram had over a million followers already."

"I know. And the movie hasn't even come out yet."

Miles's love had landed the lead role in a movie adaptation of some big romantasy book series. Rodrigo was twenty-six, but he had a boyish charm and could pass for nineteen. He'd become a celebrity almost overnight. The teenage girls went gaga for him.

"Can't say I blame them," Miles continued. "I mean, look how adorable the man is. He has dimples when he's sleeping, for God's sake."

We looked over at Rodrigo. He had a cheetah-print travel pillow hooked around his neck and was currently dozing with a slight smile on his face. And he did, in fact, still have dimples. I smiled. "I'm happy for you."

"I'm happy for both of us," Miles said. "What a difference a year makes."

I tried not to think back to anything related to a year ago, anything related to Silas Clive. But I hadn't been able to help it lately since my birthday was approaching. One year ago tomorrow, the card had arrived, setting off the chain of events that had finally allowed me to put the nightmare I'd been stuck in since my first year of college behind me.

Jagger had gotten lucky, and the police had ultimately decided not to charge him with assault. But Silas? Not so much. Two days after the police took him out of his Brooklyn apartment in handcuffs, he was charged with two counts of rape. But that was only the beginning of his troubles. Once his face had been flashed all over the news, three other women came forward who had never reported being assaulted. Two months later, he took a plea deal of sixty years in prison, rather than facing twenty-five years for each victim. He deserved life, but I was relieved not to have to testify.

Jagger came back from the bathroom and thumbed to the empty chair across the aisle that Miles had been seated in. "Beat it."

I frowned. "Jagger..."

Undeterred, Miles stood with a grin. "It's okay. With that face, he can get away with almost anything. Especially when he's being possessive about my girl."

Jagger settled back into his seat. "When do you have to be back at the office?"

"Monday, a week from tomorrow. Why?"

"Because I want to make a stop on the way home next Sunday."

"Where?"

He passed me his cell phone. There was a text from Bridget Nelson, the wife of Jagger's marine buddy.

**Bridget: I hope we didn't create a monster by letting him keep it.**

Underneath was a picture of Lucas smiling, riding his new mountain bike. Two weeks ago, Jagger had received an out-of-the-blue phone call from the thirteen-year-old. Lucas had gotten his phone number from the back of the photo his mother had put in his room—the one that told him to call Jagger if he ever needed anything and his father wasn't around. He'd called to ask for a new bike because his had been stolen. The following day, Jagger had flown down to Maryland with a bike on his private plane. Bridget had been mortified when he'd arrived. She'd had no idea her son had contacted him. But Jagger had been thrilled to put a smile on Lucas's face.

"I'd like to make a stop in Maryland. I'm going to set up a college fund for Lucas and pay off their house, if you don't mind."

"Mind? Why would I mind?"

"I figured you wouldn't, but I wasn't about to give another woman a gift without running it by you first."

I smiled. "I think that's an amazing idea."

"I'd like to visit more often, too."

I kissed Jagger's cheek. "I don't care what you say—you have a sweet side, Mr. Langston."

His eyes sparkled. "You may think so now, but I brought some toys that are going to make you question that statement. Now get your ass in the back bedroom and strip naked."

•  •  •

St. Lucia was heaven—lush rainforests that smelled like hibiscus, twin pitons cloaked in vibrant greenery that rose from the azure-colored Caribbean, and miles and miles of white-sand beaches dotted with lazy coves. We'd spent the last two days scuba diving, sipping piña coladas, and swaying to the music of steel-drum bands at tucked-away bars. This afternoon we'd said goodbye to Miles and his boyfriend. Rodrigo had to go back home to continue shooting his movie, and tonight Jagger and I were having our first dinner alone.

The house we were staying in was located on the beach, and each evening we'd walked along the shoreline to find a different place to have dinner. I'd thought that's what we were doing again tonight. But when we got to the water's edge, there was a table set for two. A waiter appeared out of nowhere, holding a silver tray with two champagne flutes.

"Good evening, Ms. Holland." He nodded and passed me a glass. "Mr. Langston."

A breeze blew the bottom of the white tablecloth around and brought with it the smell of something delicious. I looked around as music started to play in the distance. "Wow. This is amazing. When did you plan all this?"

He smiled. "The music wasn't me. I'm not even sure where it's coming from."

The waiter pulled out a chair for me, but Jagger waved him away. "Give us a few minutes, please."

He bowed. "Of course, sir."

Jagger took both my hands. When I felt his shaking, I jumped to the only logical conclusion. "Are you cold?"

He shook his head.

"But you're shivering."

He smiled. "I guess I'm a little more nervous than I thought I'd be."

"Nervous about…"

Jagger bent down on one knee.

Oh. My. God. *I'm a total idiot!* Romantic setting, hands trembling… I'd never seen this man nervous before, so it hadn't dawned on me that could be an option. I pulled a hand away and covered my mouth.

Jagger took a box out of his pocket. "If someone would've told me fifteen months ago that I was going to meet the love of my life—a twenty-four-year-old virgin about to start an internship at my company, oh and her stepfather was one of my executives—I would've told them they were out of their minds. We were never supposed to work. I was all business, including in my personal life. I was pessimistic, controlling, and didn't believe in love. And you—you had been through hell and back, yet you were still optimistic, still open to new things, and held out hope that your Prince Charming was out there."

Jagger smiled. "I'm no Prince Charming. But somehow you got me to start thinking the unthinkable—that maybe the world wasn't such a bad place, that maybe some things were worth the risk, even if I couldn't control the outcome, and maybe—maybe the reason I'd never wanted more from a woman was because I hadn't met you yet."

I felt tears in my eyes.

"Sutton, I love you because despite how different we are, you never try to change me. You don't run away when I push. You stay and fight for what you believe in, and you have believed in us from the start."

Jagger took a deep breath. "I still like rules and order. But a wise woman once told me that every rule needs an exception. Because while rules keep your life organized, it's the exceptions that make it interesting." He opened the little black box, and inside was a gorgeous, princess-cut diamond set in white gold. The entire band was encrusted with teeny-tiny pearls. He took it from the box and held it out to me.

"Sutton Holland, you are my pearl. You are my forever exception. You are my world. You brought me back to life, and there is nothing I want to do but live every day of that life trying to be the man you deserve. So, please tell me you'll marry me, because there is nothing I want more than to be your husband."

I practically knocked him over, rushing into his arms. "Yes! Yes! I can't wait to marry you."

Jagger slipped the ring on my finger while tears streamed down my face.

"My God, Jagger. That was the most beautiful and romantic proposal. I can't believe you had that in you."

Jagger tugged me against him, wrapped the back of my hair in his hand, and pulled me in for a kiss. "I had it in me, and now you're about to have me in you."

**THE END**

# ACKNOWLEDGEMENTS

To you – the *readers*. Thank you for every message, review, recommendation, and moment you've spent in my fictional worlds. Your support has meant more than words can express, and I'm so thankful to share this journey with you.

To Penelope – Thank you for keeping me (mostly) sane and always being there to listen and talk me down.

To Cheri – Books brought us together, *who you are* made us true friends.

To Julie – Thank you for your friendship. I can't wait for something new from you!

To Luna – Thank you for more than a decade of support and being such a loyal friend.

To my amazing Facebook reader group, Vi's Violets – More than 26,000 smart ladies (and a few awesome men) who love books! You've turned a community into a family. Thanks for always showing up with humor, heart, and a healthy dose of book obsession.

To Sommer – Thank you for creating not just one, but TWO beautiful covers for each of my books now!

To Jessica, Elaine, and Julia – Thank you for smoothing out the all the rough edges and making me shine!

To Kylie and Jo at Give Me Books –Thank you for everything you do.

To all of the influencers, reviewers, and bloggers who shine a spotlight on my books—Thank you! Your passion and your platforms help books find the readers who need them most. I'm endlessly grateful for the time, energy, and love you share with each story you champion!

Much love,
Vi

# OTHER ROMANCE NOVELS BY VI KEELAND

Indiscretion
What Happens at the Lake
Something Unexpected
The Game
The Boss Project
The Summer Proposal
The Spark
The Invitation
The Rivals
Inappropriate
All Grown Up
We Shouldn't
The Naked Truth
Something Borrowed, Something You
Beautiful Mistake
Egomaniac
Bossman
The Baller
Left Behind
Beat
Throb
Worth the Fight
Worth the Chance
Worth Forgiving
Belong to You
Made for You
Jilted

## THRILLER NOVELS BY VI KEELAND

The Unraveling
Someone Knows


## ROMANCE NOVELS CO-WRITTEN BY VI KEELAND AND PENELOPE WARD

Denim & Diamonds
The Rules of Dating
The Rules of Dating My Best Friend's Sister
The Rules of Dating My One-Night Stand
The Rules of Dating a Younger Man
Well Played
Not Pretending Anymore
Happily Letter After
My Favorite Souvenir
Dirty Letters
Hate Notes
Rebel Heir
Rebel Heart
Cocky Bastard
Stuck-Up Suit
Playboy Pilot
Mister Moneybags
British Bedmate
Park Avenue Player

# ABOUT THE AUTHOR

VI KEELAND is a #1 *New York Times,* #1 *Wall Street Journal,* and *USA Today* Bestselling author. With millions of books sold, her titles are currently translated in twenty-six languages and have appeared on bestseller lists in the US, Germany, Brazil, Bulgaria, Israel, and Hungary. Three of her short stories have been turned into films by Passionflix, and two of her books are currently optioned for movies. She resides in New York with her husband and their three children where she is living out her own happily ever after with the boy she met at age six.